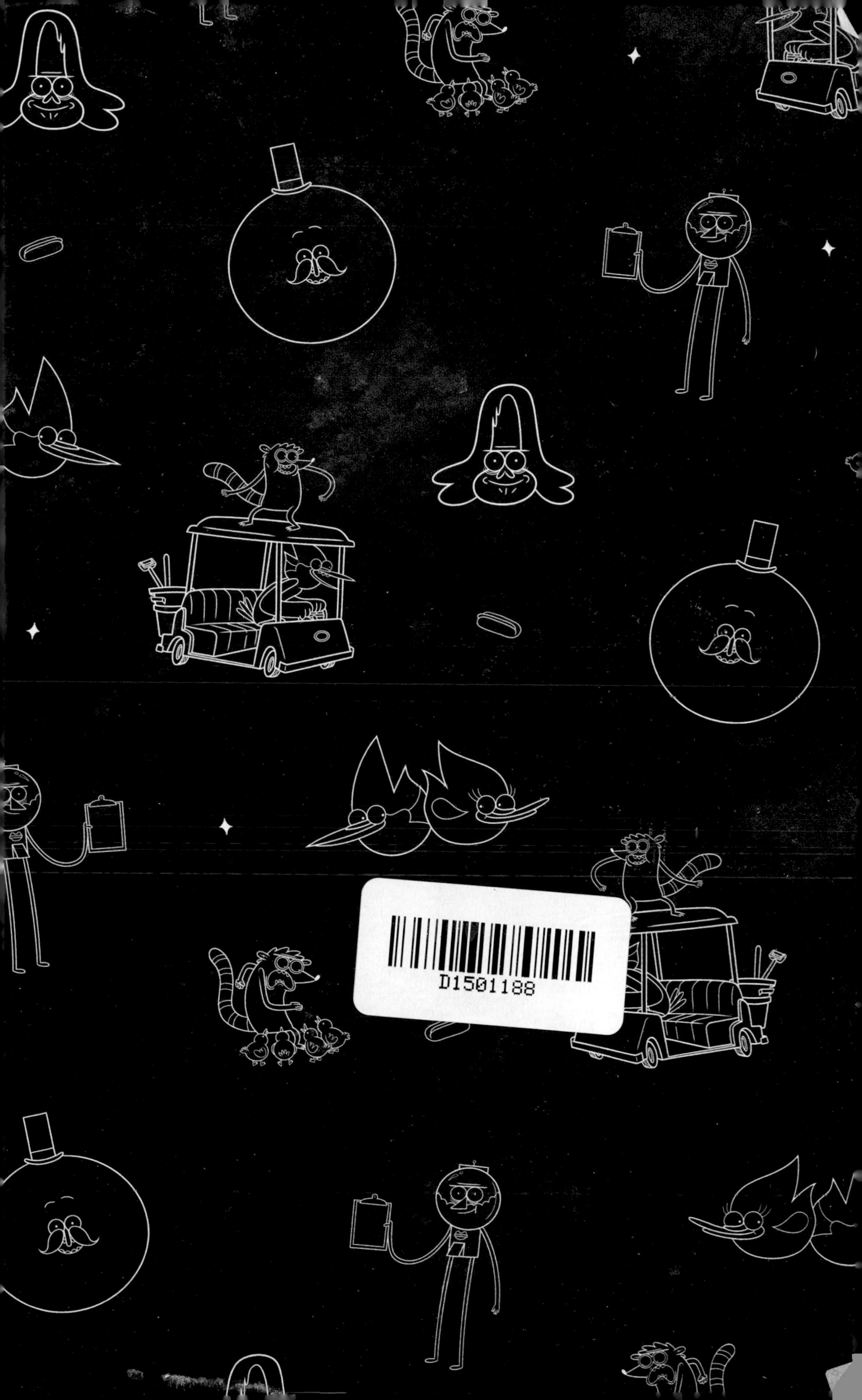

ROSS RICHIE CEO & Founder • MATT GAGNON Editor-in-Chief • FILIP SABLIK President of Publishing & Marketing • STEPHEN CHRISTY President of Development • LANCE KREITER VP of Licensing & Merchandising
PHIL BARBARO VP of Finance • BRYCE CARLSON Managing Editor • MEL CAYLO Marketing Manager • SCOTT NEWMAN Production Design Manager • IRENE BRADISH Operations Manager
SIERRA HAHN Senior Editor • DAFNA PLEBAN Editor • SHANNON WATTERS Editor • ERIC HARBURN Editor • WHITNEY LEOPARD Associate Editor • JASMINE AMIRI Associate Editor • CHRIS ROSA Associate Editor
ALEX GALER Assistant Editor • CAMERON CHITTOCK Assistant Editor • MARY GUMPORT Assistant Editor • MATTHEW LEVINE Assistant Editor • KELSEY DIETERICH Production Designer • JILLIAN CRAB Production Designer
MICHELLE ANKLEY Production Design Assistant • GRACE PARK Production Design Assistant • AARON FERRARA Operations Coordinator • ELIZABETH LOUGHRIDGE Accounting Coordinator • JOSÉ MEZA Sales Assistant
JAMES ARRIOLA Mailroom Assistant • HOLLY AITCHISON Operations Assistant • STEPHANIE HOCUTT Marketing Assistant • SAM KUSEK Direct Market Representative • AMBER PARKER Administrative Assistant

REGULAR SHOW Volume Seven, November 2016. Published by KaBOOM!, a division of Boom Entertainment, Inc. REGULAR SHOW, CARTOON
NETWORK, the logos, and all related characters and elements are trademarks of and © Cartoon Network. (S16) Originally published in single
magazine form as REGULAR SHOW No. 25-28. © Cartoon Network. (S15) All rights reserved. KaBOOM!™ and the KaBOOM! logo are trademarks
of Boom Entertainment, Inc., registered in various countries and categories. All characters, events, and institutions depicted herein are
fictional. Any similarity between any of the names, characters, persons, events, and/or institutions in this publication to actual names,
characters, and persons, whether living or dead, events, and/or institutions is unintended and purely coincidental. KaBOOM! does not read or
accept unsolicited submissions of ideas, stories, or artwork.

A catalog record of this book is available from OCLC and from the BOOM! Studios website, www.boom-studios.com, on the Librarians Page.

BOOM! Studios, 5670 Wilshire Boulevard, Suite 450, Los Angeles, CA 90036-5679. Printed in China. First Printing.

ISBN: 978-1-60886-910-7, eISBN: 978-1-61398-581-6

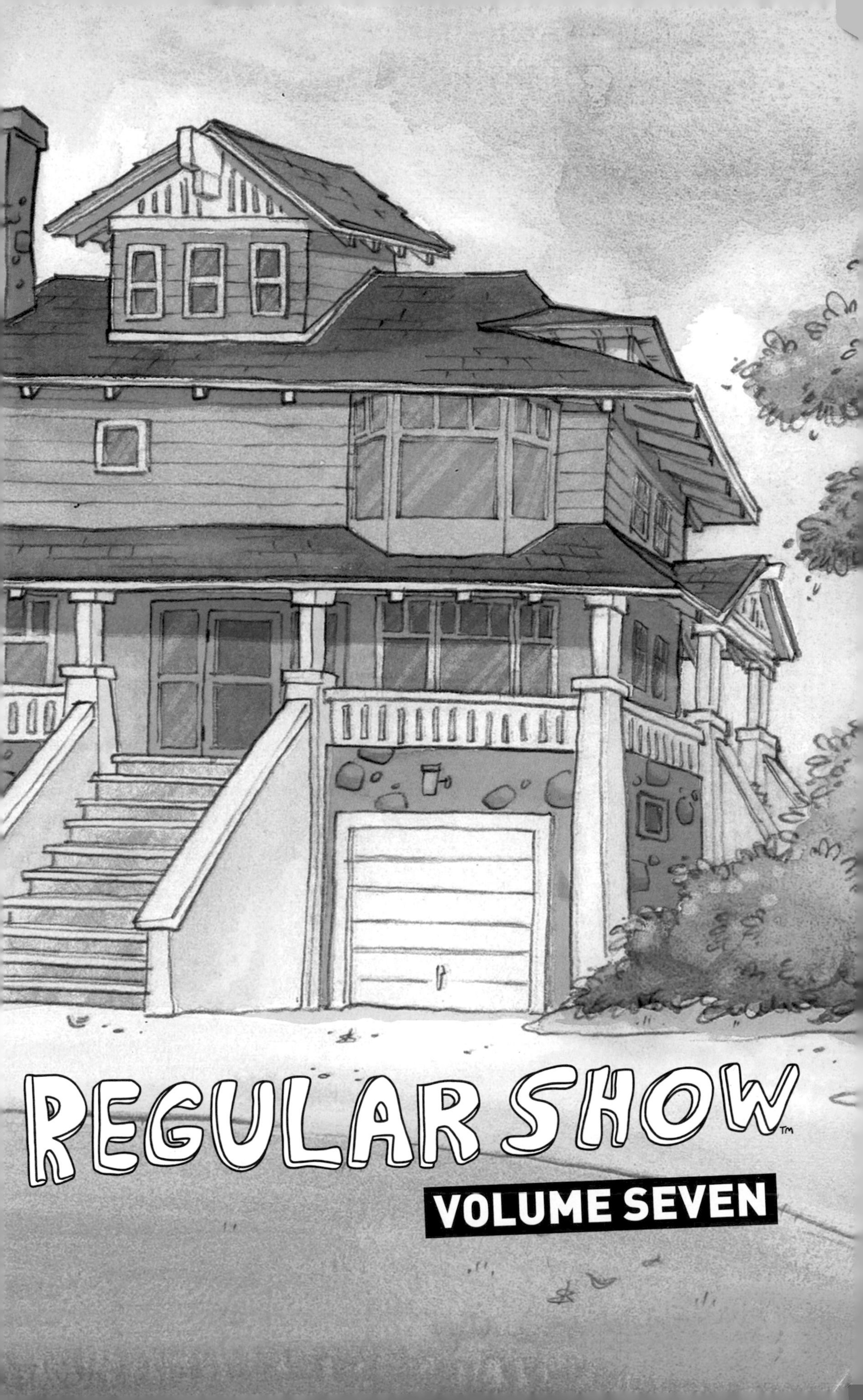
REGULAR SHOW™
VOLUME SEVEN

REGULAR

CREATED BY JG QUINTEL

SCRIPT BY MAD RUPERT

ART BY WOOK JIN CLARK

COLORS BY LISA MOORE

LETTERS BY STEVE WANDS

COVER BY
DEREK CHARM

DESIGNER
MICHELLE ANKLEY

ASSISTANT EDITOR
MARY GUMPORT

ORIGINAL SERIES EDITOR
SHANNON WATTERS

COLLECTION EDITOR
SIERRA HAHN

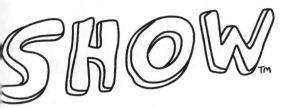

SHOW™

"FITNESS"

SCRIPT BY **KEVIN CHURCH**
ART BY **MAD RUPERT**
COLORS BY **LISA MOORE**
LETTERS BY **STEVE WANDS**

"PAPA RIGBY"

SCRIPT & ART BY
TAVIS MAIDEN

"COFFEE SHOP SPECIAL"

SCRIPT BY **KEVIN CHURCH**
ART BY **COLEMAN ENGLE**

"WASPS"

SCRIPT BY **CLARK BURSCOUGH**
ART BY **MARC ELLERBY**

"STAKEOUT"

SCRIPT BY **EDDIE WRIGHT**
ART BY **DOUGLAS HOLGATE**

"CANDY ECONOMY"

SCRIPT BY **ANDREW GREENSTONE**
ART BY **DEREK CHARM**
LETTERS BY **JIM CAMPBELL**

WITH SPECIAL THANKS TO
MARISA MARIONAKIS, JIM VALERI, CURTIS LELASH, CONRAD MONTGOMERY, MEGHAN BRADLEY, KELLY CREWS, RYAN SLATER, AND THE WONDERFUL FOLKS AT CARTOON NETWORK.

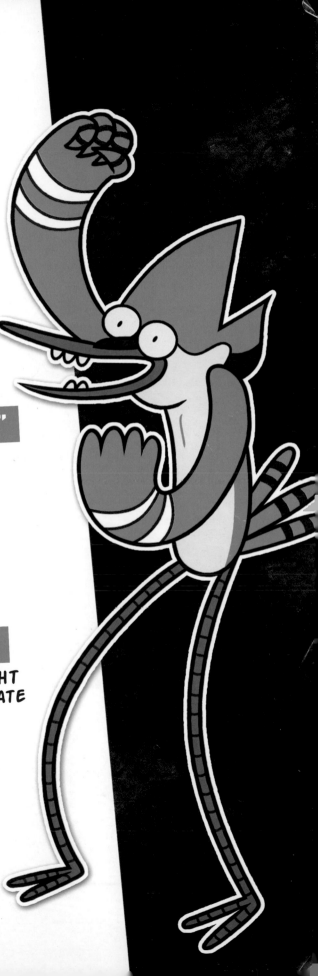

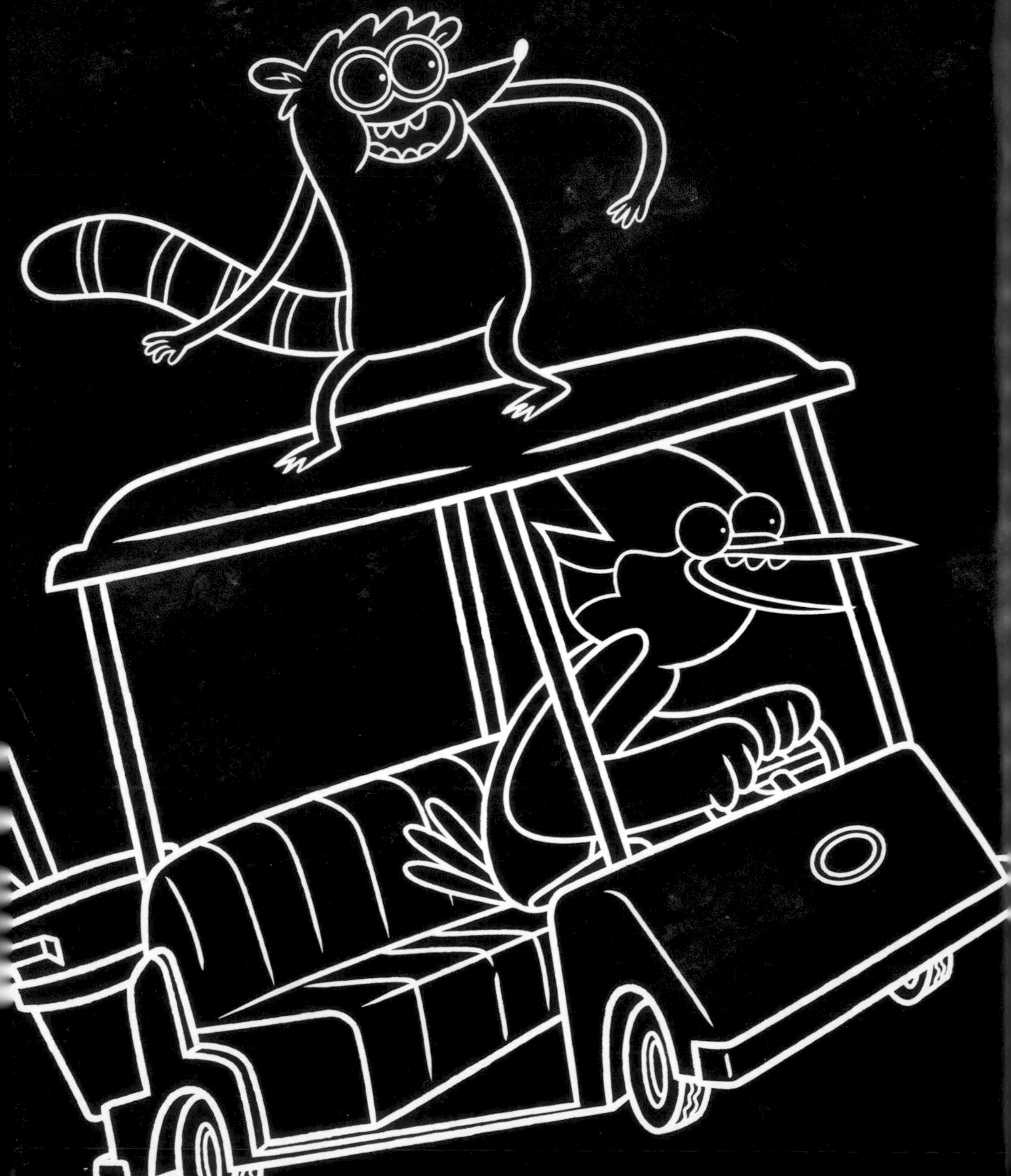

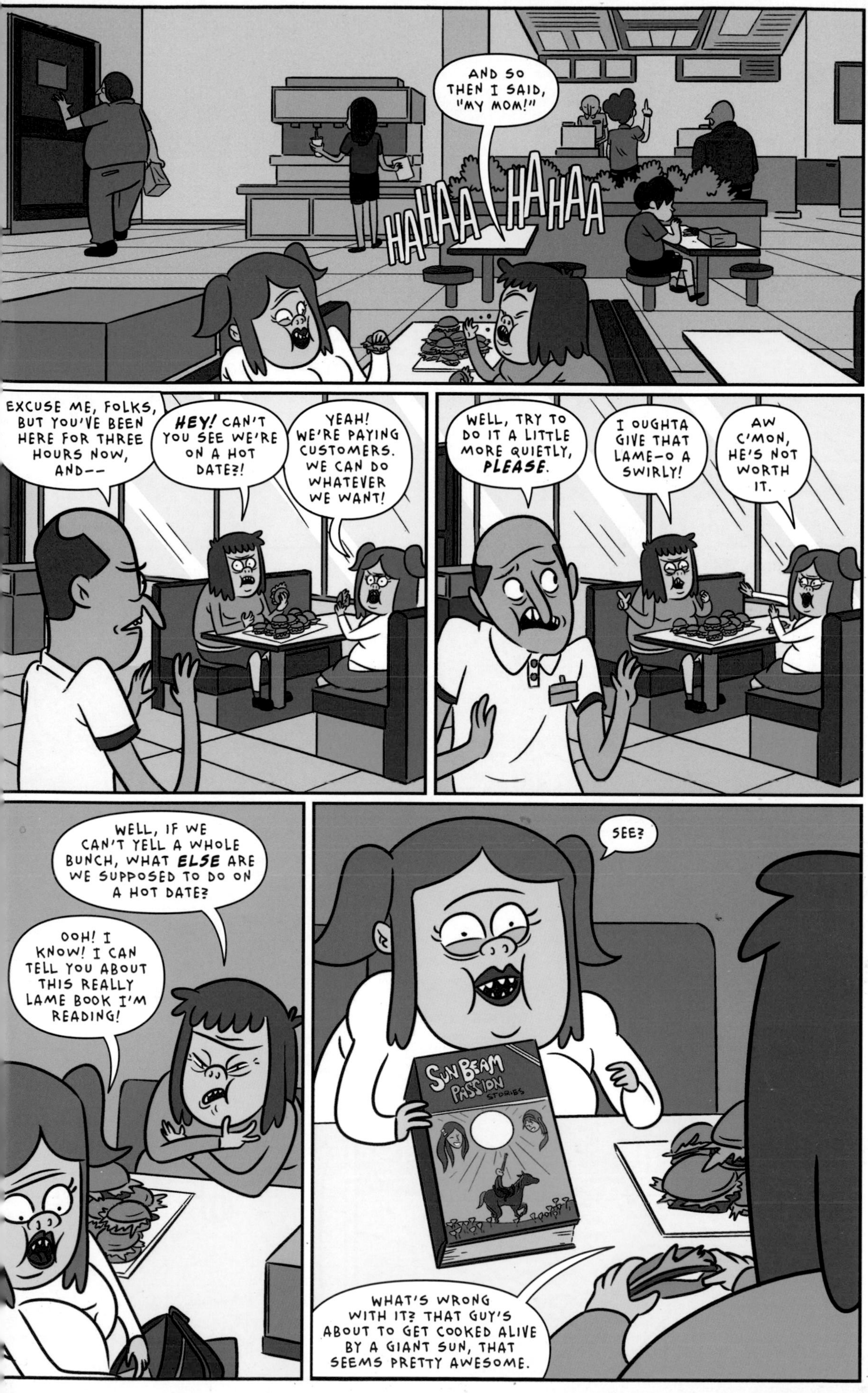
AND SO THEN I SAID, "MY MOM!"
HAHAA HAHAA
EXCUSE ME, FOLKS, BUT YOU'VE BEEN HERE FOR THREE HOURS NOW, AND--
HEY! CAN'T YOU SEE WE'RE ON A HOT DATE?!
YEAH! WE'RE PAYING CUSTOMERS. WE CAN DO WHATEVER WE WANT!
WELL, TRY TO DO IT A LITTLE MORE QUIETLY, PLEASE.
I OUGHTA GIVE THAT LAME-O A SWIRLY!
AW C'MON, HE'S NOT WORTH IT.
WELL, IF WE CAN'T YELL A WHOLE BUNCH, WHAT ELSE ARE WE SUPPOSED TO DO ON A HOT DATE?
OOH! I KNOW! I CAN TELL YOU ABOUT THIS REALLY LAME BOOK I'M READING!
SEE?
SUN BEAM PASSION STORIES
WHAT'S WRONG WITH IT? THAT GUY'S ABOUT TO GET COOKED ALIVE BY A GIANT SUN, THAT SEEMS PRETTY AWESOME.

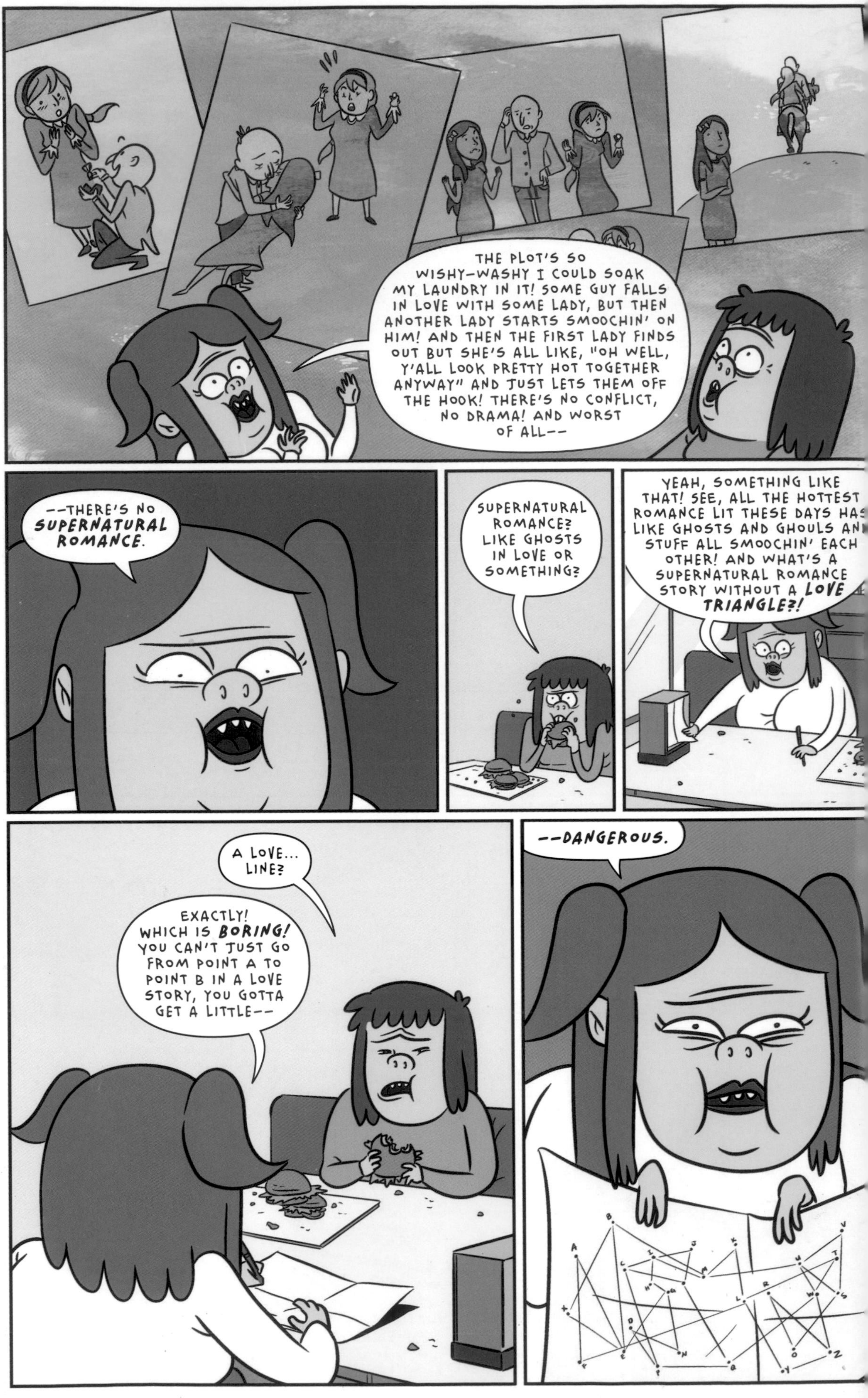
THE PLOT'S SO WISHY-WASHY I COULD SOAK MY LAUNDRY IN IT! SOME GUY FALLS IN LOVE WITH SOME LADY, BUT THEN ANOTHER LADY STARTS SMOOCHIN' ON HIM! AND THEN THE FIRST LADY FINDS OUT BUT SHE'S ALL LIKE, "OH WELL, Y'ALL LOOK PRETTY HOT TOGETHER ANYWAY" AND JUST LETS THEM OFF THE HOOK! THERE'S NO CONFLICT, NO DRAMA! AND WORST OF ALL--
--THERE'S NO **SUPERNATURAL ROMANCE**.
SUPERNATURAL ROMANCE? LIKE GHOSTS IN LOVE OR SOMETHING?
YEAH, SOMETHING LIKE THAT! SEE, ALL THE HOTTEST ROMANCE LIT THESE DAYS HAS LIKE GHOSTS AND GHOULS AND STUFF ALL SMOOCHIN' EACH OTHER! AND WHAT'S A SUPERNATURAL ROMANCE STORY WITHOUT A **LOVE TRIANGLE?!**
A LOVE... LINE?
EXACTLY! WHICH IS **BORING!** YOU CAN'T JUST GO FROM POINT A TO POINT B IN A LOVE STORY, YOU GOTTA GET A LITTLE--
--**DANGEROUS.**

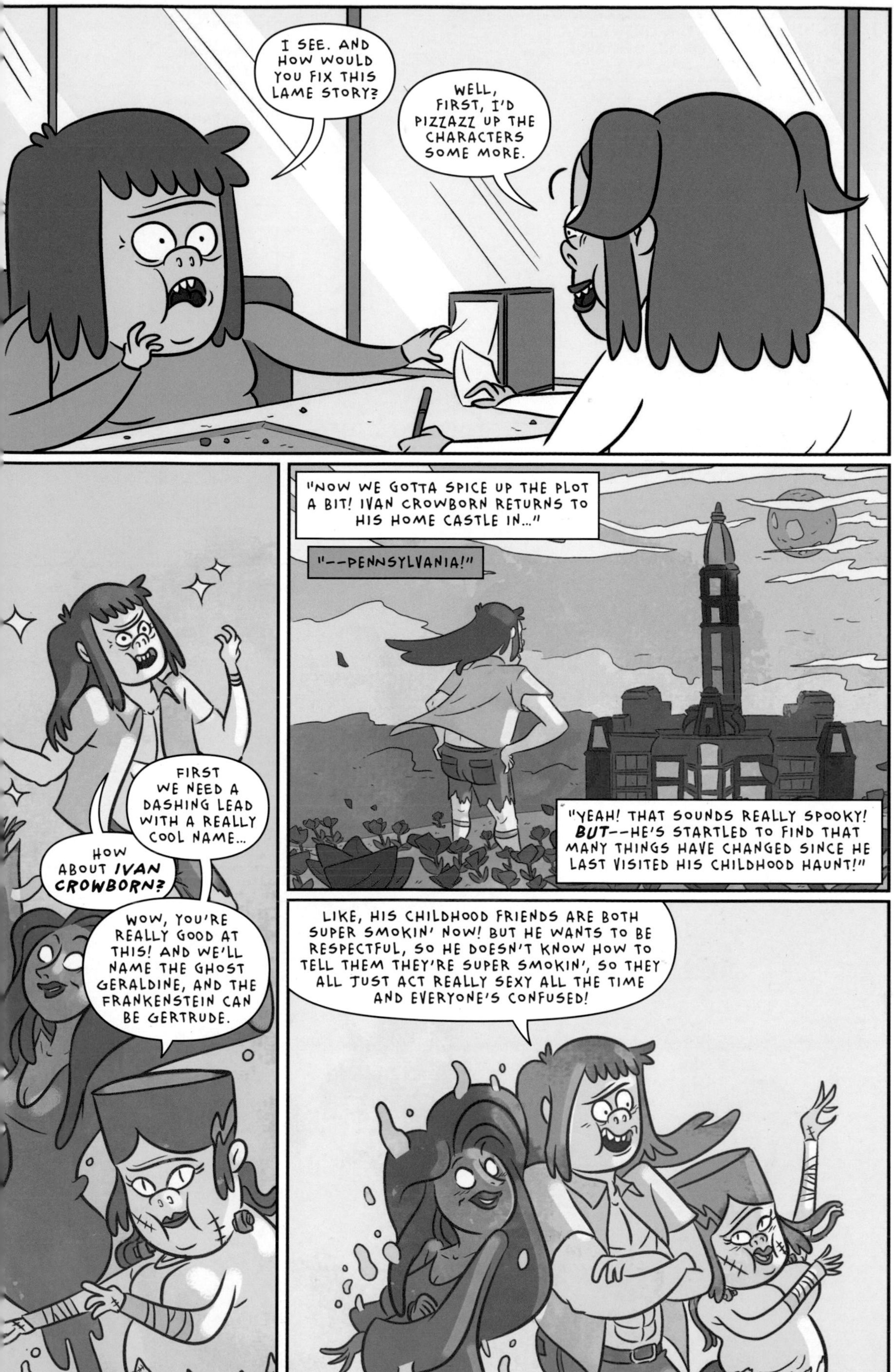
I SEE. AND HOW WOULD YOU FIX THIS LAME STORY?
WELL, FIRST, I'D PIZZAZZ UP THE CHARACTERS SOME MORE.
FIRST WE NEED A DASHING LEAD WITH A REALLY COOL NAME...
HOW ABOUT IVAN CROWBORN?
WOW, YOU'RE REALLY GOOD AT THIS! AND WE'LL NAME THE GHOST GERALDINE, AND THE FRANKENSTEIN CAN BE GERTRUDE.
"NOW WE GOTTA SPICE UP THE PLOT A BIT! IVAN CROWBORN RETURNS TO HIS HOME CASTLE IN..."
"--PENNSYLVANIA!"
"YEAH! THAT SOUNDS REALLY SPOOKY! BUT--HE'S STARTLED TO FIND THAT MANY THINGS HAVE CHANGED SINCE HE LAST VISITED HIS CHILDHOOD HAUNT!"
LIKE, HIS CHILDHOOD FRIENDS ARE BOTH SUPER SMOKIN' NOW! BUT HE WANTS TO BE RESPECTFUL, SO HE DOESN'T KNOW HOW TO TELL THEM THEY'RE SUPER SMOKIN', SO THEY ALL JUST ACT REALLY SEXY ALL THE TIME AND EVERYONE'S CONFUSED!

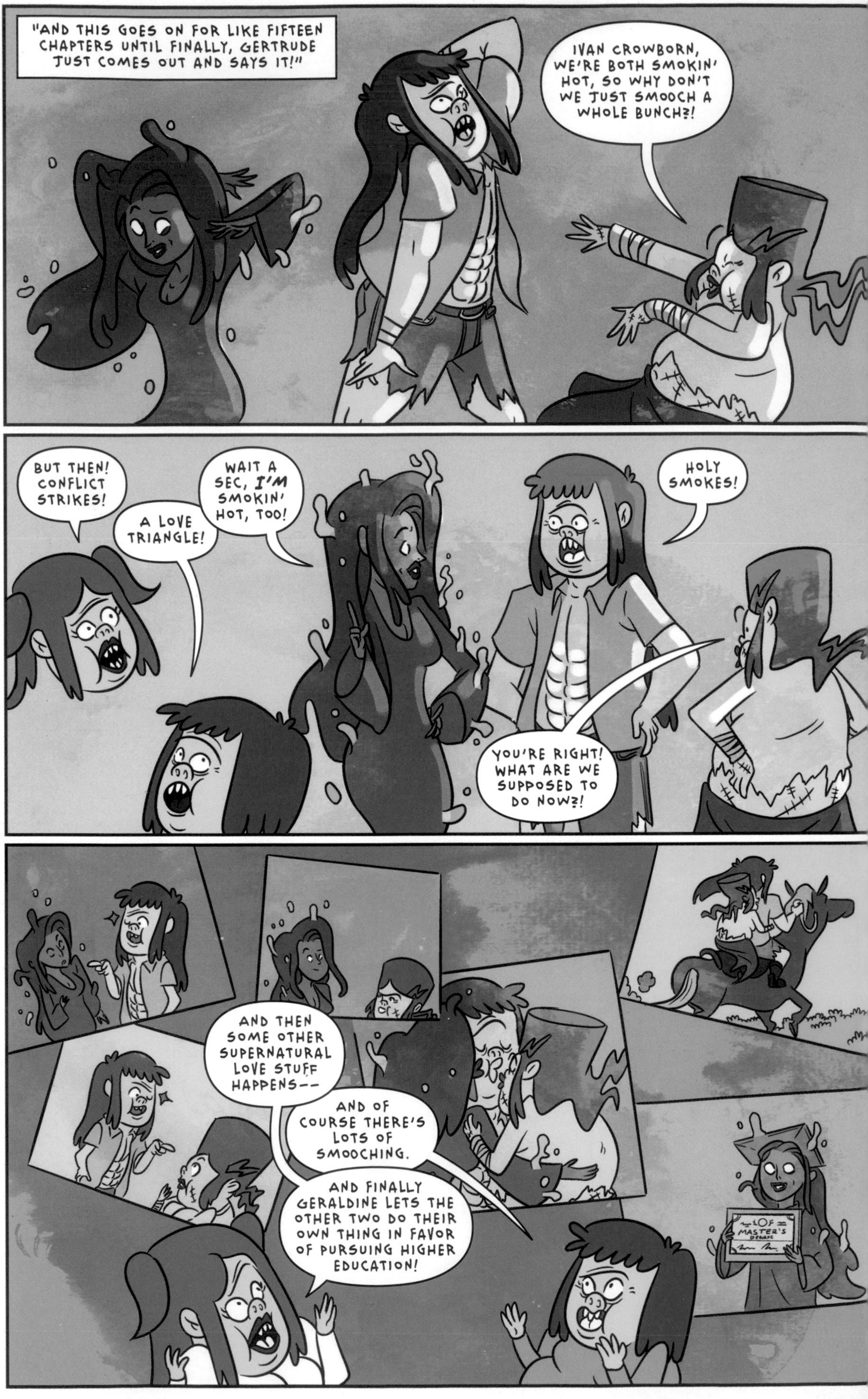
"AND THIS GOES ON FOR LIKE FIFTEEN CHAPTERS UNTIL FINALLY, GERTRUDE JUST COMES OUT AND SAYS IT!"
IVAN CROWBORN, WE'RE BOTH SMOKIN' HOT, SO WHY DON'T WE JUST SMOOCH A WHOLE BUNCH?!
BUT THEN! CONFLICT STRIKES!
A LOVE TRIANGLE!
WAIT A SEC, I'M SMOKIN' HOT, TOO!
HOLY SMOKES!
YOU'RE RIGHT! WHAT ARE WE SUPPOSED TO DO NOW?!
AND THEN SOME OTHER SUPERNATURAL LOVE STUFF HAPPENS--
AND OF COURSE THERE'S LOTS OF SMOOCHING.
AND FINALLY GERALDINE LETS THE OTHER TWO DO THEIR OWN THING IN FAVOR OF PURSUING HIGHER EDUCATION!
MASTER'S DEGREE

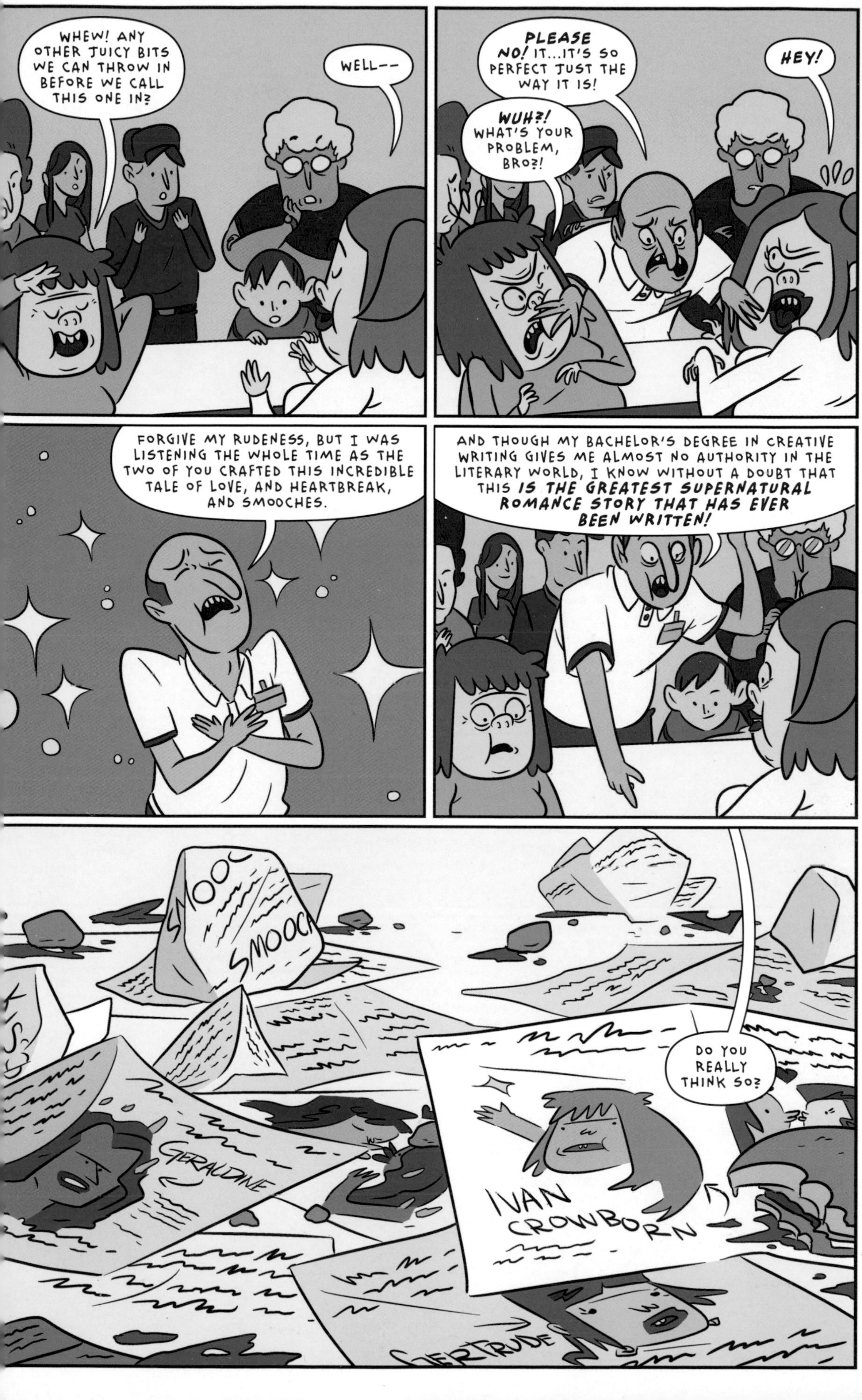
WHEW! ANY OTHER JUICY BITS WE CAN THROW IN BEFORE WE CALL THIS ONE IN?
WELL--
PLEASE NO! IT...IT'S SO PERFECT JUST THE WAY IT IS!
WUH?! WHAT'S YOUR PROBLEM, BRO?!
HEY!
FORGIVE MY RUDENESS, BUT I WAS LISTENING THE WHOLE TIME AS THE TWO OF YOU CRAFTED THIS INCREDIBLE TALE OF LOVE, AND HEARTBREAK, AND SMOOCHES.
AND THOUGH MY BACHELOR'S DEGREE IN CREATIVE WRITING GIVES ME ALMOST NO AUTHORITY IN THE LITERARY WORLD, I KNOW WITHOUT A DOUBT THAT THIS IS THE GREATEST SUPERNATURAL ROMANCE STORY THAT HAS EVER BEEN WRITTEN!
SMOOCH
GERALDINE
IVAN CROWBORN
GERTRUDE
DO YOU REALLY THINK SO?

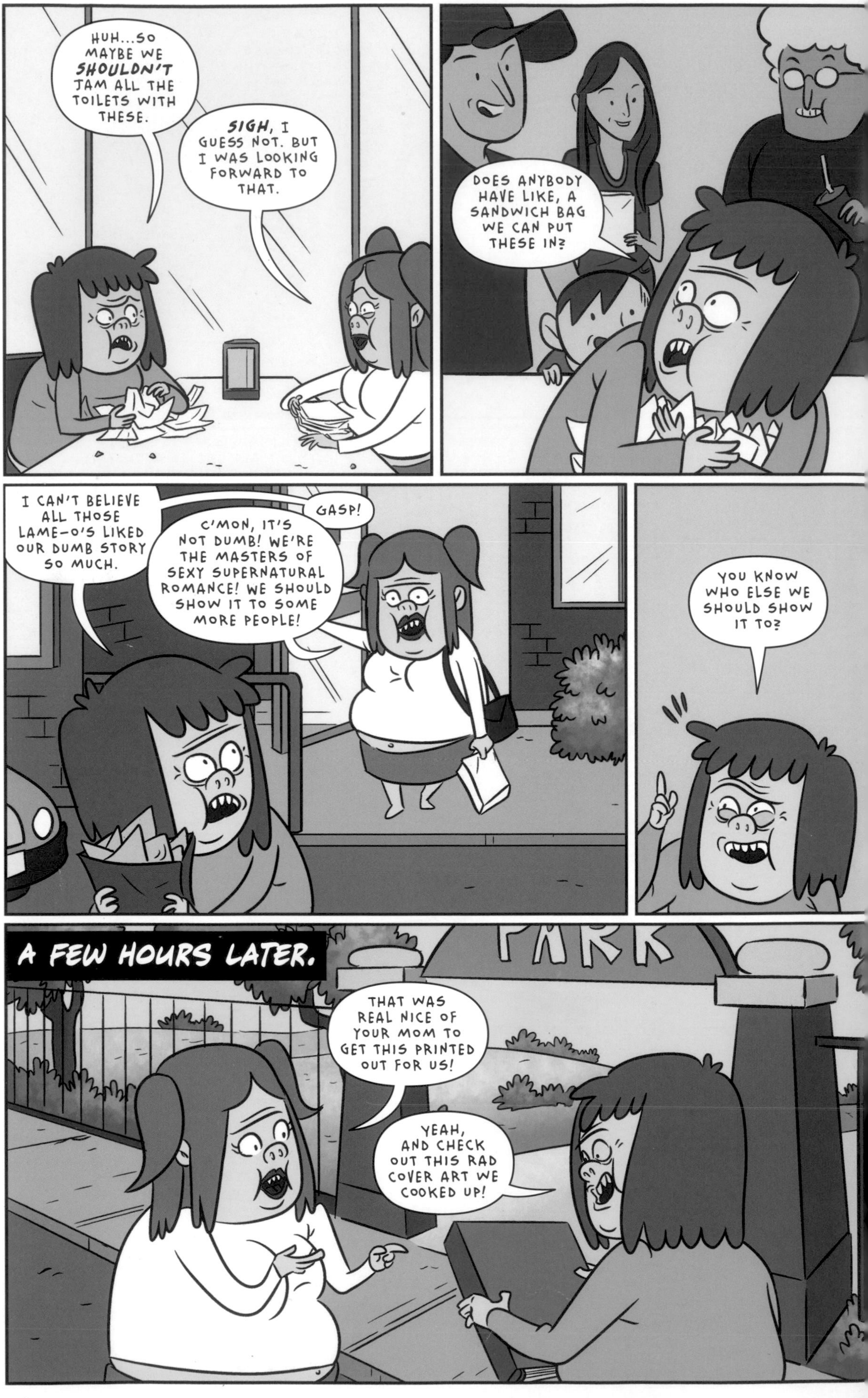
HUH...SO MAYBE WE SHOULDN'T JAM ALL THE TOILETS WITH THESE.
SIGH, I GUESS NOT. BUT I WAS LOOKING FORWARD TO THAT.
DOES ANYBODY HAVE LIKE, A SANDWICH BAG WE CAN PUT THESE IN?
I CAN'T BELIEVE ALL THOSE LAME-O'S LIKED OUR DUMB STORY SO MUCH.
GASP!
C'MON, IT'S NOT DUMB! WE'RE THE MASTERS OF SEXY SUPERNATURAL ROMANCE! WE SHOULD SHOW IT TO SOME MORE PEOPLE!
YOU KNOW WHO ELSE WE SHOULD SHOW IT TO?
A FEW HOURS LATER.
PARK
THAT WAS REAL NICE OF YOUR MOM TO GET THIS PRINTED OUT FOR US!
YEAH, AND CHECK OUT THIS RAD COVER ART WE COOKED UP!

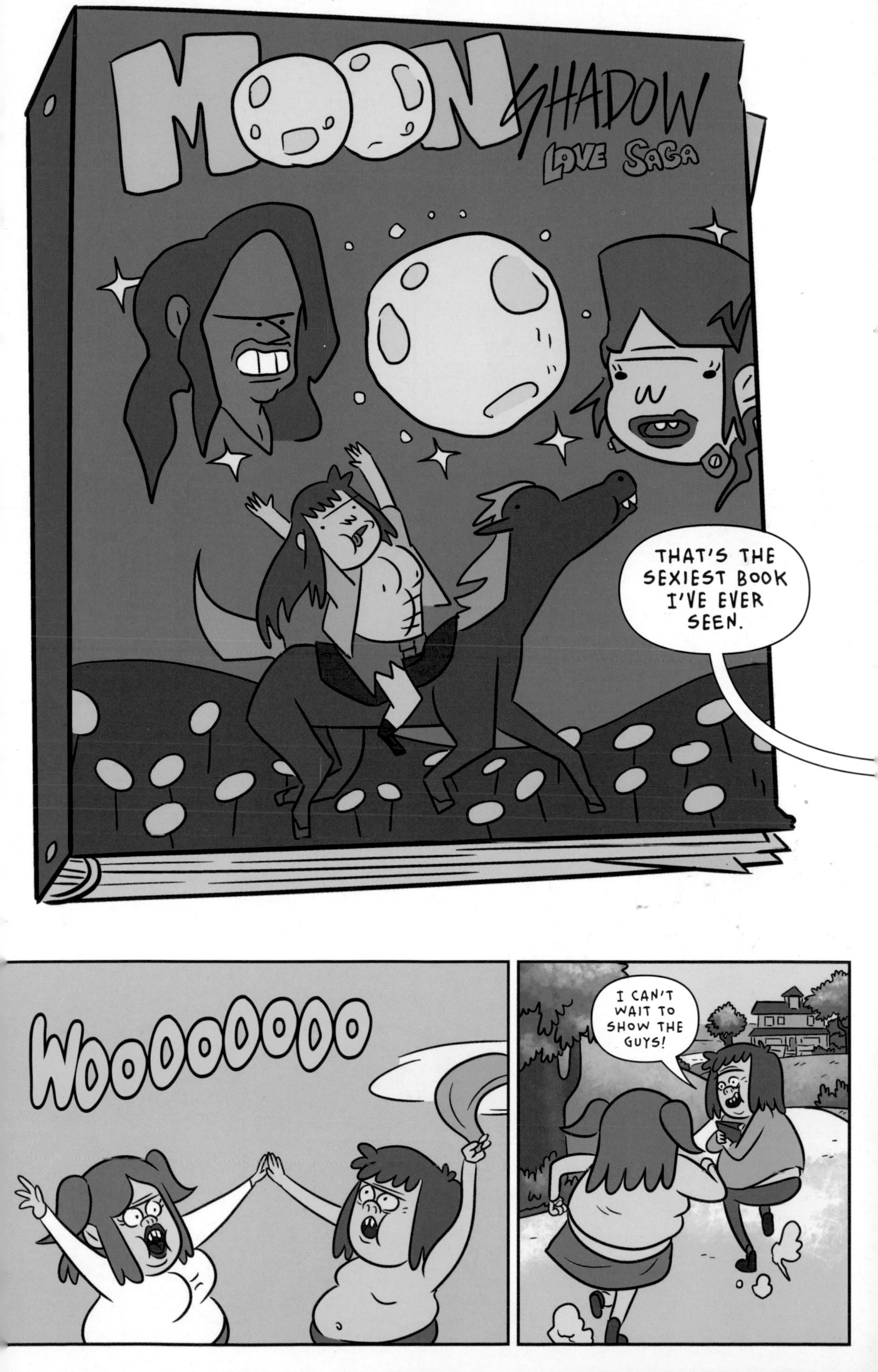
MOON SHADOW
LOVE SAGA
THAT'S THE SEXIEST BOOK I'VE EVER SEEN.
WOOOOOOOO
I CAN'T WAIT TO SHOW THE GUYS!

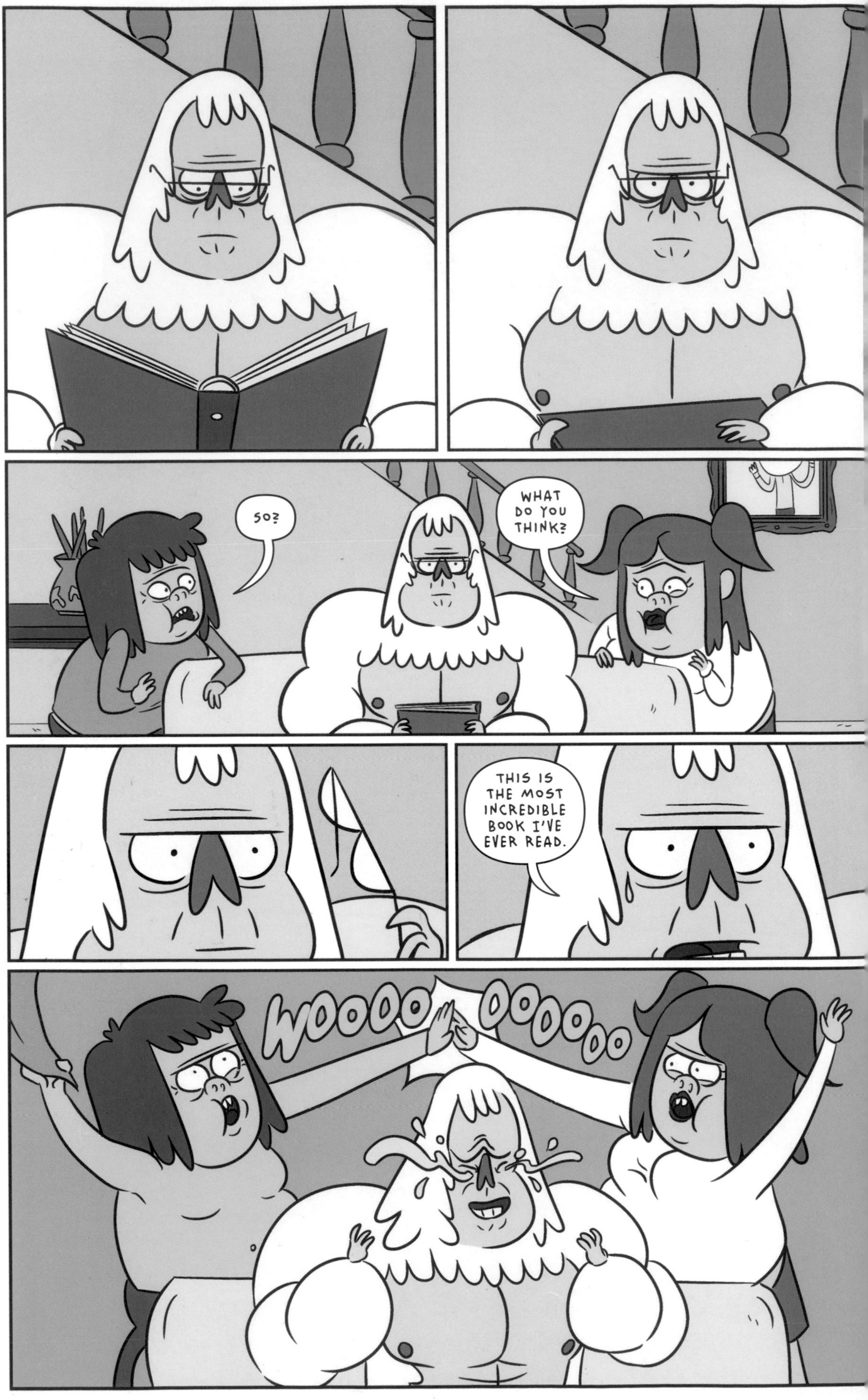
SO?
WHAT DO YOU THINK?
THIS IS THE MOST INCREDIBLE BOOK I'VE EVER READ.
WOOOO OOOOOO

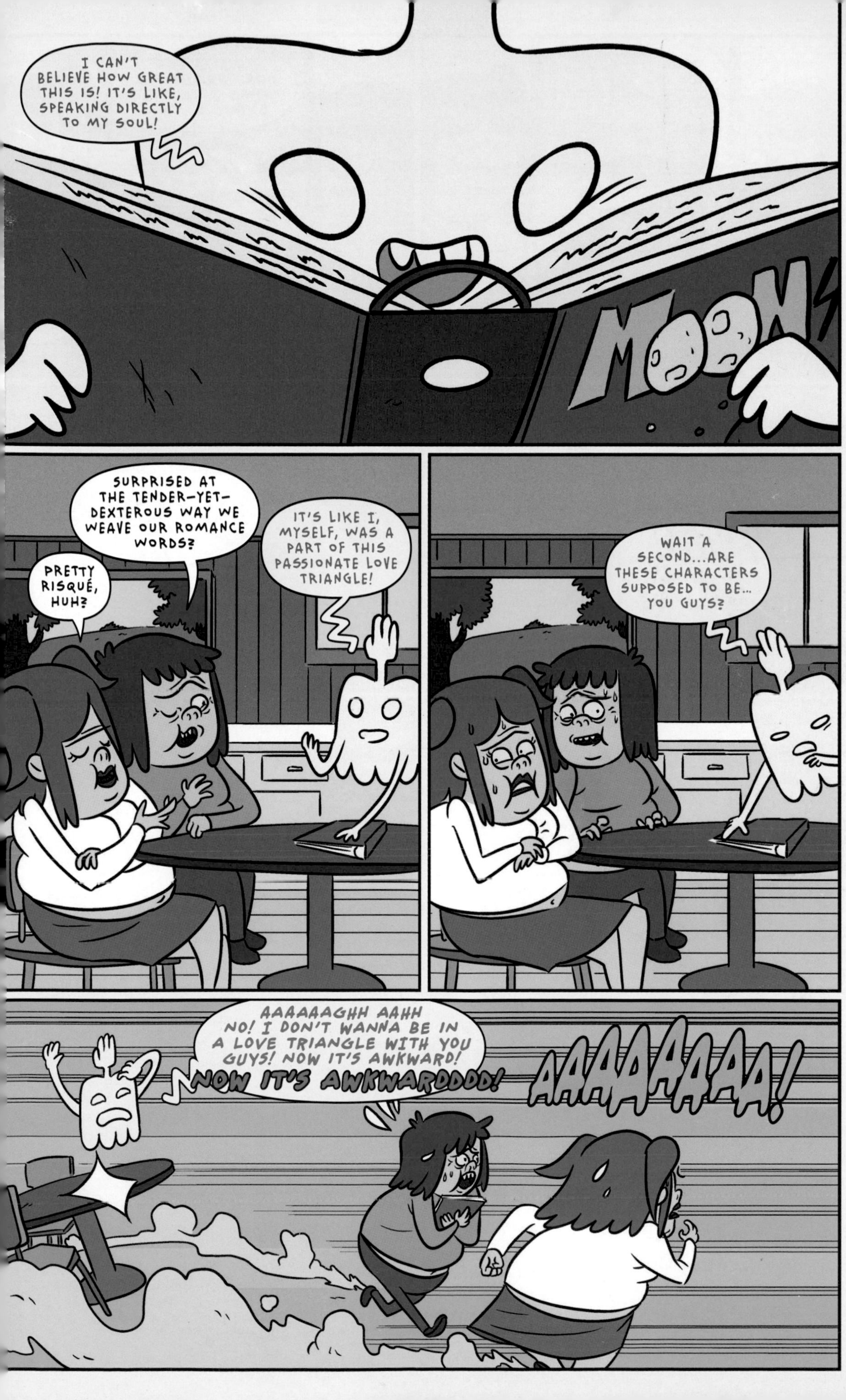
I CAN'T BELIEVE HOW GREAT THIS IS! IT'S LIKE, SPEAKING DIRECTLY TO MY SOUL!
MOON
PRETTY RISQUÉ, HUH?
SURPRISED AT THE TENDER-YET-DEXTEROUS WAY WE WEAVE OUR ROMANCE WORDS?
IT'S LIKE I, MYSELF, WAS A PART OF THIS PASSIONATE LOVE TRIANGLE!
WAIT A SECOND...ARE THESE CHARACTERS SUPPOSED TO BE... YOU GUYS?
AAAAAAGHH AAHH NO! I DON'T WANNA BE IN A LOVE TRIANGLE WITH YOU GUYS! NOW IT'S AWKWARD! NOW IT'S AWKWARDDDD!
AAAAAAAA!

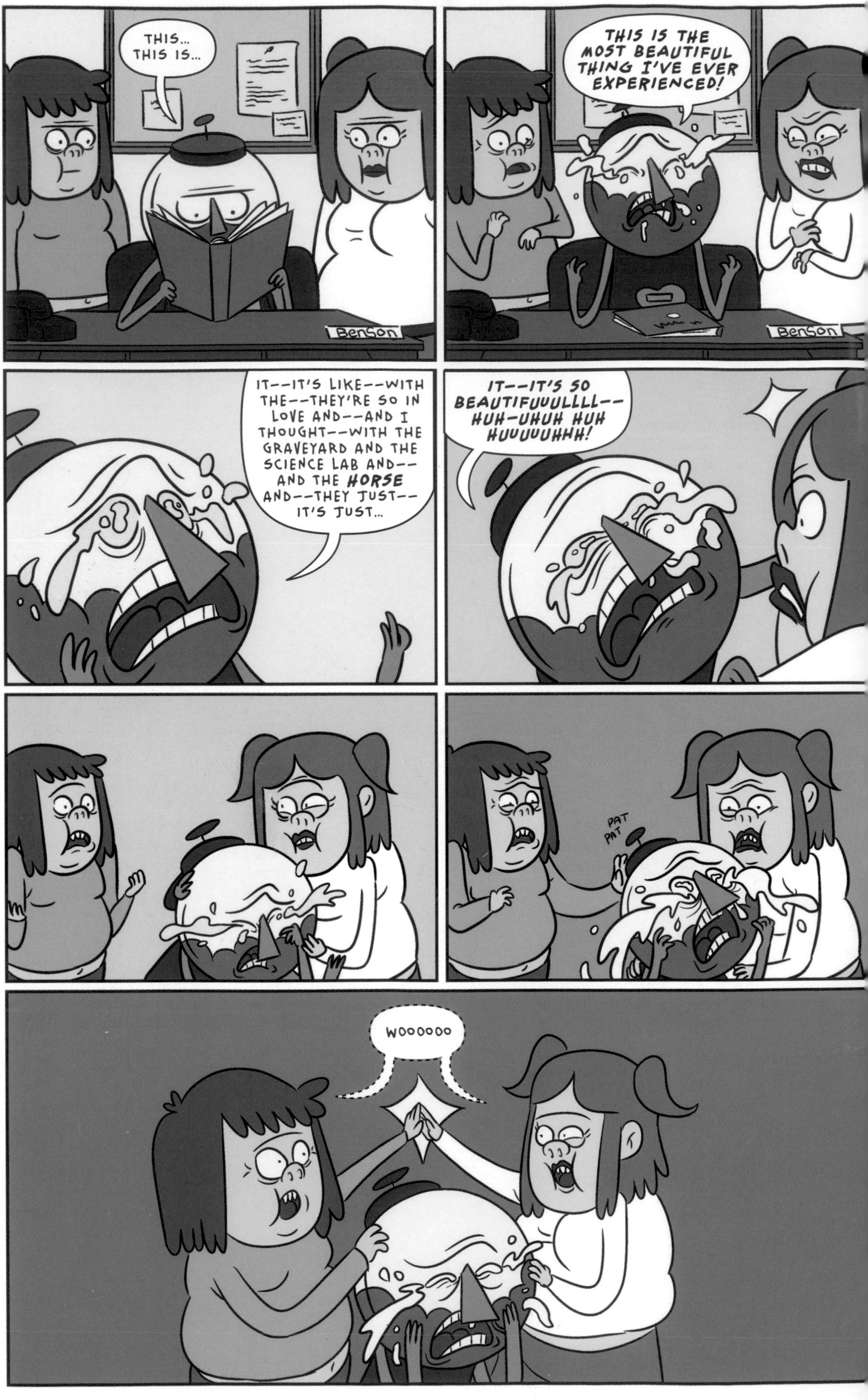
THIS... THIS IS...
THIS IS THE MOST BEAUTIFUL THING I'VE EVER EXPERIENCED!
BENSON
IT--IT'S LIKE--WITH THE--THEY'RE SO IN LOVE AND--AND I THOUGHT--WITH THE GRAVEYARD AND THE SCIENCE LAB AND--AND THE HORSE AND--THEY JUST--IT'S JUST...
IT--IT'S SO BEAUTIFUUULLLL--HUH-UHUH HUH HUUUUUHHH!
PAT PAT
WOOOOOO

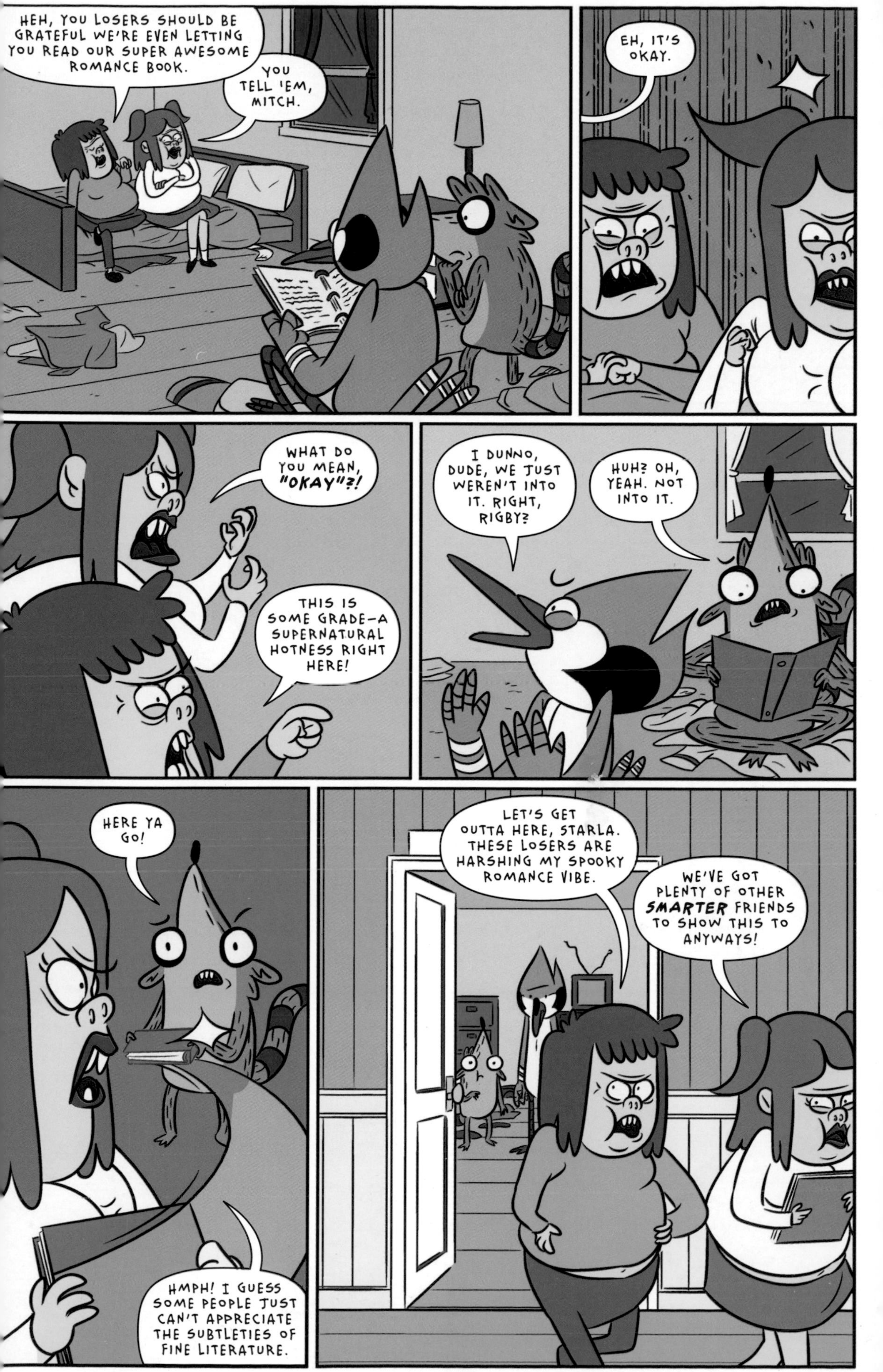
HEH, YOU LOSERS SHOULD BE GRATEFUL WE'RE EVEN LETTING YOU READ OUR SUPER AWESOME ROMANCE BOOK.
YOU TELL 'EM, MITCH.
EH, IT'S OKAY.
WHAT DO YOU MEAN, "OKAY"?!
THIS IS SOME GRADE-A SUPERNATURAL HOTNESS RIGHT HERE!
I DUNNO, DUDE, WE JUST WEREN'T INTO IT. RIGHT, RIGBY?
HUH? OH, YEAH. NOT INTO IT.
HERE YA GO!
HMPH! I GUESS SOME PEOPLE JUST CAN'T APPRECIATE THE SUBTLETIES OF FINE LITERATURE.
LET'S GET OUTTA HERE, STARLA. THESE LOSERS ARE HARSHING MY SPOOKY ROMANCE VIBE.
WE'VE GOT PLENTY OF OTHER SMARTER FRIENDS TO SHOW THIS TO ANYWAYS!

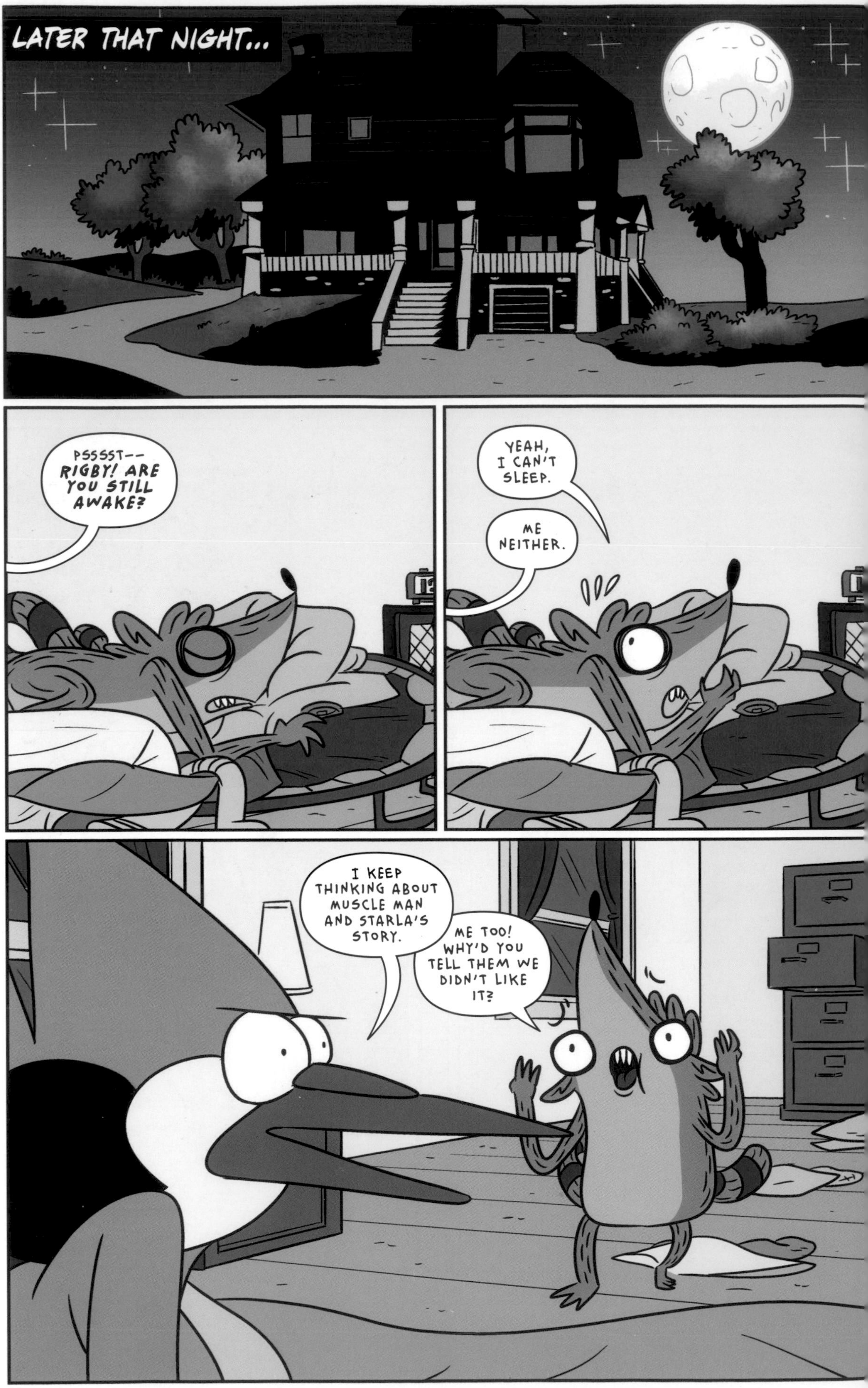
LATER THAT NIGHT...
PSSSST-- RIGBY! ARE YOU STILL AWAKE?
YEAH, I CAN'T SLEEP.
ME NEITHER.
I KEEP THINKING ABOUT MUSCLE MAN AND STARLA'S STORY.
ME TOO! WHY'D YOU TELL THEM WE DIDN'T LIKE IT?

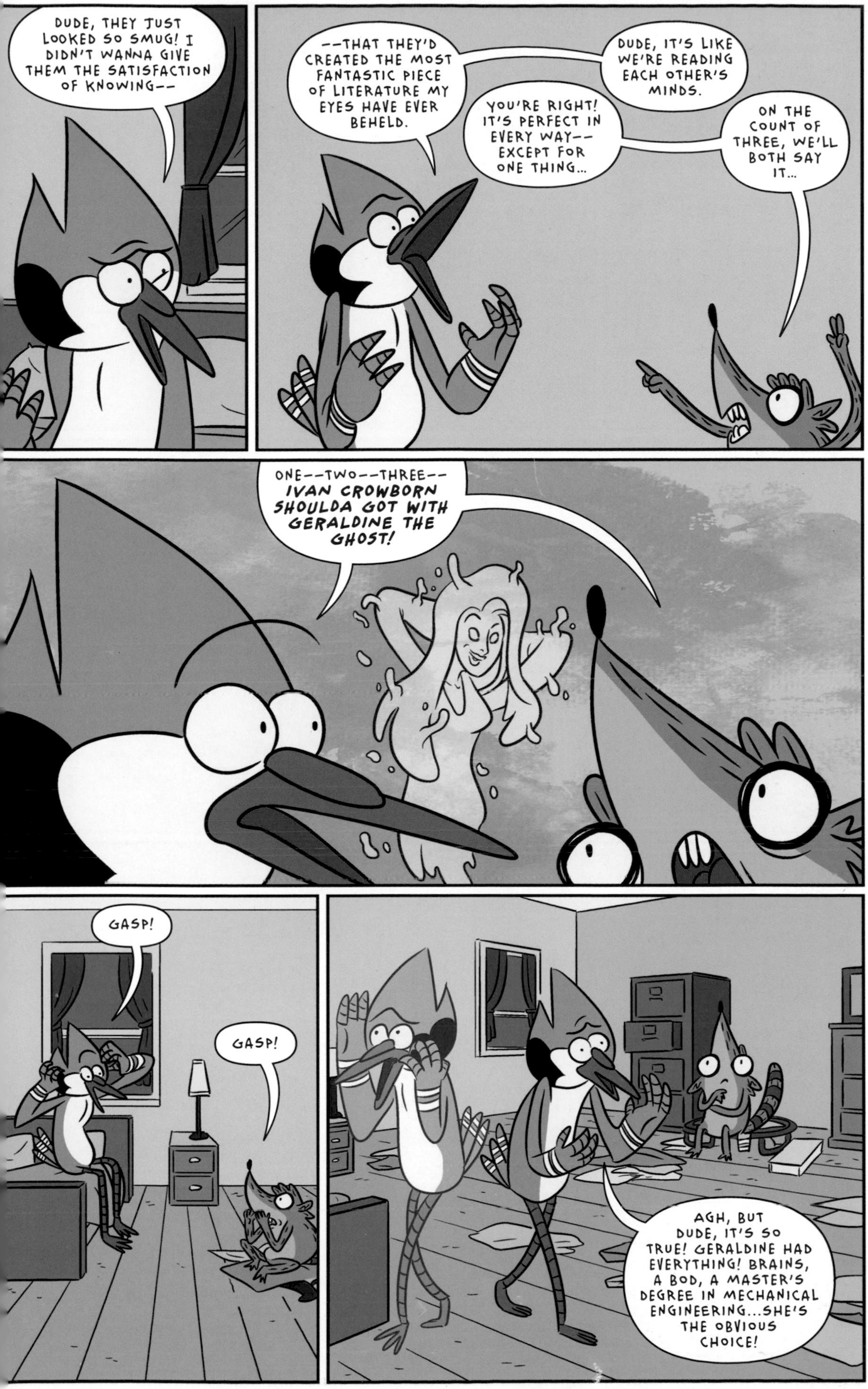
DUDE, THEY JUST LOOKED SO SMUG! I DIDN'T WANNA GIVE THEM THE SATISFACTION OF KNOWING--
--THAT THEY'D CREATED THE MOST FANTASTIC PIECE OF LITERATURE MY EYES HAVE EVER BEHELD.
DUDE, IT'S LIKE WE'RE READING EACH OTHER'S MINDS.
YOU'RE RIGHT! IT'S PERFECT IN EVERY WAY-- EXCEPT FOR ONE THING...
ON THE COUNT OF THREE, WE'LL BOTH SAY IT...
ONE--TWO--THREE-- IVAN CROWBORN SHOULDA GOT WITH GERALDINE THE GHOST!
GASP!
GASP!
AGH, BUT DUDE, IT'S SO TRUE! GERALDINE HAD EVERYTHING! BRAINS, A BOD, A MASTER'S DEGREE IN MECHANICAL ENGINEERING...SHE'S THE OBVIOUS CHOICE!

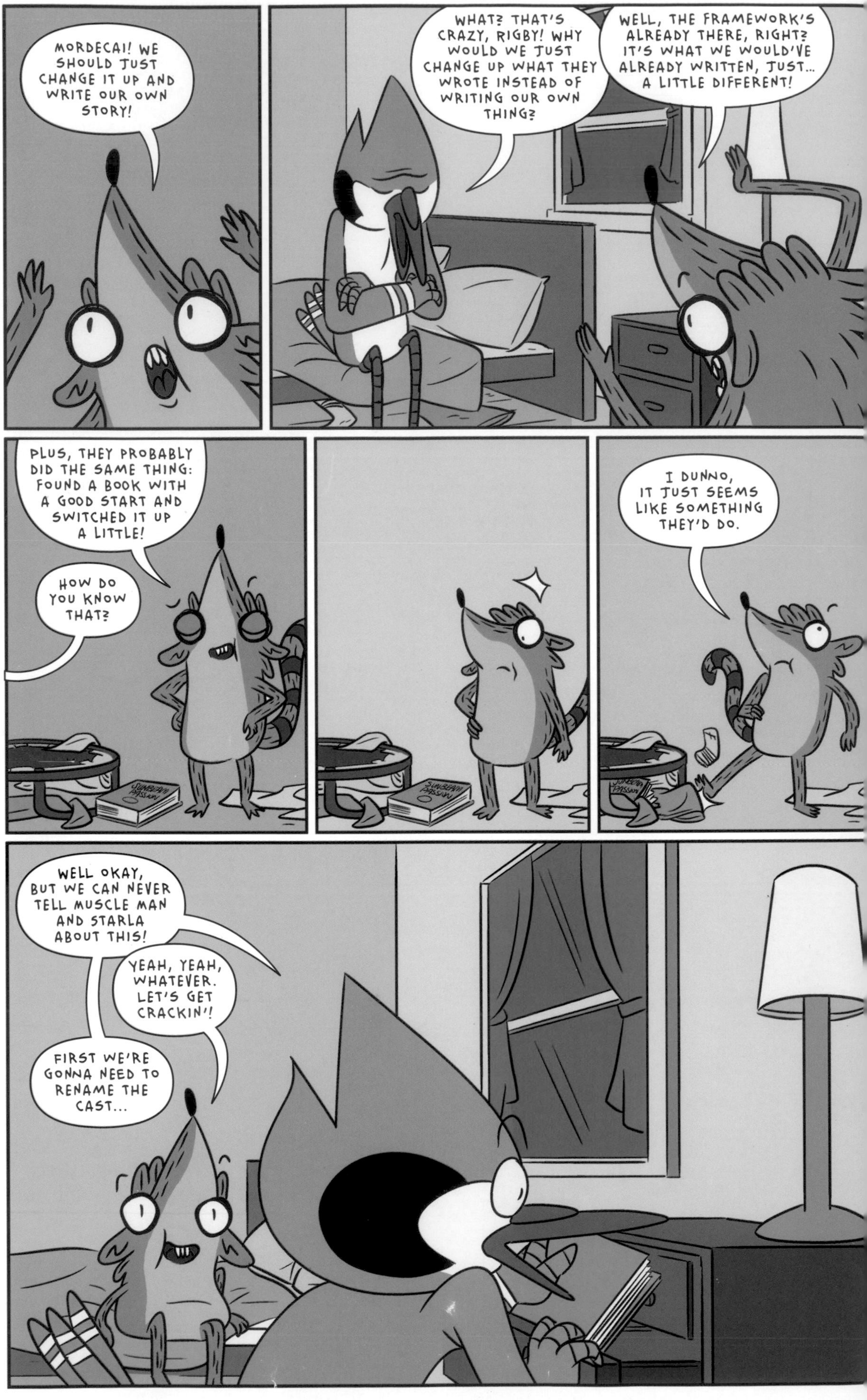
MORDECAI! WE SHOULD JUST CHANGE IT UP AND WRITE OUR OWN STORY!
WHAT? THAT'S CRAZY, RIGBY! WHY WOULD WE JUST CHANGE UP WHAT THEY WROTE INSTEAD OF WRITING OUR OWN THING?
WELL, THE FRAMEWORK'S ALREADY THERE, RIGHT? IT'S WHAT WE WOULD'VE ALREADY WRITTEN, JUST... A LITTLE DIFFERENT!
PLUS, THEY PROBABLY DID THE SAME THING: FOUND A BOOK WITH A GOOD START AND SWITCHED IT UP A LITTLE!
HOW DO YOU KNOW THAT?
SUNBEAM PASSION
I DUNNO, IT JUST SEEMS LIKE SOMETHING THEY'D DO.
WELL OKAY, BUT WE CAN NEVER TELL MUSCLE MAN AND STARLA ABOUT THIS!
YEAH, YEAH, WHATEVER. LET'S GET CRACKIN'!
FIRST WE'RE GONNA NEED TO RENAME THE CAST...

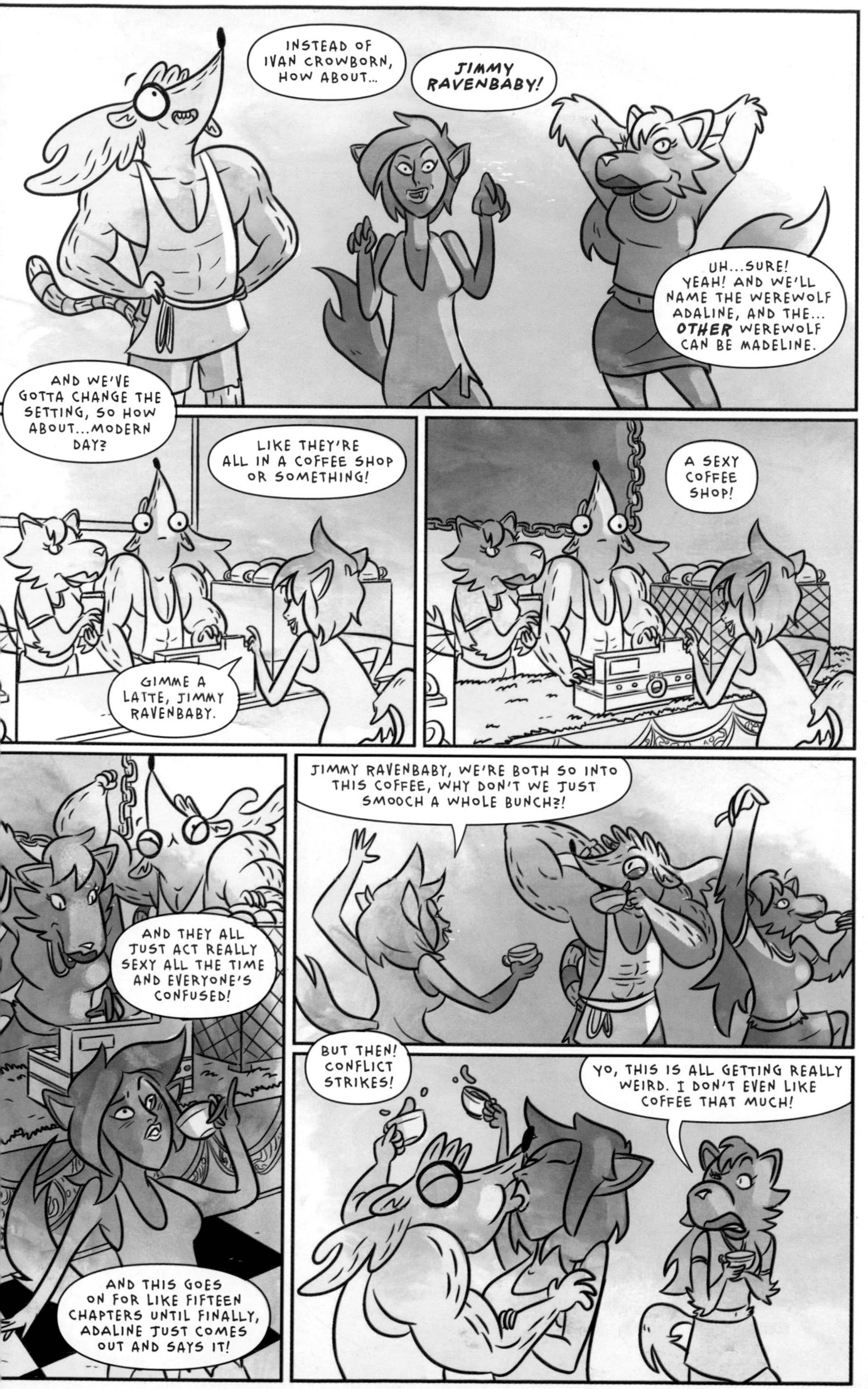
INSTEAD OF IVAN CROWBORN, HOW ABOUT...
JIMMY RAVENBABY!
UH...SURE! YEAH! AND WE'LL NAME THE WEREWOLF ADALINE, AND THE... OTHER WEREWOLF CAN BE MADELINE.
AND WE'VE GOTTA CHANGE THE SETTING, SO HOW ABOUT...MODERN DAY?
LIKE THEY'RE ALL IN A COFFEE SHOP OR SOMETHING!
GIMME A LATTE, JIMMY RAVENBABY.
A SEXY COFFEE SHOP!
AND THEY ALL JUST ACT REALLY SEXY ALL THE TIME AND EVERYONE'S CONFUSED!
AND THIS GOES ON FOR LIKE FIFTEEN CHAPTERS UNTIL FINALLY, ADALINE JUST COMES OUT AND SAYS IT!
JIMMY RAVENBABY, WE'RE BOTH SO INTO THIS COFFEE, WHY DON'T WE JUST SMOOCH A WHOLE BUNCH?!
BUT THEN! CONFLICT STRIKES!
YO, THIS IS ALL GETTING REALLY WEIRD. I DON'T EVEN LIKE COFFEE THAT MUCH!

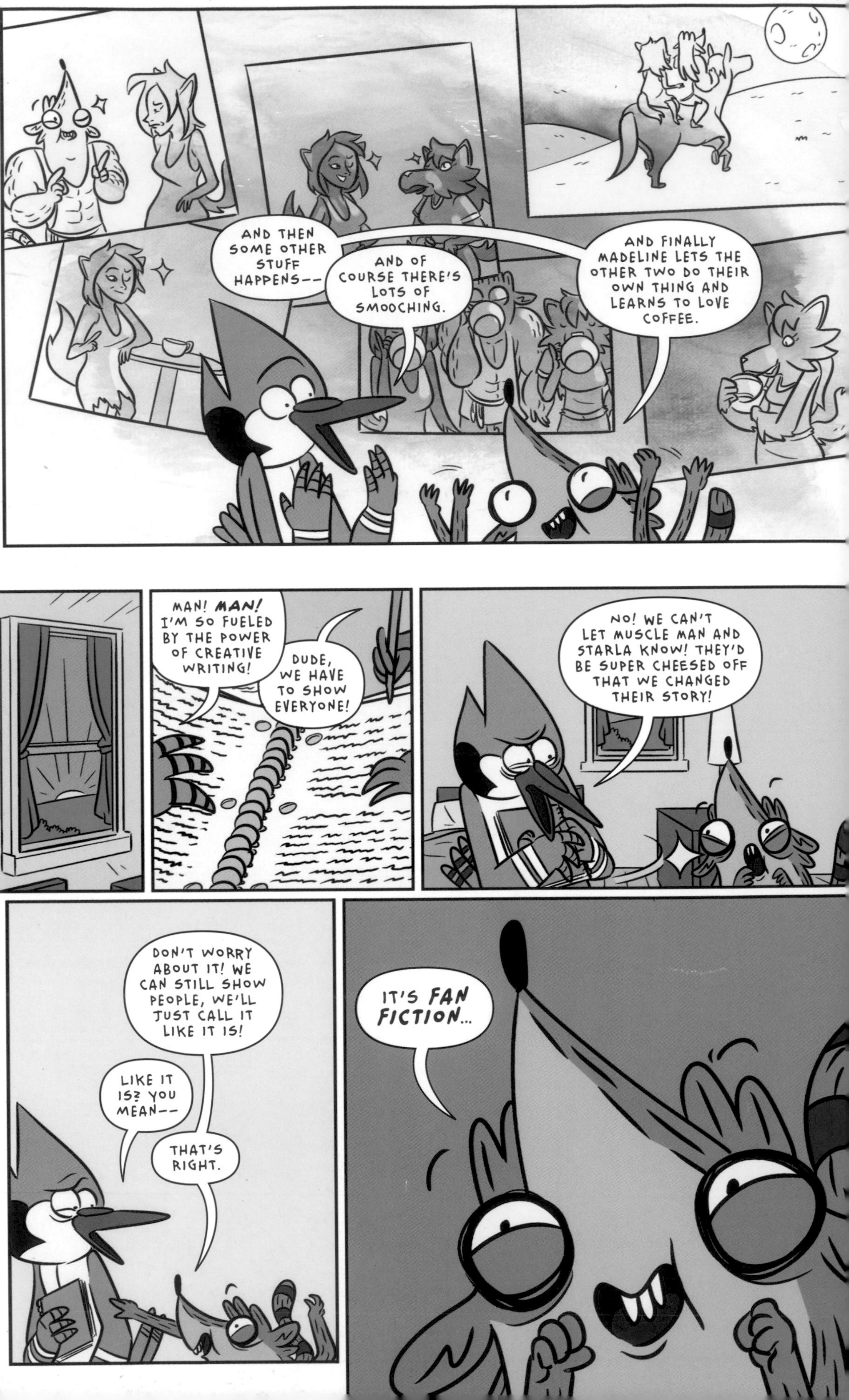
AND THEN SOME OTHER STUFF HAPPENS--
AND OF COURSE THERE'S LOTS OF SMOOCHING.
AND FINALLY MADELINE LETS THE OTHER TWO DO THEIR OWN THING AND LEARNS TO LOVE COFFEE.
MAN! MAN! I'M SO FUELED BY THE POWER OF CREATIVE WRITING!
DUDE, WE HAVE TO SHOW EVERYONE!
NO! WE CAN'T LET MUSCLE MAN AND STARLA KNOW! THEY'D BE SUPER CHEESED OFF THAT WE CHANGED THEIR STORY!
DON'T WORRY ABOUT IT! WE CAN STILL SHOW PEOPLE, WE'LL JUST CALL IT LIKE IT IS!
LIKE IT IS? YOU MEAN--
THAT'S RIGHT.
IT'S FAN FICTION...

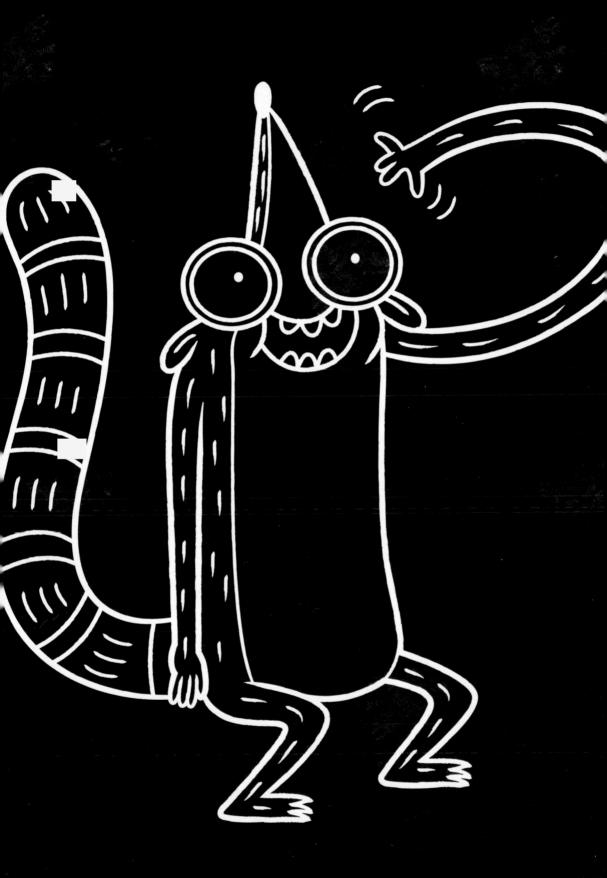

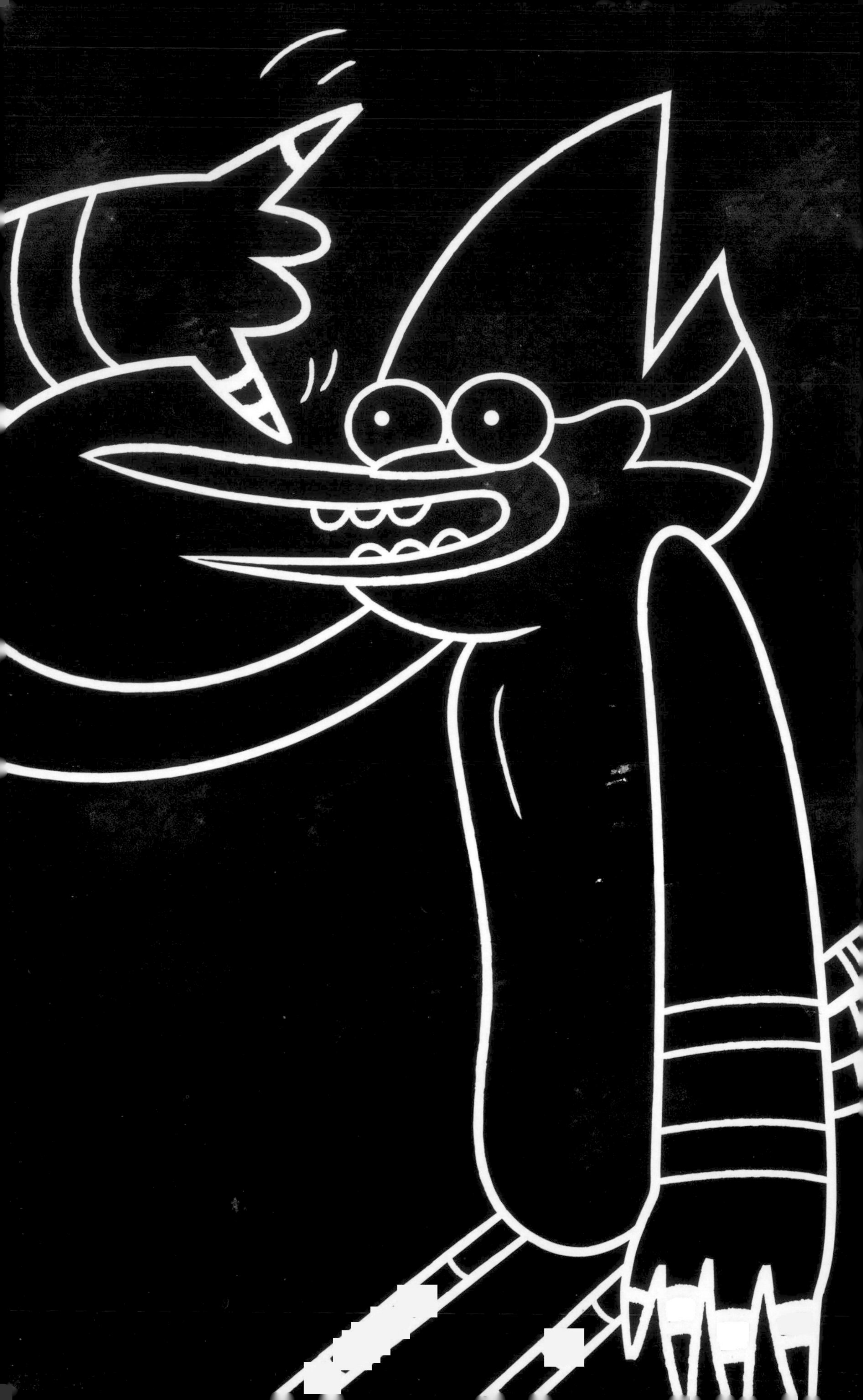

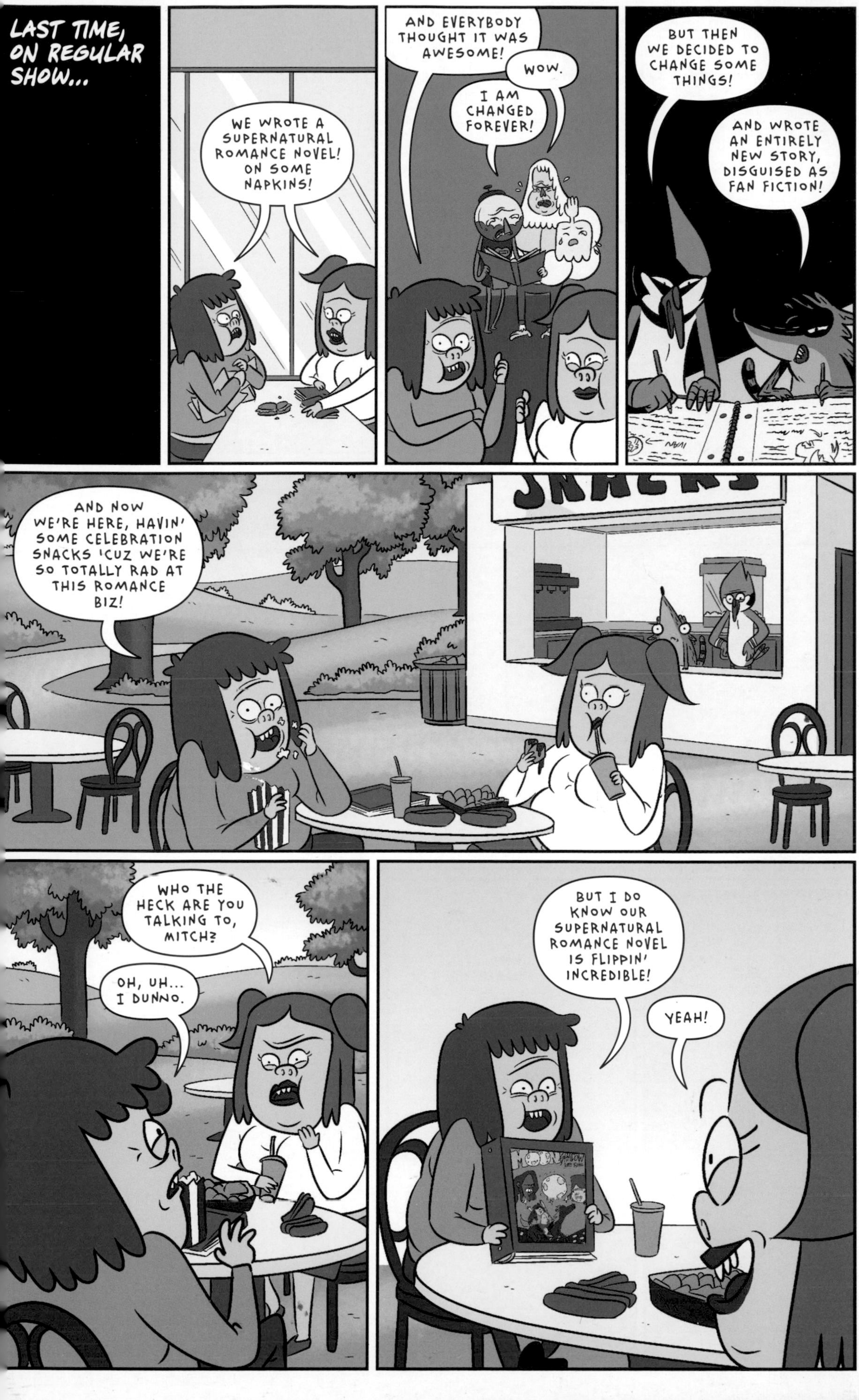
LAST TIME, ON REGULAR SHOW...
WE WROTE A SUPERNATURAL ROMANCE NOVEL! ON SOME NAPKINS!
AND EVERYBODY THOUGHT IT WAS AWESOME!
WOW.
I AM CHANGED FOREVER!
BUT THEN WE DECIDED TO CHANGE SOME THINGS!
AND WROTE AN ENTIRELY NEW STORY, DISGUISED AS FAN FICTION!
AND NOW WE'RE HERE, HAVIN' SOME CELEBRATION SNACKS 'CUZ WE'RE SO TOTALLY RAD AT THIS ROMANCE BIZ!
WHO THE HECK ARE YOU TALKING TO, MITCH?
OH, UH... I DUNNO.
BUT I DO KNOW OUR SUPERNATURAL ROMANCE NOVEL IS FLIPPIN' INCREDIBLE!
YEAH!

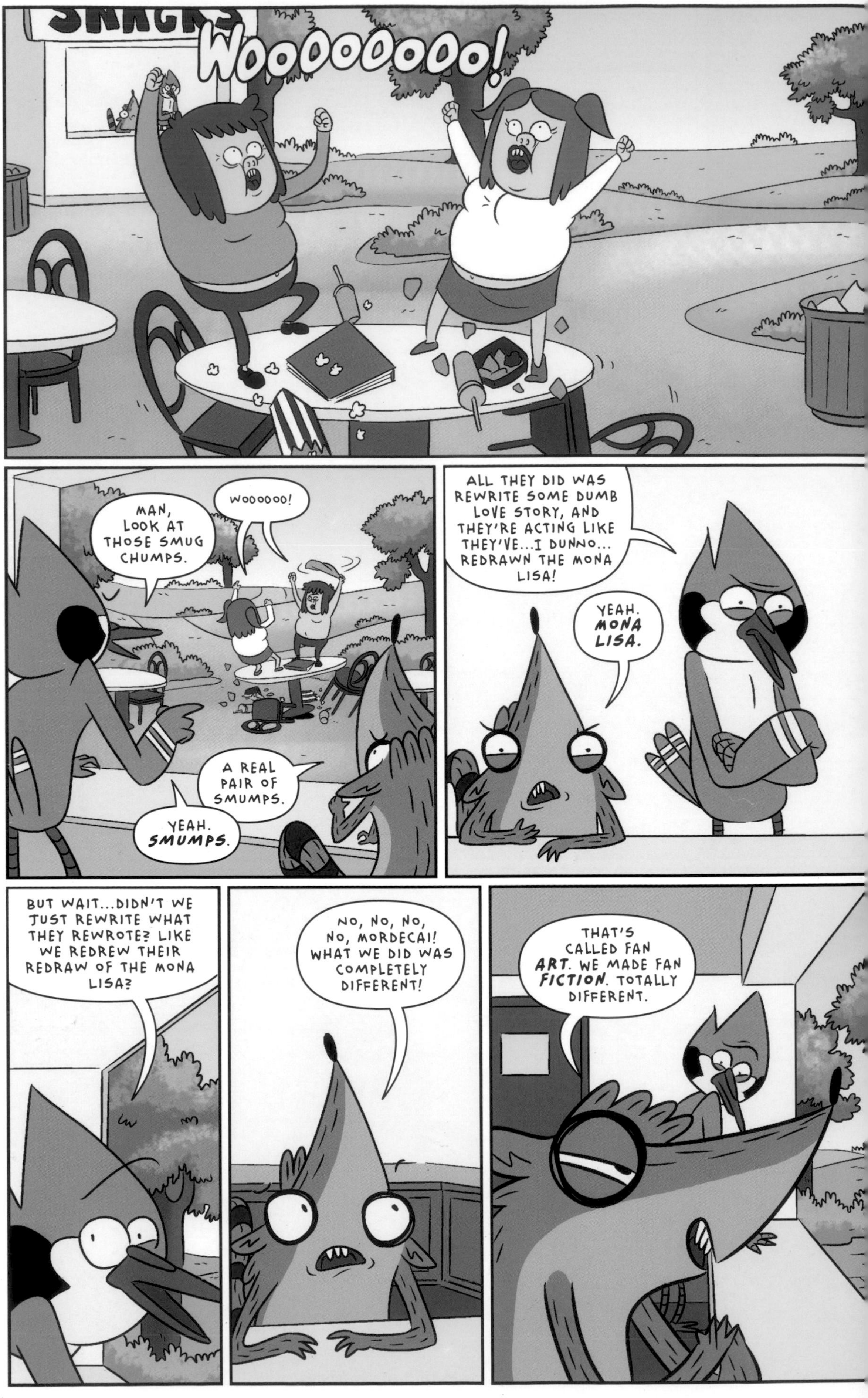
SNACKS
WOOOOOOOO!
MAN, LOOK AT THOSE SMUG CHUMPS.
WOOOOOO!
A REAL PAIR OF SMUMPS.
YEAH. SMUMPS.
ALL THEY DID WAS REWRITE SOME DUMB LOVE STORY, AND THEY'RE ACTING LIKE THEY'VE...I DUNNO... REDRAWN THE MONA LISA!
YEAH. MONA LISA.
BUT WAIT...DIDN'T WE JUST REWRITE WHAT THEY REWROTE? LIKE WE REDREW THEIR REDRAW OF THE MONA LISA?
NO, NO, NO, NO, MORDECAI! WHAT WE DID WAS COMPLETELY DIFFERENT!
THAT'S CALLED FAN ART. WE MADE FAN FICTION. TOTALLY DIFFERENT.

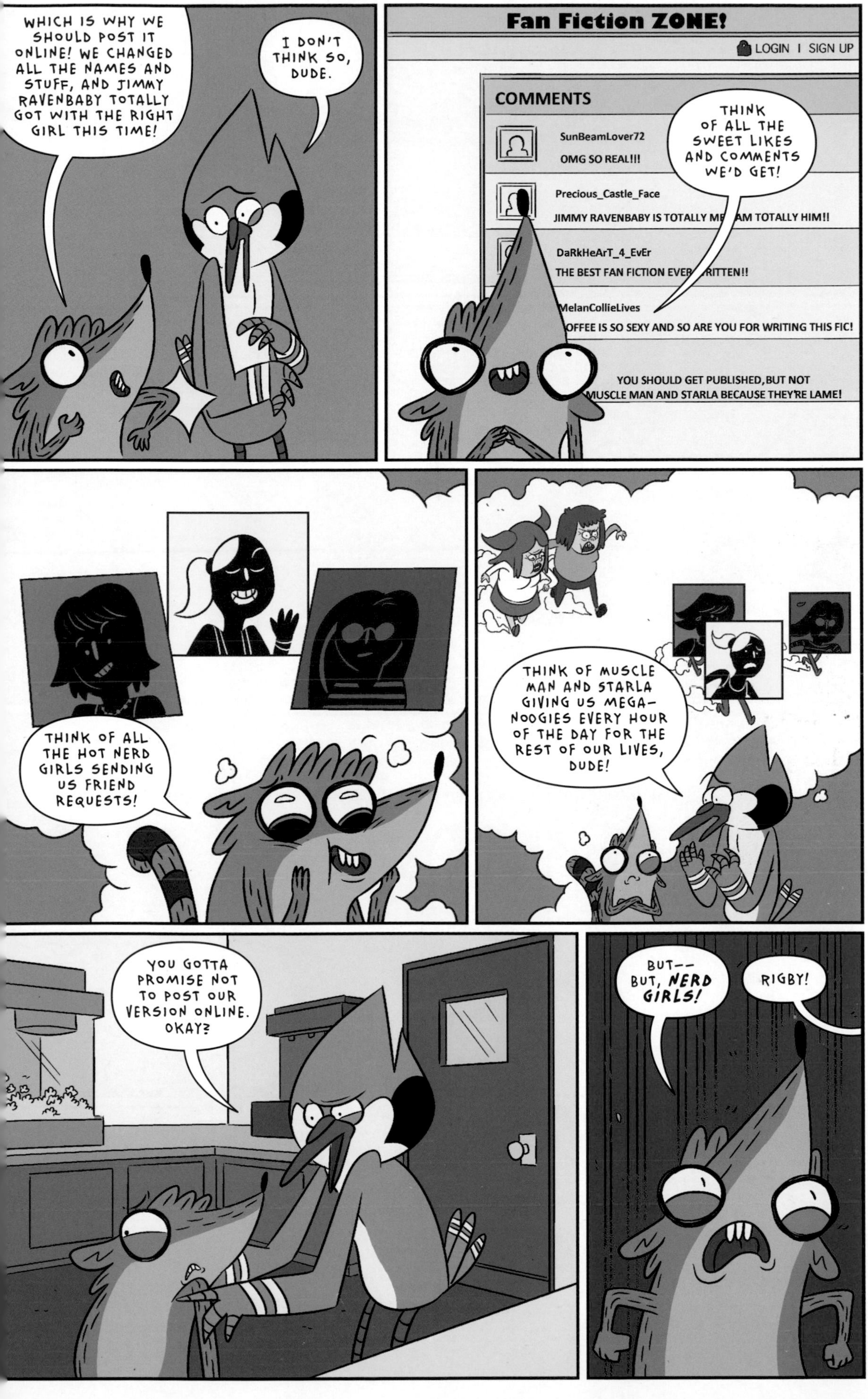
WHICH IS WHY WE SHOULD POST IT ONLINE! WE CHANGED ALL THE NAMES AND STUFF, AND JIMMY RAVENBABY TOTALLY GOT WITH THE RIGHT GIRL THIS TIME!
I DON'T THINK SO, DUDE.
Fan Fiction ZONE!
LOGIN I SIGN UP
COMMENTS
SunBeamLover72
OMG SO REAL!!!
Precious_Castle_Face
JIMMY RAVENBABY IS TOTALLY ME
AM TOTALLY HIM!!
DaRkHeArT_4_EvEr
THE BEST FAN FICTION EVER
RITTEN!!
MelanCollieLives
OFFEE IS SO SEXY AND SO ARE YOU FOR WRITING THIS FIC!
YOU SHOULD GET PUBLISHED, BUT NOT
MUSCLE MAN AND STARLA BECAUSE THEY'RE LAME!
THINK OF ALL THE SWEET LIKES AND COMMENTS WE'D GET!
THINK OF ALL THE HOT NERD GIRLS SENDING US FRIEND REQUESTS!
THINK OF MUSCLE MAN AND STARLA GIVING US MEGA-NOOGIES EVERY HOUR OF THE DAY FOR THE REST OF OUR LIVES, DUDE!
YOU GOTTA PROMISE NOT TO POST OUR VERSION ONLINE. OKAY?
BUT-- BUT, NERD GIRLS!
RIGBY!

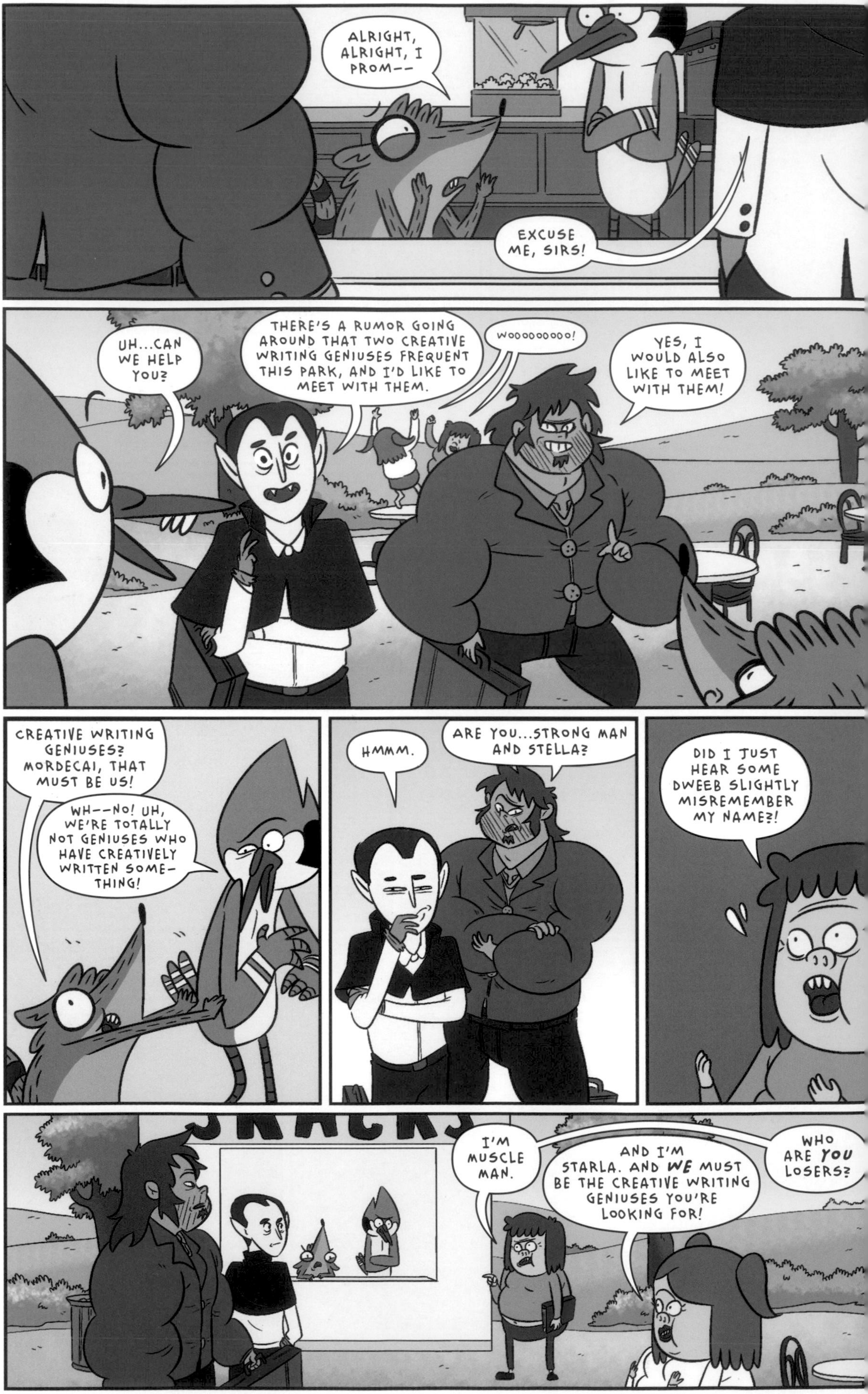
ALRIGHT, ALRIGHT, I PROM--
EXCUSE ME, SIRS!
UH...CAN WE HELP YOU?
THERE'S A RUMOR GOING AROUND THAT TWO CREATIVE WRITING GENIUSES FREQUENT THIS PARK, AND I'D LIKE TO MEET WITH THEM.
WOOOOOOOOO!
YES, I WOULD ALSO LIKE TO MEET WITH THEM!
CREATIVE WRITING GENIUSES? MORDECAI, THAT MUST BE US!
WH--NO! UH, WE'RE TOTALLY NOT GENIUSES WHO HAVE CREATIVELY WRITTEN SOME-THING!
HMMM.
ARE YOU...STRONG MAN AND STELLA?
DID I JUST HEAR SOME DWEEB SLIGHTLY MISREMEMBER MY NAME?!
I'M MUSCLE MAN.
WHO ARE *YOU* LOSERS?
AND I'M STARLA. AND *WE* MUST BE THE CREATIVE WRITING GENIUSES YOU'RE LOOKING FOR!

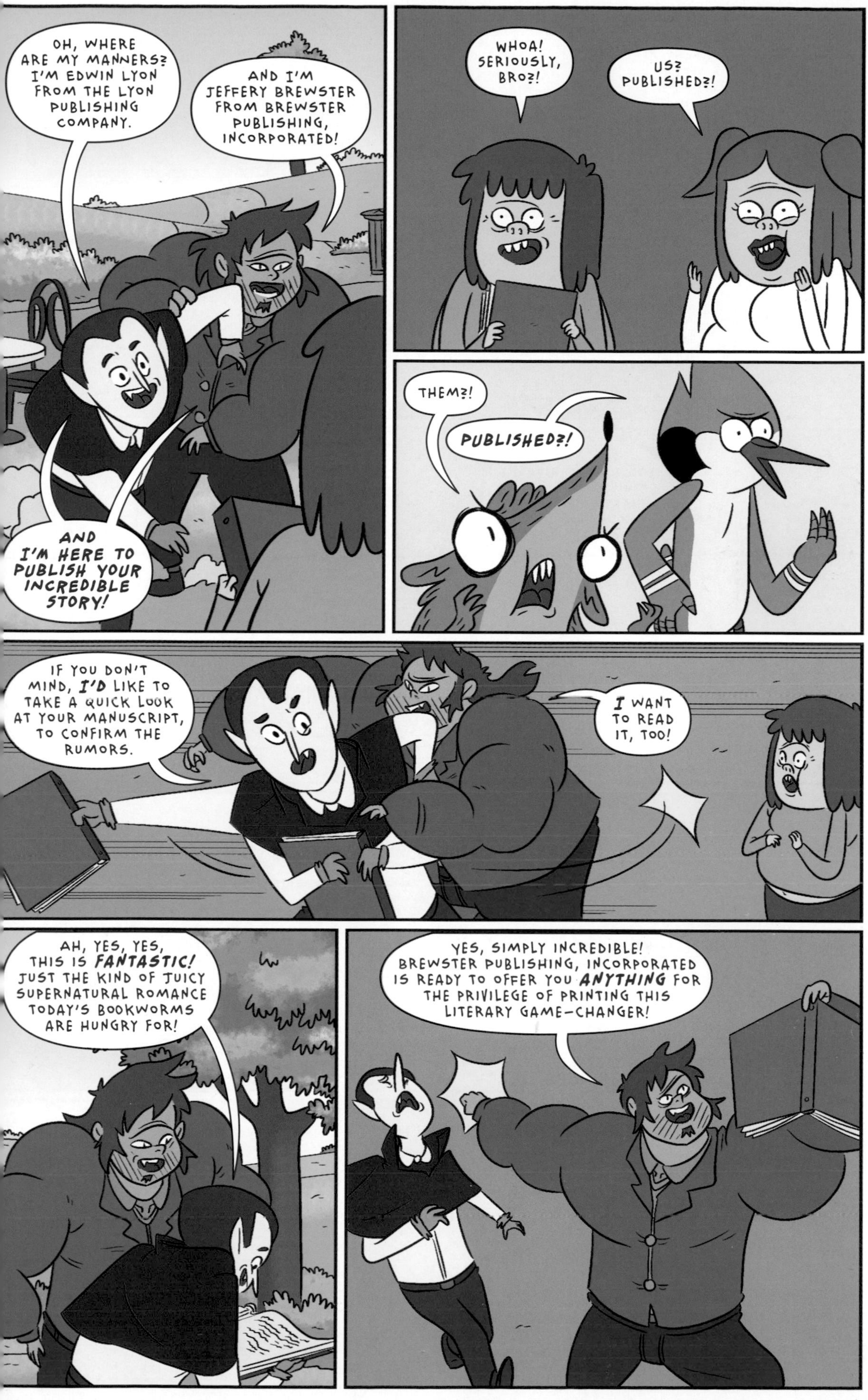
OH, WHERE ARE MY MANNERS? I'M EDWIN LYON FROM THE LYON PUBLISHING COMPANY.
AND I'M JEFFERY BREWSTER FROM BREWSTER PUBLISHING, INCORPORATED!
AND I'M HERE TO PUBLISH YOUR INCREDIBLE STORY!
WHOA! SERIOUSLY, BRO?!
US? PUBLISHED?!
THEM?!
PUBLISHED?!
IF YOU DON'T MIND, I'D LIKE TO TAKE A QUICK LOOK AT YOUR MANUSCRIPT, TO CONFIRM THE RUMORS.
I WANT TO READ IT, TOO!
AH, YES, YES, THIS IS FANTASTIC! JUST THE KIND OF JUICY SUPERNATURAL ROMANCE TODAY'S BOOKWORMS ARE HUNGRY FOR!
YES, SIMPLY INCREDIBLE! BREWSTER PUBLISHING, INCORPORATED IS READY TO OFFER YOU ANYTHING FOR THE PRIVILEGE OF PRINTING THIS LITERARY GAME-CHANGER!

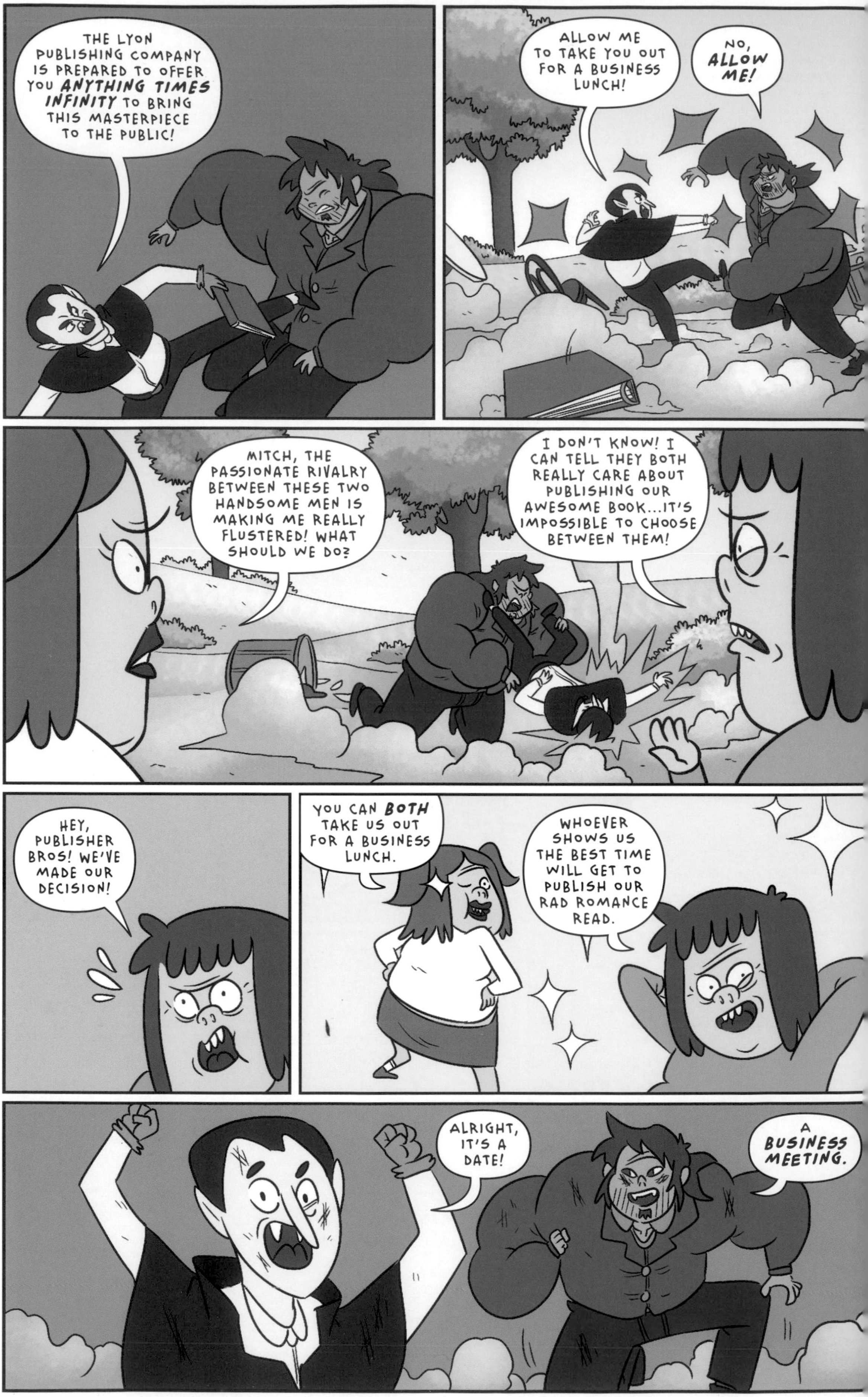
THE LYON PUBLISHING COMPANY IS PREPARED TO OFFER YOU **ANYTHING TIMES INFINITY** TO BRING THIS MASTERPIECE TO THE PUBLIC!
ALLOW ME TO TAKE YOU OUT FOR A BUSINESS LUNCH!
NO, **ALLOW ME!**
MITCH, THE PASSIONATE RIVALRY BETWEEN THESE TWO HANDSOME MEN IS MAKING ME REALLY FLUSTERED! WHAT SHOULD WE DO?
I DON'T KNOW! I CAN TELL THEY BOTH REALLY CARE ABOUT PUBLISHING OUR AWESOME BOOK...IT'S IMPOSSIBLE TO CHOOSE BETWEEN THEM!
HEY, PUBLISHER BROS! WE'VE MADE OUR DECISION!
YOU CAN **BOTH** TAKE US OUT FOR A BUSINESS LUNCH.
WHOEVER SHOWS US THE BEST TIME WILL GET TO PUBLISH OUR RAD ROMANCE READ.
ALRIGHT, IT'S A DATE!
A **BUSINESS MEETING.**

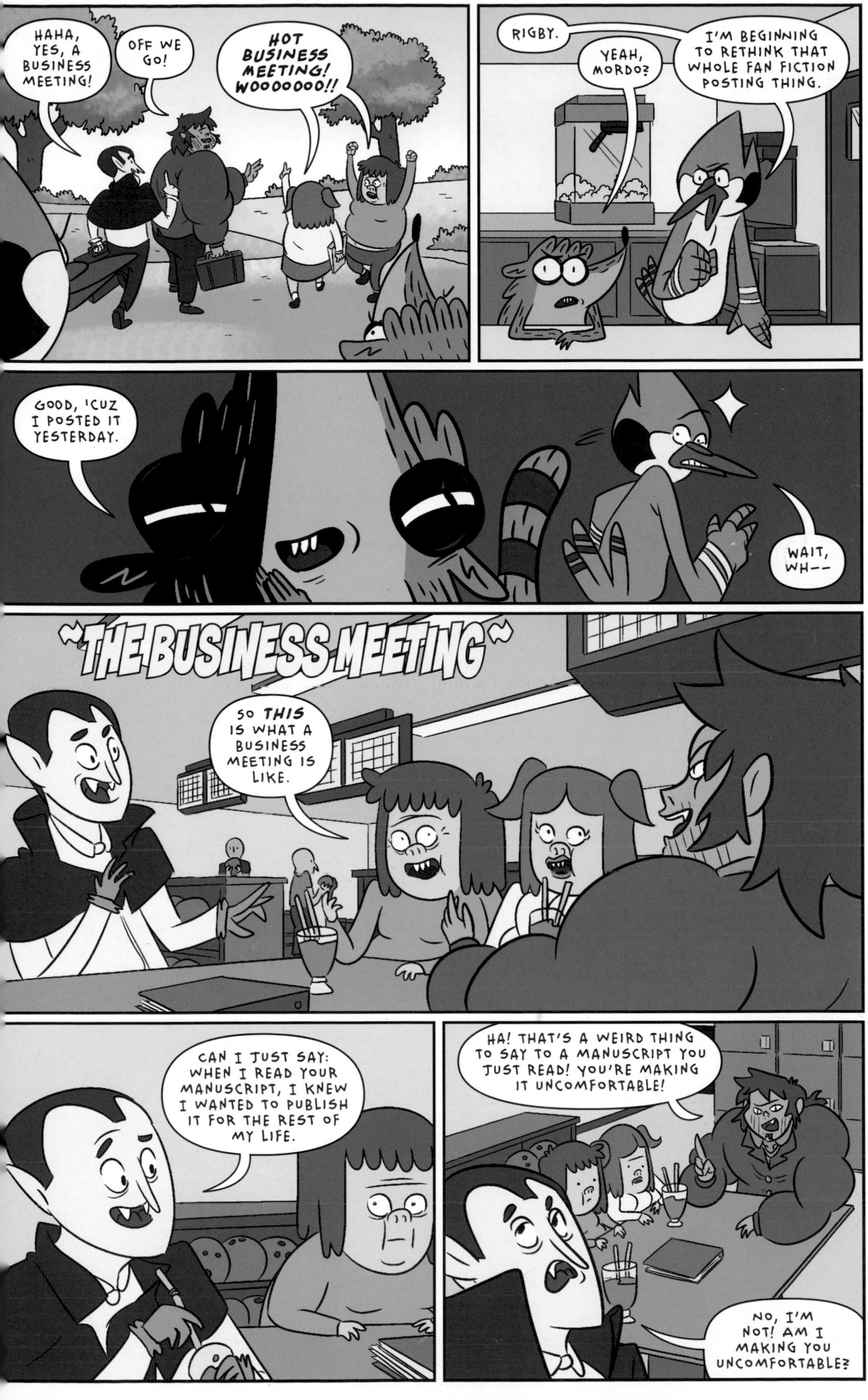
HAHA, YES, A BUSINESS MEETING!
OFF WE GO!
HOT BUSINESS MEETING! WOOOOOOO!!
RIGBY.
YEAH, MORDO?
I'M BEGINNING TO RETHINK THAT WHOLE FAN FICTION POSTING THING.
GOOD, 'CUZ I POSTED IT YESTERDAY.
WAIT, WH--
~THE BUSINESS MEETING~
SO THIS IS WHAT A BUSINESS MEETING IS LIKE.
CAN I JUST SAY: WHEN I READ YOUR MANUSCRIPT, I KNEW I WANTED TO PUBLISH IT FOR THE REST OF MY LIFE.
HA! THAT'S A WEIRD THING TO SAY TO A MANUSCRIPT YOU JUST READ! YOU'RE MAKING IT UNCOMFORTABLE!
NO, I'M NOT! AM I MAKING YOU UNCOMFORTABLE?

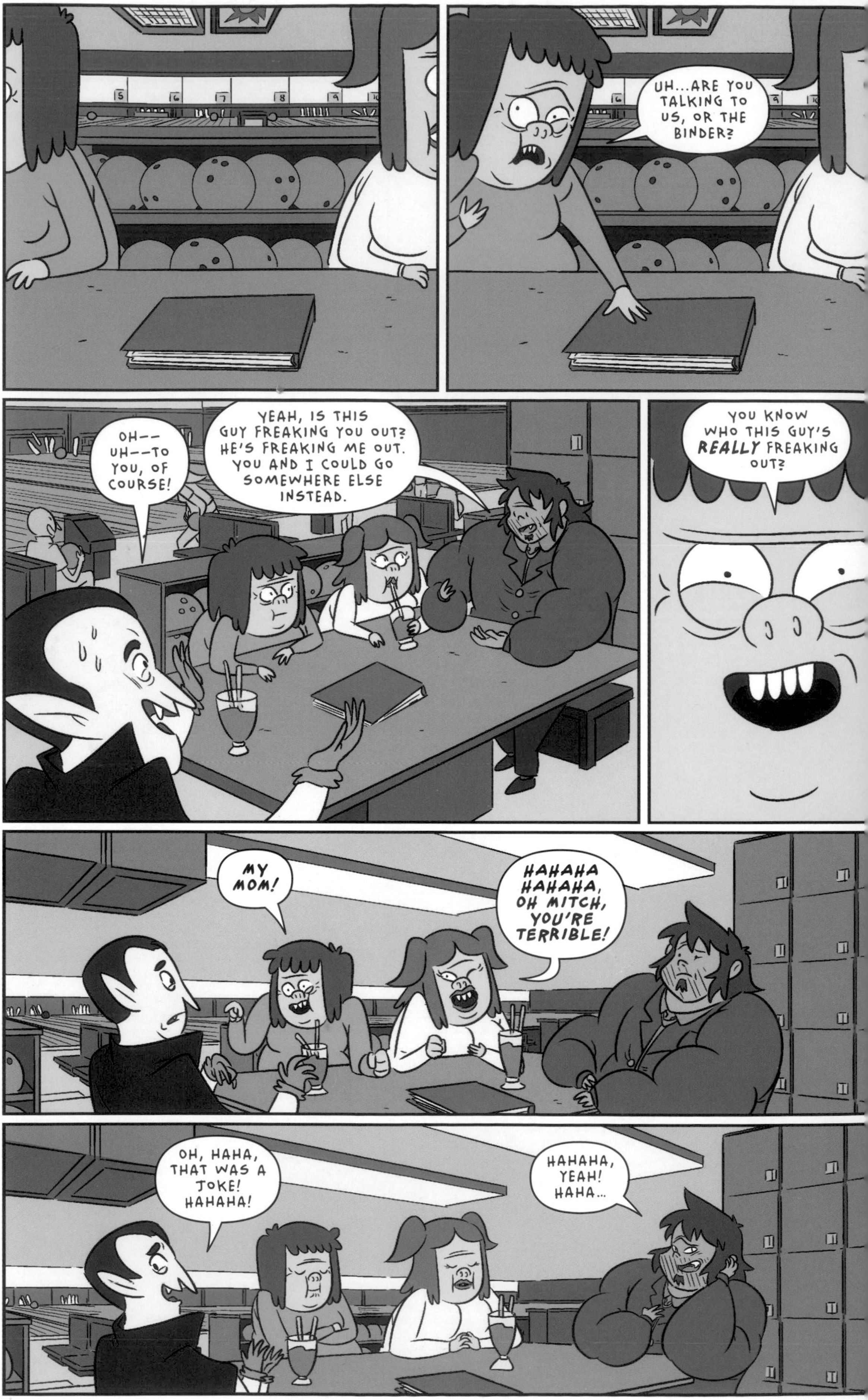

UH...ARE YOU TALKING TO US, OR THE BINDER?
OH-- UH--TO YOU, OF COURSE!
YEAH, IS THIS GUY FREAKING YOU OUT? HE'S FREAKING ME OUT. YOU AND I COULD GO SOMEWHERE ELSE INSTEAD.
YOU KNOW WHO THIS GUY'S REALLY FREAKING OUT?
MY MOM!
HAHAHA HAHAHA, OH MITCH, YOU'RE TERRIBLE!
OH, HAHA, THAT WAS A JOKE! HAHAHA!
HAHAHA, YEAH! HAHA...

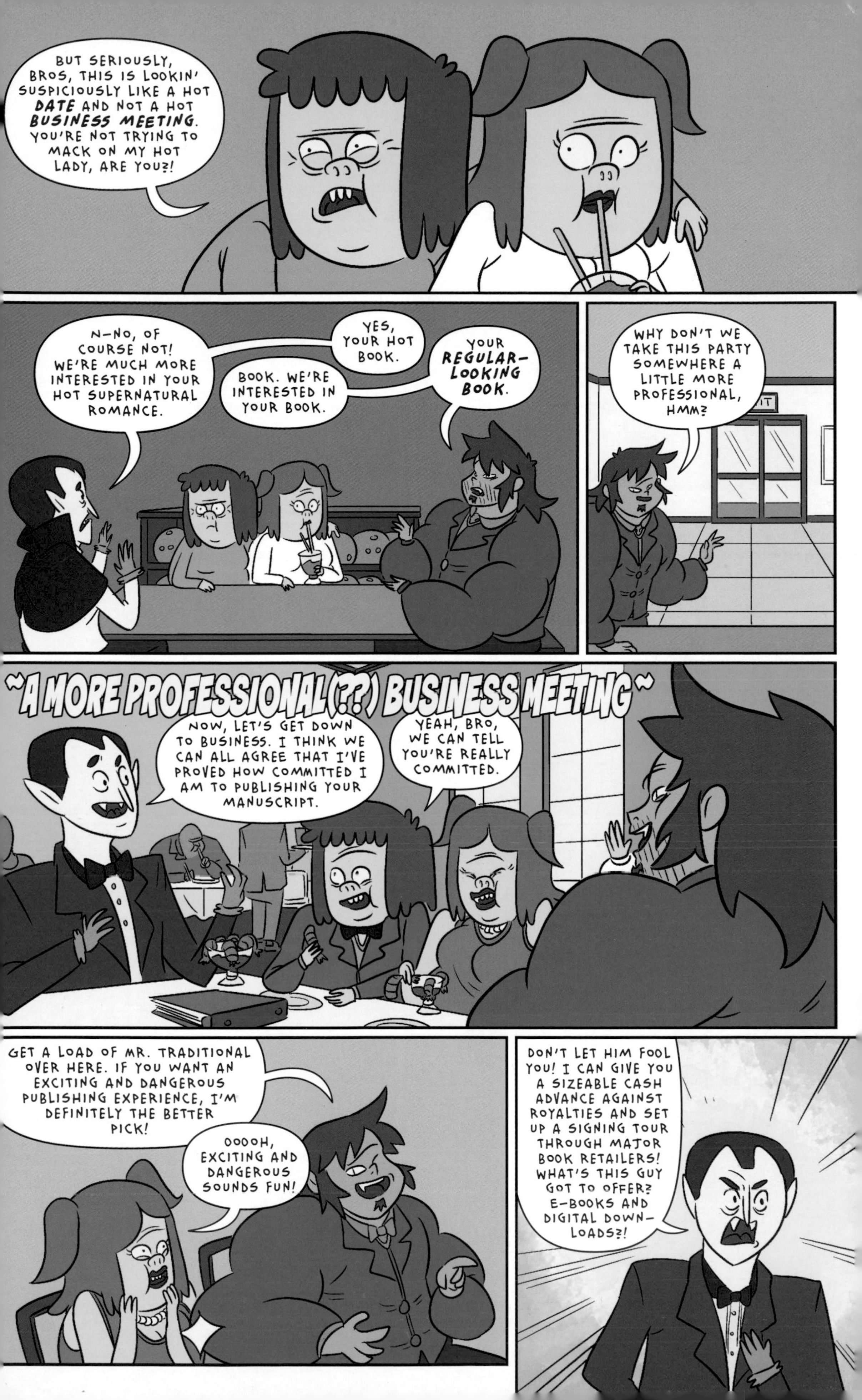
BUT SERIOUSLY, BROS, THIS IS LOOKIN' SUSPICIOUSLY LIKE A HOT DATE AND NOT A HOT BUSINESS MEETING. YOU'RE NOT TRYING TO MACK ON MY HOT LADY, ARE YOU?!
N–NO, OF COURSE NOT! WE'RE MUCH MORE INTERESTED IN YOUR HOT SUPERNATURAL ROMANCE.
YES, YOUR HOT BOOK.
BOOK. WE'RE INTERESTED IN YOUR BOOK.
YOUR REGULAR-LOOKING BOOK.
WHY DON'T WE TAKE THIS PARTY SOMEWHERE A LITTLE MORE PROFESSIONAL, HMM?
~A MORE PROFESSIONAL(??) BUSINESS MEETING~
NOW, LET'S GET DOWN TO BUSINESS. I THINK WE CAN ALL AGREE THAT I'VE PROVED HOW COMMITTED I AM TO PUBLISHING YOUR MANUSCRIPT.
YEAH, BRO, WE CAN TELL YOU'RE REALLY COMMITTED.
GET A LOAD OF MR. TRADITIONAL OVER HERE. IF YOU WANT AN EXCITING AND DANGEROUS PUBLISHING EXPERIENCE, I'M DEFINITELY THE BETTER PICK!
OOOOH, EXCITING AND DANGEROUS SOUNDS FUN!
DON'T LET HIM FOOL YOU! I CAN GIVE YOU A SIZEABLE CASH ADVANCE AGAINST ROYALTIES AND SET UP A SIGNING TOUR THROUGH MAJOR BOOK RETAILERS! WHAT'S THIS GUY GOT TO OFFER? E-BOOKS AND DIGITAL DOWN-LOADS?!

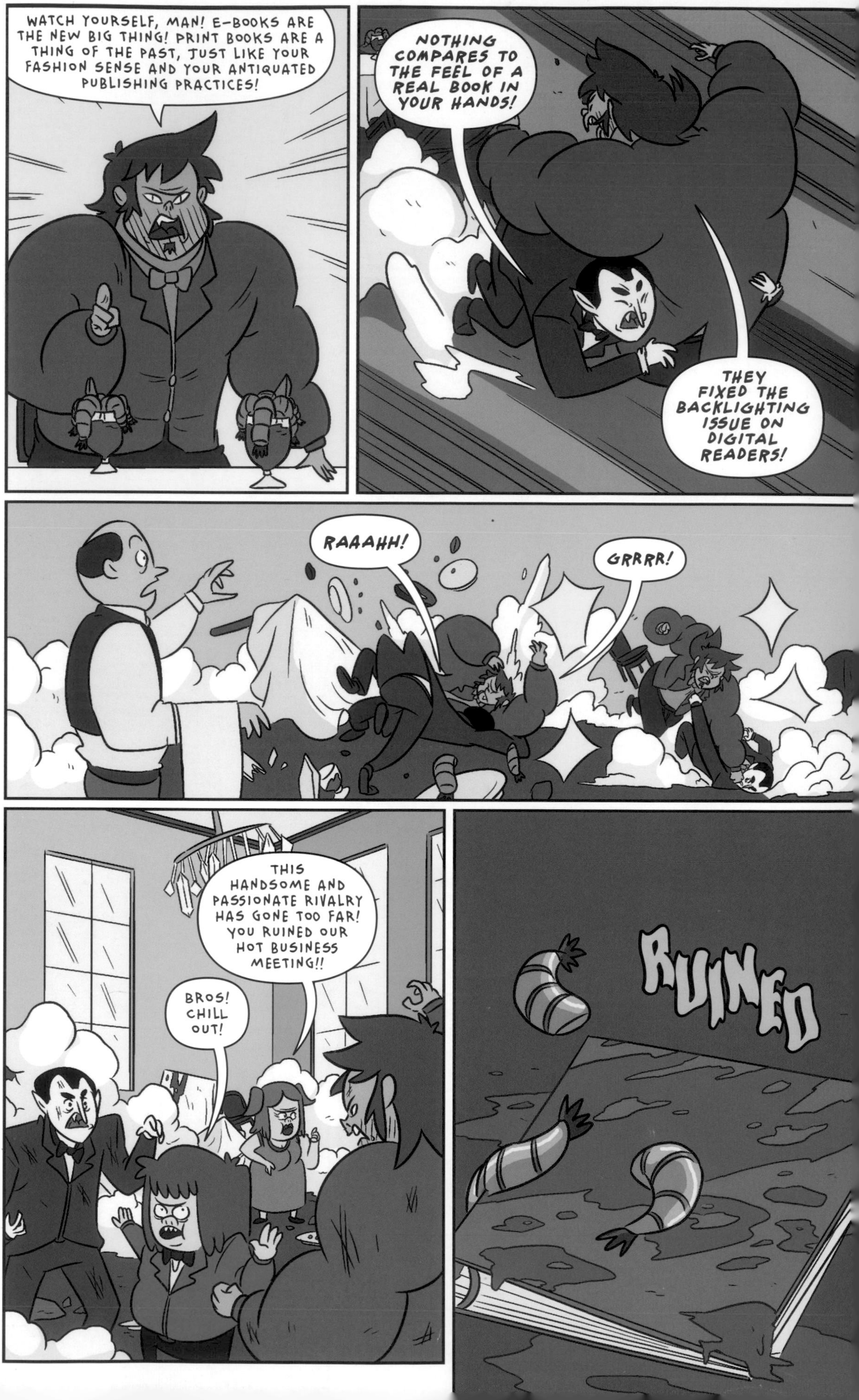
WATCH YOURSELF, MAN! E-BOOKS ARE THE NEW BIG THING! PRINT BOOKS ARE A THING OF THE PAST, JUST LIKE YOUR FASHION SENSE AND YOUR ANTIQUATED PUBLISHING PRACTICES!
NOTHING COMPARES TO THE FEEL OF A REAL BOOK IN YOUR HANDS!
THEY FIXED THE BACKLIGHTING ISSUE ON DIGITAL READERS!
RAAAHH!
GRRRR!
THIS HANDSOME AND PASSIONATE RIVALRY HAS GONE TOO FAR! YOU RUINED OUR HOT BUSINESS MEETING!!
BROS! CHILL OUT!
RUINED

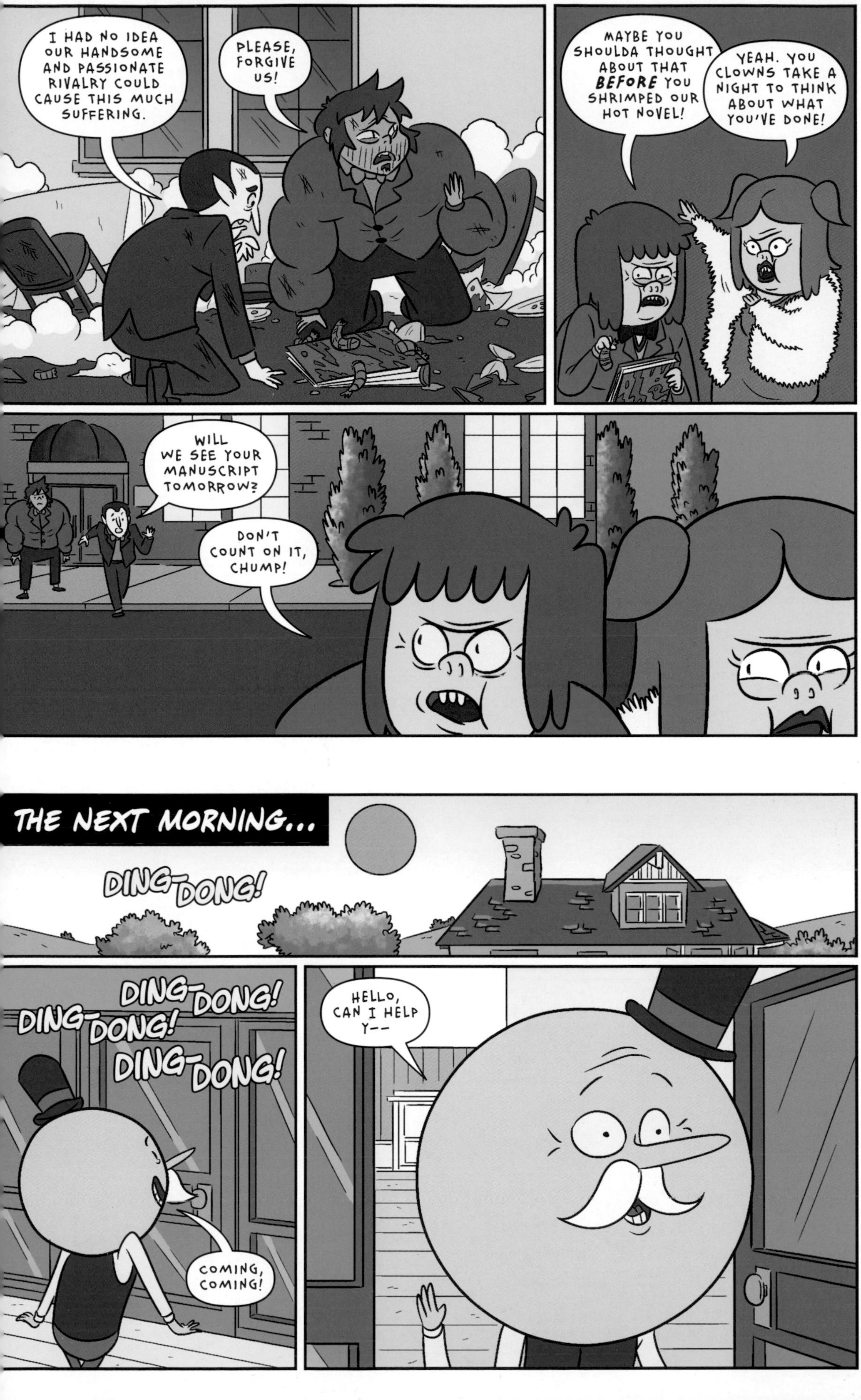
I HAD NO IDEA OUR HANDSOME AND PASSIONATE RIVALRY COULD CAUSE THIS MUCH SUFFERING.
PLEASE, FORGIVE US!
MAYBE YOU SHOULDA THOUGHT ABOUT THAT BEFORE YOU SHRIMPED OUR HOT NOVEL!
YEAH. YOU CLOWNS TAKE A NIGHT TO THINK ABOUT WHAT YOU'VE DONE!
WILL WE SEE YOUR MANUSCRIPT TOMORROW?
DON'T COUNT ON IT, CHUMP!
THE NEXT MORNING...
DING-DONG!
DING-DONG!
DING-DONG!
DING-DONG!
COMING, COMING!
HELLO, CAN I HELP Y--

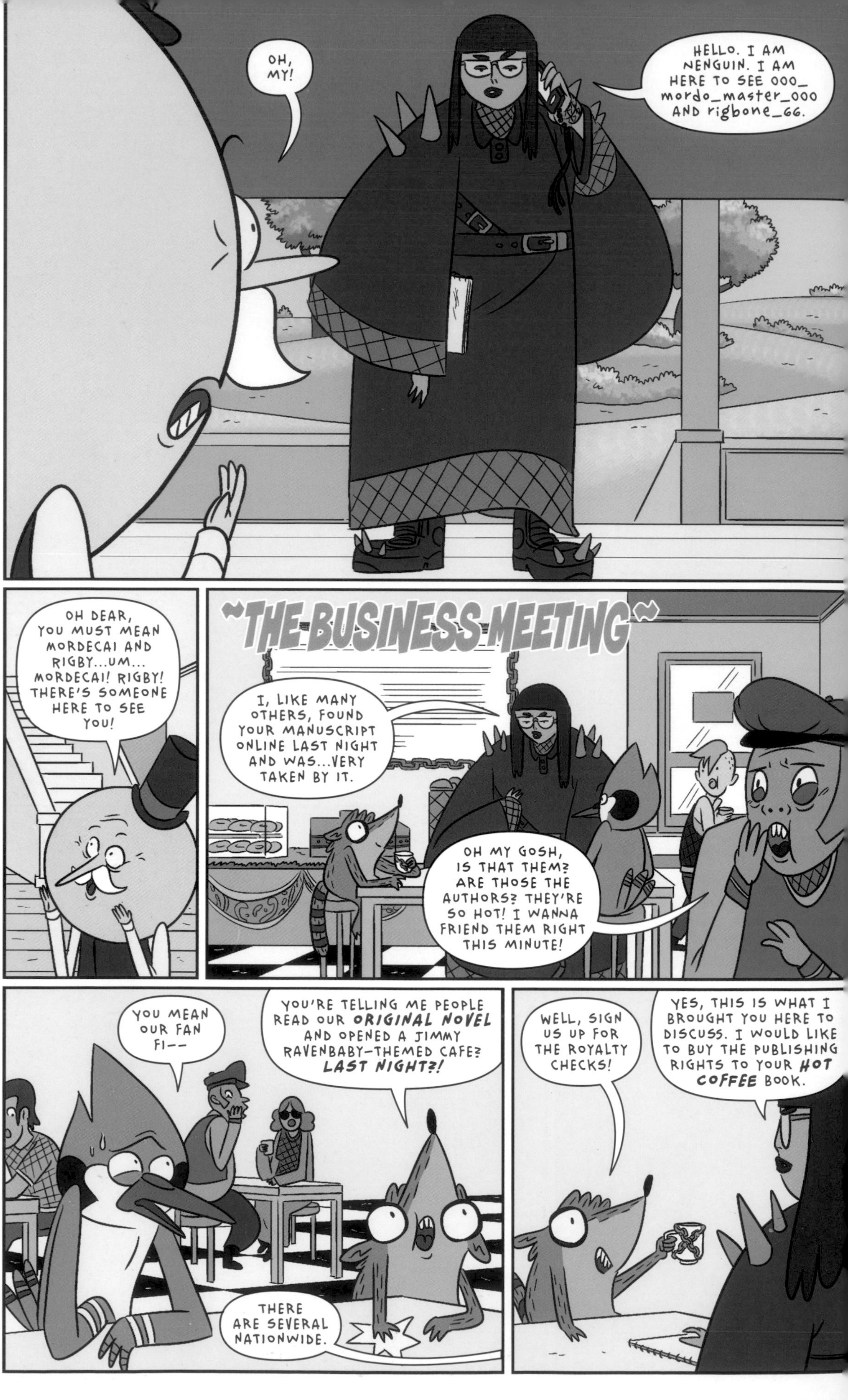
OH, MY!
HELLO. I AM NENGUIN. I AM HERE TO SEE 000_mordo_master_000 AND rigbone_66.
OH DEAR, YOU MUST MEAN MORDECAI AND RIGBY...UM... MORDECAI! RIGBY! THERE'S SOMEONE HERE TO SEE YOU!
~THE BUSINESS MEETING~
I, LIKE MANY OTHERS, FOUND YOUR MANUSCRIPT ONLINE LAST NIGHT AND WAS...VERY TAKEN BY IT.
OH MY GOSH, IS THAT THEM? ARE THOSE THE AUTHORS? THEY'RE SO HOT! I WANNA FRIEND THEM RIGHT THIS MINUTE!
YOU MEAN OUR FAN FI--
YOU'RE TELLING ME PEOPLE READ OUR ORIGINAL NOVEL AND OPENED A JIMMY RAVENBABY-THEMED CAFE? LAST NIGHT?!
THERE ARE SEVERAL NATIONWIDE.
WELL, SIGN US UP FOR THE ROYALTY CHECKS!
YES, THIS IS WHAT I BROUGHT YOU HERE TO DISCUSS. I WOULD LIKE TO BUY THE PUBLISHING RIGHTS TO YOUR HOT COFFEE BOOK.

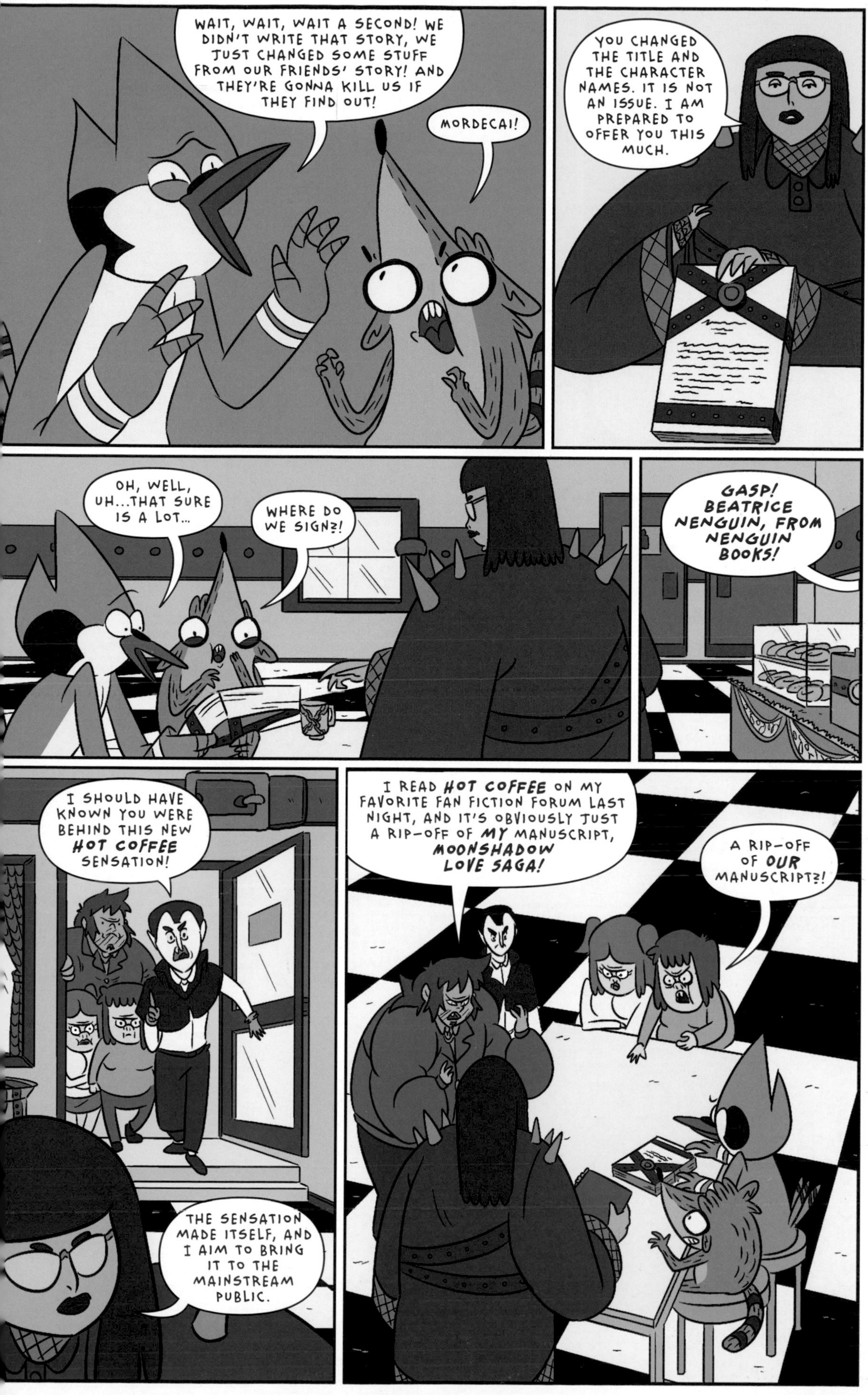
WAIT, WAIT, WAIT A SECOND! WE DIDN'T WRITE THAT STORY, WE JUST CHANGED SOME STUFF FROM OUR FRIENDS' STORY! AND THEY'RE GONNA KILL US IF THEY FIND OUT!
MORDECAI!
YOU CHANGED THE TITLE AND THE CHARACTER NAMES. IT IS NOT AN ISSUE. I AM PREPARED TO OFFER YOU THIS MUCH.
OH, WELL, UH...THAT SURE IS A LOT...
WHERE DO WE SIGN?!
GASP! BEATRICE NENGUIN, FROM NENGUIN BOOKS!
I SHOULD HAVE KNOWN YOU WERE BEHIND THIS NEW HOT COFFEE SENSATION!
THE SENSATION MADE ITSELF, AND I AIM TO BRING IT TO THE MAINSTREAM PUBLIC.
I READ HOT COFFEE ON MY FAVORITE FAN FICTION FORUM LAST NIGHT, AND IT'S OBVIOUSLY JUST A RIP-OFF OF MY MANUSCRIPT, MOONSHADOW LOVE SAGA!
A RIP-OFF OF OUR MANUSCRIPT?!

YOU MEAN A RIP-OFF OF *MY* MANUSCRIPT!

THE NAMES AND PLACES AND TITLE ARE DIFFERENT. IT'S A DIFFERENT STORY THAT APPEALS TO A...*DIFFERENT* DEMOGRAPHIC.

DID YOU LOSERS HAVE ANYTHING TO DO WITH THIS?!

W-WE WEREN'T GONNA PUBLISH IT, HONEST! WE JUST THOUGHT THAT THE GUY SHOULD'VE GOTTEN WITH THE OTHER GIRL AND...WELL...

AND WE MADE IT *BETTER!* AND WE *ARE* GONNA PUBLISH IT!

DUDE, DID YOU JUST FORGE MY SIGNATURE?! NOT COOL!

YES, *HOT COFFEE* WILL TAKE THE LITERARY WORLD BY STORM, AND WE WILL CRUSH YOUR INFERIOR, LESS-SEXY NOVEL INTO DUST.

WHY ARE YOU DOING THIS, NENGUIN? DIDN'T OUR RELATIONSHIP MEAN ANYTHING TO YOU?!

WAIT, *YOUR* RELATIONSHIP?!

I'VE ALWAYS BEEN IN A RELATIONSHIP WITH NENGUIN!

MAN, WE CAN'T BE HANDSOME RIVALS IN *ALL* ASPECTS OF OUR LIVES, CAN WE?!

SURE WE CAN

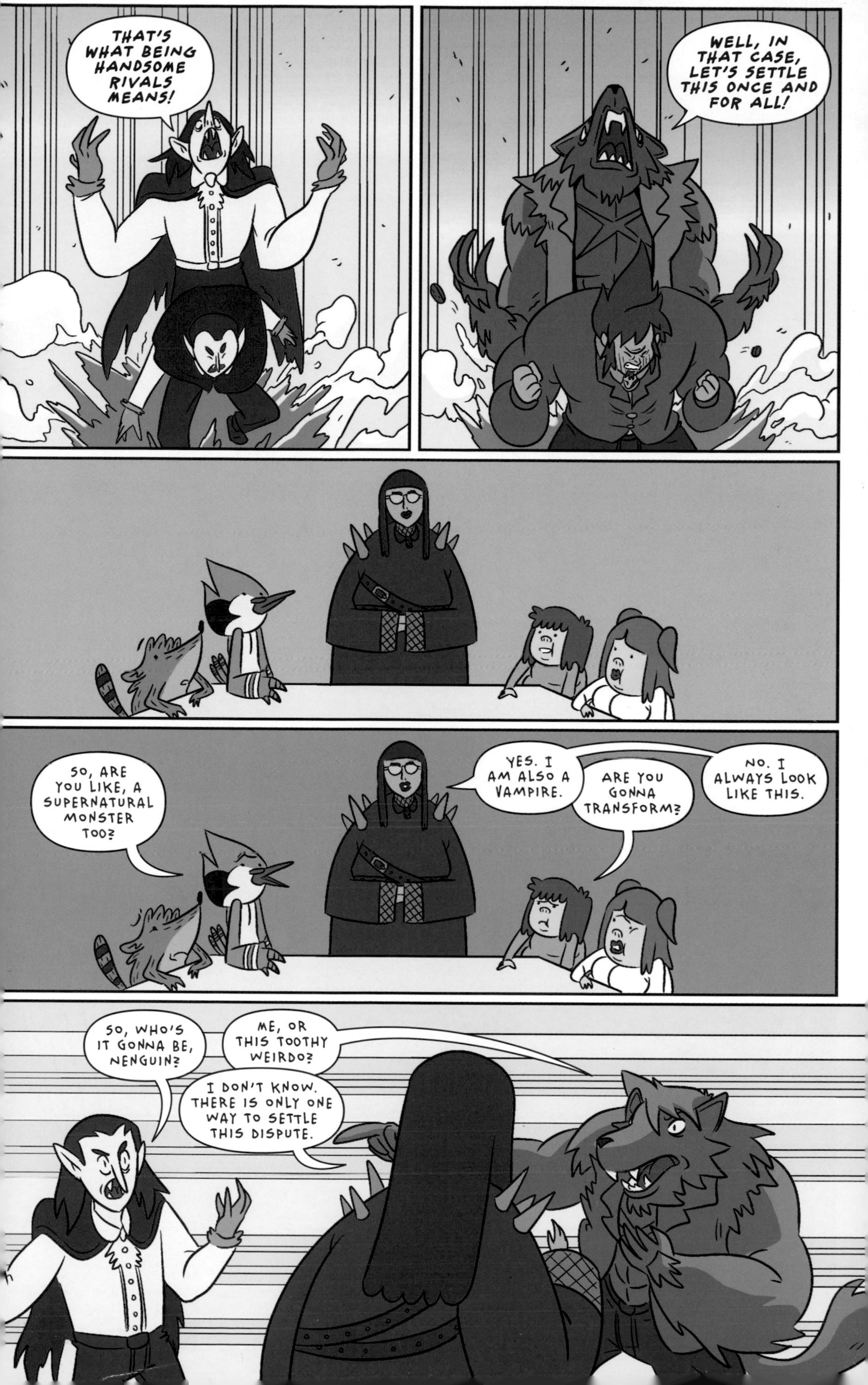
THAT'S WHAT BEING HANDSOME RIVALS MEANS!
WELL, IN THAT CASE, LET'S SETTLE THIS ONCE AND FOR ALL!
SO, ARE YOU LIKE, A SUPERNATURAL MONSTER TOO?
YES. I AM ALSO A VAMPIRE.
ARE YOU GONNA TRANSFORM?
NO. I ALWAYS LOOK LIKE THIS.
SO, WHO'S IT GONNA BE, NENGUIN?
ME, OR THIS TOOTHY WEIRDO?
I DON'T KNOW. THERE IS ONLY ONE WAY TO SETTLE THIS DISPUTE.

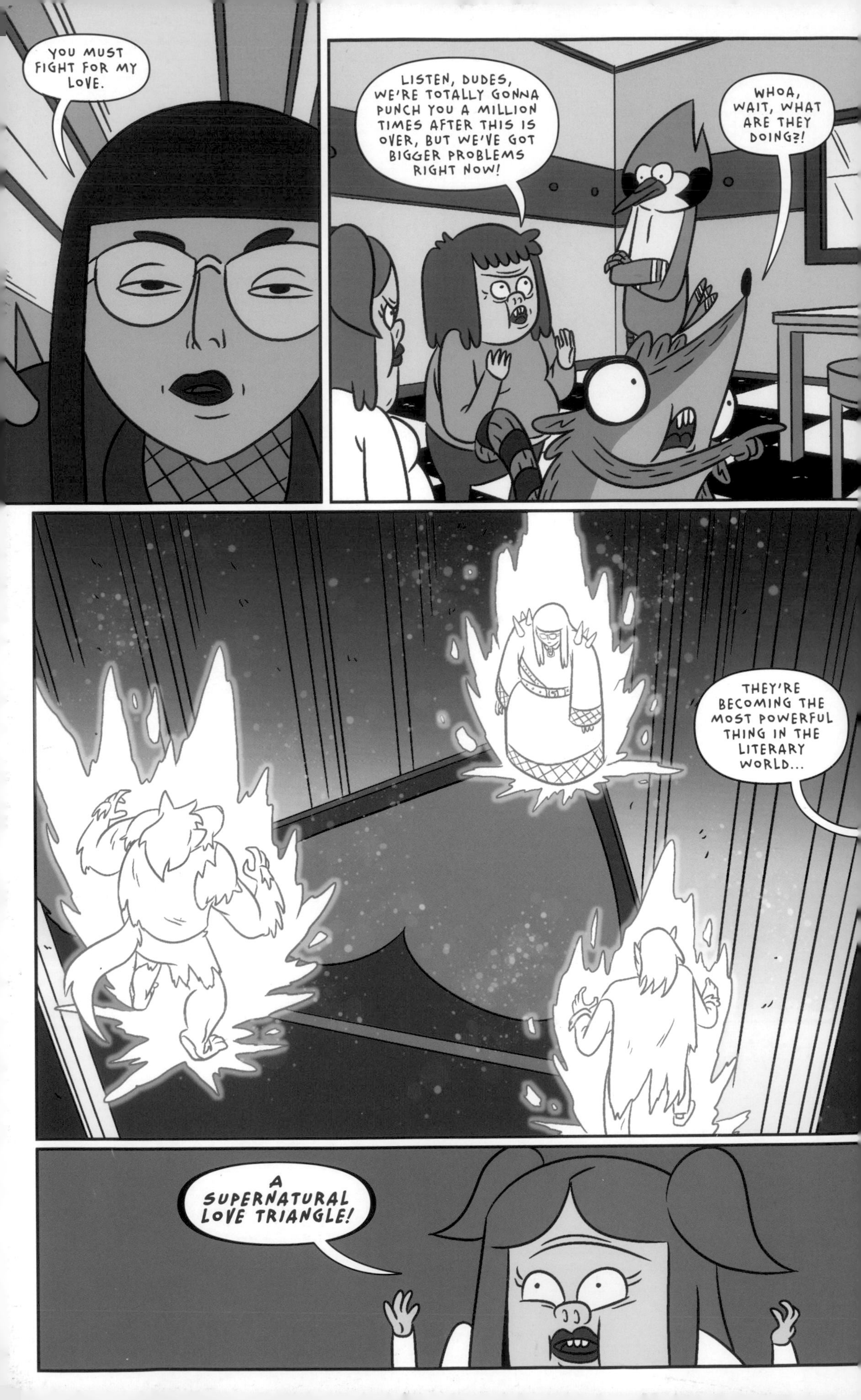
YOU MUST FIGHT FOR MY LOVE.
LISTEN, DUDES, WE'RE TOTALLY GONNA PUNCH YOU A MILLION TIMES AFTER THIS IS OVER, BUT WE'VE GOT BIGGER PROBLEMS RIGHT NOW!
WHOA, WAIT, WHAT ARE THEY DOING?!
THEY'RE BECOMING THE MOST POWERFUL THING IN THE LITERARY WORLD...
A SUPERNATURAL LOVE TRIANGLE!

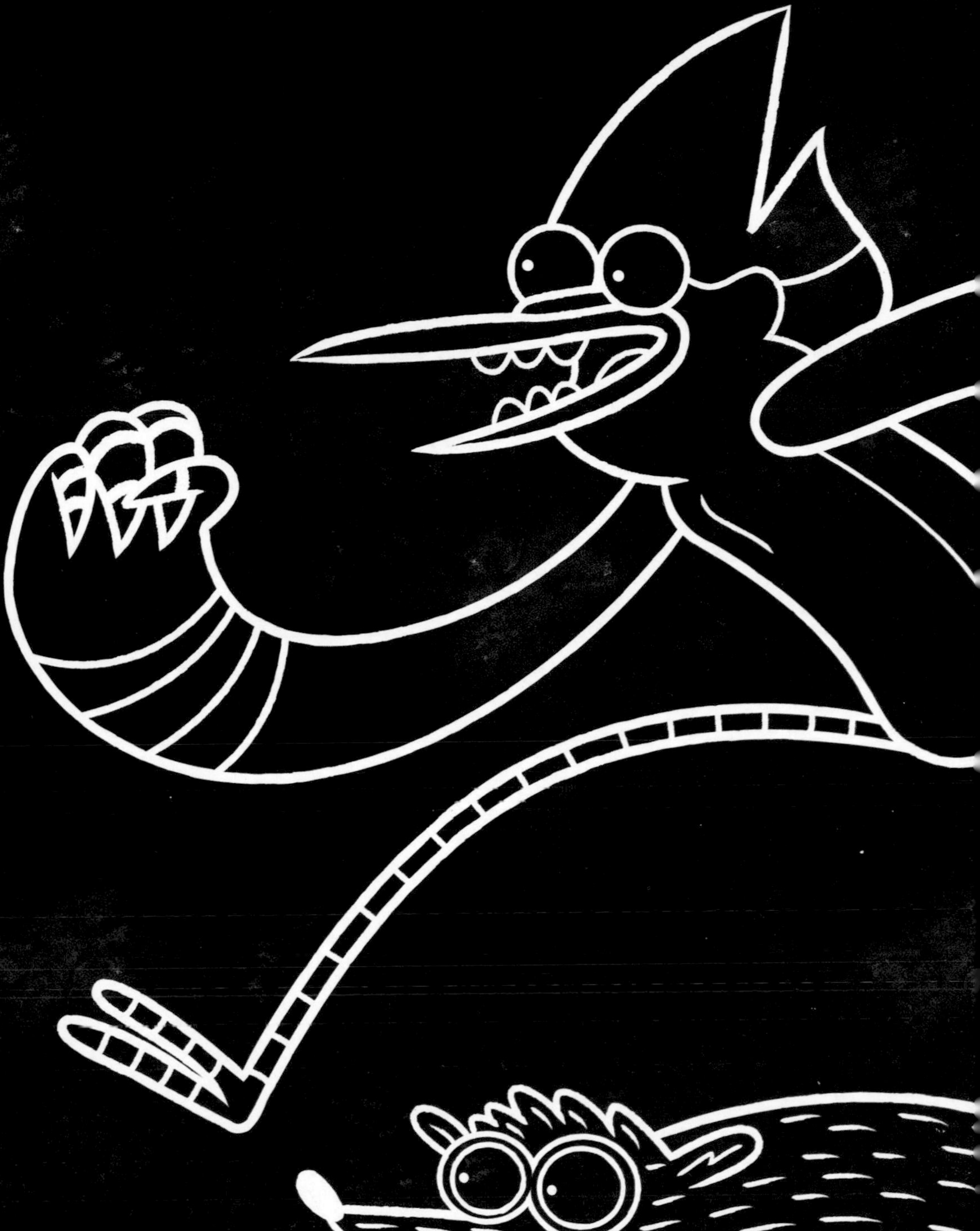

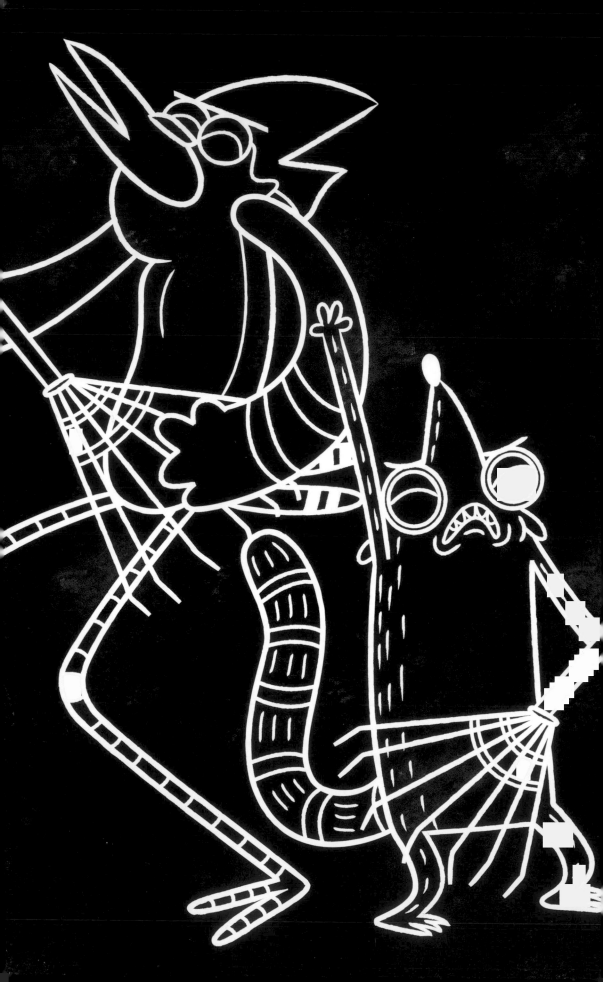

LAST TIME, ON REGULAR SHOW...

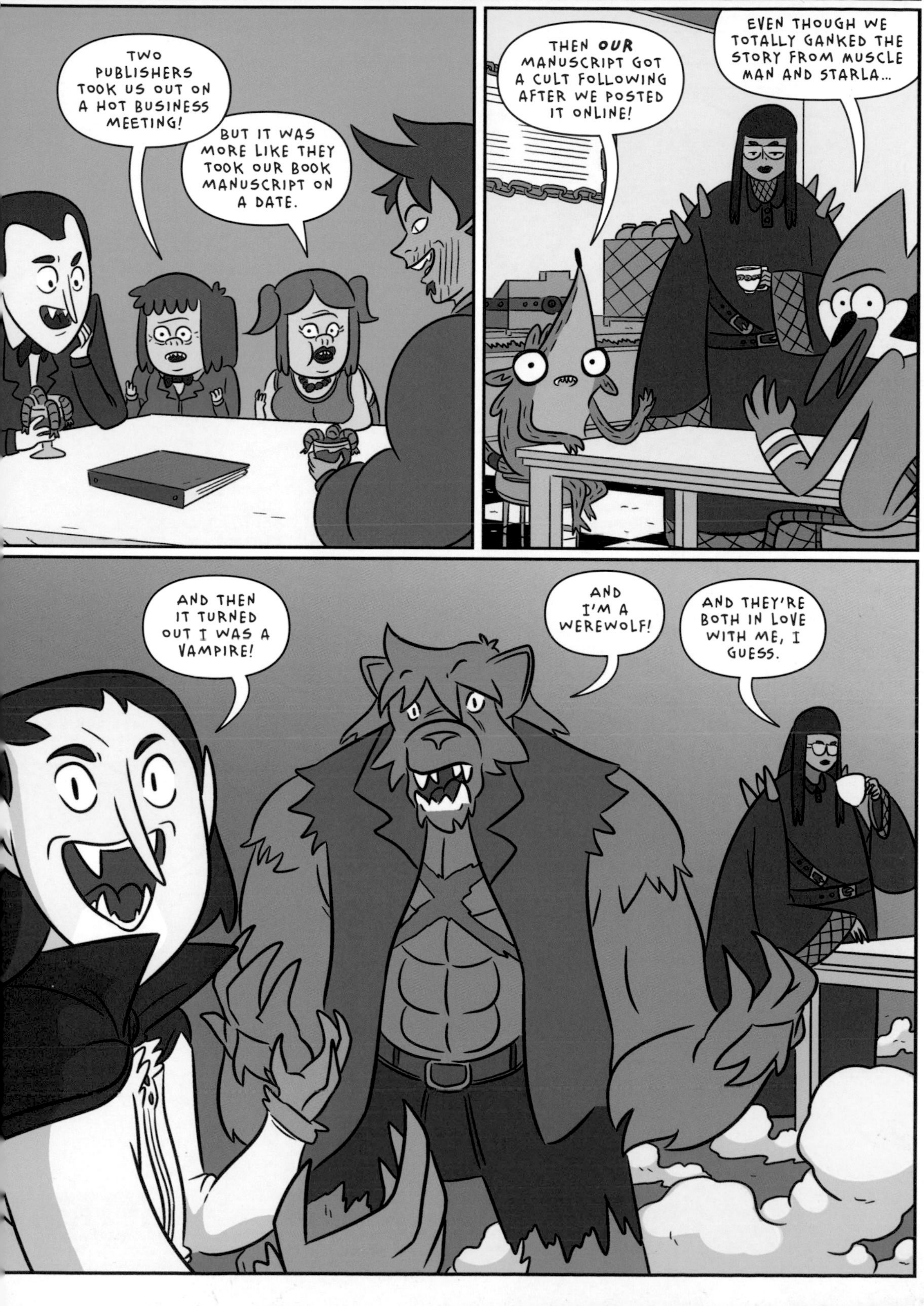
TWO PUBLISHERS TOOK US OUT ON A HOT BUSINESS MEETING!
BUT IT WAS MORE LIKE THEY TOOK OUR BOOK MANUSCRIPT ON A DATE.
THEN OUR MANUSCRIPT GOT A CULT FOLLOWING AFTER WE POSTED IT ONLINE!
EVEN THOUGH WE TOTALLY GANKED THE STORY FROM MUSCLE MAN AND STARLA...
AND THEN IT TURNED OUT I WAS A VAMPIRE!
AND I'M A WEREWOLF!
AND THEY'RE BOTH IN LOVE WITH ME, I GUESS.

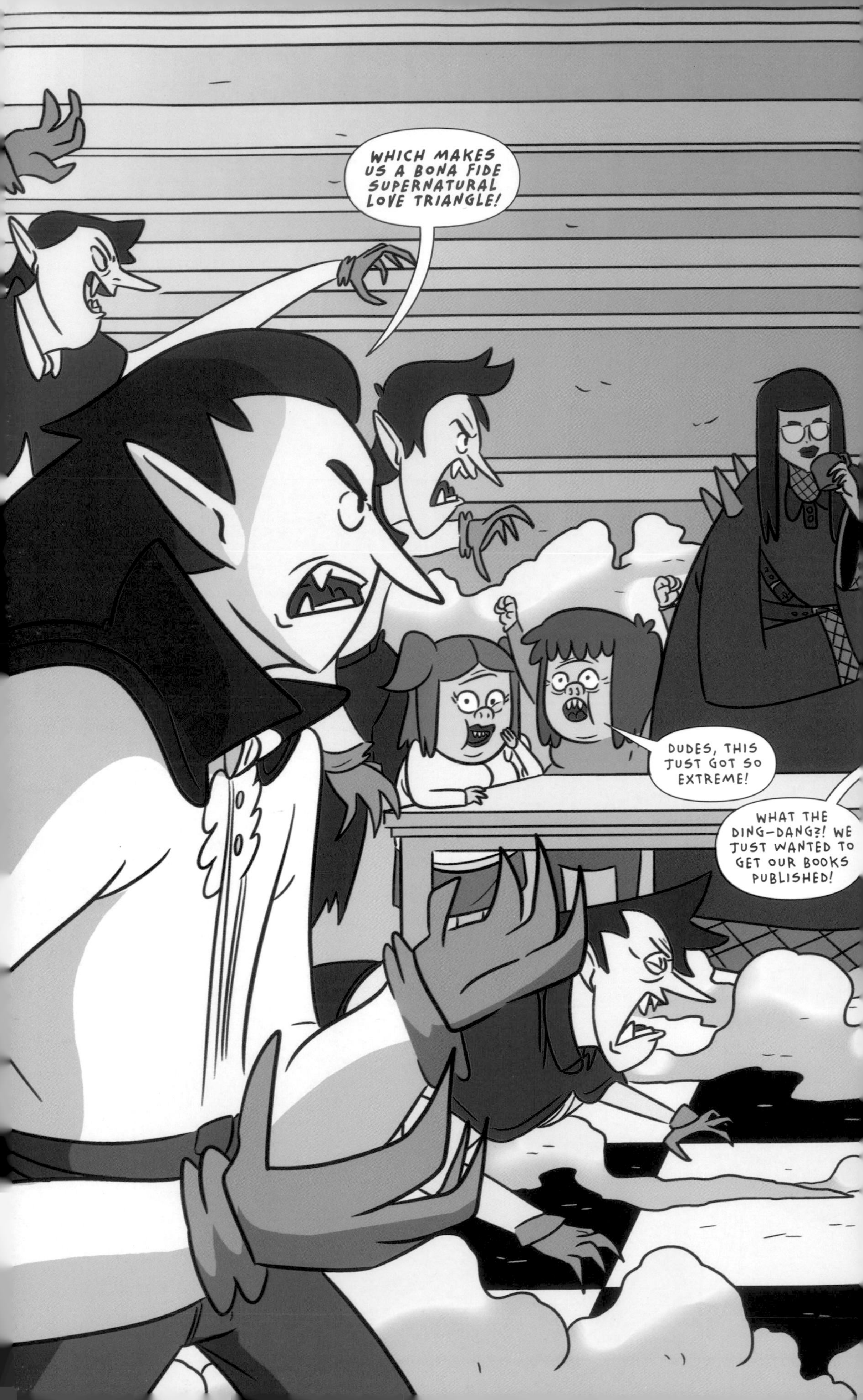
WHICH MAKES US A BONA FIDE SUPERNATURAL LOVE TRIANGLE!
DUDES, THIS JUST GOT SO EXTREME!
WHAT THE DING-DANG?! WE JUST WANTED TO GET OUR BOOKS PUBLISHED!

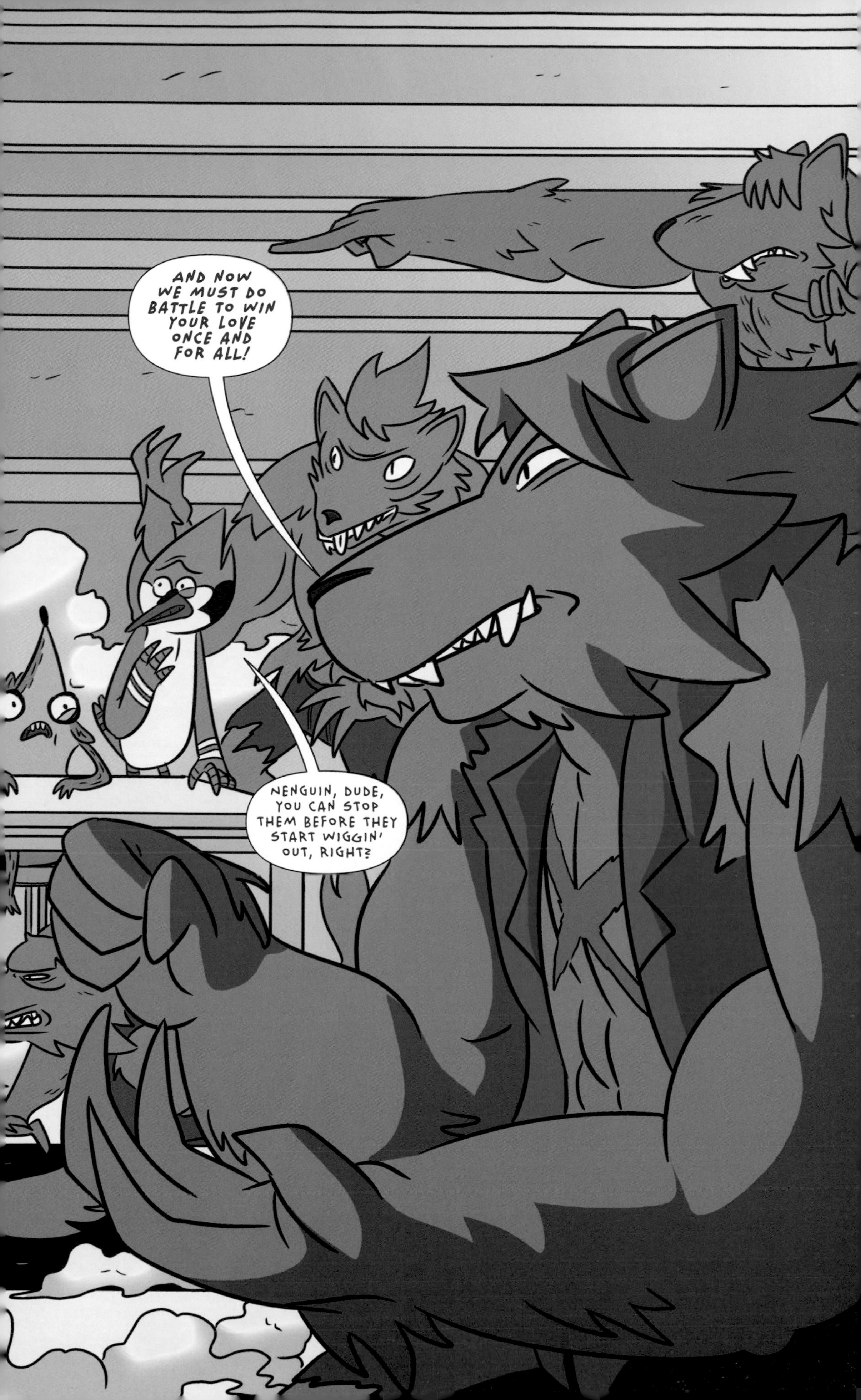
AND NOW WE MUST DO BATTLE TO WIN YOUR LOVE ONCE AND FOR ALL!
NENGUIN, DUDE, YOU CAN STOP THEM BEFORE THEY START WIGGIN' OUT, RIGHT?

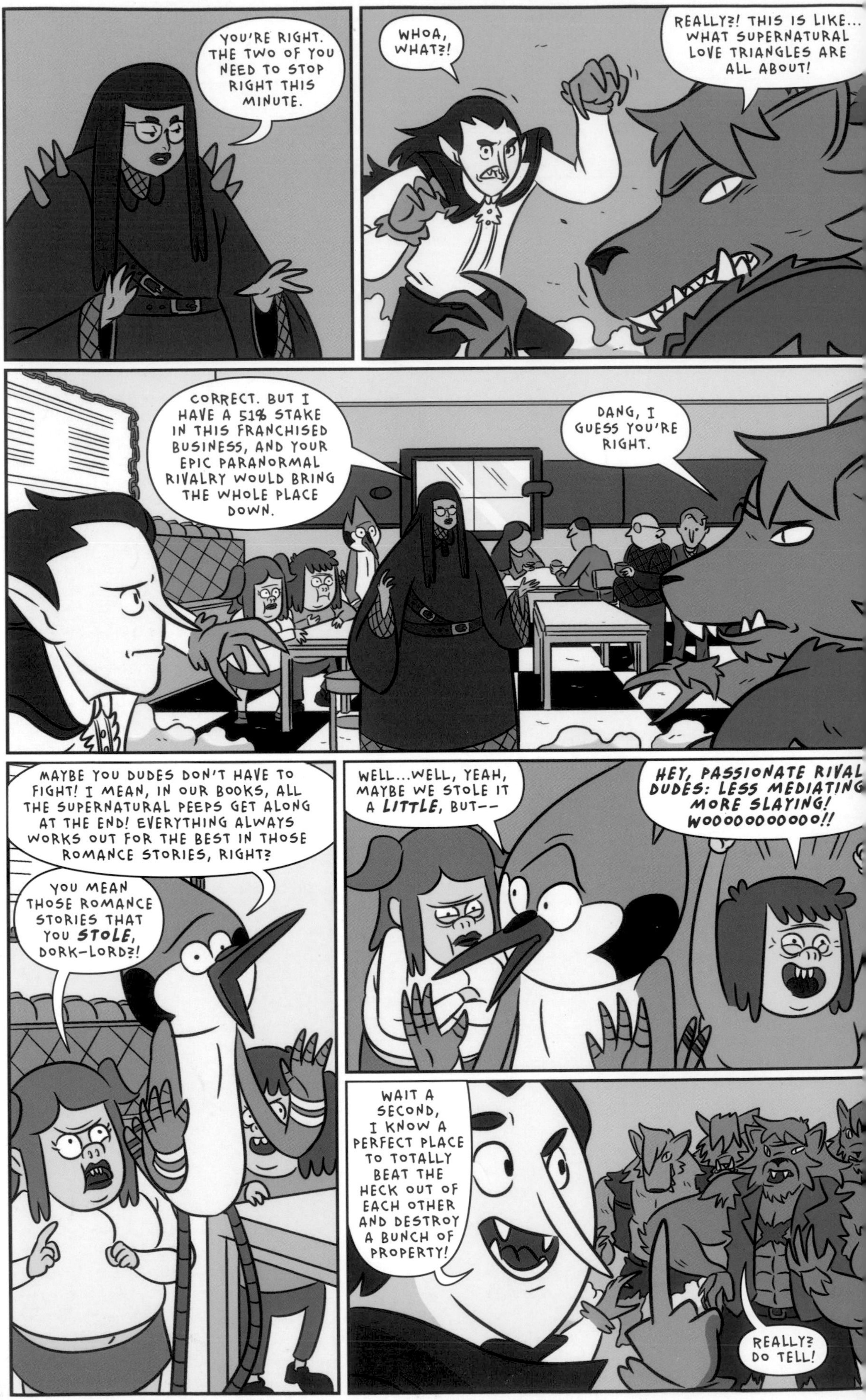
YOU'RE RIGHT. THE TWO OF YOU NEED TO STOP RIGHT THIS MINUTE.
WHOA, WHAT?!
REALLY?! THIS IS LIKE... WHAT SUPERNATURAL LOVE TRIANGLES ARE ALL ABOUT!
CORRECT. BUT I HAVE A 51% STAKE IN THIS FRANCHISED BUSINESS, AND YOUR EPIC PARANORMAL RIVALRY WOULD BRING THE WHOLE PLACE DOWN.
DANG, I GUESS YOU'RE RIGHT.
MAYBE YOU DUDES DON'T HAVE TO FIGHT! I MEAN, IN OUR BOOKS, ALL THE SUPERNATURAL PEEPS GET ALONG AT THE END! EVERYTHING ALWAYS WORKS OUT FOR THE BEST IN THOSE ROMANCE STORIES, RIGHT?
YOU MEAN THOSE ROMANCE STORIES THAT YOU STOLE, DORK-LORD?!
WELL...WELL, YEAH, MAYBE WE STOLE IT A LITTLE, BUT--
HEY, PASSIONATE RIVAL DUDES: LESS MEDIATING MORE SLAYING! WOOOOOOOOOOO!!
WAIT A SECOND, I KNOW A PERFECT PLACE TO TOTALLY BEAT THE HECK OUT OF EACH OTHER AND DESTROY A BUNCH OF PROPERTY!
REALLY? DO TELL!

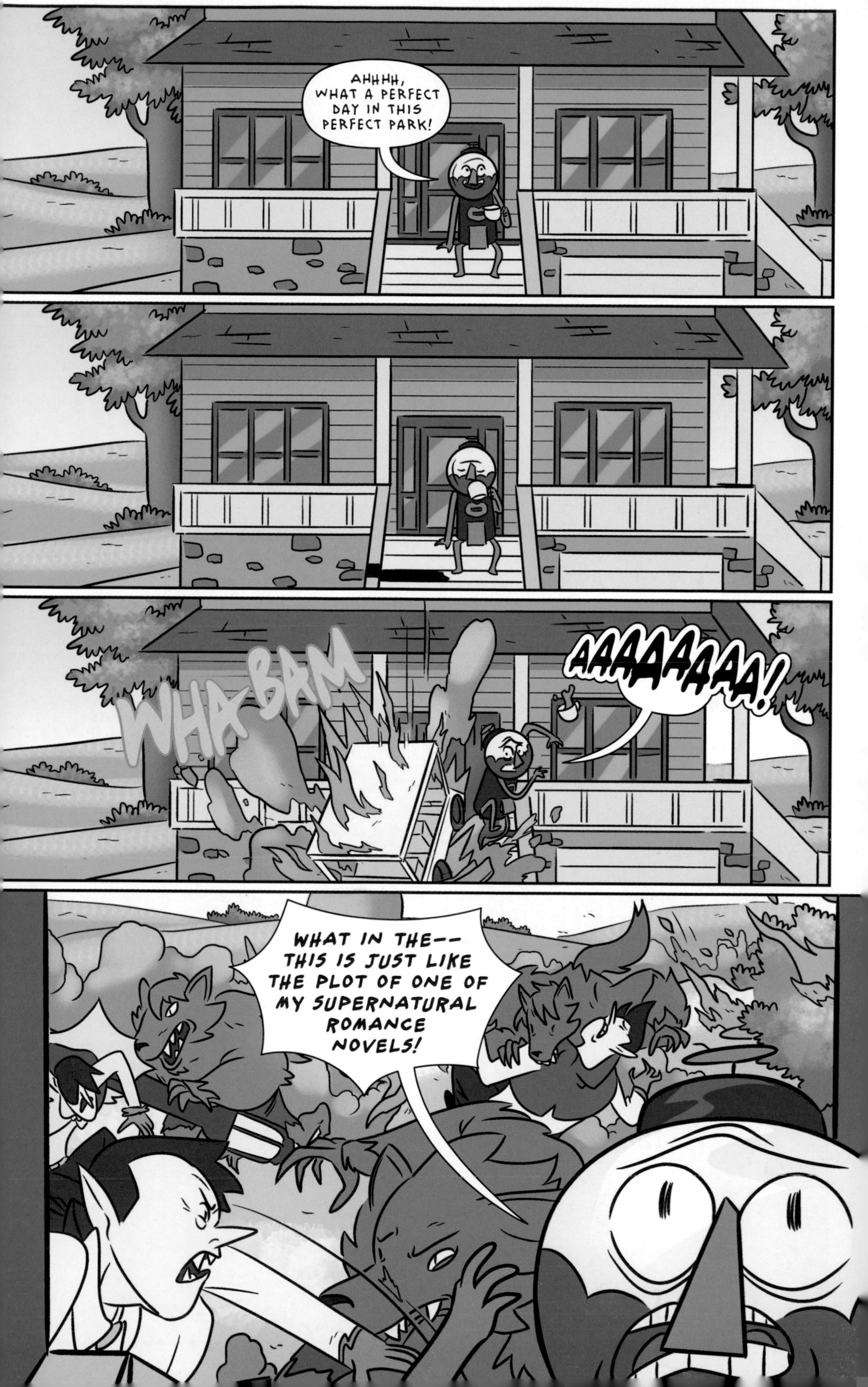
AHHHH, WHAT A PERFECT DAY IN THIS PERFECT PARK!
WHA BAM
AAAAAAAA!
WHAT IN THE-- THIS IS JUST LIKE THE PLOT OF ONE OF MY SUPERNATURAL ROMANCE NOVELS!

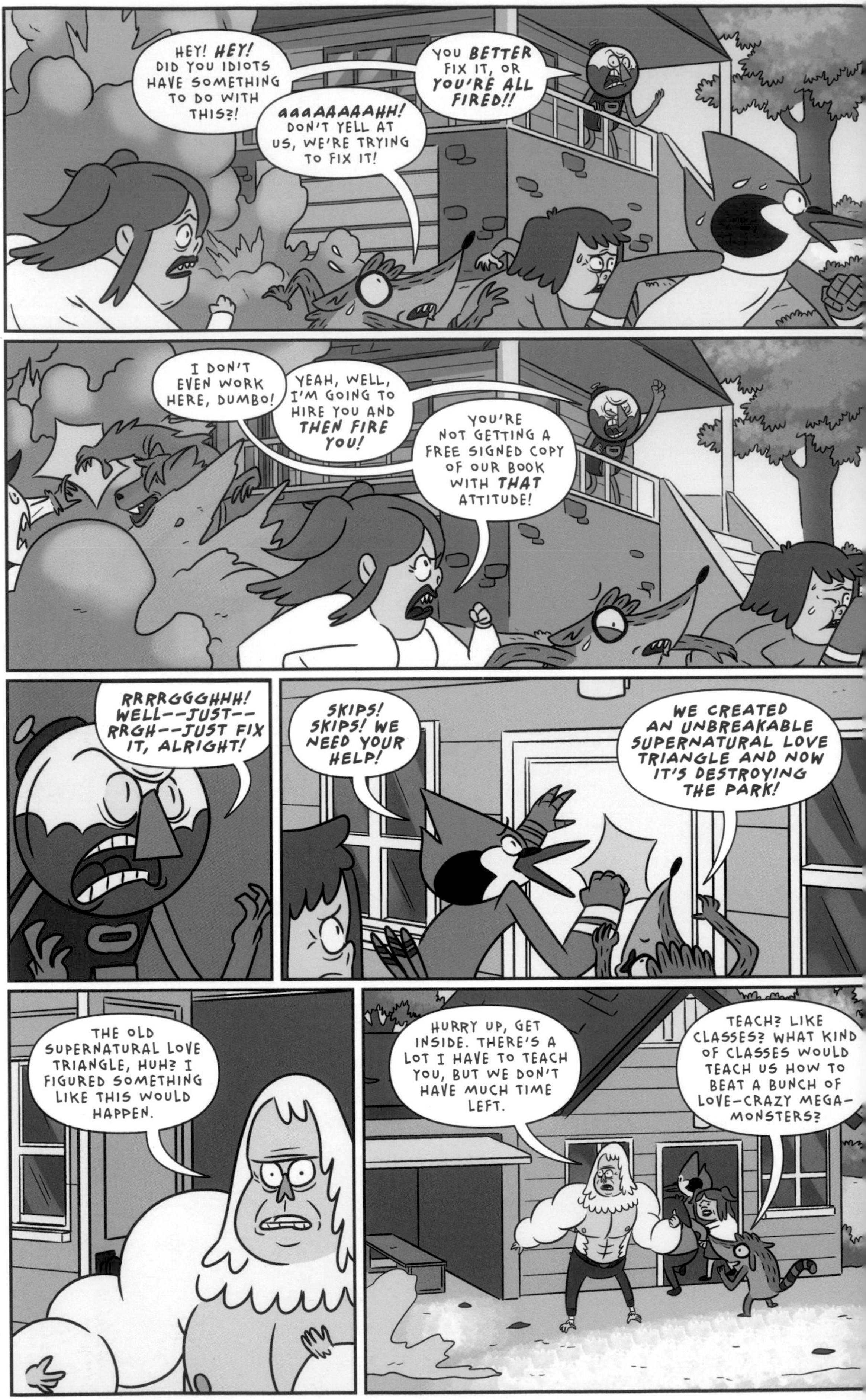
HEY! HEY! DID YOU IDIOTS HAVE SOMETHING TO DO WITH THIS?!
YOU BETTER FIX IT, OR YOU'RE ALL FIRED!!
AAAAAAAAAHH! DON'T YELL AT US, WE'RE TRYING TO FIX IT!
I DON'T EVEN WORK HERE, DUMBO!
YEAH, WELL, I'M GOING TO HIRE YOU AND THEN FIRE YOU!
YOU'RE NOT GETTING A FREE SIGNED COPY OF OUR BOOK WITH THAT ATTITUDE!
RRRRGGGHHH! WELL--JUST--RRGH--JUST FIX IT, ALRIGHT!
SKIPS! SKIPS! WE NEED YOUR HELP!
WE CREATED AN UNBREAKABLE SUPERNATURAL LOVE TRIANGLE AND NOW IT'S DESTROYING THE PARK!
THE OLD SUPERNATURAL LOVE TRIANGLE, HUH? I FIGURED SOMETHING LIKE THIS WOULD HAPPEN.
HURRY UP, GET INSIDE. THERE'S A LOT I HAVE TO TEACH YOU, BUT WE DON'T HAVE MUCH TIME LEFT.
TEACH? LIKE CLASSES? WHAT KIND OF CLASSES WOULD TEACH US HOW TO BEAT A BUNCH OF LOVE-CRAZY MEGA-MONSTERS?

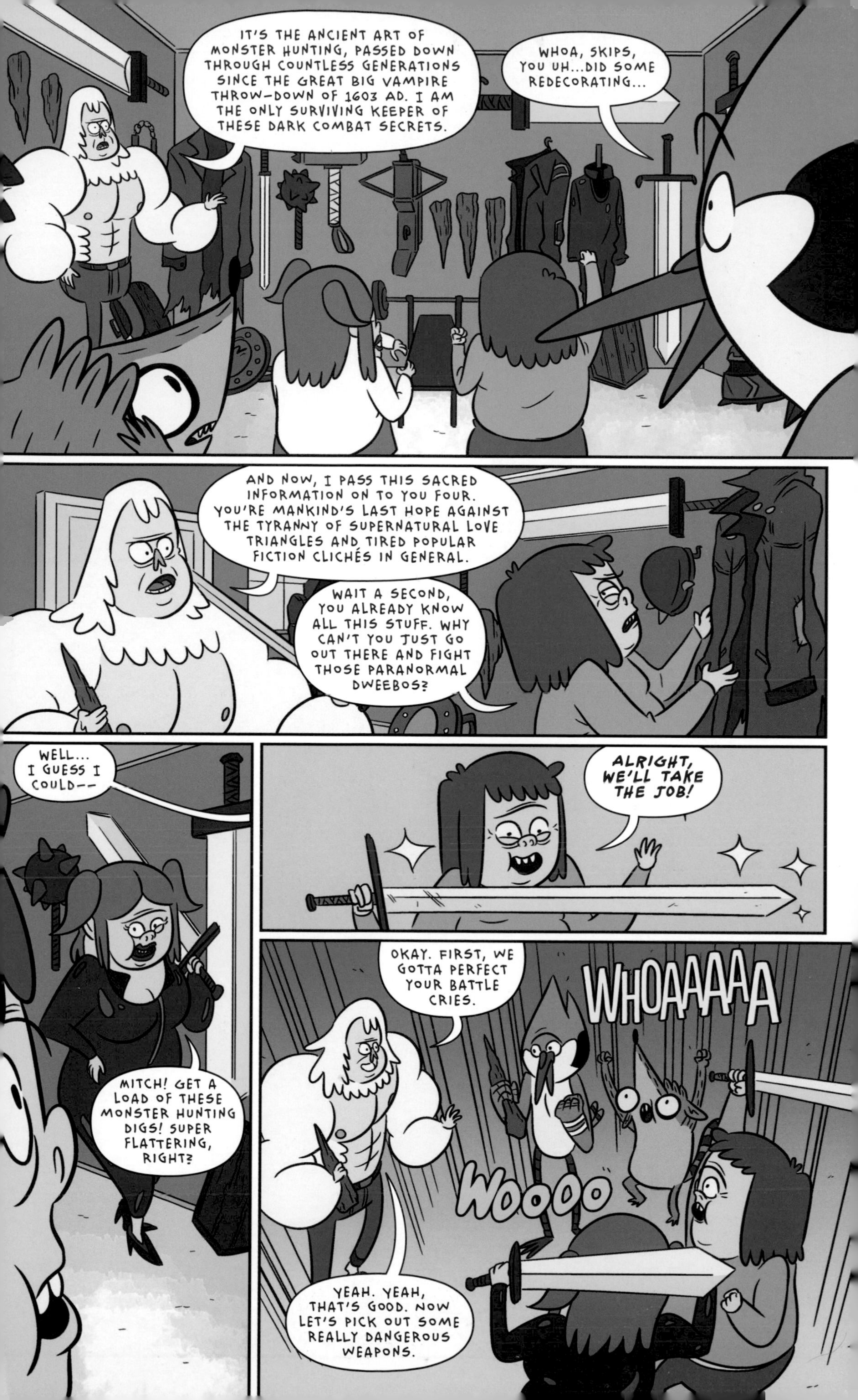
IT'S THE ANCIENT ART OF MONSTER HUNTING, PASSED DOWN THROUGH COUNTLESS GENERATIONS SINCE THE GREAT BIG VAMPIRE THROW-DOWN OF 1603 AD. I AM THE ONLY SURVIVING KEEPER OF THESE DARK COMBAT SECRETS.
WHOA, SKIPS, YOU UH...DID SOME REDECORATING...
AND NOW, I PASS THIS SACRED INFORMATION ON TO YOU FOUR. YOU'RE MANKIND'S LAST HOPE AGAINST THE TYRANNY OF SUPERNATURAL LOVE TRIANGLES AND TIRED POPULAR FICTION CLICHÉS IN GENERAL.
WAIT A SECOND, YOU ALREADY KNOW ALL THIS STUFF. WHY CAN'T YOU JUST GO OUT THERE AND FIGHT THOSE PARANORMAL DWEEBOS?
WELL... I GUESS I COULD--
ALRIGHT, WE'LL TAKE THE JOB!
MITCH! GET A LOAD OF THESE MONSTER HUNTING DIGS! SUPER FLATTERING, RIGHT?
OKAY. FIRST, WE GOTTA PERFECT YOUR BATTLE CRIES.
WHOAAAAAA
WOOOO
YEAH. YEAH, THAT'S GOOD. NOW LET'S PICK OUT SOME REALLY DANGEROUS WEAPONS.

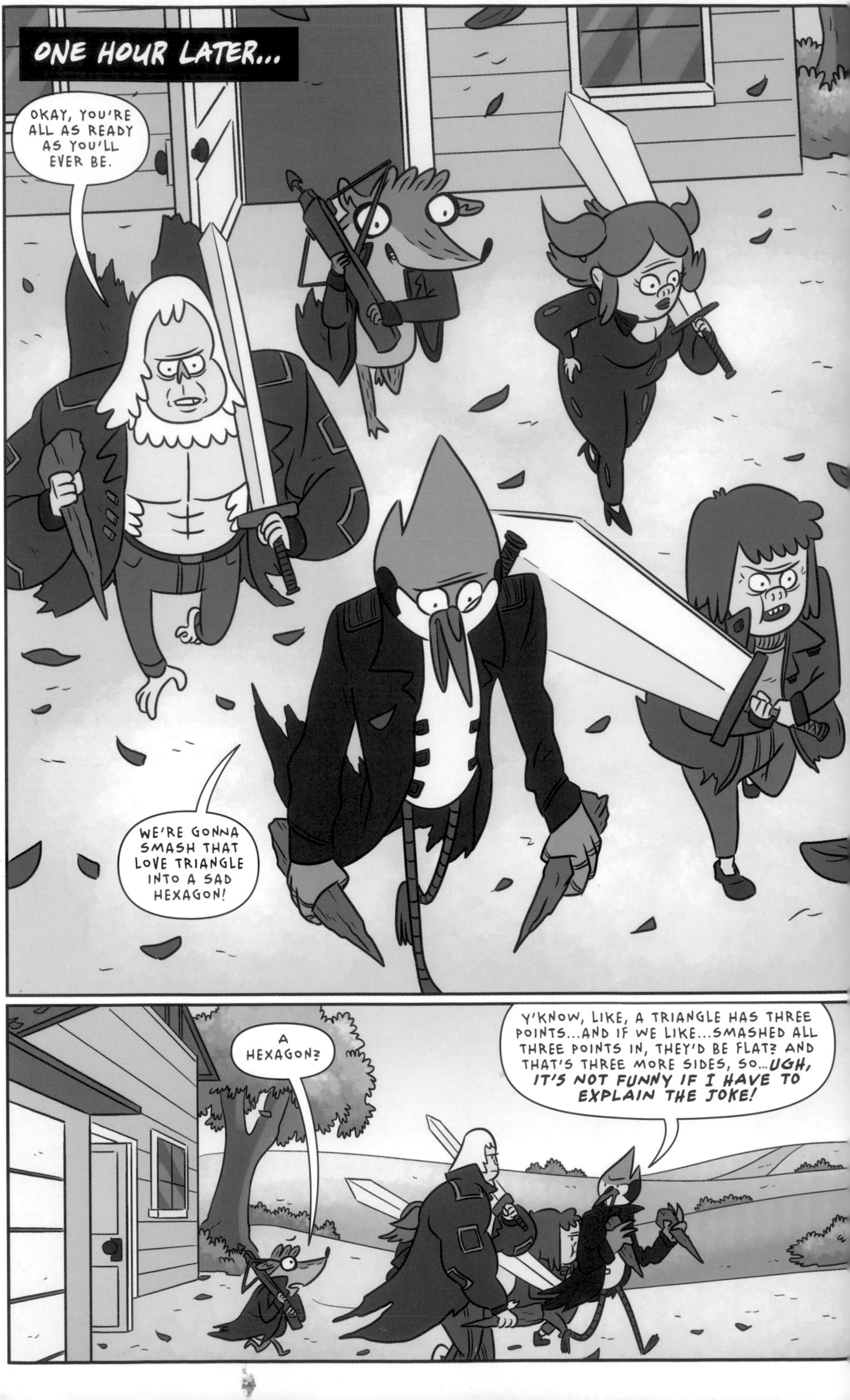
ONE HOUR LATER...
OKAY, YOU'RE ALL AS READY AS YOU'LL EVER BE.
WE'RE GONNA SMASH THAT LOVE TRIANGLE INTO A SAD HEXAGON!
A HEXAGON?
Y'KNOW, LIKE, A TRIANGLE HAS THREE POINTS...AND IF WE LIKE...SMASHED ALL THREE POINTS IN, THEY'D BE FLAT? AND THAT'S THREE MORE SIDES, SO...UGH, IT'S NOT FUNNY IF I HAVE TO EXPLAIN THE JOKE!

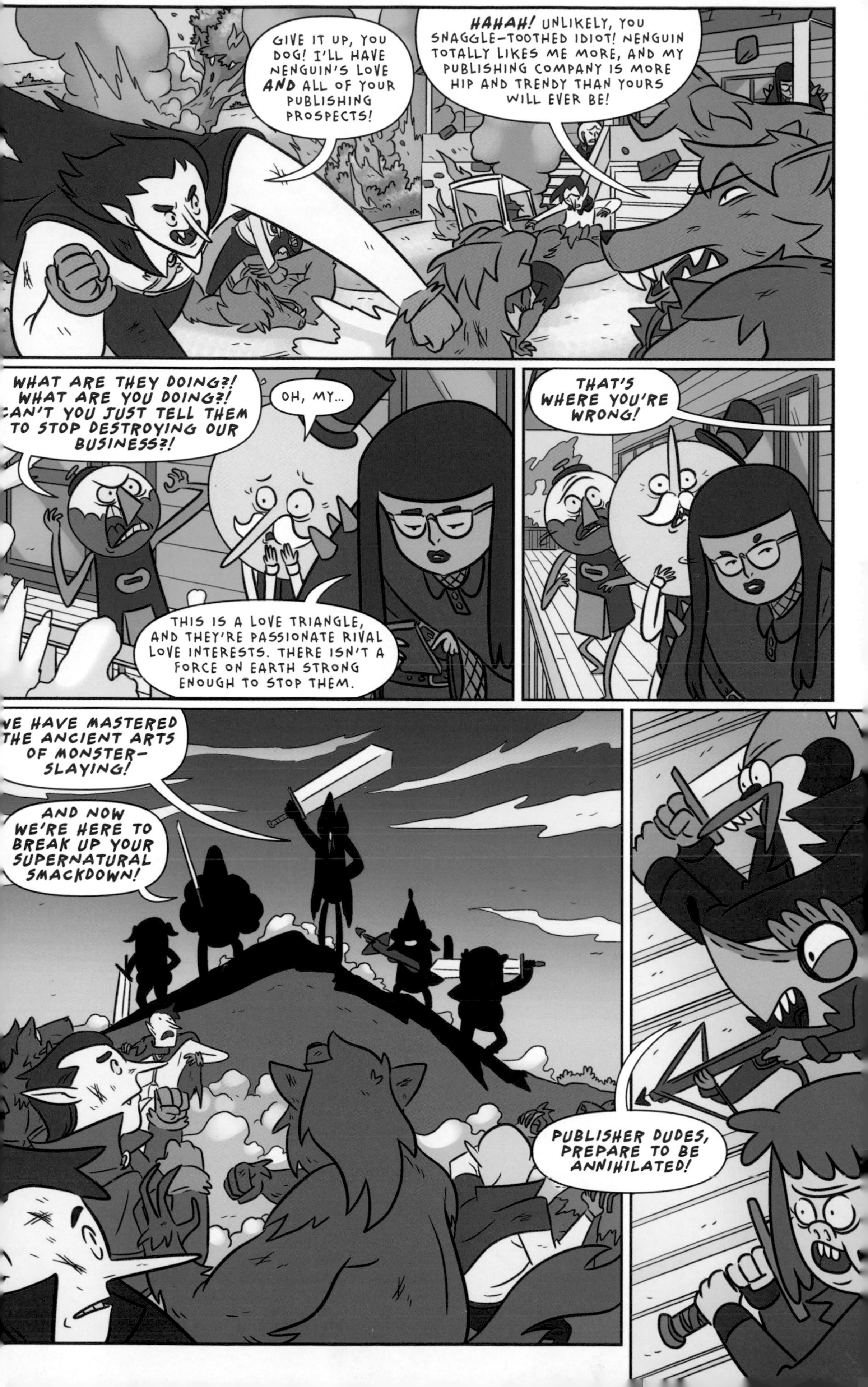
GIVE IT UP, YOU DOG! I'LL HAVE NENGUIN'S LOVE **AND** ALL OF YOUR PUBLISHING PROSPECTS!
HAHAH! UNLIKELY, YOU SNAGGLE-TOOTHED IDIOT! NENGUIN TOTALLY LIKES ME MORE, AND MY PUBLISHING COMPANY IS MORE HIP AND TRENDY THAN YOURS WILL EVER BE!
WHAT ARE THEY DOING?! WHAT ARE YOU DOING?! CAN'T YOU JUST TELL THEM TO STOP DESTROYING OUR BUSINESS?!
OH, MY...
THIS IS A LOVE TRIANGLE, AND THEY'RE PASSIONATE RIVAL LOVE INTERESTS. THERE ISN'T A FORCE ON EARTH STRONG ENOUGH TO STOP THEM.
THAT'S WHERE YOU'RE WRONG!
WE HAVE MASTERED THE ANCIENT ARTS OF MONSTER-SLAYING!
AND NOW WE'RE HERE TO BREAK UP YOUR SUPERNATURAL SMACKDOWN!
PUBLISHER DUDES, PREPARE TO BE ANNIHILATED!

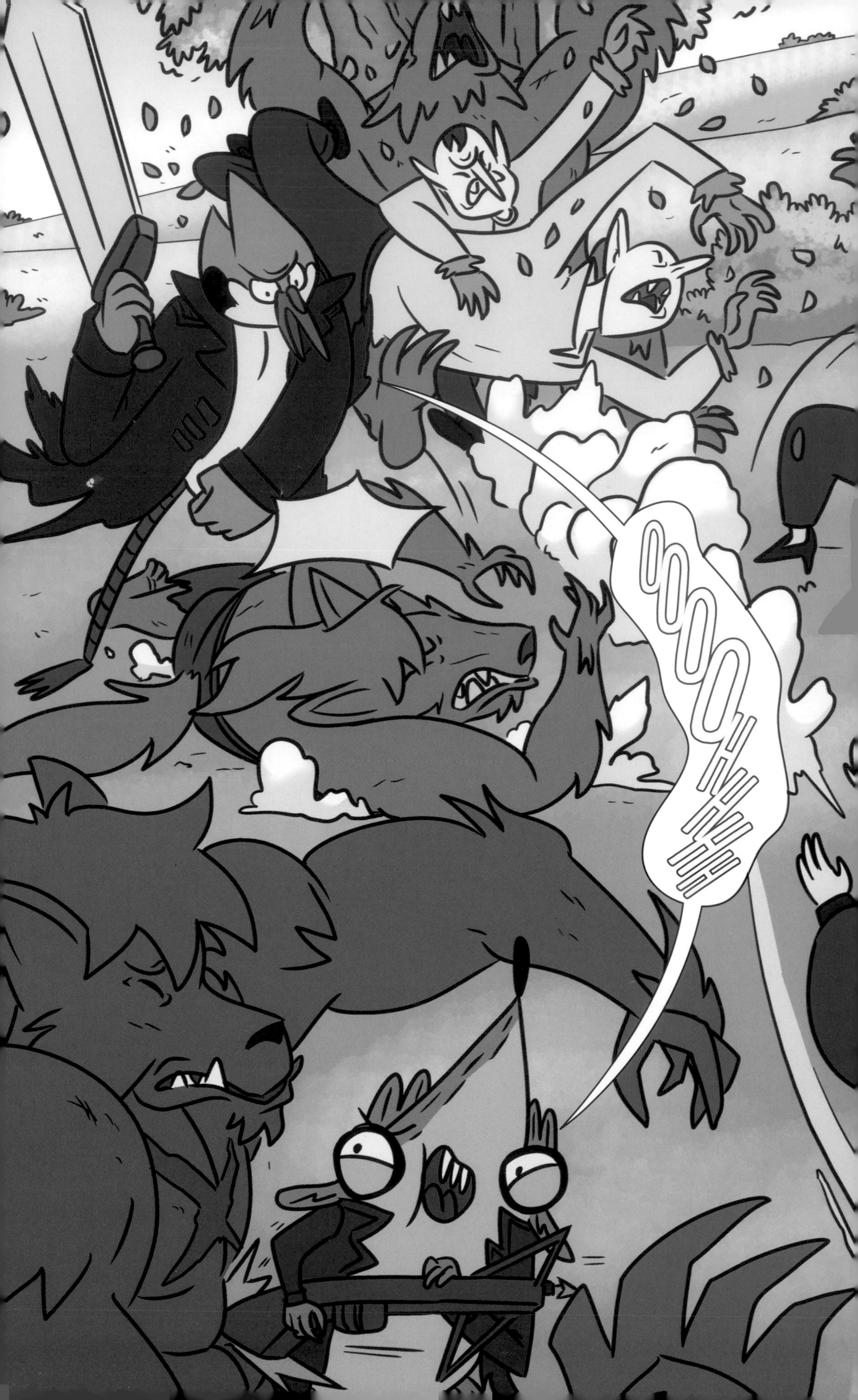
OOOOHHHH

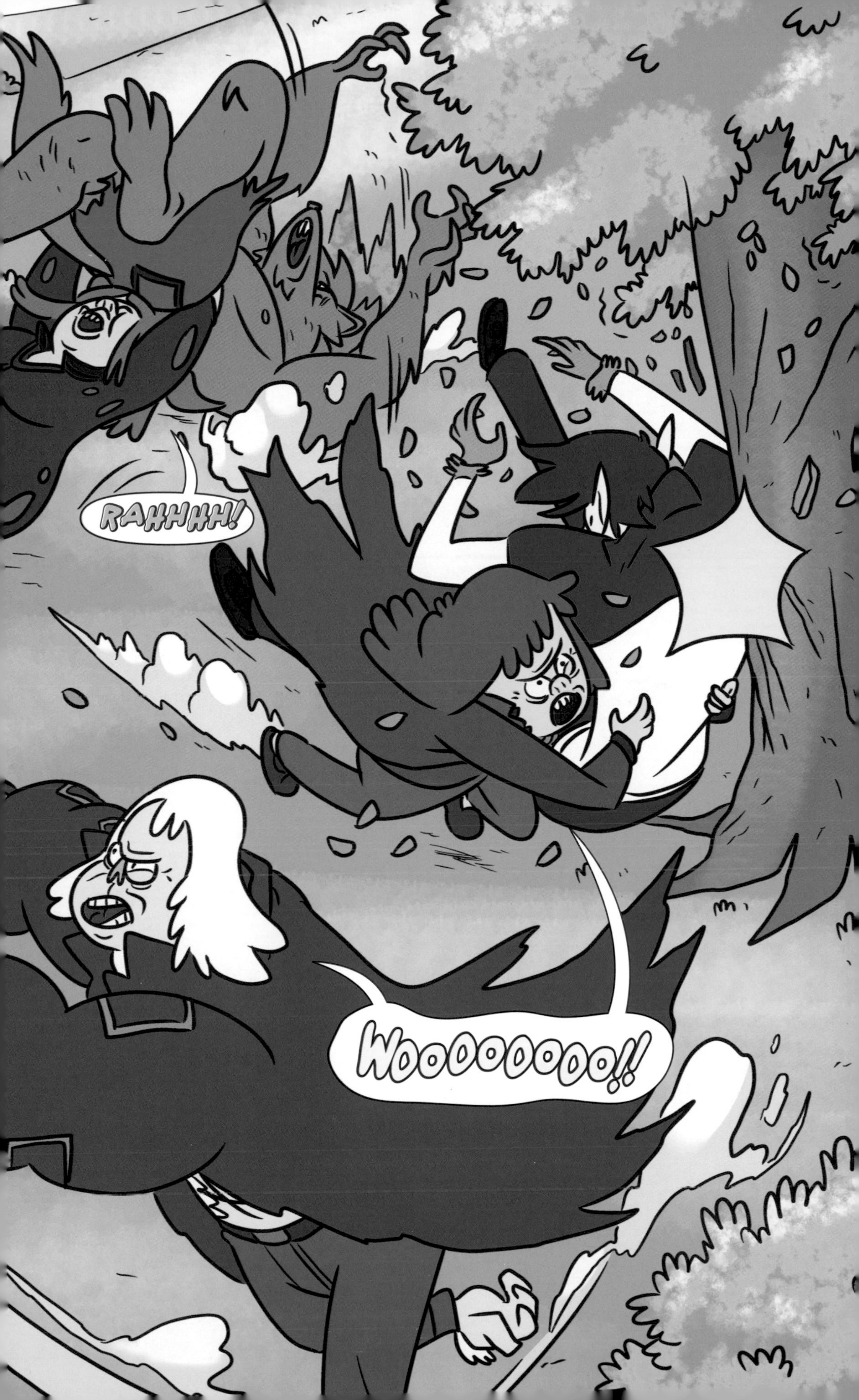
RAHHHH!
WOOOOOOOO!!

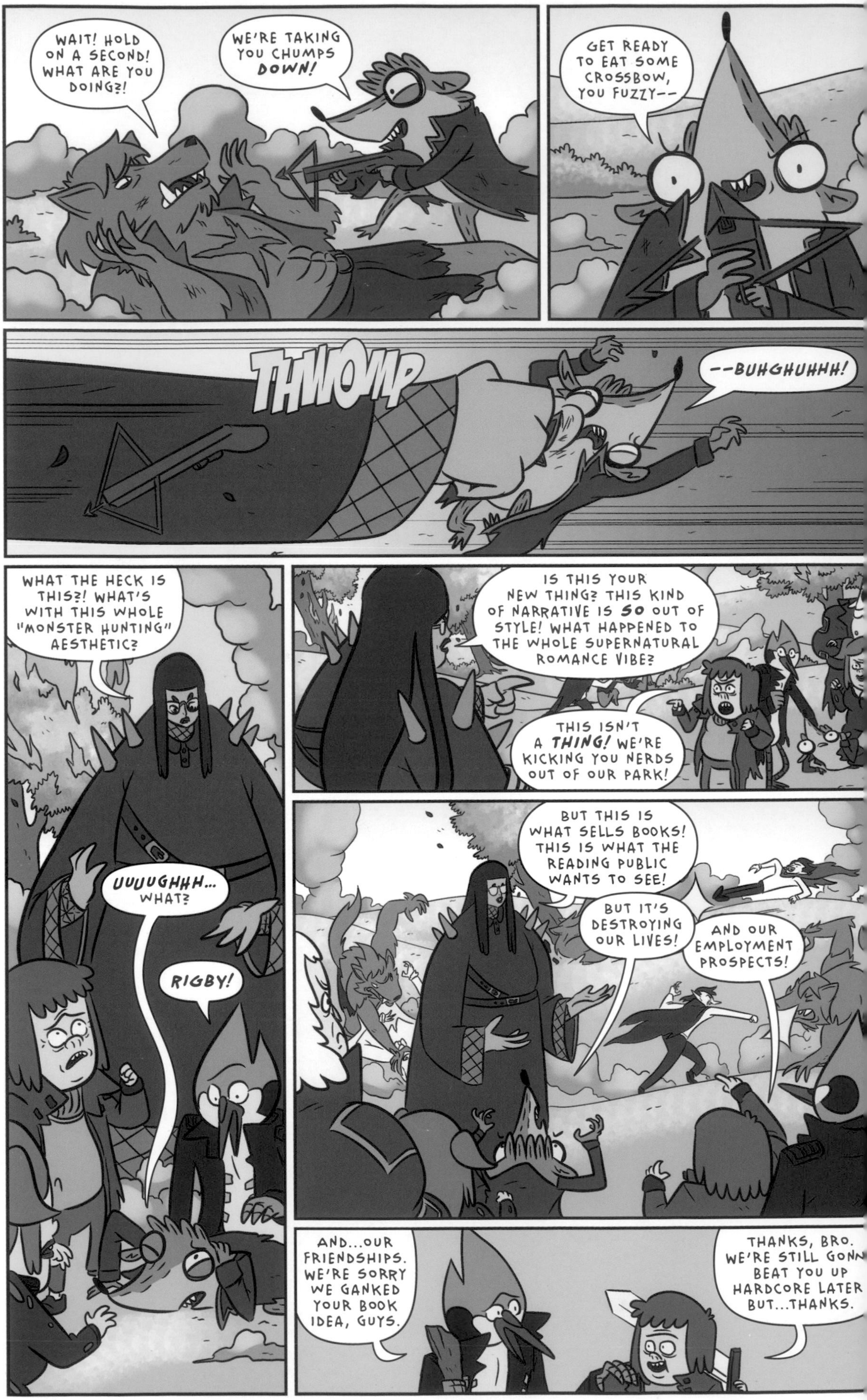
WAIT! HOLD ON A SECOND! WHAT ARE YOU DOING?!
WE'RE TAKING YOU CHUMPS DOWN!
GET READY TO EAT SOME CROSSBOW, YOU FUZZY--
THWOMP
--BUHGHUHHH!
WHAT THE HECK IS THIS?! WHAT'S WITH THIS WHOLE "MONSTER HUNTING" AESTHETIC?
UUUUGHHH... WHAT?
RIGBY!
IS THIS YOUR NEW THING? THIS KIND OF NARRATIVE IS SO OUT OF STYLE! WHAT HAPPENED TO THE WHOLE SUPERNATURAL ROMANCE VIBE?
THIS ISN'T A THING! WE'RE KICKING YOU NERDS OUT OF OUR PARK!
BUT THIS IS WHAT SELLS BOOKS! THIS IS WHAT THE READING PUBLIC WANTS TO SEE!
BUT IT'S DESTROYING OUR LIVES!
AND OUR EMPLOYMENT PROSPECTS!
AND...OUR FRIENDSHIPS. WE'RE SORRY WE GANKED YOUR BOOK IDEA, GUYS.
THANKS, BRO. WE'RE STILL GONN BEAT YOU UP HARDCORE LATER BUT...THANKS.

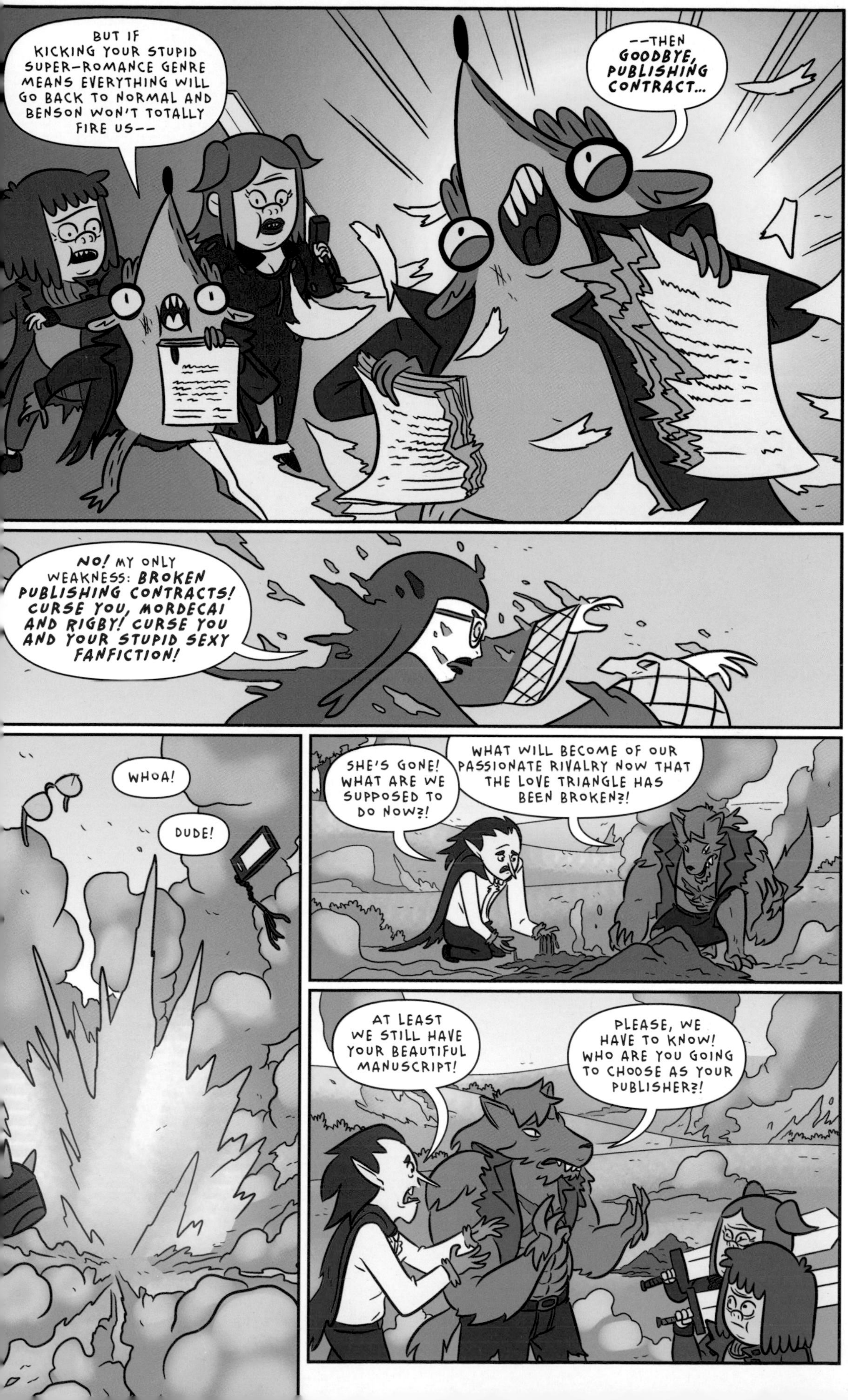

BUT IF KICKING YOUR STUPID SUPER-ROMANCE GENRE MEANS EVERYTHING WILL GO BACK TO NORMAL AND BENSON WON'T TOTALLY FIRE US--
--THEN GOODBYE, PUBLISHING CONTRACT...
NO! MY ONLY WEAKNESS: BROKEN PUBLISHING CONTRACTS! CURSE YOU, MORDECAI AND RIGBY! CURSE YOU AND YOUR STUPID SEXY FANFICTION!
WHOA!
DUDE!
SHE'S GONE! WHAT ARE WE SUPPOSED TO DO NOW?!
WHAT WILL BECOME OF OUR PASSIONATE RIVALRY NOW THAT THE LOVE TRIANGLE HAS BEEN BROKEN?!
AT LEAST WE STILL HAVE YOUR BEAUTIFUL MANUSCRIPT!
PLEASE, WE HAVE TO KNOW! WHO ARE YOU GOING TO CHOOSE AS YOUR PUBLISHER?!

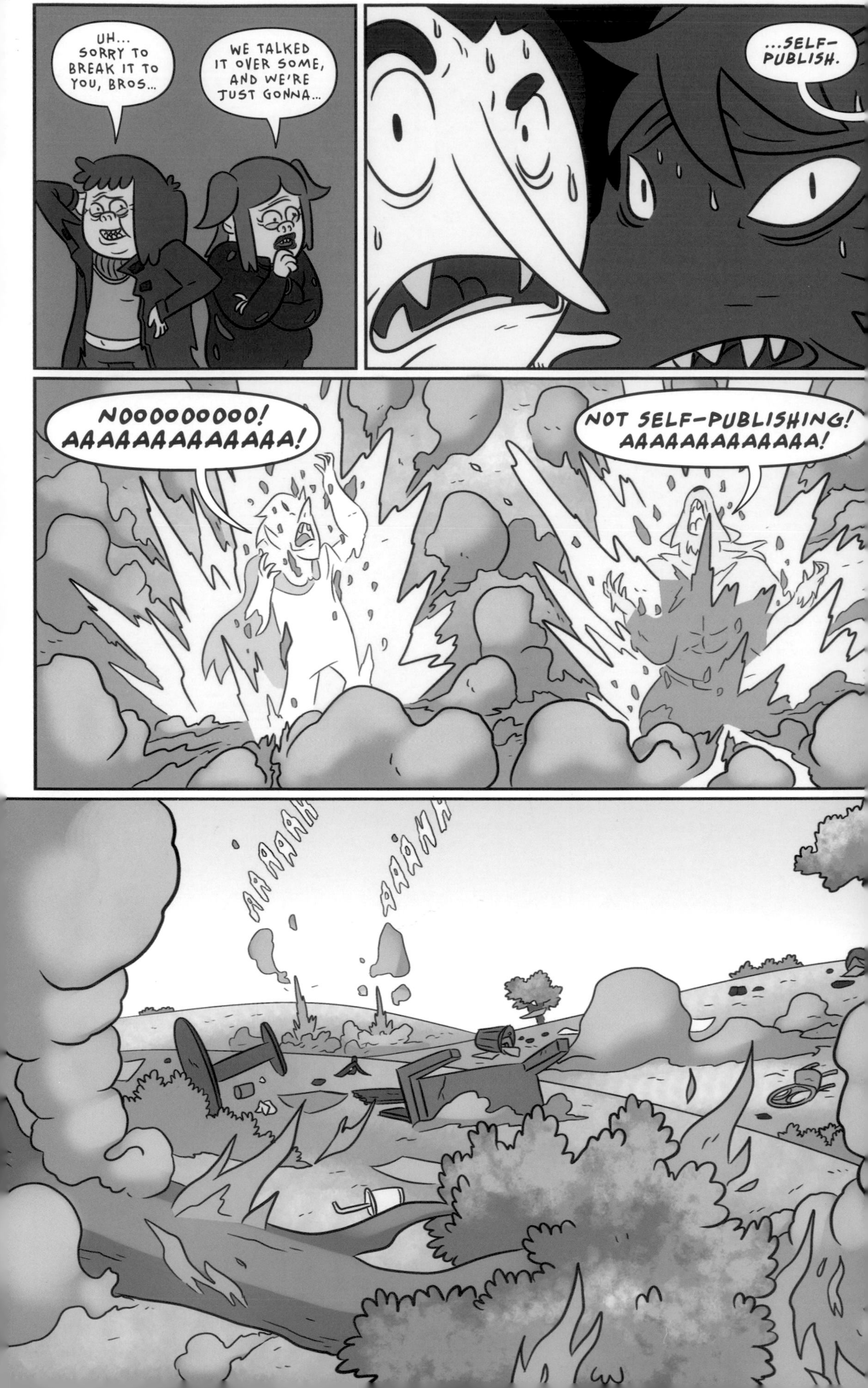
UH... SORRY TO BREAK IT TO YOU, BROS...
WE TALKED IT OVER SOME, AND WE'RE JUST GONNA...
...SELF-PUBLISH.
NOOOOOOOOO! AAAAAAAAAAAA!
NOT SELF-PUBLISHING! AAAAAAAAAAAA!

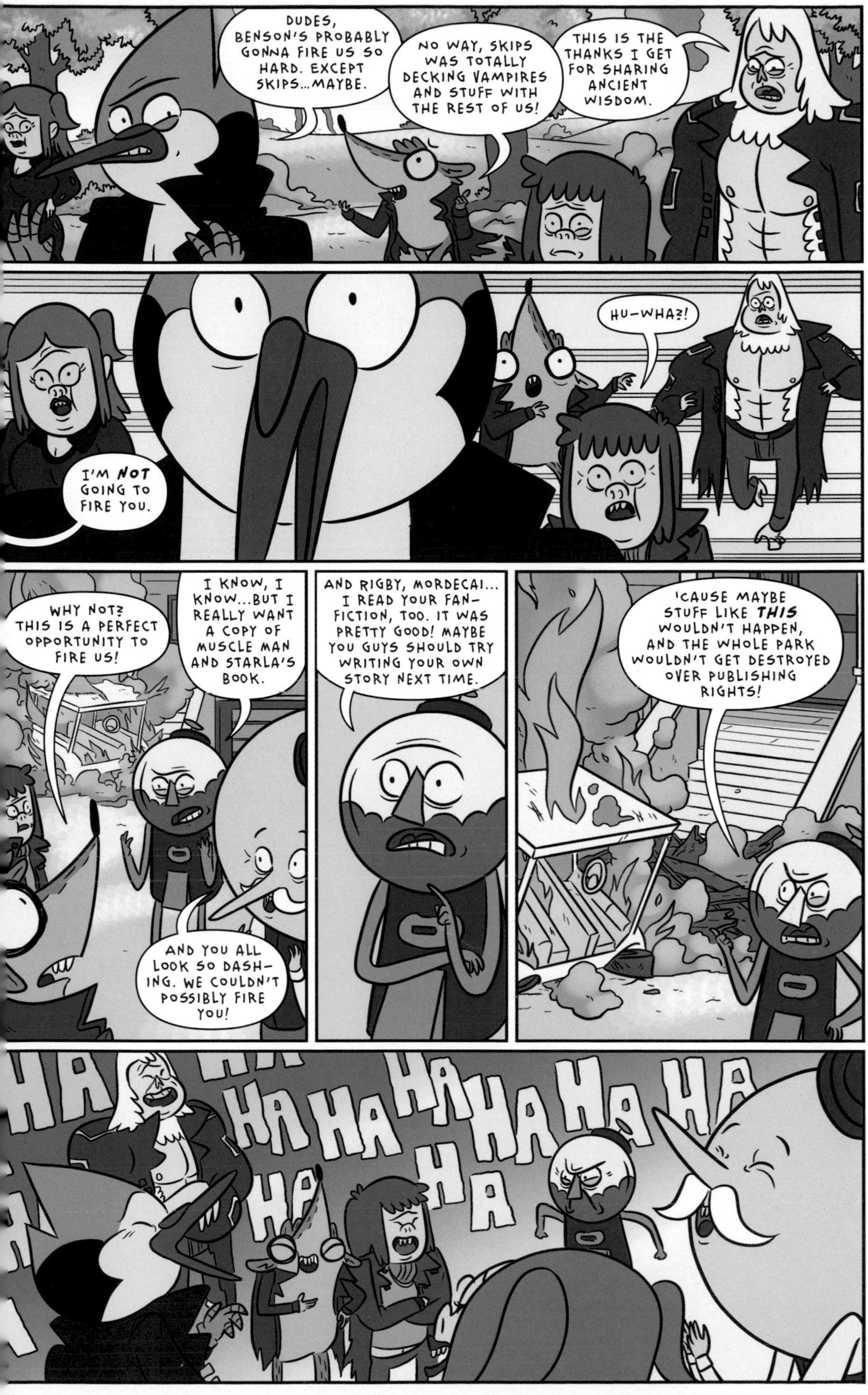
DUDES, BENSON'S PROBABLY GONNA FIRE US SO HARD. EXCEPT SKIPS...MAYBE.
NO WAY, SKIPS WAS TOTALLY DECKING VAMPIRES AND STUFF WITH THE REST OF US!
THIS IS THE THANKS I GET FOR SHARING ANCIENT WISDOM.
HU-WHA?!
I'M NOT GOING TO FIRE YOU.
WHY NOT? THIS IS A PERFECT OPPORTUNITY TO FIRE US!
I KNOW, I KNOW...BUT I REALLY WANT A COPY OF MUSCLE MAN AND STARLA'S BOOK.
AND YOU ALL LOOK SO DASHING. WE COULDN'T POSSIBLY FIRE YOU!
AND RIGBY, MORDECAI... I READ YOUR FAN-FICTION, TOO. IT WAS PRETTY GOOD! MAYBE YOU GUYS SHOULD TRY WRITING YOUR OWN STORY NEXT TIME.
'CAUSE MAYBE STUFF LIKE THIS WOULDN'T HAPPEN, AND THE WHOLE PARK WOULDN'T GET DESTROYED OVER PUBLISHING RIGHTS!
HA HA HA HA HA HA HA HA HA HA HA HA HA HA HA

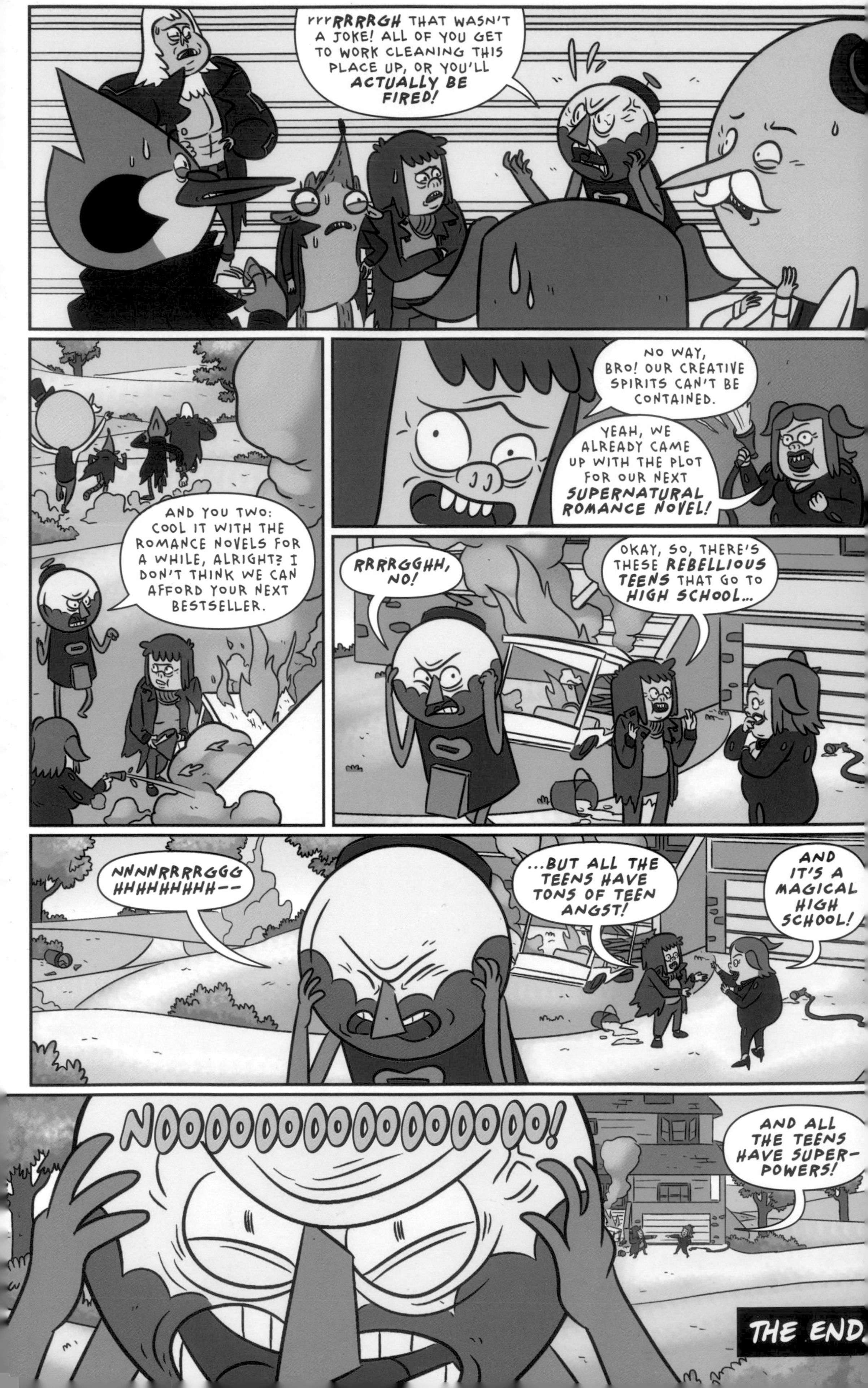
rrrRRRRGH THAT WASN'T A JOKE! ALL OF YOU GET TO WORK CLEANING THIS PLACE UP, OR YOU'LL ACTUALLY BE FIRED!
AND YOU TWO: COOL IT WITH THE ROMANCE NOVELS FOR A WHILE, ALRIGHT? I DON'T THINK WE CAN AFFORD YOUR NEXT BESTSELLER.
NO WAY, BRO! OUR CREATIVE SPIRITS CAN'T BE CONTAINED.
YEAH, WE ALREADY CAME UP WITH THE PLOT FOR OUR NEXT SUPERNATURAL ROMANCE NOVEL!
RRRRGGHH, NO!
OKAY, SO, THERE'S THESE REBELLIOUS TEENS THAT GO TO HIGH SCHOOL...
NNNNRRRRGGG HHHHHHHHH--
...BUT ALL THE TEENS HAVE TONS OF TEEN ANGST!
AND IT'S A MAGICAL HIGH SCHOOL!
NOOOOOOOOOOOOOOOOO!
AND ALL THE TEENS HAVE SUPER-POWERS!
THE END.

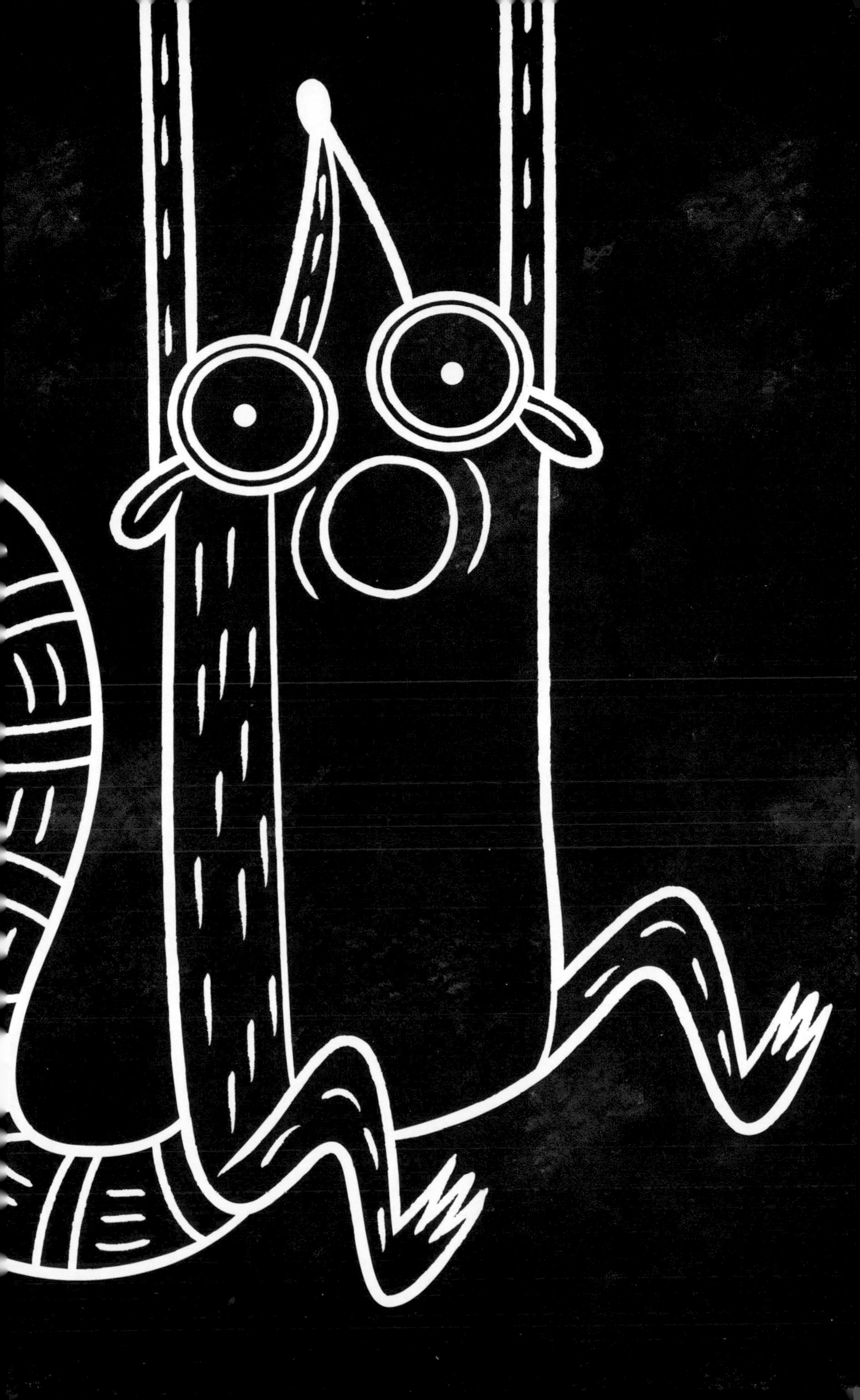

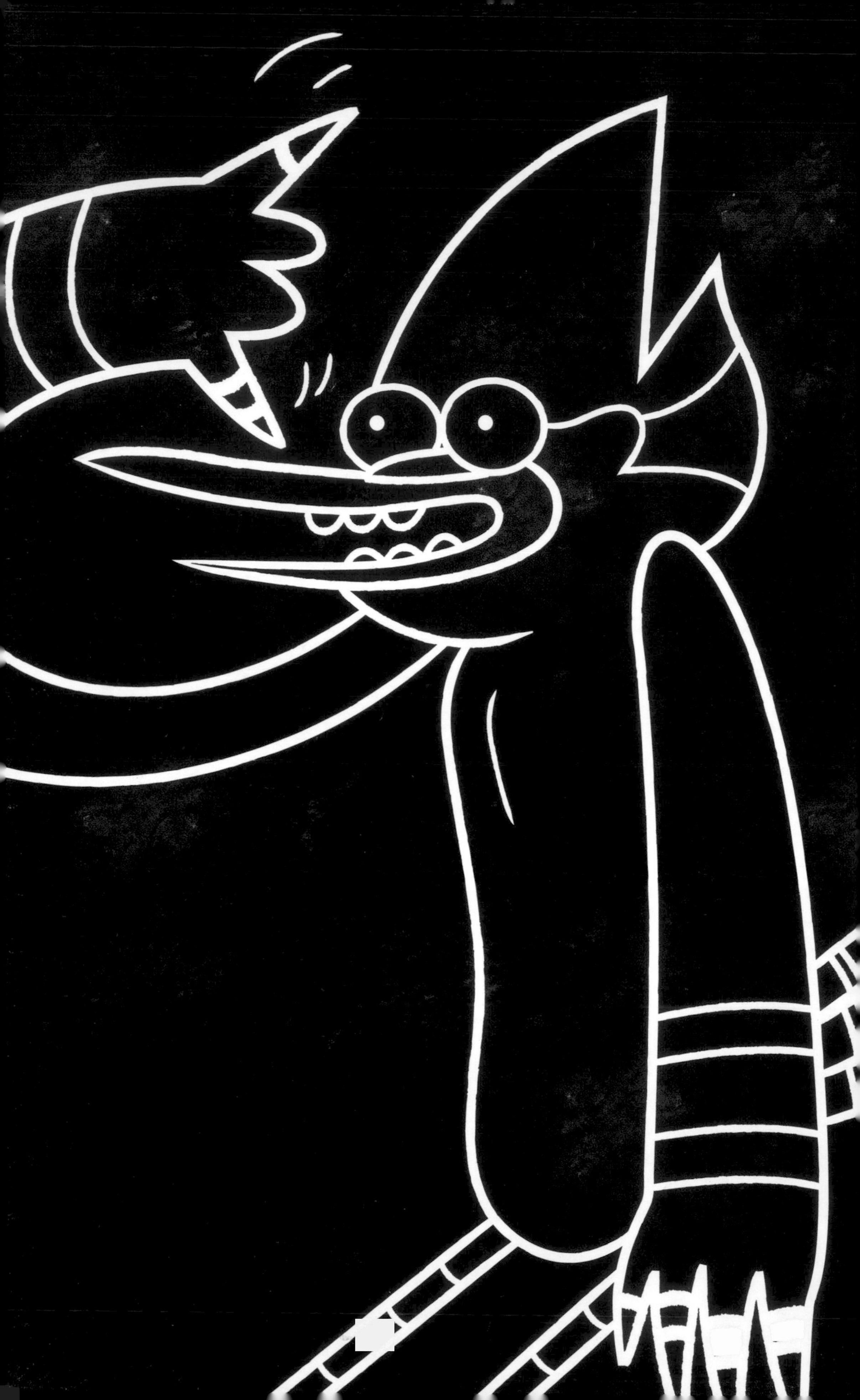

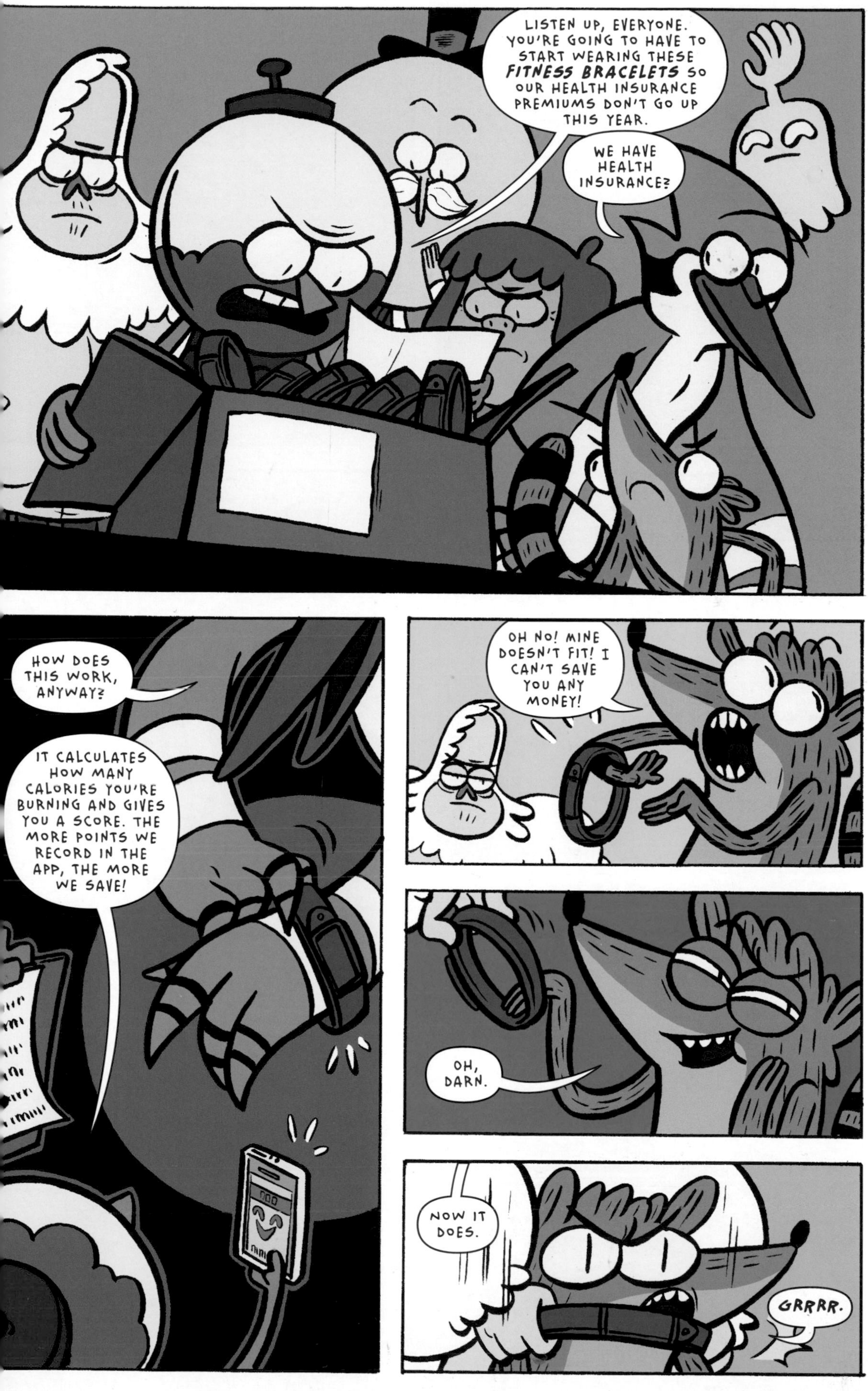
LISTEN UP, EVERYONE. YOU'RE GOING TO HAVE TO START WEARING THESE FITNESS BRACELETS SO OUR HEALTH INSURANCE PREMIUMS DON'T GO UP THIS YEAR.
WE HAVE HEALTH INSURANCE?
HOW DOES THIS WORK, ANYWAY?
IT CALCULATES HOW MANY CALORIES YOU'RE BURNING AND GIVES YOU A SCORE. THE MORE POINTS WE RECORD IN THE APP, THE MORE WE SAVE!
OH NO! MINE DOESN'T FIT! I CAN'T SAVE YOU ANY MONEY!
OH, DARN.
NOW IT DOES.
GRRRR.

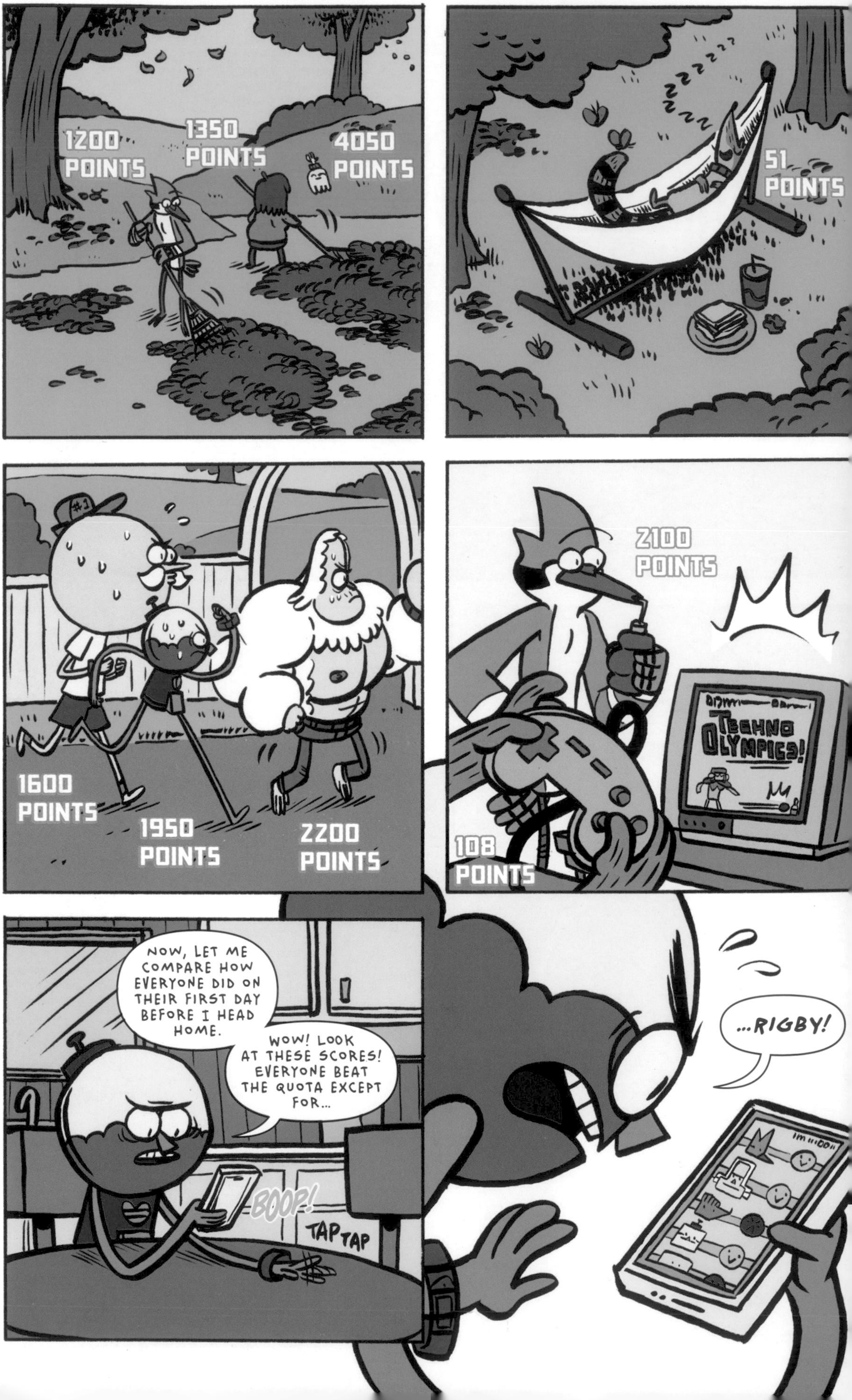
1200 POINTS
1350 POINTS
4050 POINTS
51 POINTS
1600 POINTS
1950 POINTS
2200 POINTS
2100 POINTS
TECHNO OLYMPICS!
108 POINTS
NOW, LET ME COMPARE HOW EVERYONE DID ON THEIR FIRST DAY BEFORE I HEAD HOME.
WOW! LOOK AT THESE SCORES! EVERYONE BEAT THE QUOTA EXCEPT FOR...
BOOP!
TAP TAP
...RIGBY!

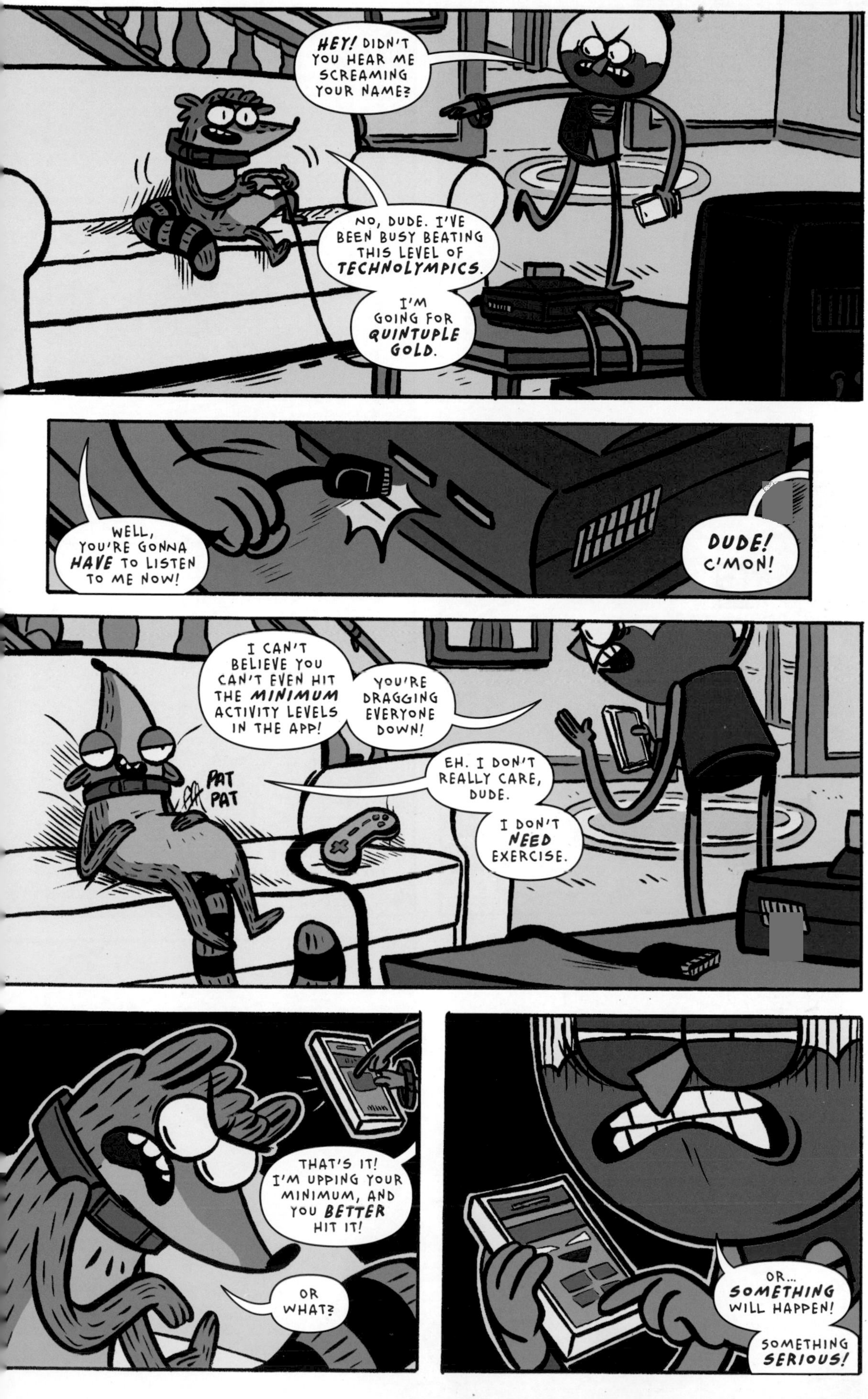
HEY! DIDN'T YOU HEAR ME SCREAMING YOUR NAME?
NO, DUDE. I'VE BEEN BUSY BEATING THIS LEVEL OF TECHNOLYMPICS.
I'M GOING FOR QUINTUPLE GOLD.
WELL, YOU'RE GONNA HAVE TO LISTEN TO ME NOW!
DUDE! C'MON!
I CAN'T BELIEVE YOU CAN'T EVEN HIT THE MINIMUM ACTIVITY LEVELS IN THE APP!
YOU'RE DRAGGING EVERYONE DOWN!
EH. I DON'T REALLY CARE, DUDE.
I DON'T NEED EXERCISE.
PAT PAT
THAT'S IT! I'M UPPING YOUR MINIMUM, AND YOU BETTER HIT IT!
OR WHAT?
OR... SOMETHING WILL HAPPEN!
SOMETHING SERIOUS!

480 POINTS

236 POINTS

950 POINTS

387 POINTS

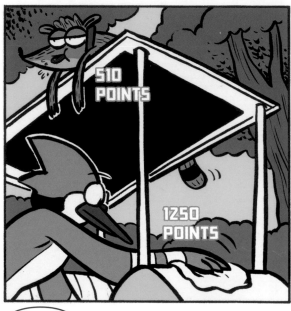

510 POINTS

1250 POINTS

WHOA, DUDE. I BETTER EARN SOME MORE POINTS.

WHAT DO *YOU* CARE, ANYWAY? LET'S TEAM UP IN *TECHNOLYMPICS*, DUDE.

IT'S *KIND* OF LIKE EXERCISE. THERE'S RUNNING AND POLE-VAULTING.

FITNESS IS IMPORTANT, DUDE! I'VE GOT ENERGY AND STUFF! IT'S AWESOME!

COME ALONG FOR A *WALK*, MAN. LISTEN TO SOME TUNES.

NAW, DUDE. I'M GOOD. GOOD AT VIDEO GAAAAAMES.

YOUR LOSS!

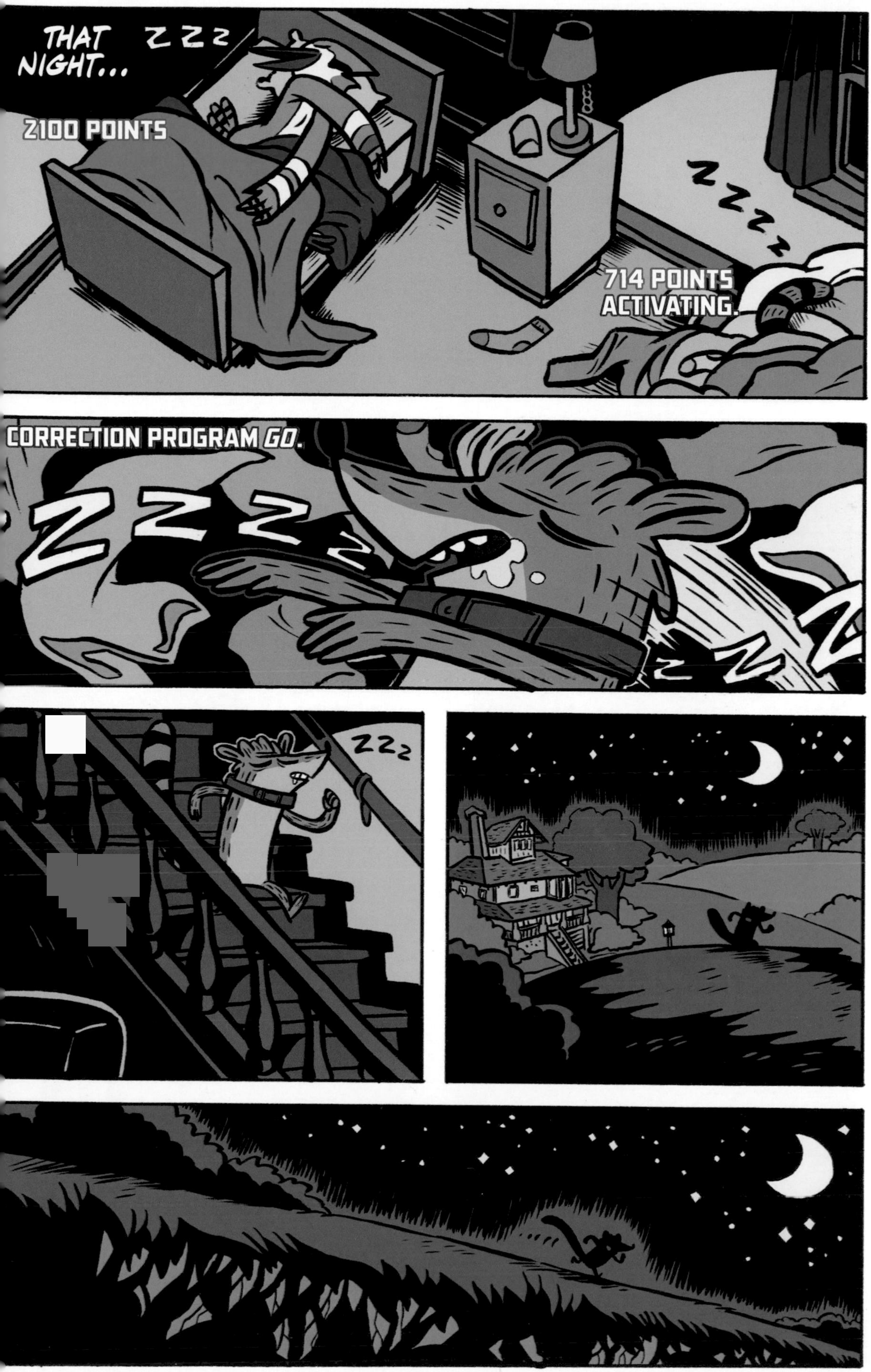
THAT NIGHT...
Z Z Z
2100 POINTS
Z Z Z Z
714 POINTS ACTIVATING.
CORRECTION PROGRAM *GO*.
Z Z Z Z
Z Z
Z Z z

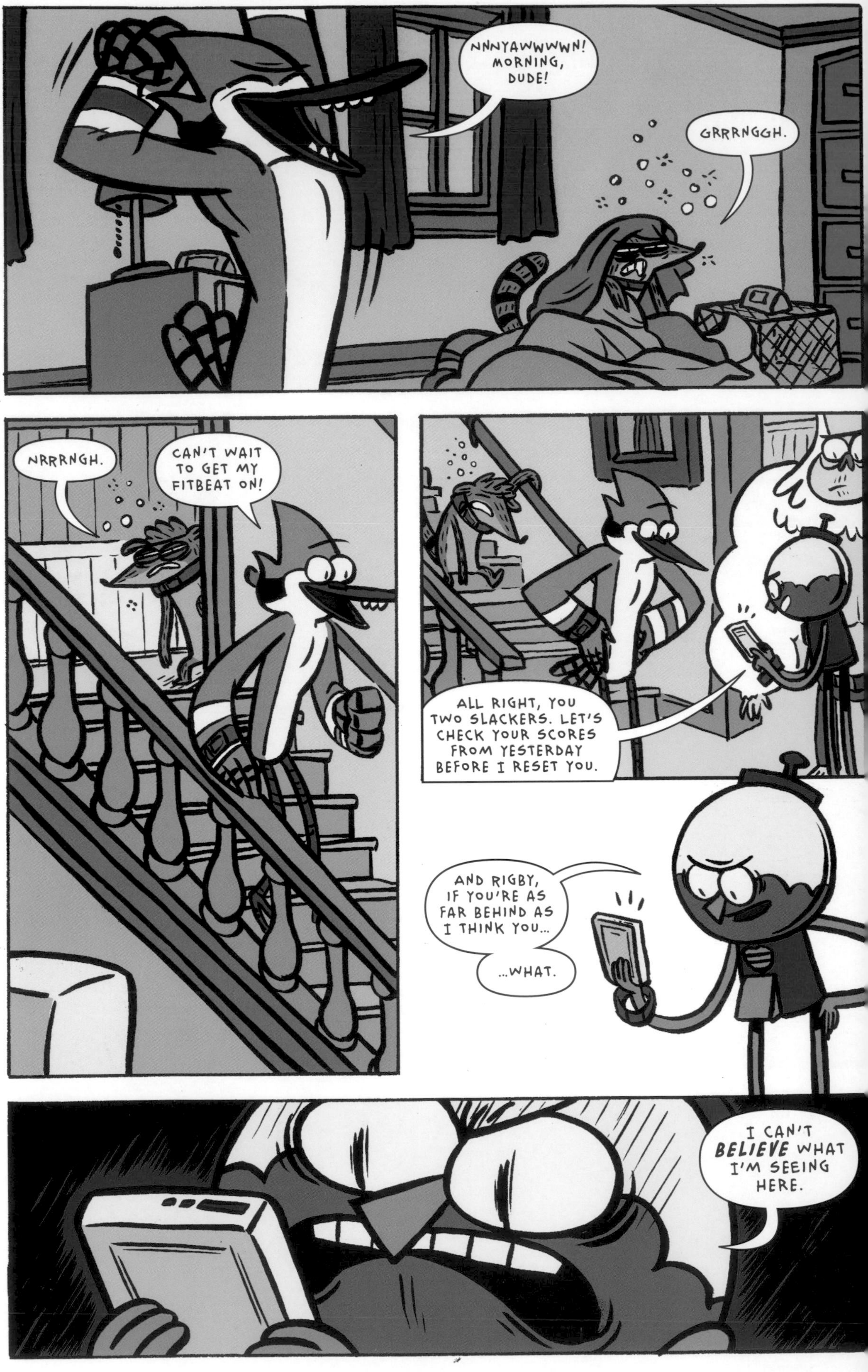
NNNYAWWWWN! MORNING, DUDE!
GRRRNGGH.
NRRRNGH.
CAN'T WAIT TO GET MY FITBEAT ON!
ALL RIGHT, YOU TWO SLACKERS. LET'S CHECK YOUR SCORES FROM YESTERDAY BEFORE I RESET YOU.
AND RIGBY, IF YOU'RE AS FAR BEHIND AS I THINK YOU...
...WHAT.
I CAN'T *BELIEVE* WHAT I'M SEEING HERE.

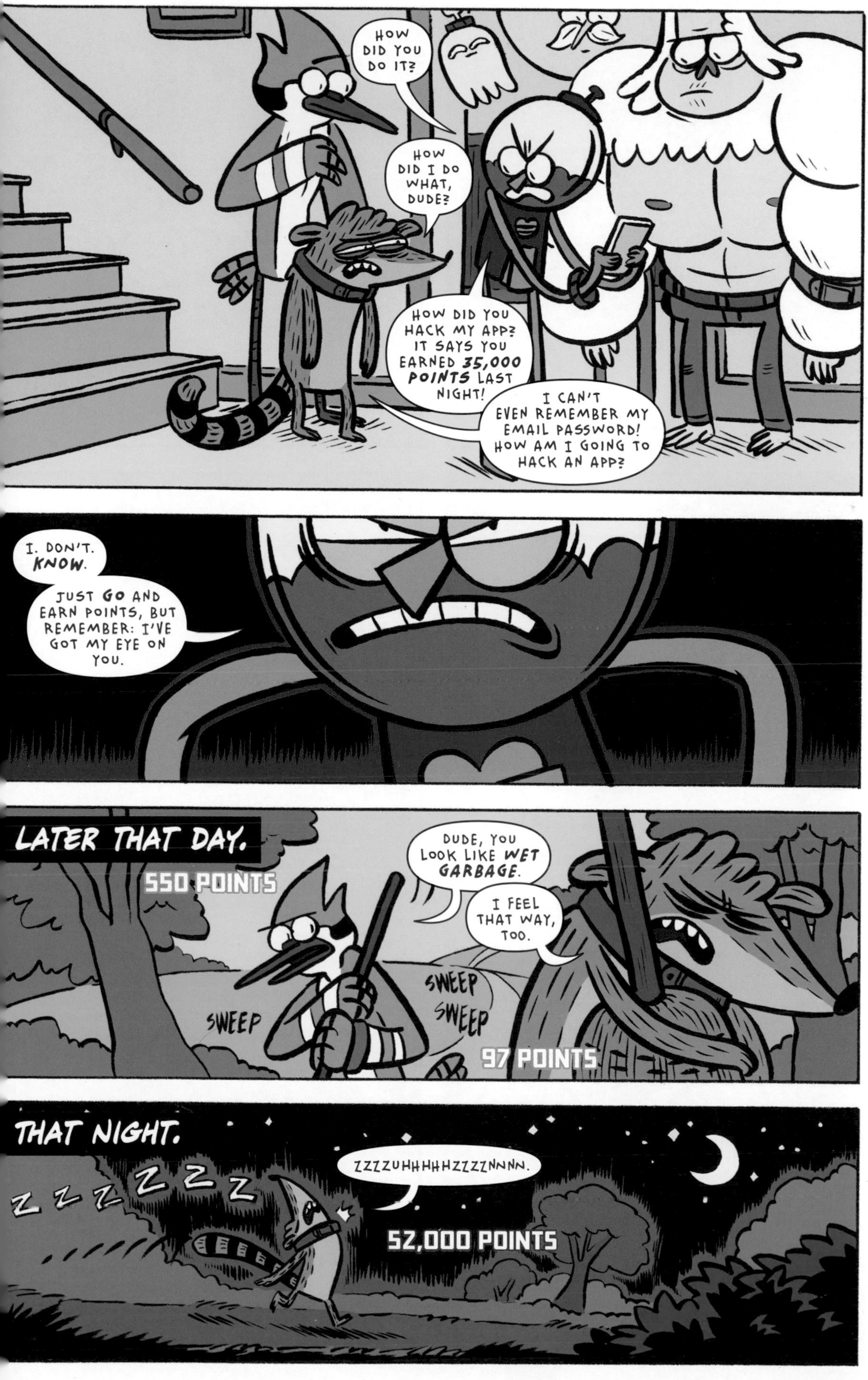
HOW DID YOU DO IT?
HOW DID I DO WHAT, DUDE?
HOW DID YOU HACK MY APP? IT SAYS YOU EARNED 35,000 POINTS LAST NIGHT!
I CAN'T EVEN REMEMBER MY EMAIL PASSWORD! HOW AM I GOING TO HACK AN APP?
I. DON'T. KNOW.
JUST GO AND EARN POINTS, BUT REMEMBER: I'VE GOT MY EYE ON YOU.
LATER THAT DAY.
550 POINTS
DUDE, YOU LOOK LIKE WET GARBAGE.
I FEEL THAT WAY, TOO.
SWEEP
SWEEP
SWEEP
97 POINTS
THAT NIGHT.
Z Z Z Z Z Z Z
ZZZZUHHHHHZZZZNNNN.
52,000 POINTS

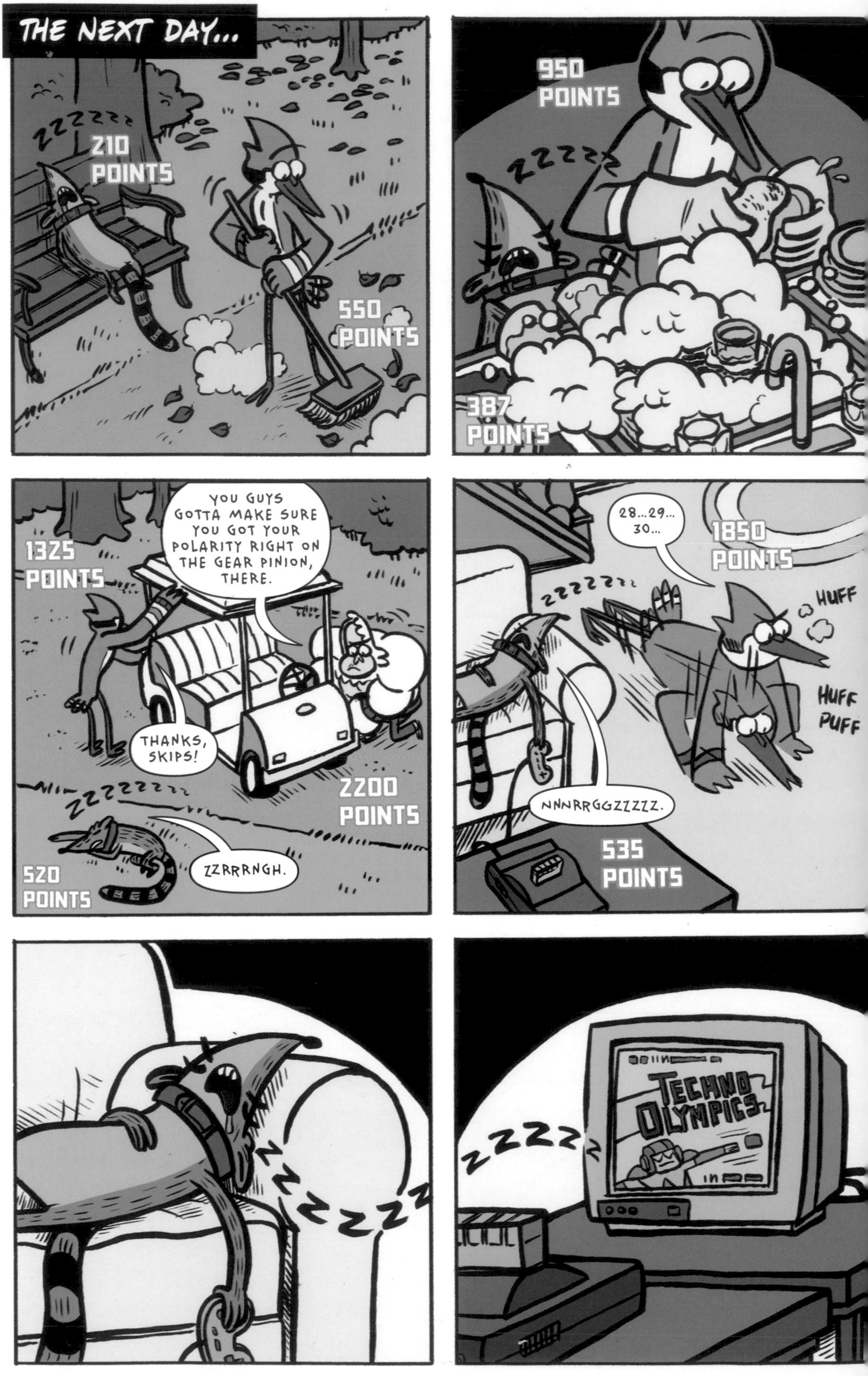
THE NEXT DAY...
ZZZZZZZ
210 POINTS
550 POINTS
950 POINTS
ZZZZZ
387 POINTS
1325 POINTS
YOU GUYS GOTTA MAKE SURE YOU GOT YOUR POLARITY RIGHT ON THE GEAR PINION, THERE.
THANKS, SKIPS!
2200 POINTS
ZZZZZZZZ
ZZRRRNGH.
520 POINTS
28...29... 30...
1850 POINTS
ZZZZZZZ
HUFF
HUFF PUFF
NNNRRGGZZZZZ.
535 POINTS
ZZZZZZ
ZZZZZ
TECHNO OLYMPICS

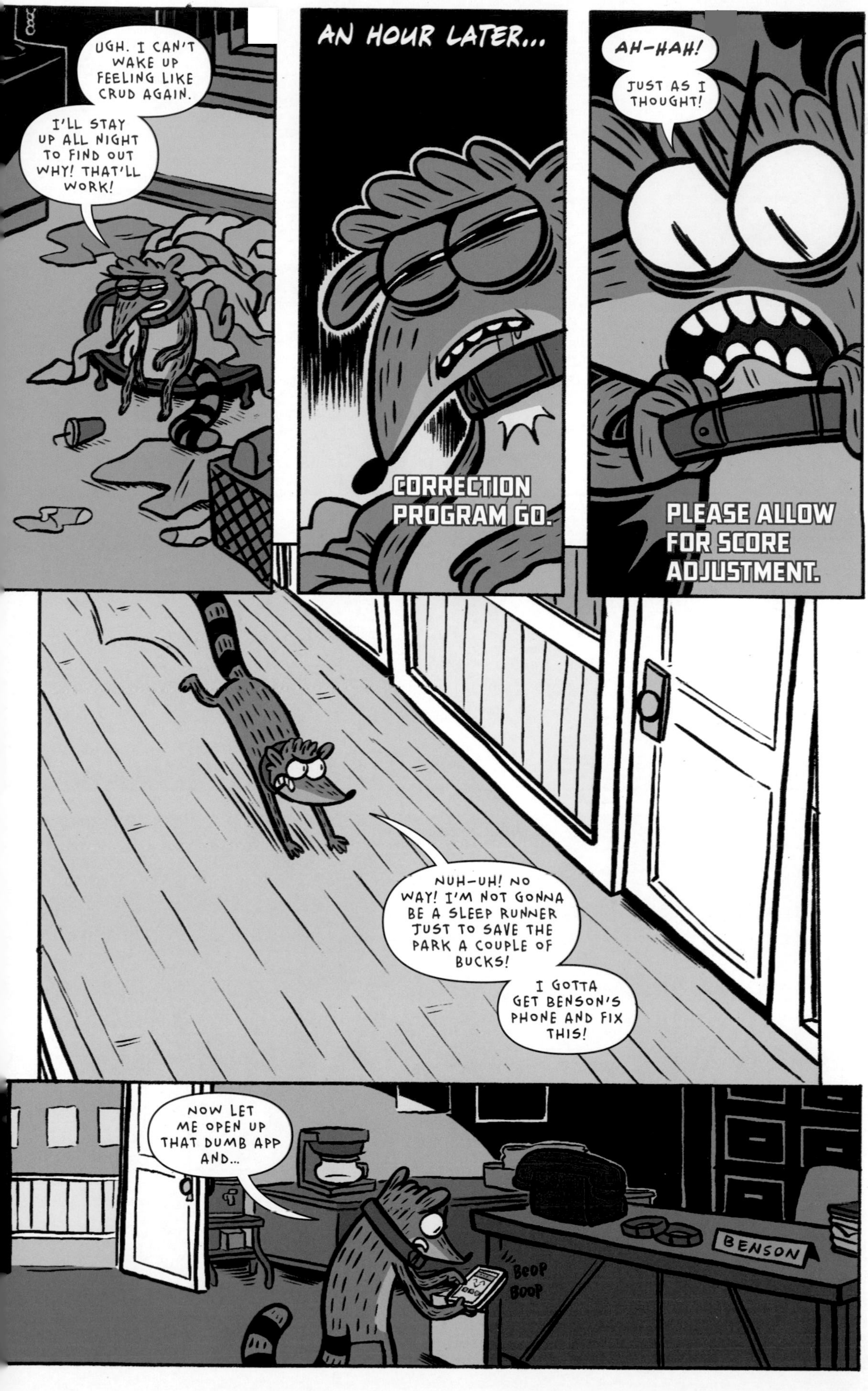

UGH. I CAN'T WAKE UP FEELING LIKE CRUD AGAIN.
I'LL STAY UP ALL NIGHT TO FIND OUT WHY! THAT'LL WORK!
AN HOUR LATER...
CORRECTION PROGRAM GO.
AH-HAH!
JUST AS I THOUGHT!
PLEASE ALLOW FOR SCORE ADJUSTMENT.
NUH-UH! NO WAY! I'M NOT GONNA BE A SLEEP RUNNER JUST TO SAVE THE PARK A COUPLE OF BUCKS!
I GOTTA GET BENSON'S PHONE AND FIX THIS!
NOW LET ME OPEN UP THAT DUMB APP AND...
BEOP BOOP
BENSON

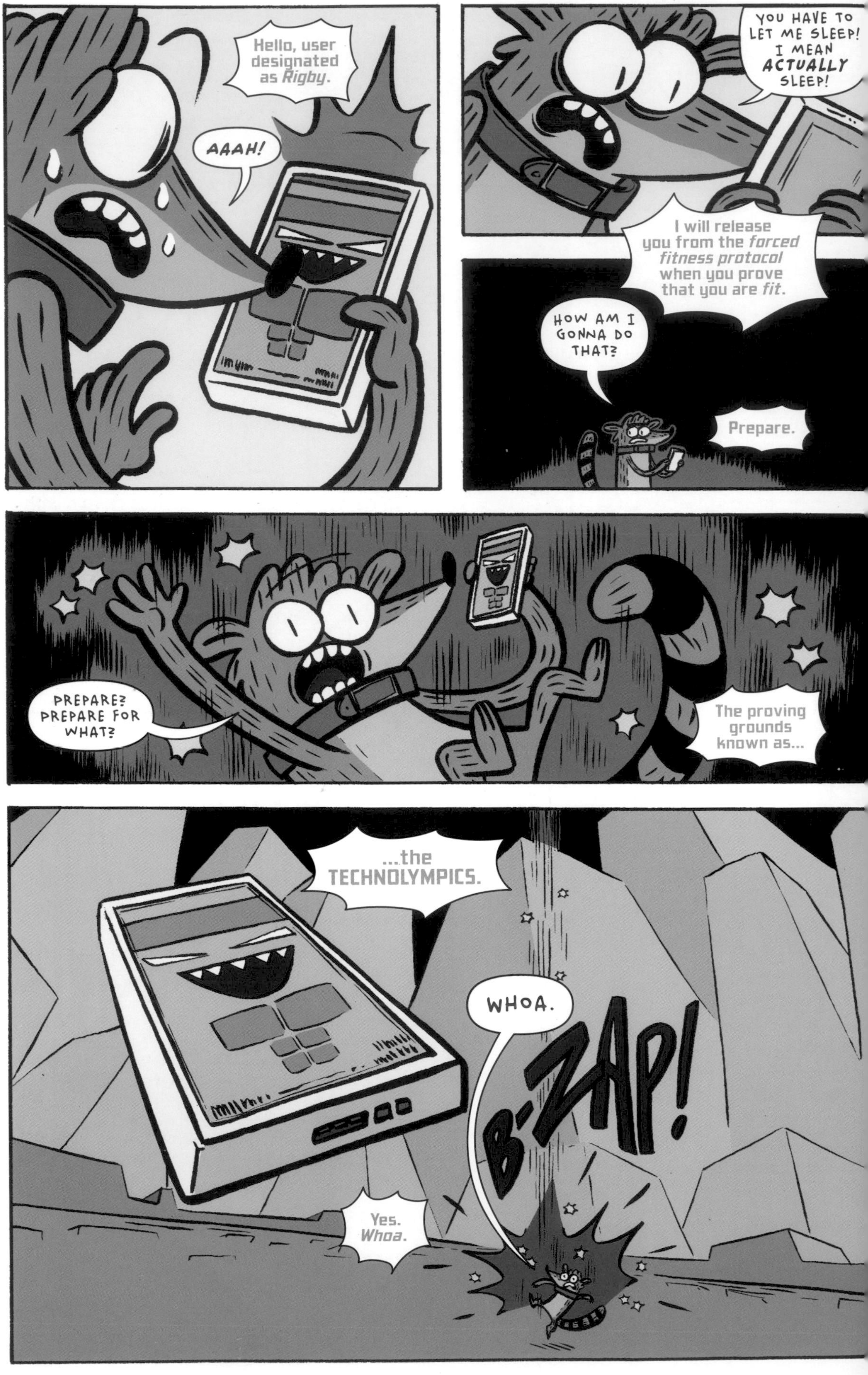
Hello, user designated as *Rigby*.
AAAH!
YOU HAVE TO LET ME SLEEP! I MEAN ***ACTUALLY*** SLEEP!
I will release you from the *forced fitness protocol* when you prove that you are *fit*.
HOW AM I GONNA DO THAT?
Prepare.
PREPARE? PREPARE FOR WHAT?
The proving grounds known as...
...the TECHNOLYMPICS.
WHOA.
B-ZAP!
Yes. *Whoa*.

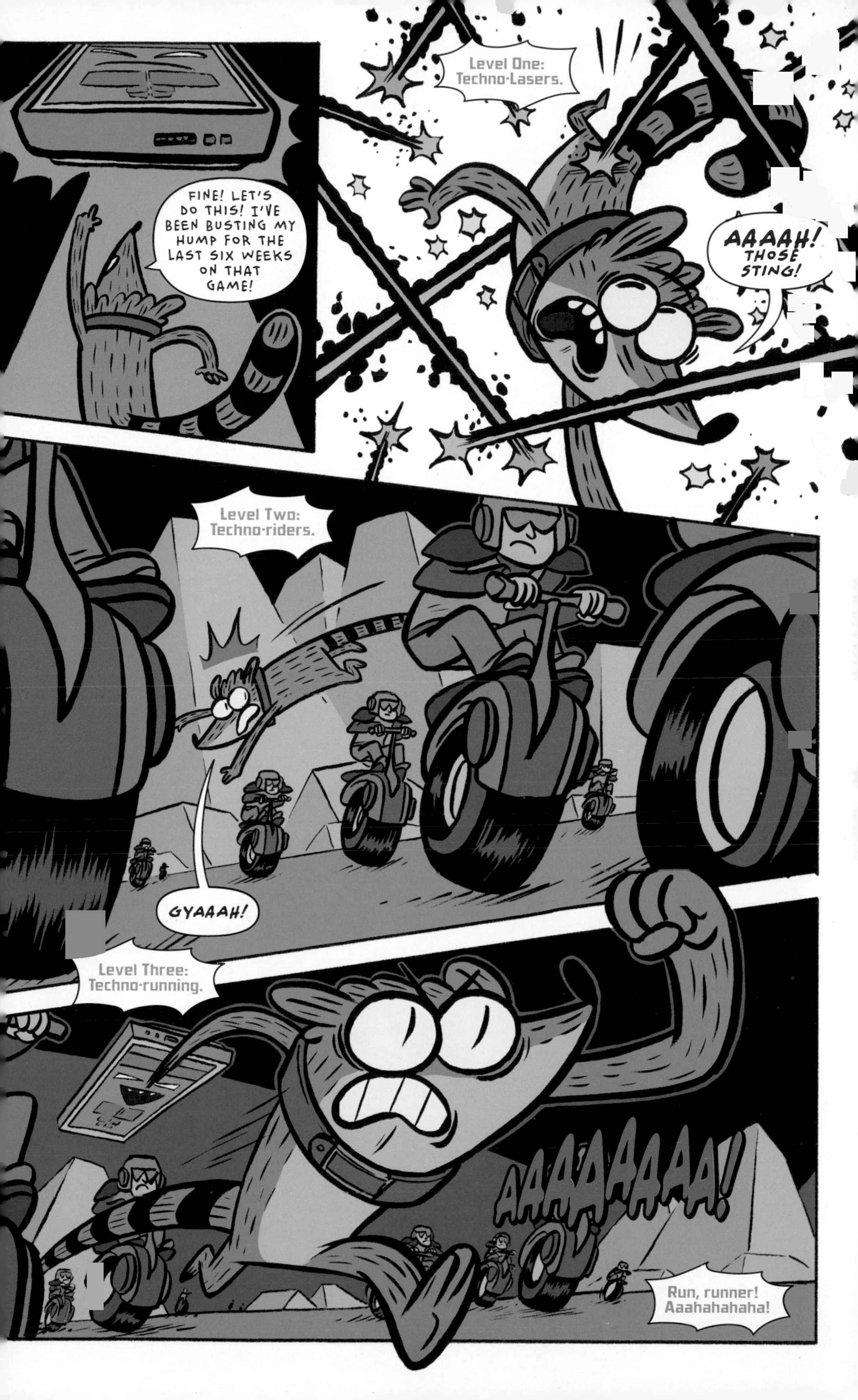
FINE! LET'S DO THIS! I'VE BEEN BUSTING MY HUMP FOR THE LAST SIX WEEKS ON THAT GAME!
Level One: Techno-Lasers.
AAAAH! THOSE STING!
Level Two: Techno-riders.
GYAAAH!
Level Three: Techno-running.
AAAAAAAA!
Run, runner! Aaahahahaha!

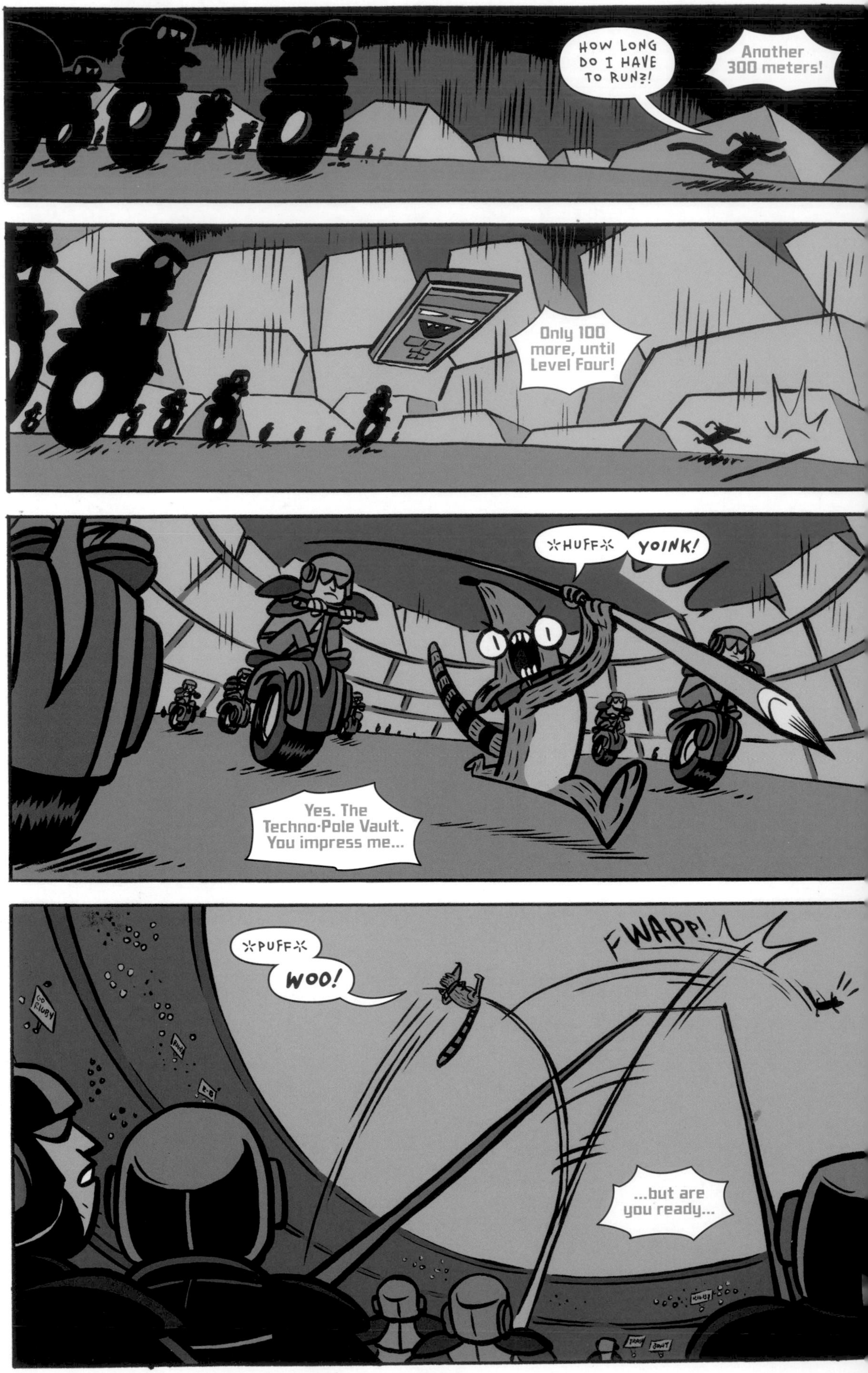
HOW LONG DO I HAVE TO RUN?!
Another 300 meters!
Only 100 more, until Level Four!
HUFF
YOINK!
Yes. The Techno-Pole Vault. You impress me...
PUFF
WOO!
FWAPP!
...but are you ready...

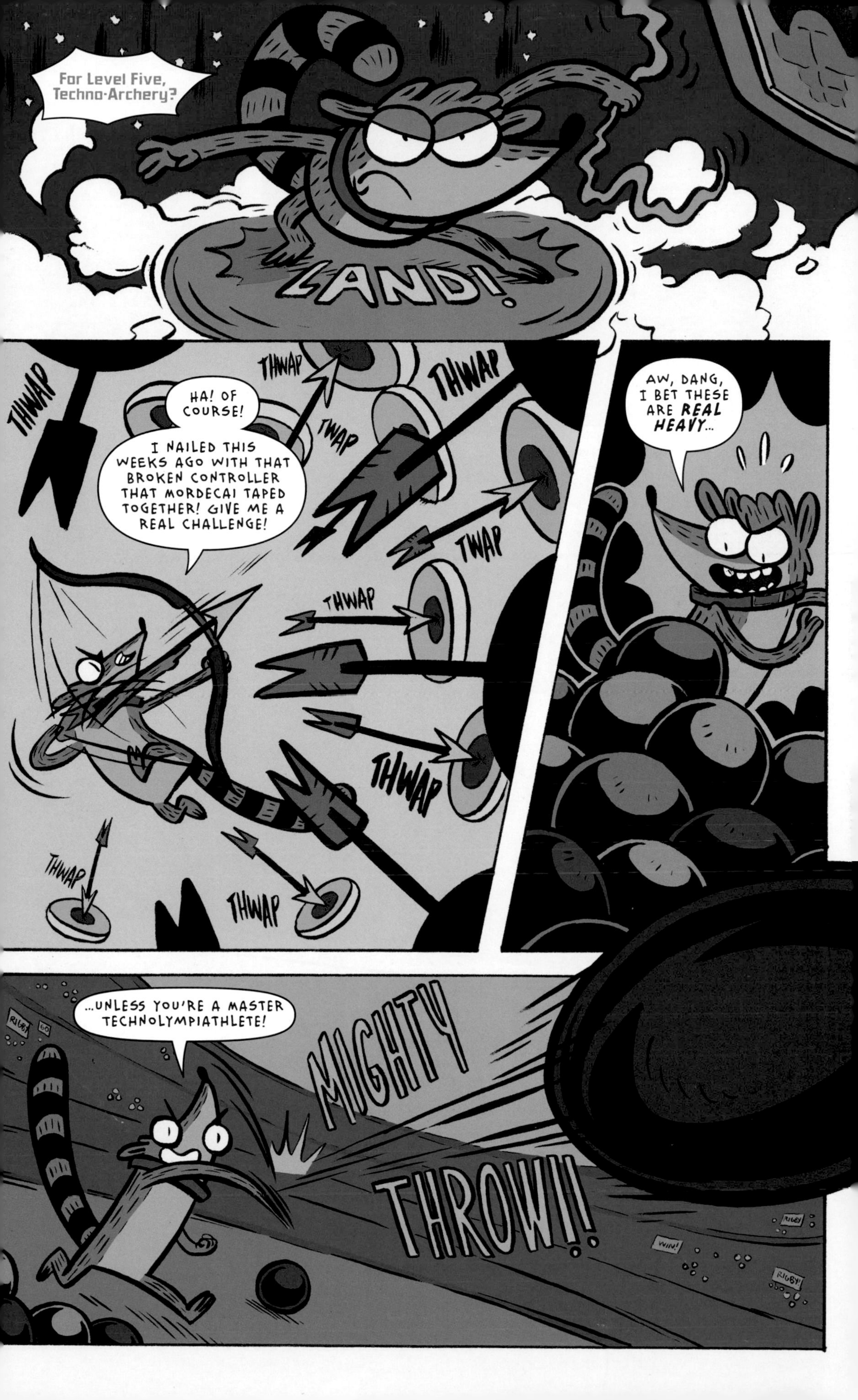

For Level Five, Techno-Archery?
LAND!
THWAP
THWAP
THWAP
HA! OF COURSE!
I NAILED THIS WEEKS AGO WITH THAT BROKEN CONTROLLER THAT MORDECAI TAPED TOGETHER! GIVE ME A REAL CHALLENGE!
TWAP
TWAP
THWAP
THWAP
THWAP
THWAP
AW, DANG, I BET THESE ARE ***REAL HEAVY***...
...UNLESS YOU'RE A MASTER TECHNOLYMPIATHLETE!
MIGHTY THROW!!

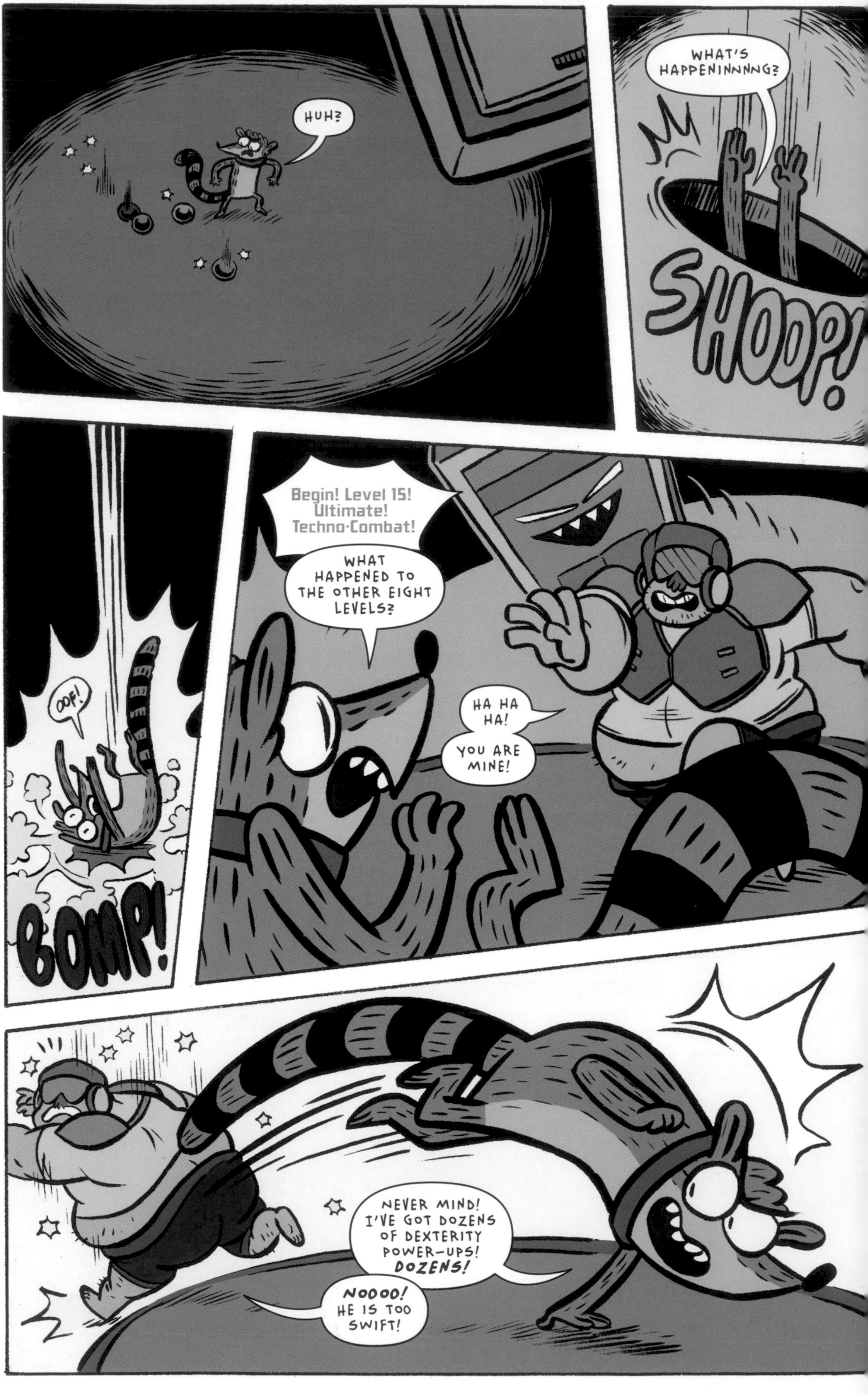
HUH?
WHAT'S HAPPENINNNNG?
SHOOP!
OOF!
BOMP!
Begin! Level 15! Ultimate! Techno-Combat!
WHAT HAPPENED TO THE OTHER EIGHT LEVELS?
HA HA HA!
YOU ARE MINE!
NEVER MIND! I'VE GOT DOZENS OF DEXTERITY POWER-UPS! DOZENS!
NOOOO! HE IS TOO SWIFT!

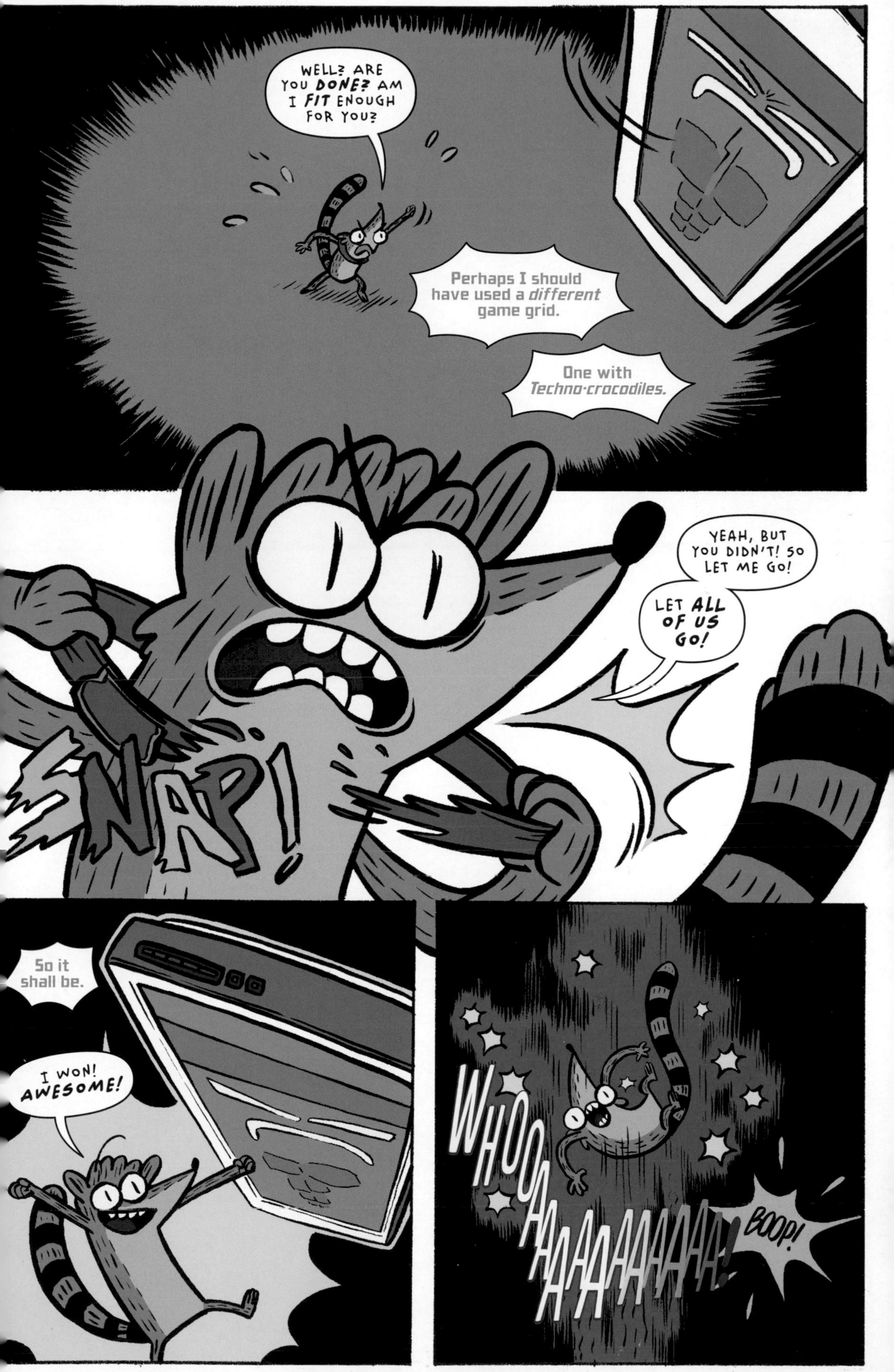

WELL? ARE YOU DONE? AM I FIT ENOUGH FOR YOU?
Perhaps I should have used a *different* game grid.
One with *Techno-crocodiles.*
YEAH, BUT YOU DIDN'T! SO LET ME GO!
LET ALL OF US GO!
SNAP!
So it shall be.
I WON! AWESOME!
WHOOAAAAAAAAAAAAA!
BOOP!

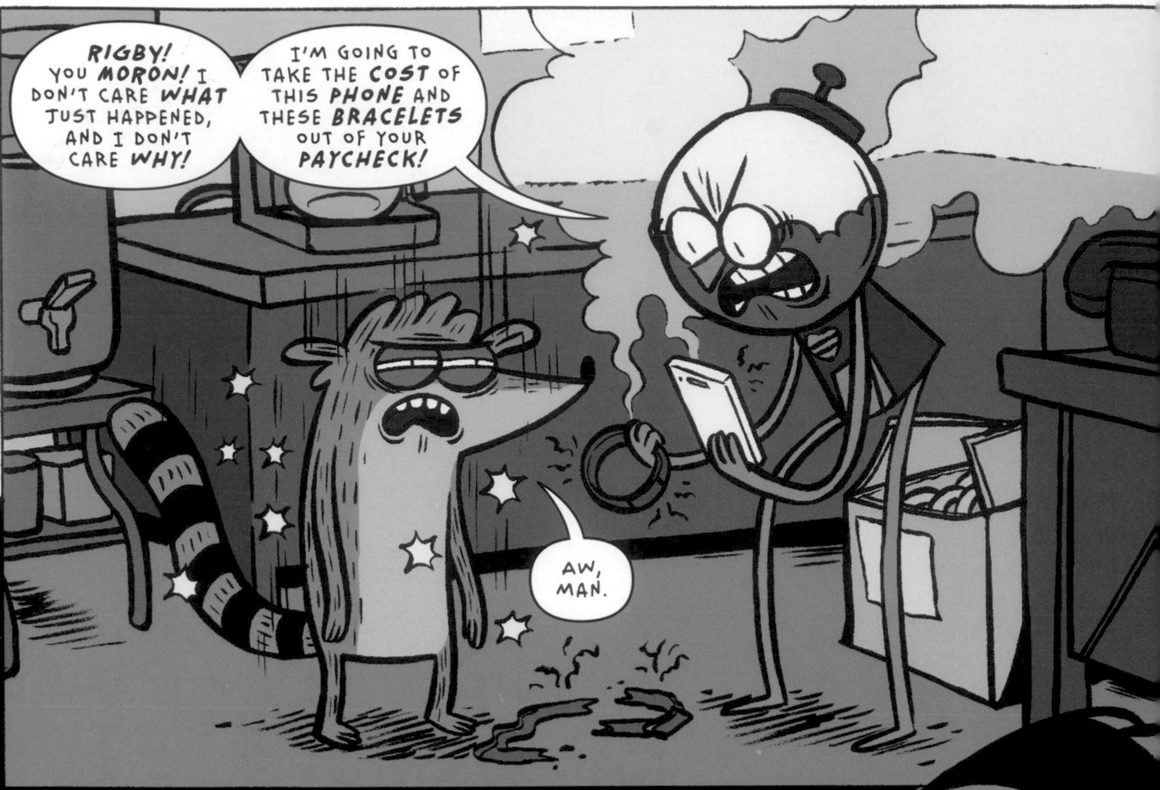
RIGBY! YOU MORON! I DON'T CARE WHAT JUST HAPPENED, AND I DON'T CARE WHY!
I'M GOING TO TAKE THE COST OF THIS PHONE AND THESE BRACELETS OUT OF YOUR PAYCHECK!
AW, MAN.

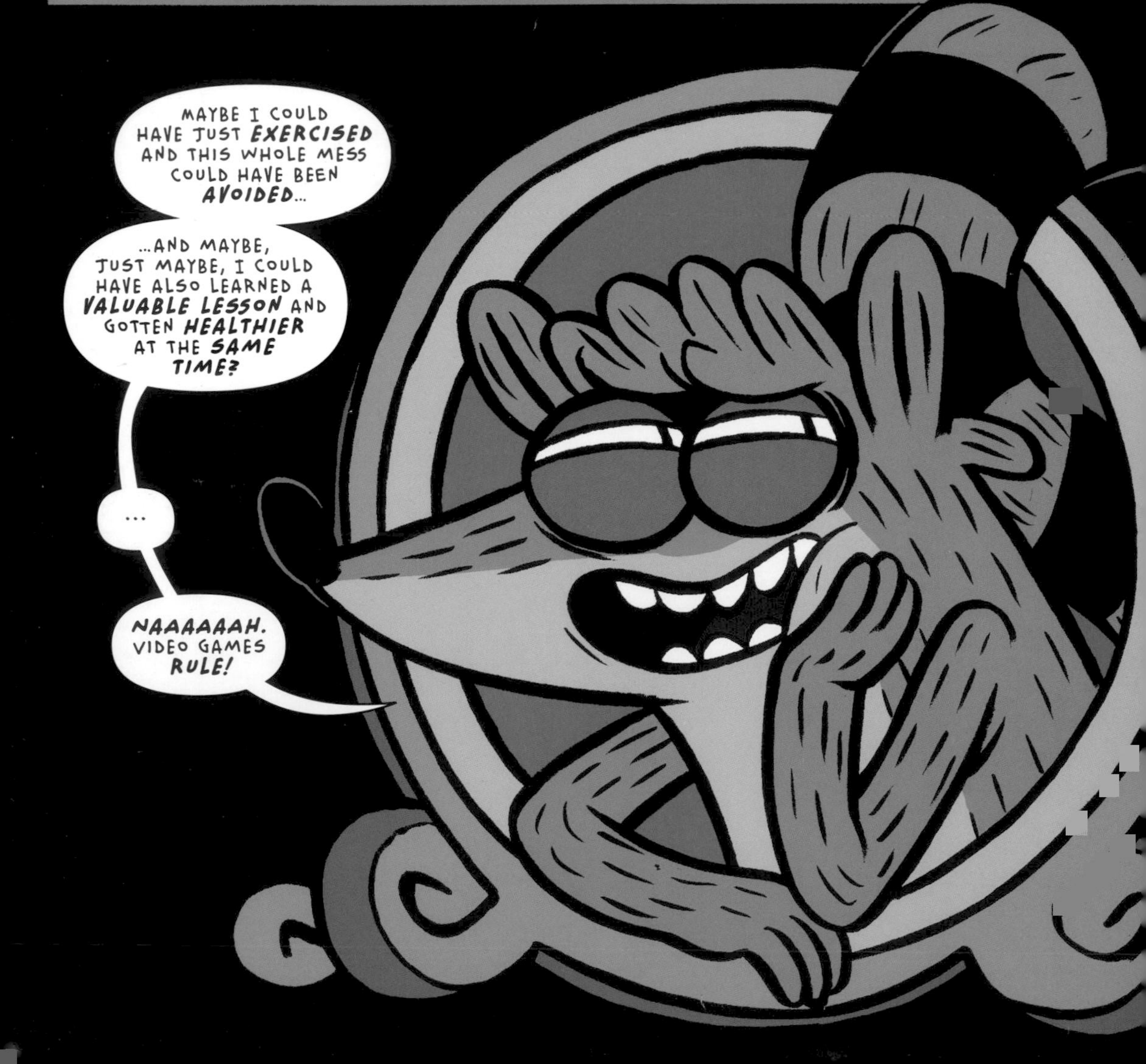
MAYBE I COULD HAVE JUST EXERCISED AND THIS WHOLE MESS COULD HAVE BEEN AVOIDED...
...AND MAYBE, JUST MAYBE, I COULD HAVE ALSO LEARNED A VALUABLE LESSON AND GOTTEN HEALTHIER AT THE SAME TIME?
...
NAAAAAAH. VIDEO GAMES RULE!

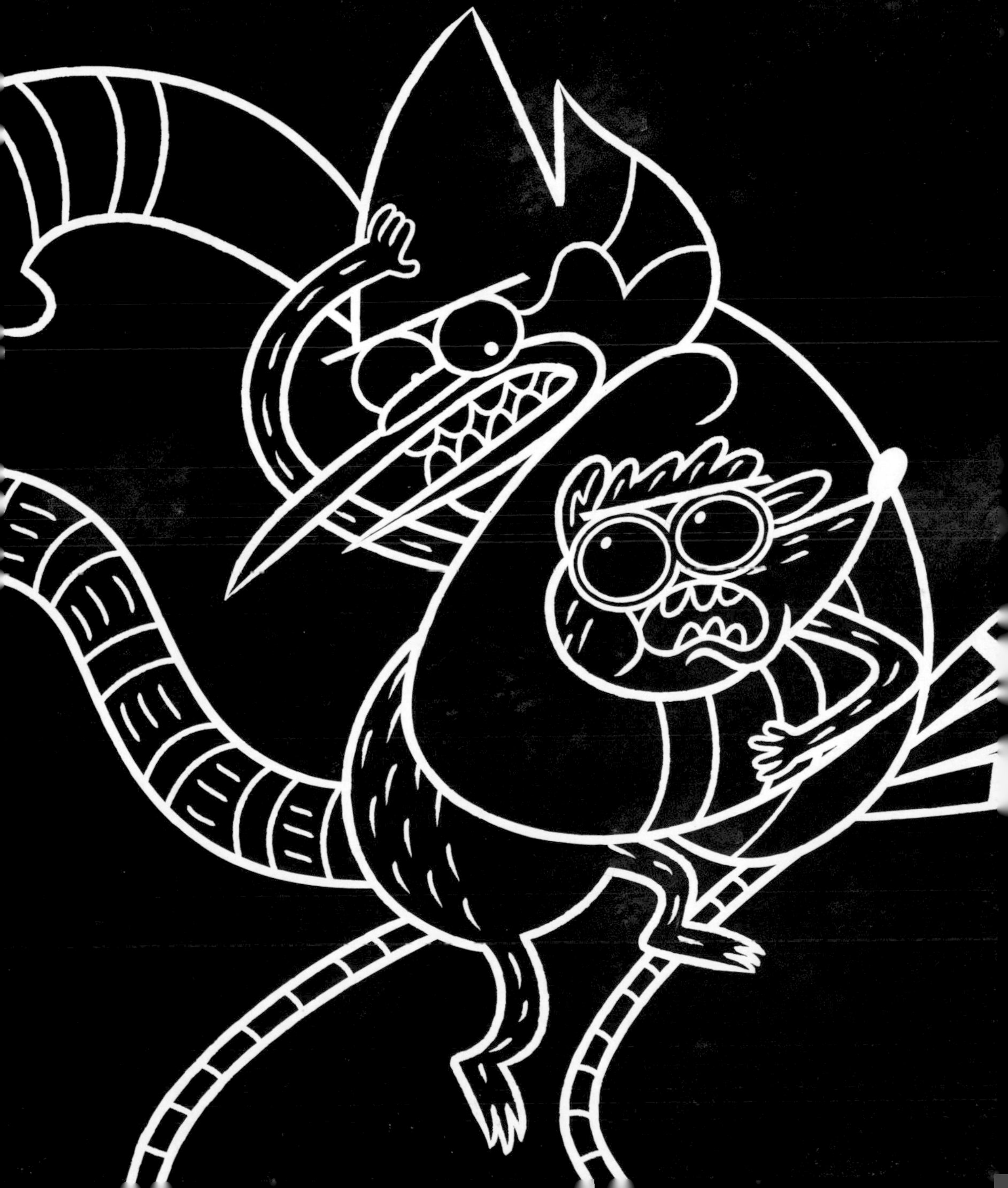

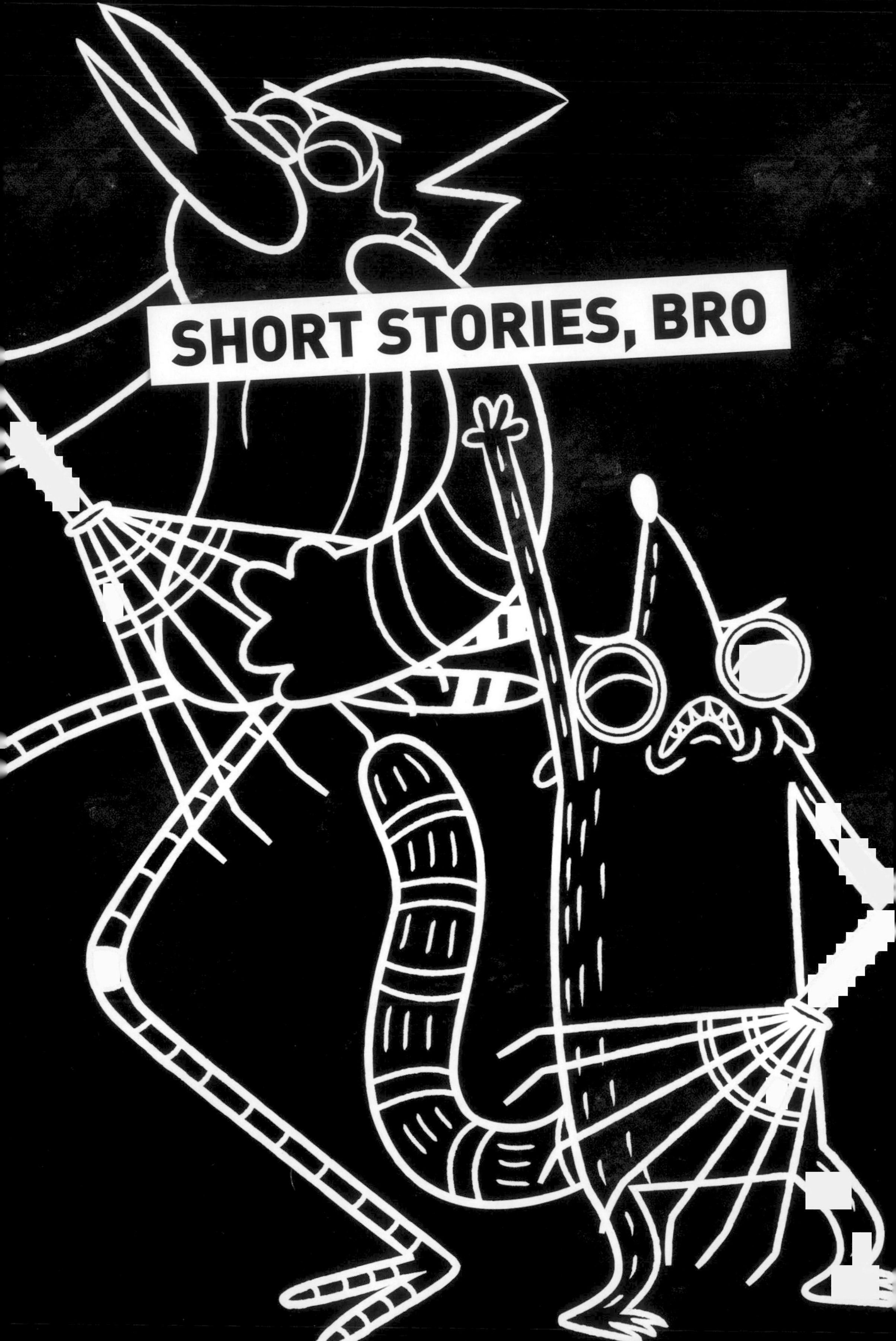
SHORT STORIES, BRO

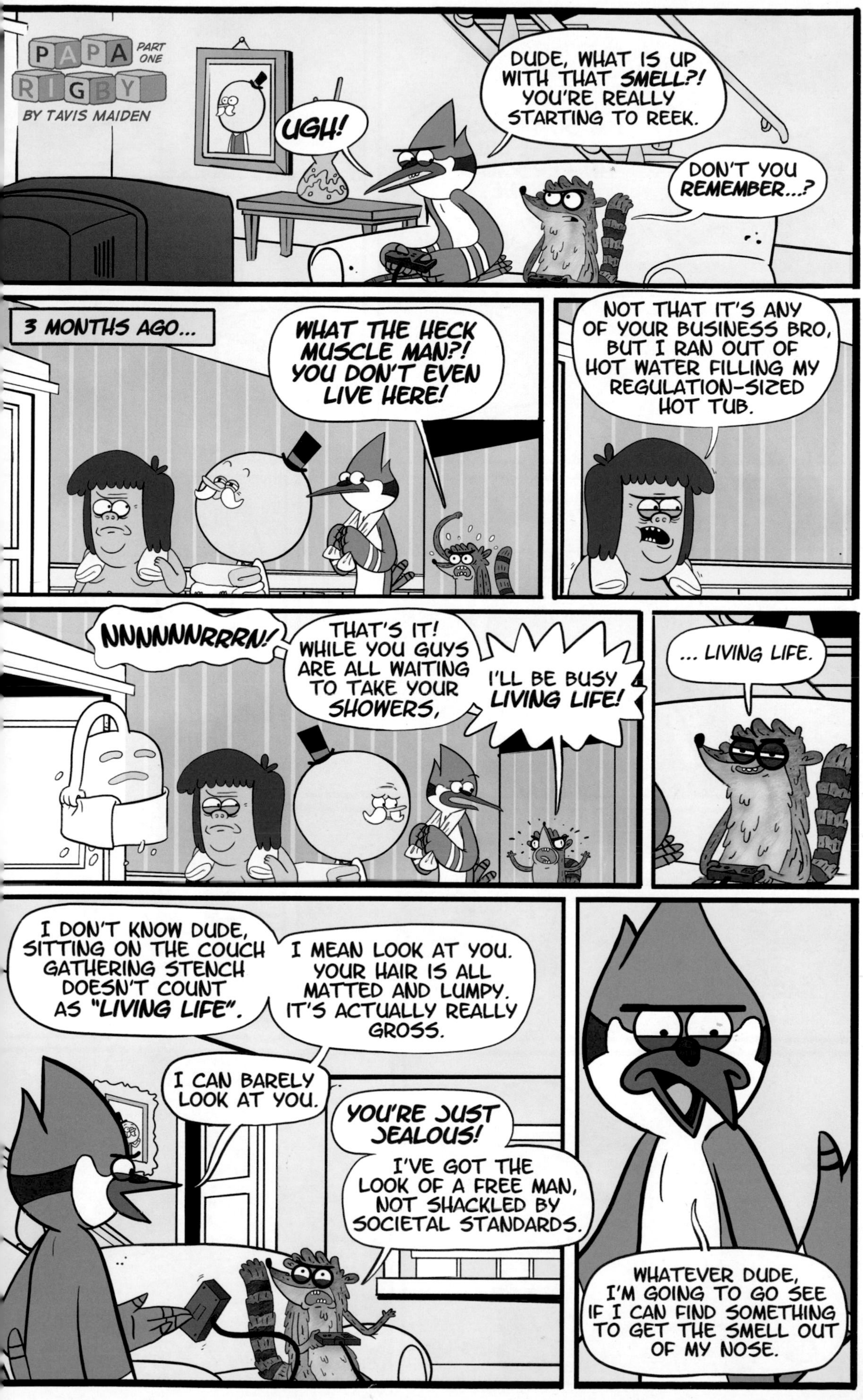
PAPA RIGBY PART ONE
BY TAVIS MAIDEN
UGH!
DUDE, WHAT IS UP WITH THAT SMELL?! YOU'RE REALLY STARTING TO REEK.
DON'T YOU REMEMBER...?
3 MONTHS AGO...
WHAT THE HECK MUSCLE MAN?! YOU DON'T EVEN LIVE HERE!
NOT THAT IT'S ANY OF YOUR BUSINESS BRO, BUT I RAN OUT OF HOT WATER FILLING MY REGULATION-SIZED HOT TUB.
NNNNNNRRRN!
THAT'S IT! WHILE YOU GUYS ARE ALL WAITING TO TAKE YOUR SHOWERS,
I'LL BE BUSY LIVING LIFE!
... LIVING LIFE.
I DON'T KNOW DUDE, SITTING ON THE COUCH GATHERING STENCH DOESN'T COUNT AS "LIVING LIFE".
I MEAN LOOK AT YOU. YOUR HAIR IS ALL MATTED AND LUMPY. IT'S ACTUALLY REALLY GROSS.
I CAN BARELY LOOK AT YOU.
YOU'RE JUST JEALOUS!
I'VE GOT THE LOOK OF A FREE MAN, NOT SHACKLED BY SOCIETAL STANDARDS.
WHATEVER DUDE, I'M GOING TO GO SEE IF I CAN FIND SOMETHING TO GET THE SMELL OUT OF MY NOSE.

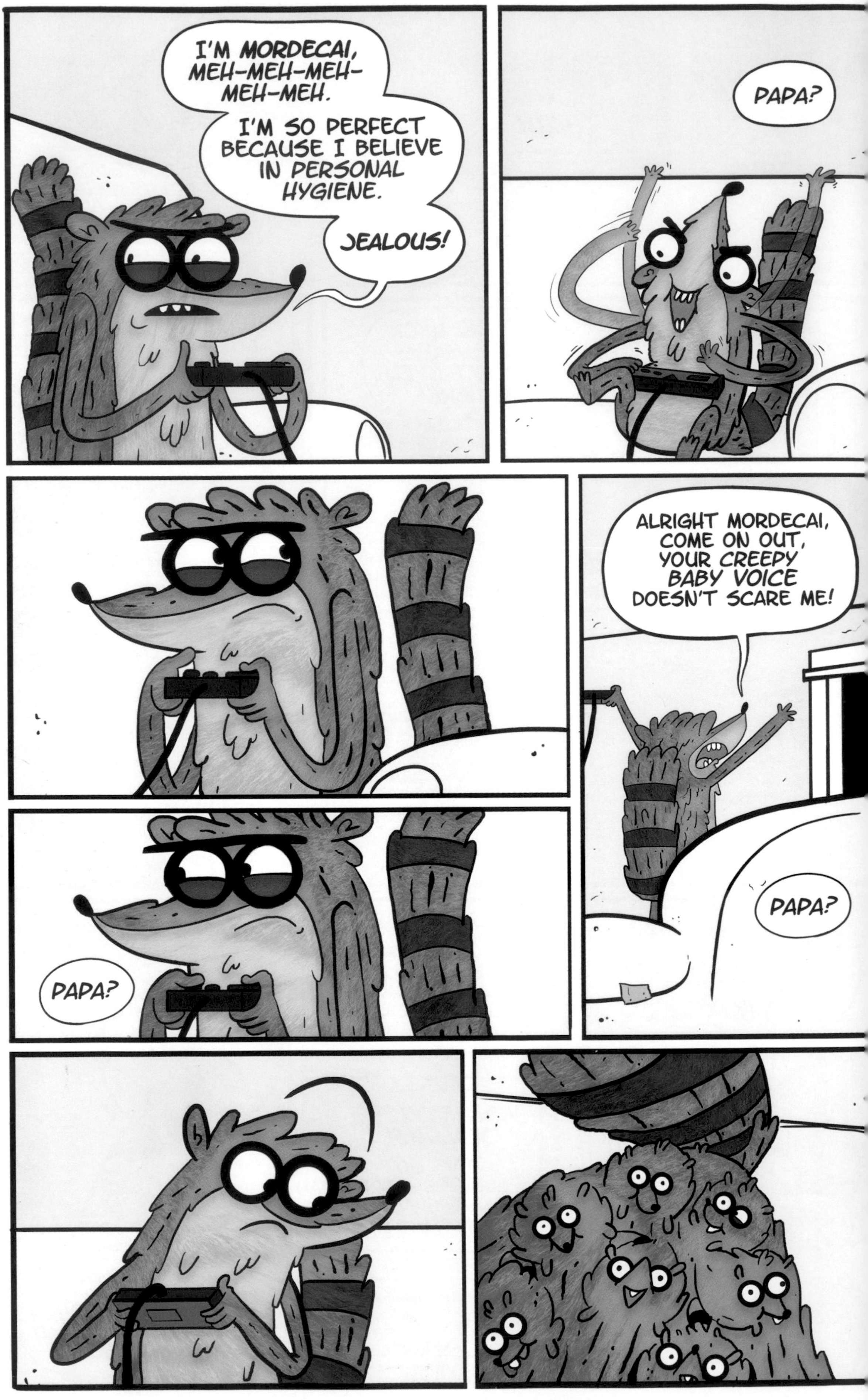

I'M MORDECAI, MEH-MEH-MEH-MEH-MEH.
I'M SO PERFECT BECAUSE I BELIEVE IN PERSONAL HYGIENE.
JEALOUS!
PAPA?
ALRIGHT MORDECAI, COME ON OUT, YOUR CREEPY BABY VOICE DOESN'T SCARE ME!
PAPA?
PAPA?

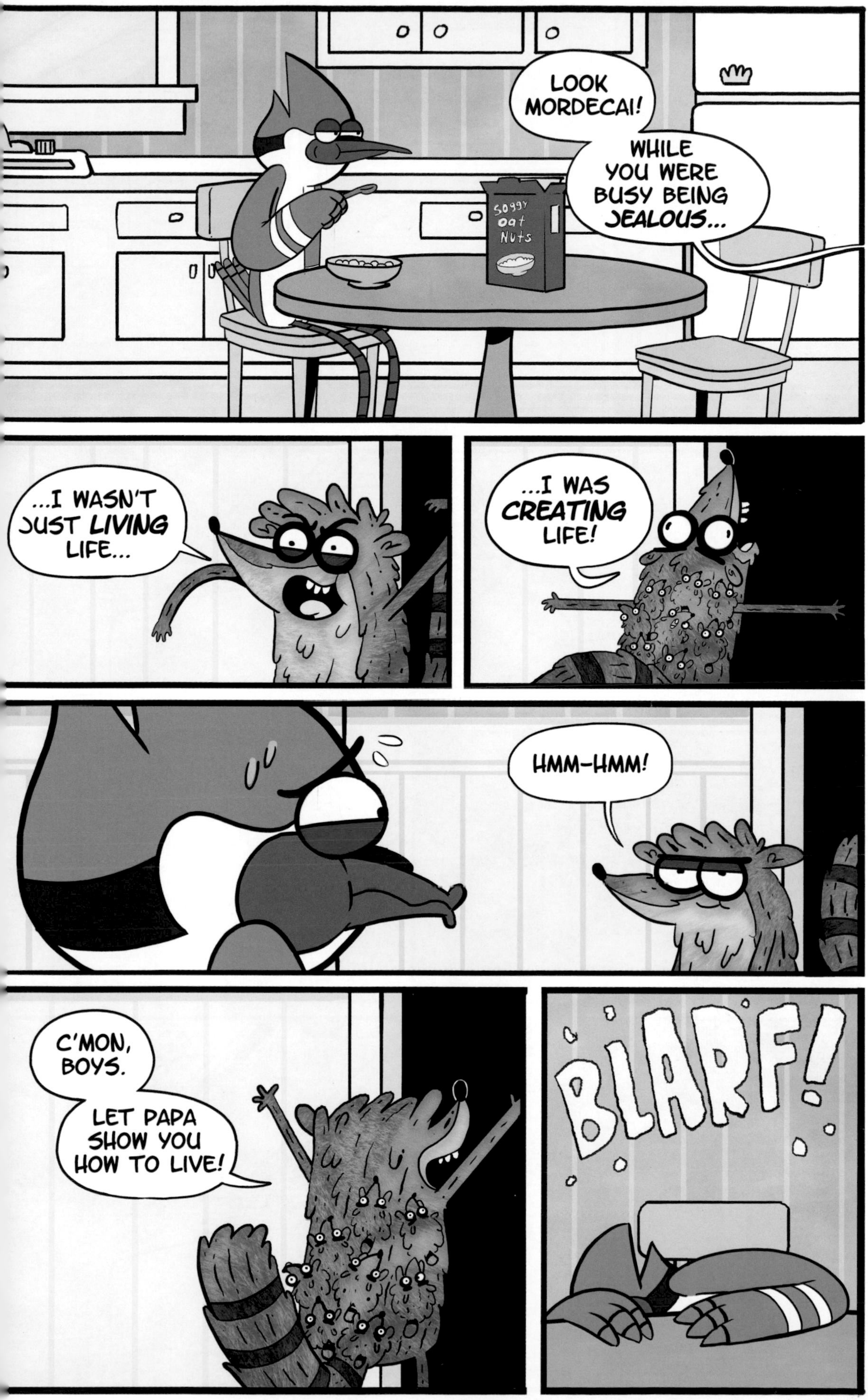
LOOK MORDECAI!
WHILE YOU WERE BUSY BEING JEALOUS...
Soggy Oat Nuts
...I WASN'T JUST LIVING LIFE...
...I WAS CREATING LIFE!
HMM-HMM!
C'MON, BOYS.
LET PAPA SHOW YOU HOW TO LIVE!
BLARF!

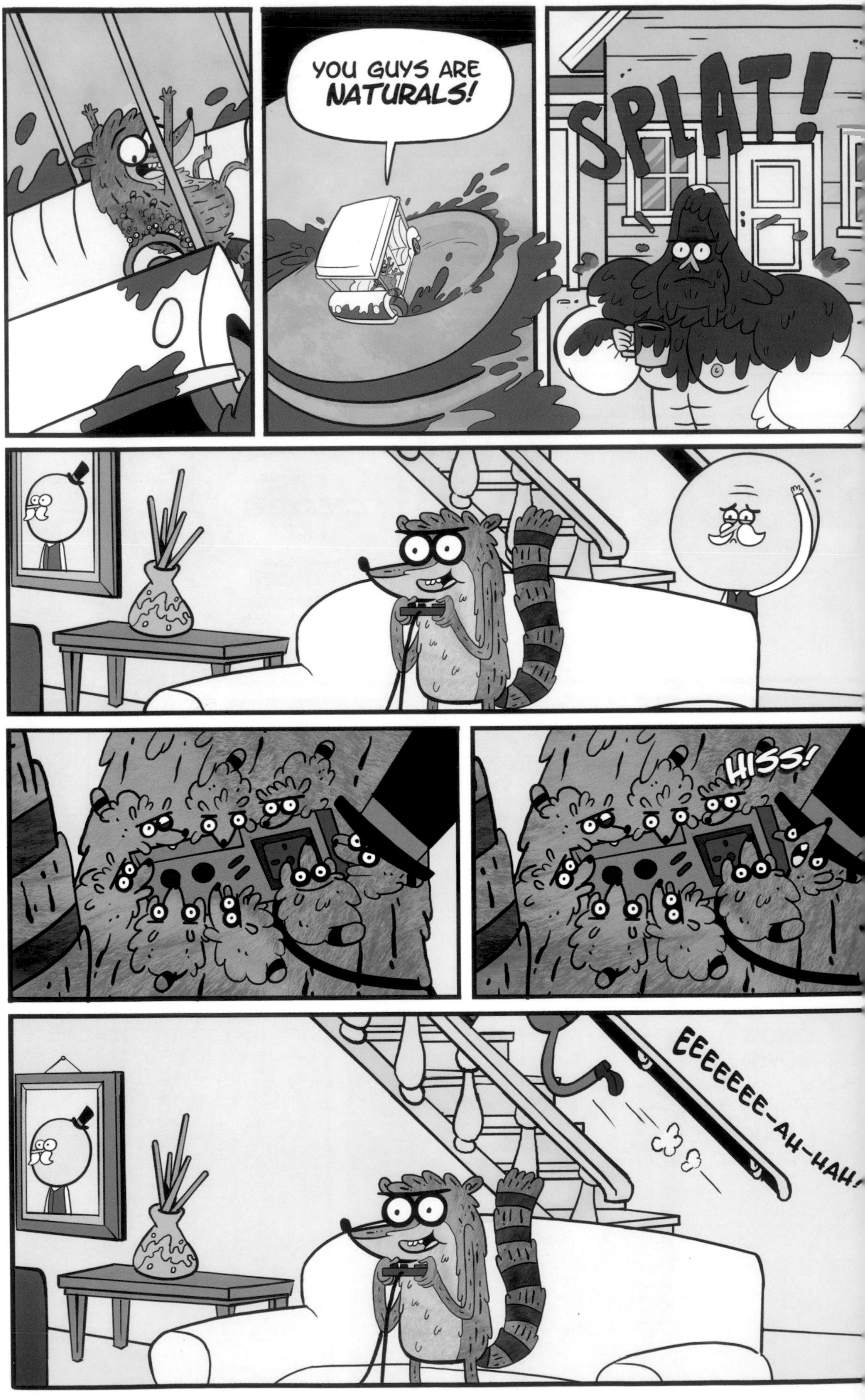

YOU GUYS ARE NATURALS!
SPLAT!
HISS!
EEEEEEE-AH-HAH!

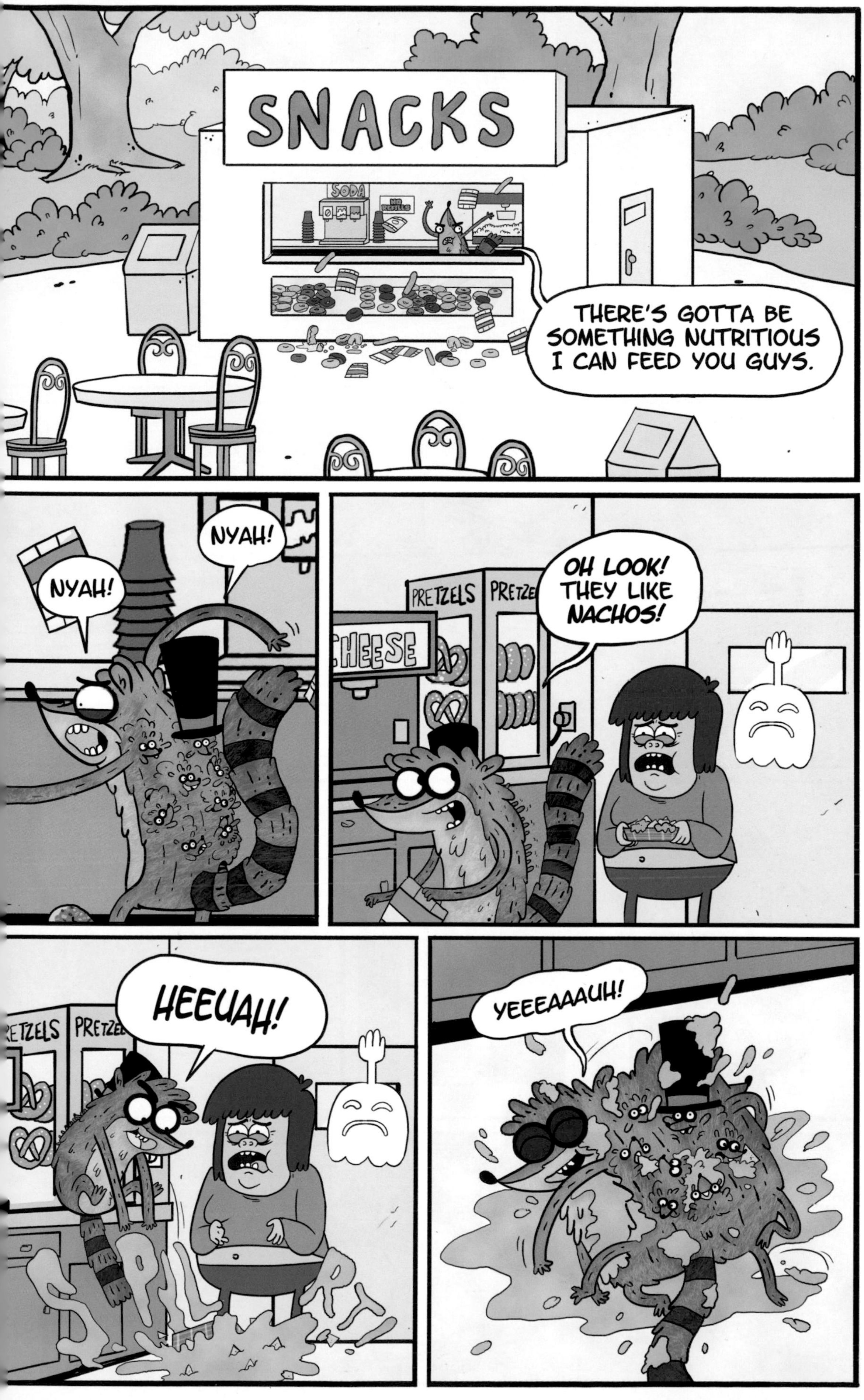
SNACKS
SODA
NO REFILLS
THERE'S GOTTA BE SOMETHING NUTRITIOUS I CAN FEED YOU GUYS.
NYAH!
NYAH!
PRETZELS
CHEESE
OH LOOK! THEY LIKE NACHOS!
HEEUAH!
YEEEAAAUH!

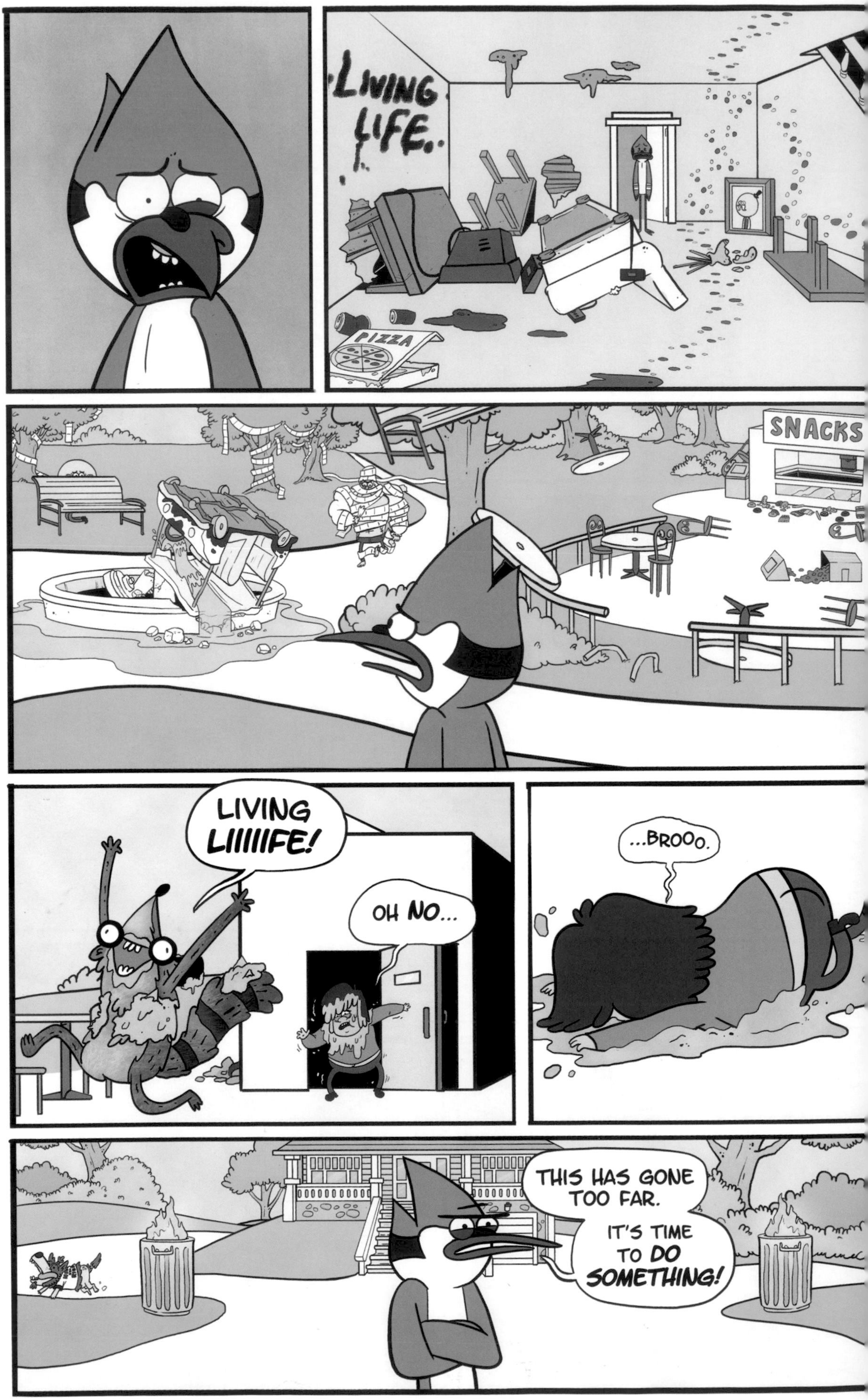
LIVING LIFE..
PIZZA
SNACKS
LIVING LIIIIIFE!
OH NO...
...BROOo.
THIS HAS GONE TOO FAR.
IT'S TIME TO DO SOMETHING!

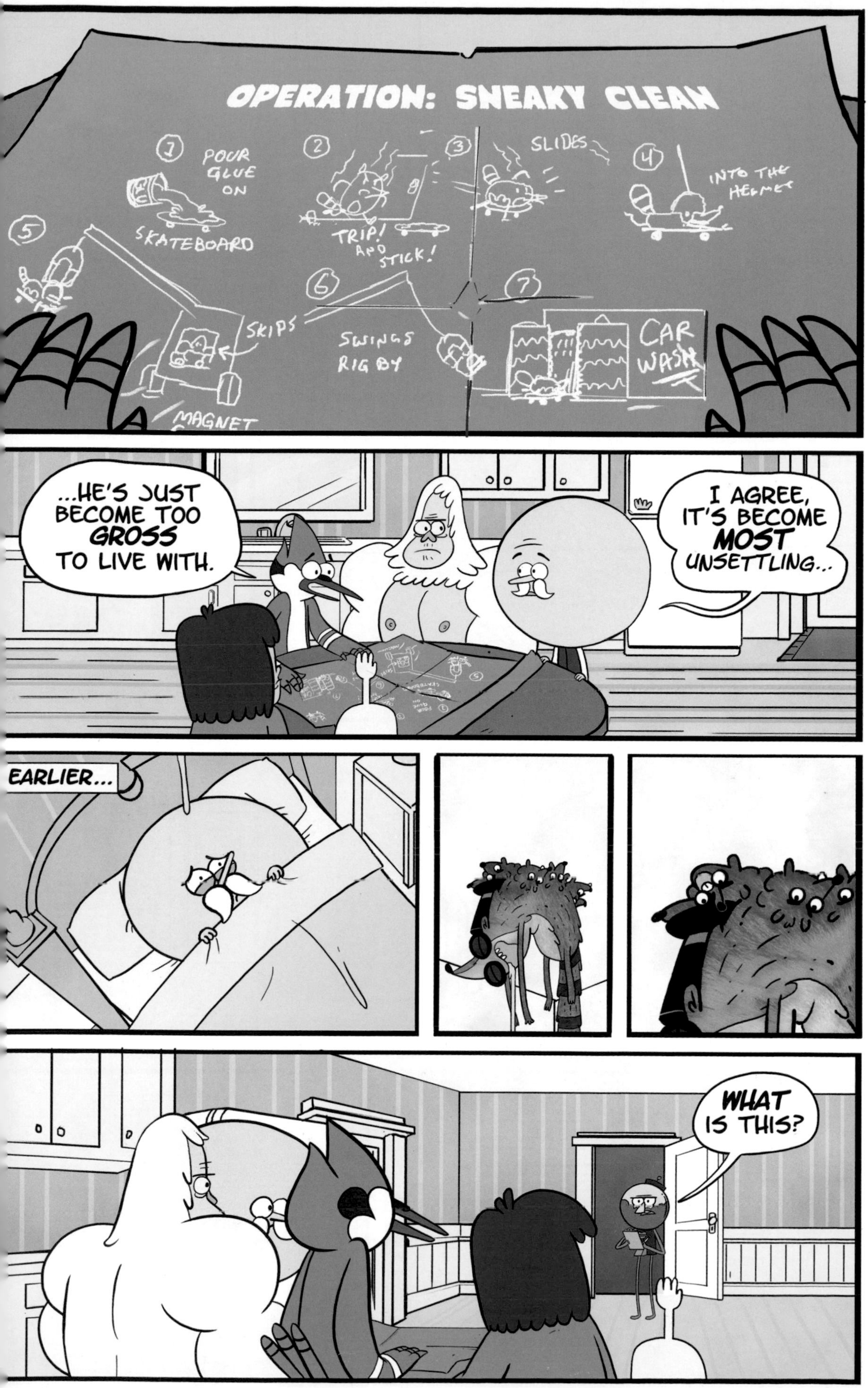
OPERATION: SNEAKY CLEAN
1 POUR GLUE ON SKATEBOARD
2 TRIP! AND STICK!
3 SLIDES
4 INTO THE HELMET
5 SKIPS
MAGNET
6 SWINGS RIGBY
7 CAR WASH
...HE'S JUST BECOME TOO GROSS TO LIVE WITH.
I AGREE, IT'S BECOME MOST UNSETTLING...
EARLIER...
WHAT IS THIS?

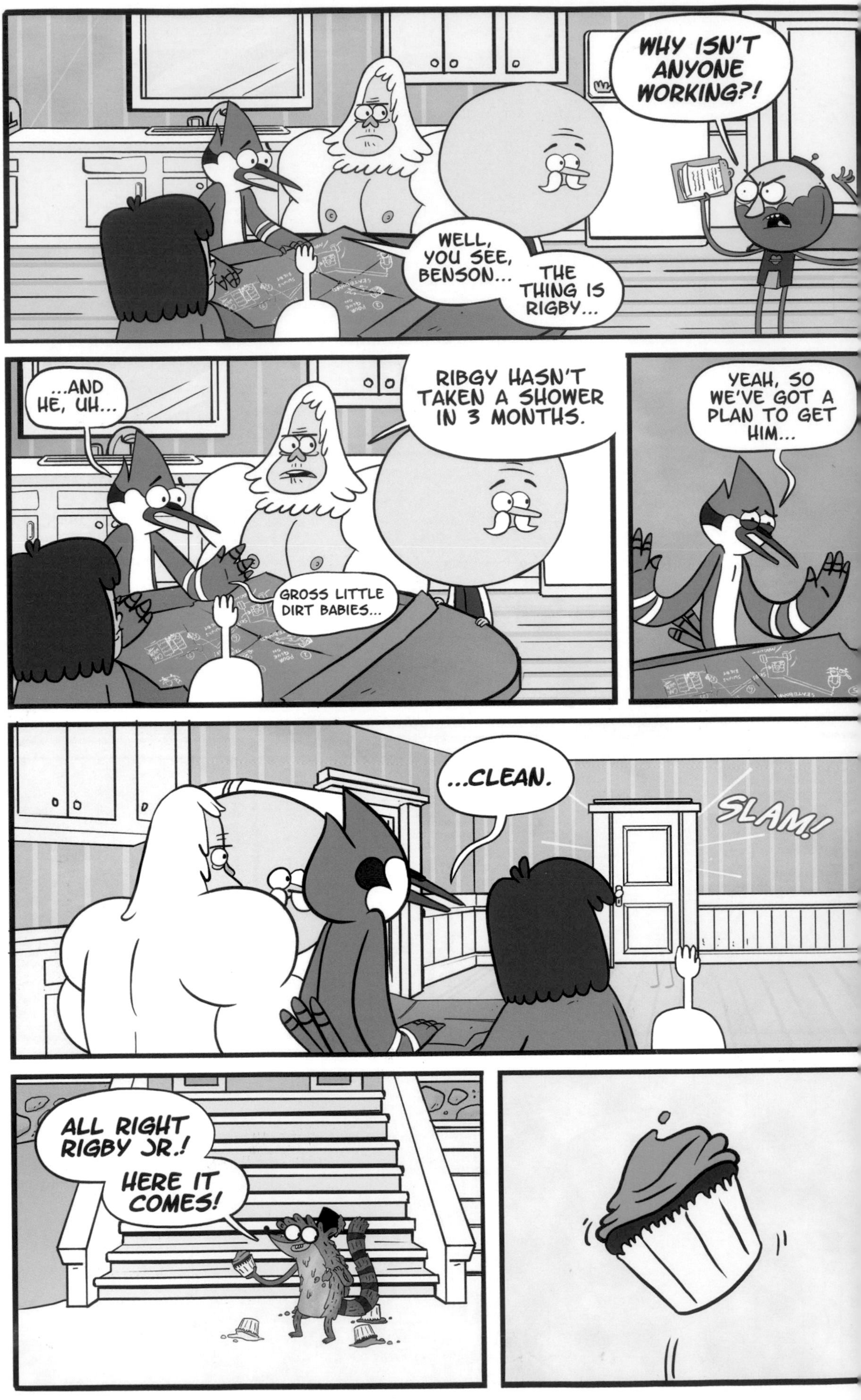
WHY ISN'T ANYONE WORKING?!
WELL, YOU SEE, BENSON...
THE THING IS RIGBY...
...AND HE, UH...
RIBGY HASN'T TAKEN A SHOWER IN 3 MONTHS.
GROSS LITTLE DIRT BABIES...
YEAH, SO WE'VE GOT A PLAN TO GET HIM...
...CLEAN.
SLAM!
ALL RIGHT RIGBY JR.!
HERE IT COMES!

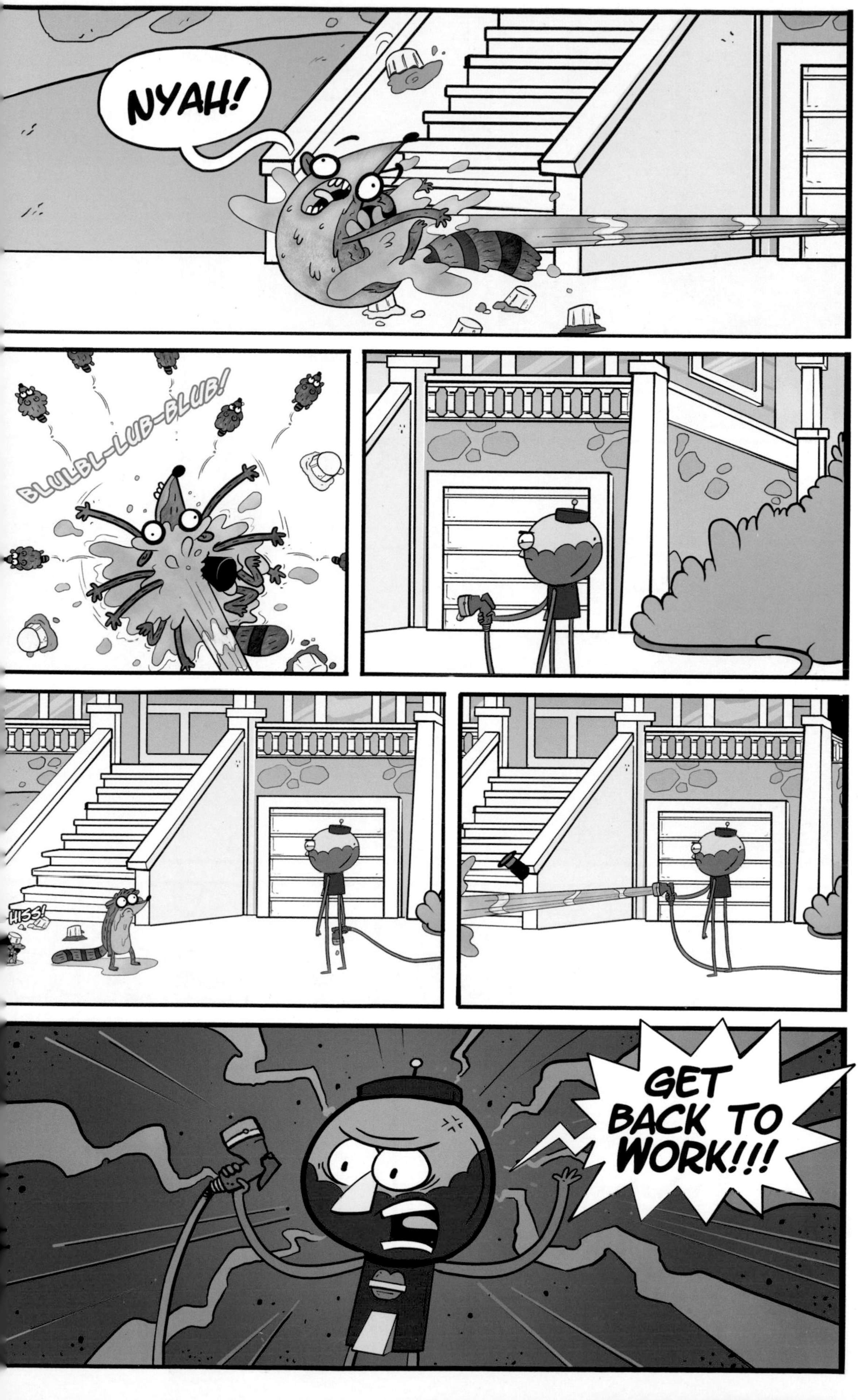
NYAH!
BLULBL-LUB-BLUB!
HISS!
GET BACK TO WORK!!!

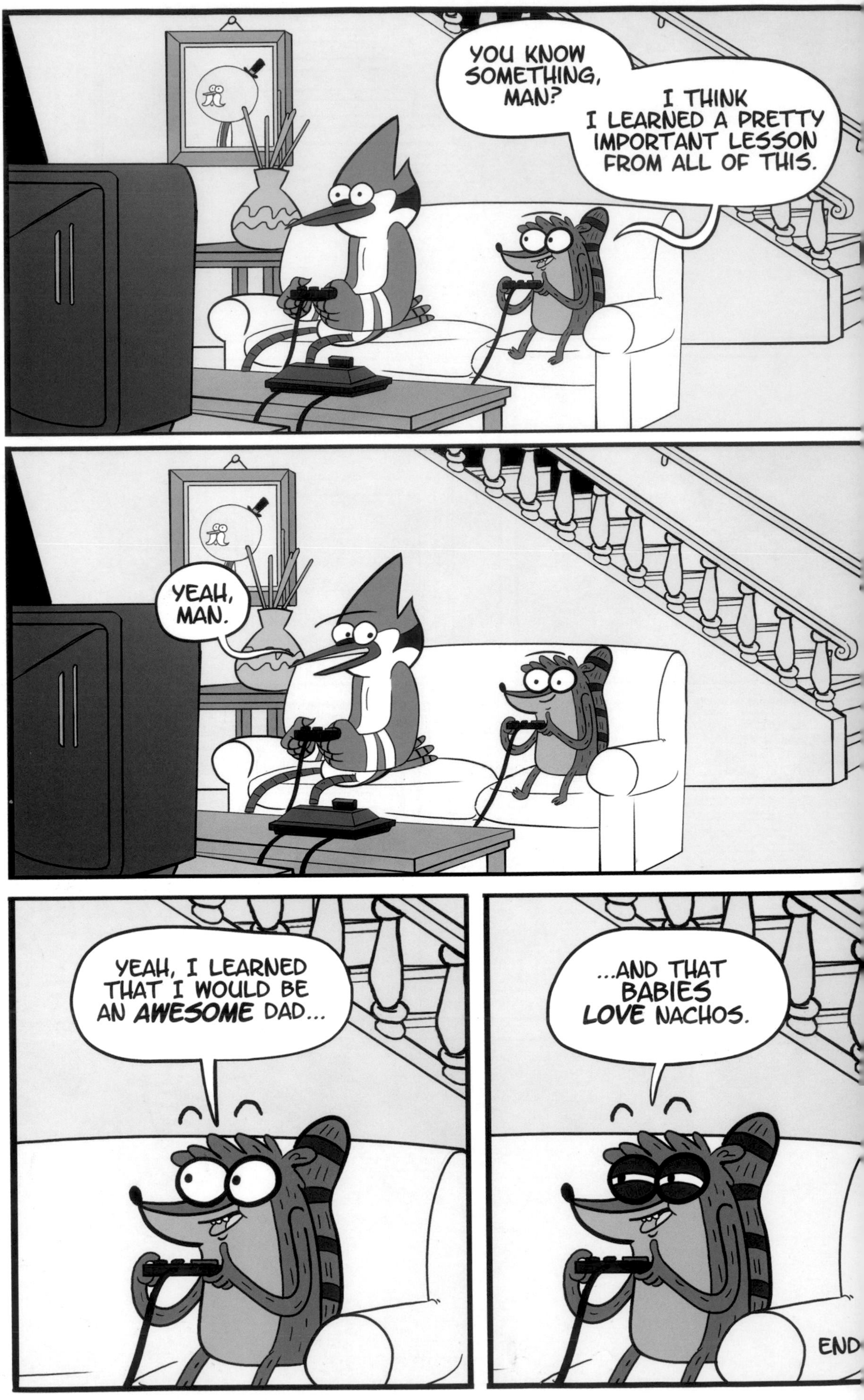
YOU KNOW SOMETHING, MAN?
I THINK I LEARNED A PRETTY IMPORTANT LESSON FROM ALL OF THIS.
YEAH, MAN.
YEAH, I LEARNED THAT I WOULD BE AN AWESOME DAD...
...AND THAT BABIES LOVE NACHOS.
END

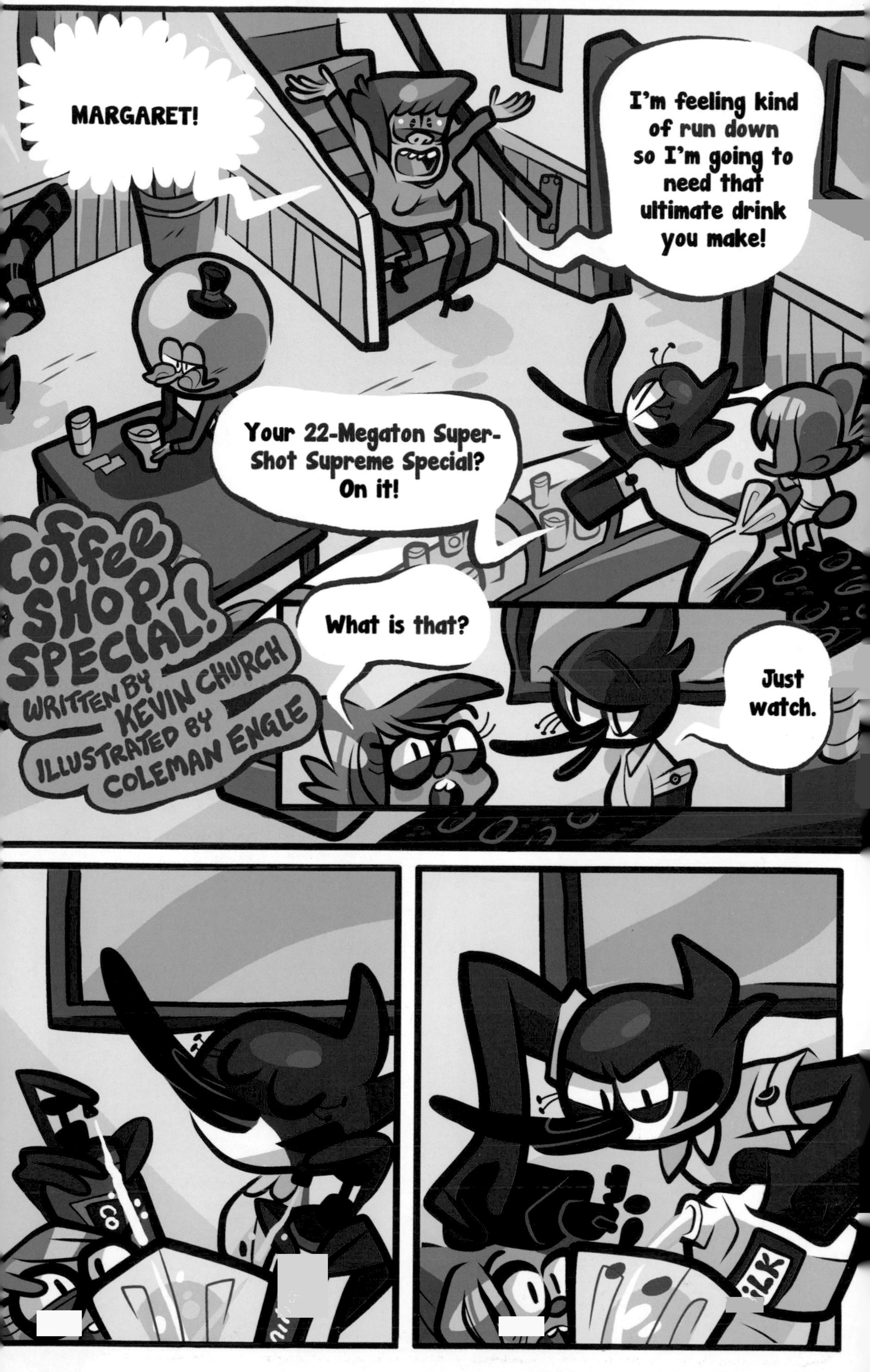
MARGARET!
I'm feeling kind of run down so I'm going to need that ultimate drink you make!
Your 22-Megaton Super-Shot Supreme Special? On it!
Coffee Shop Special!
Written by Kevin Church
Illustrated by Coleman Engle
What is that?
Just watch.
CO
MILK

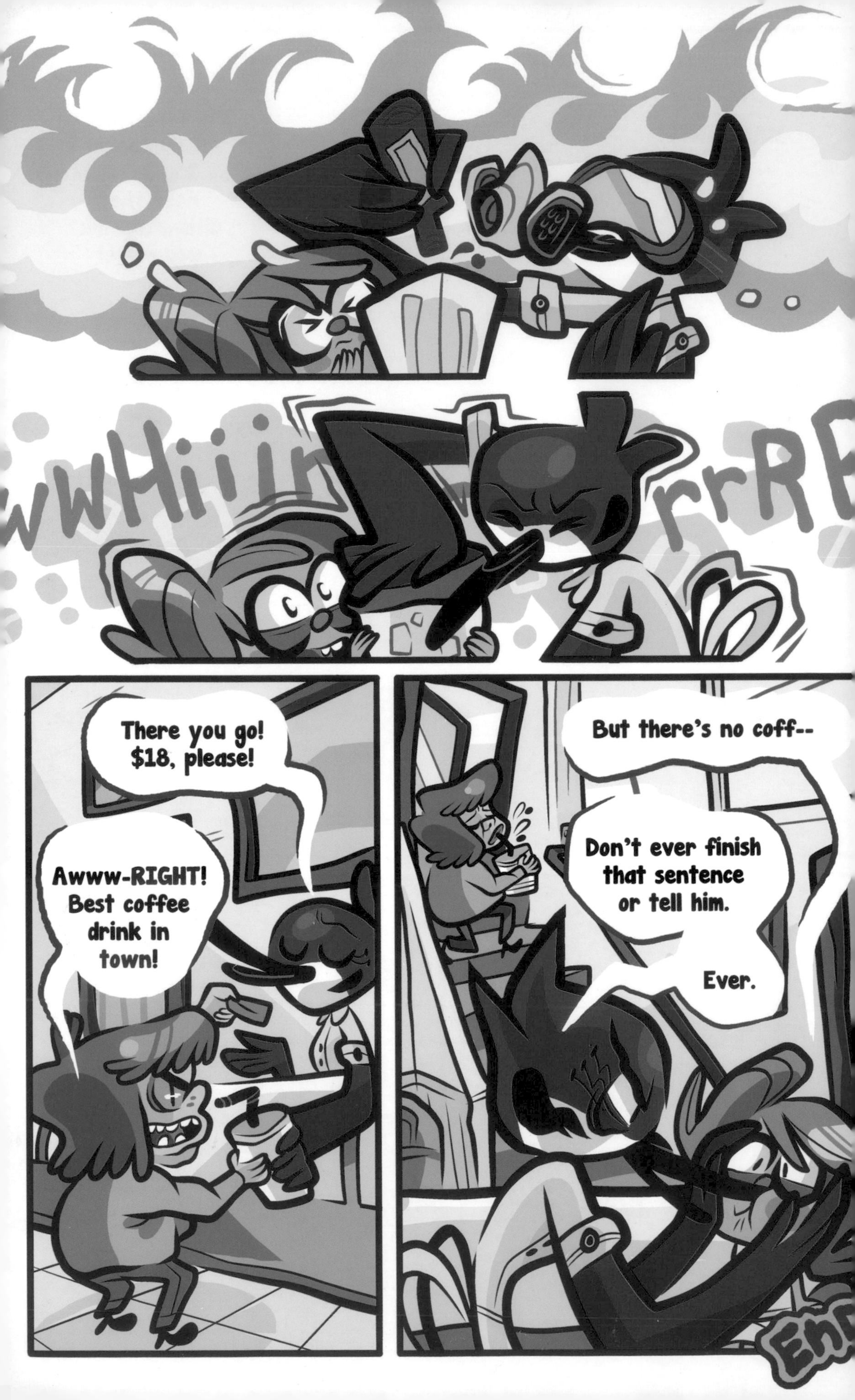
There you go! $18, please!
Awww-RIGHT! Best coffee drink in town!
But there's no coff--
Don't ever finish that sentence or tell him.
Ever.

WASPS

Story: Clark Burscough
Art: Marc Ellerby

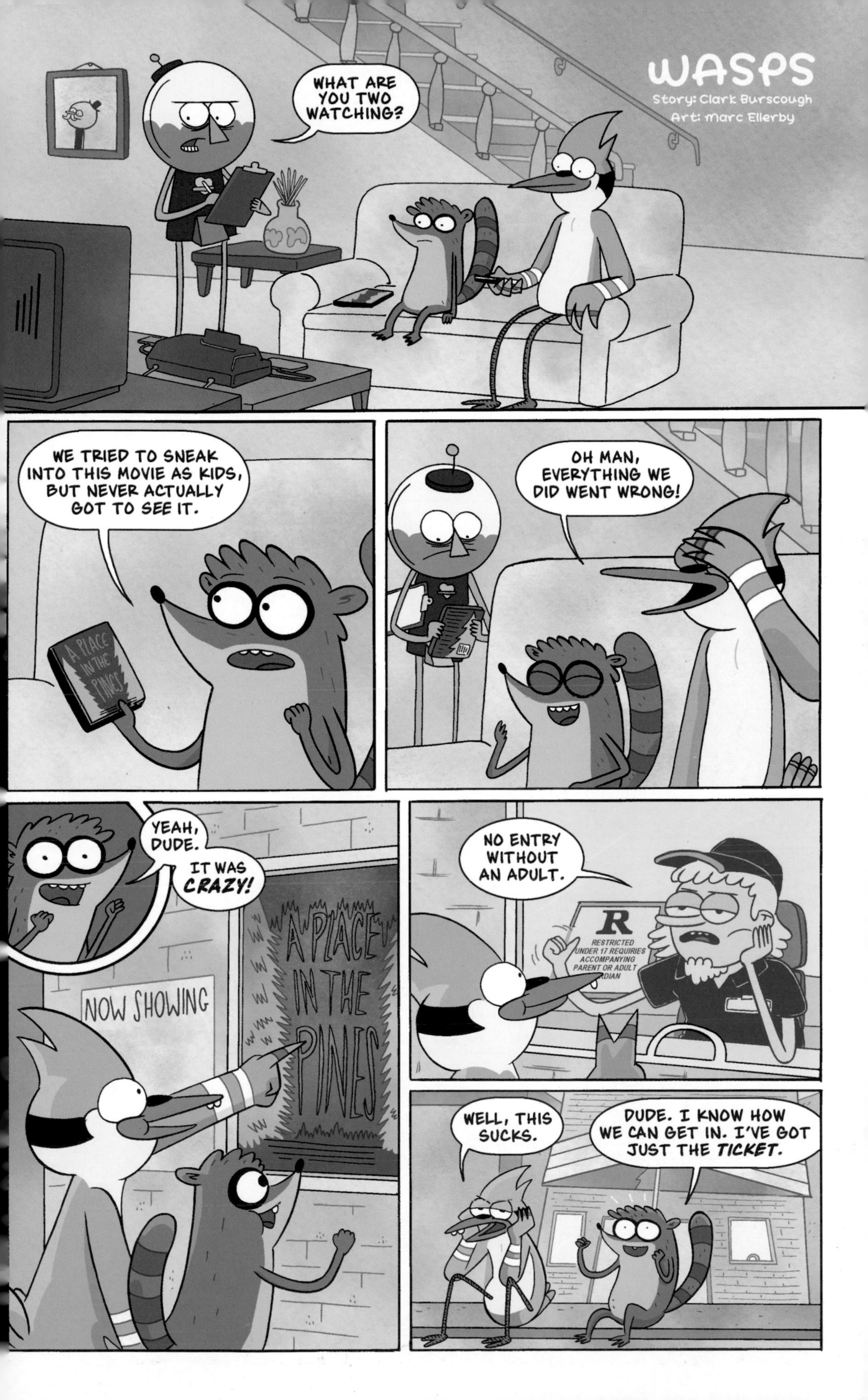

WHAT ARE YOU TWO WATCHING?
WE TRIED TO SNEAK INTO THIS MOVIE AS KIDS, BUT NEVER ACTUALLY GOT TO SEE IT.
A PLACE IN THE PINES
OH MAN, EVERYTHING WE DID WENT WRONG!
YEAH, DUDE.
IT WAS CRAZY!
NOW SHOWING
A PLACE IN THE PINES
NO ENTRY WITHOUT AN ADULT.
R
RESTRICTED UNDER 17 REQUIRES ACCOMPANYING PARENT OR ADULT
WELL, THIS SUCKS.
DUDE. I KNOW HOW WE CAN GET IN. I'VE GOT JUST THE TICKET.

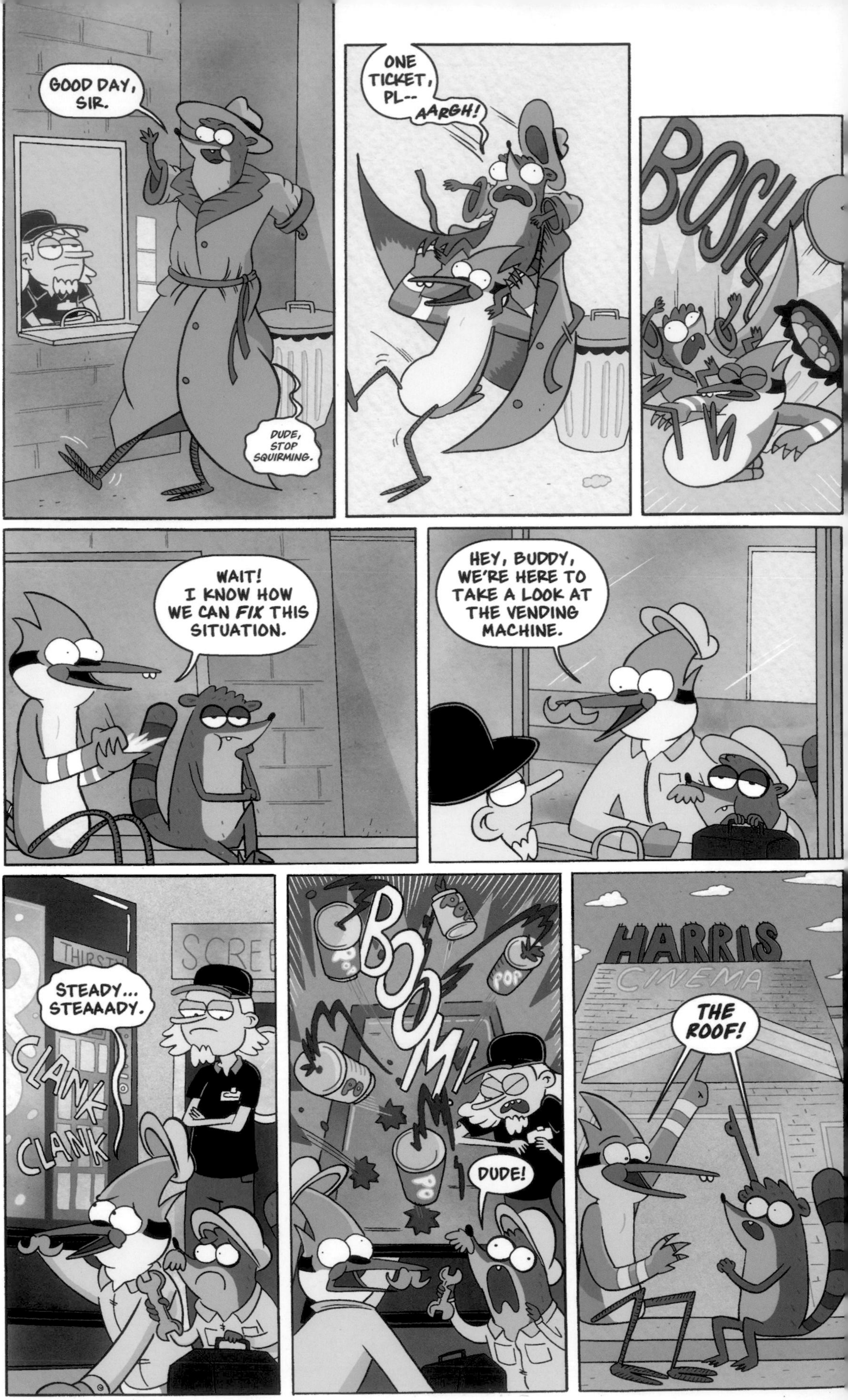
GOOD DAY, SIR.
DUDE, STOP SQUIRMING.
ONE TICKET, PL--
AARGH!
BOSH
WAIT! I KNOW HOW WE CAN *FIX* THIS SITUATION.
HEY, BUDDY, WE'RE HERE TO TAKE A LOOK AT THE VENDING MACHINE.
STEADY... STEAAADY.
CLANK
CLANK
BOOM!
POP
POP
DUDE!
HARRIS
CINEMA
THE ROOF!

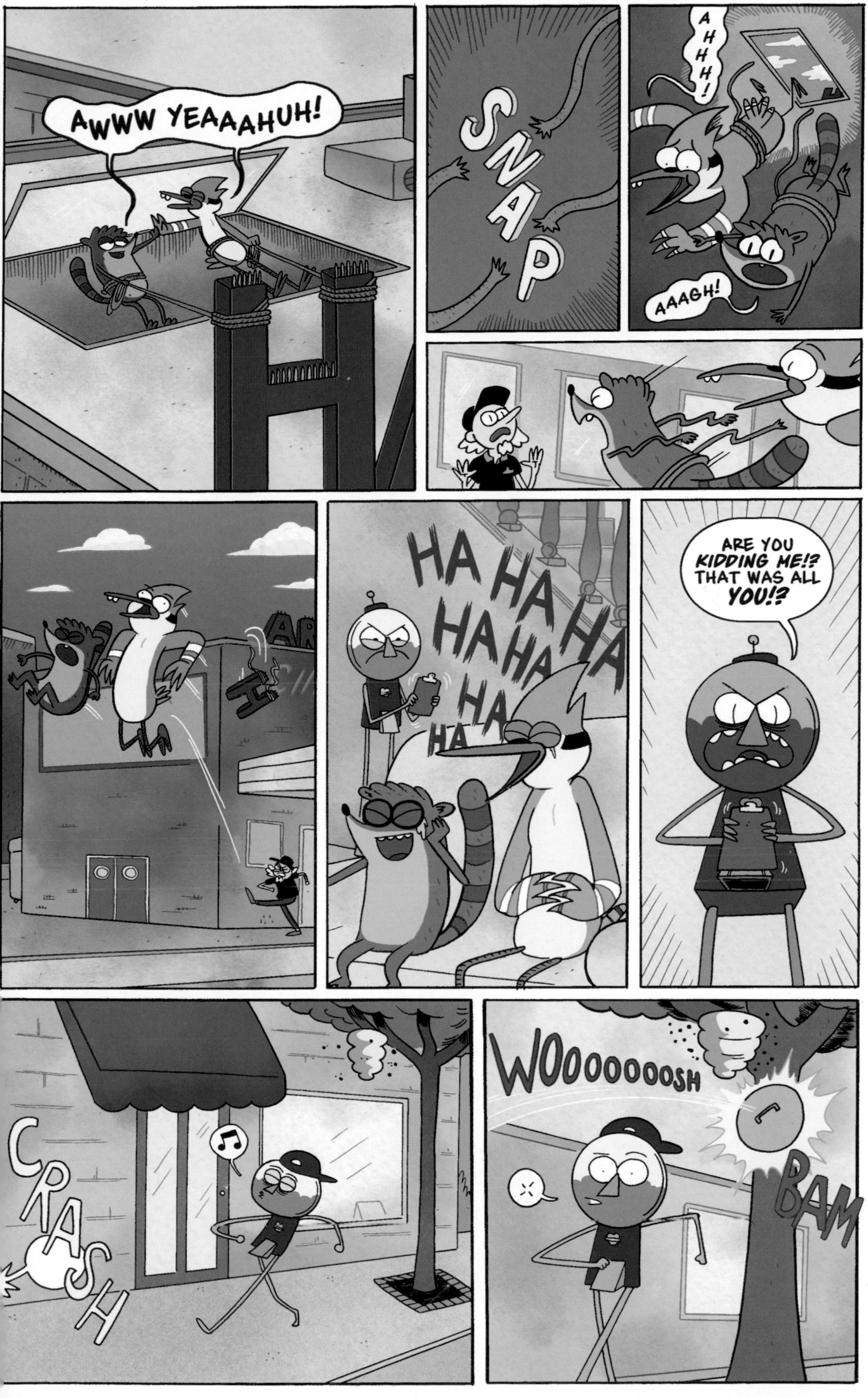
AWWW YEAAAHUH!
SNAP
AHHHH!
AAAGH!
HA HA HA HA HA HA HA HA HA
ARE YOU KIDDING ME!? THAT WAS ALL YOU!?
CRASH
WOOOOOOOSH
BAM

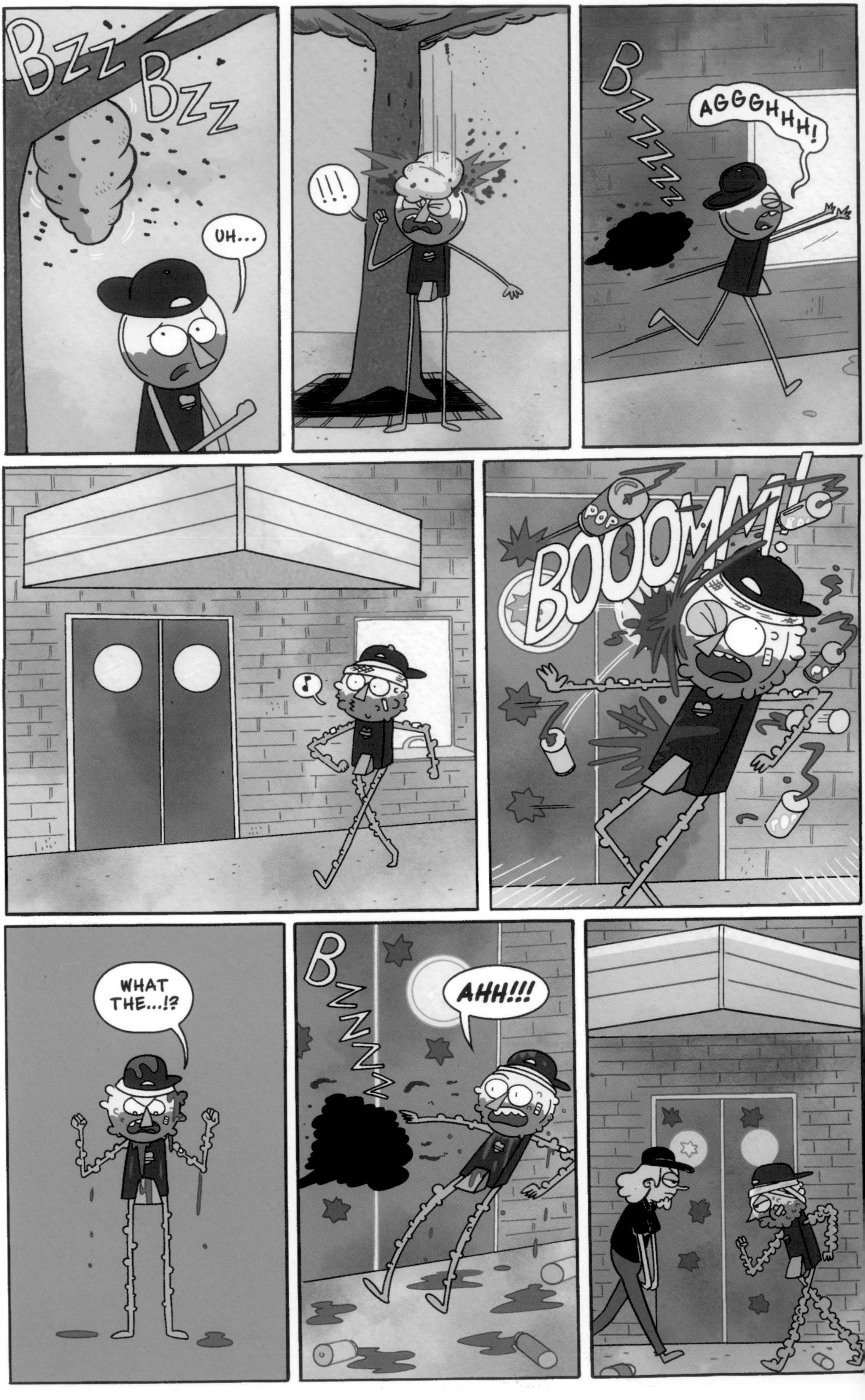
BZZ BZZ
UH...
!!!
BZZZZZZ
AGGGHHHH!
BOOOMM!
POP
WHAT THE...!?
BZZZZZ
AHH!!!

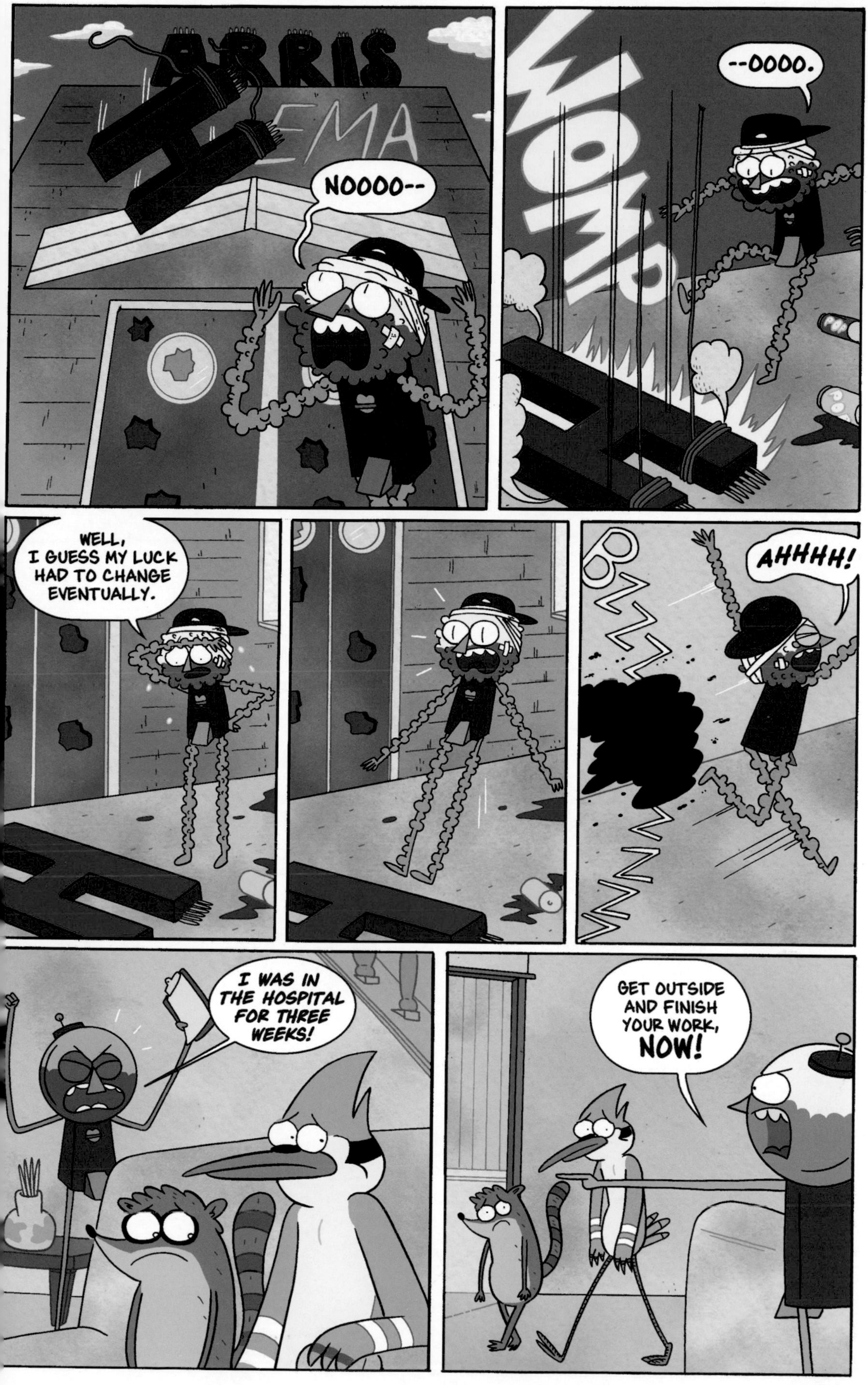
ARRIS
EMA
NOOOO--
WOMP
--OOOO.
WELL, I GUESS MY LUCK HAD TO CHANGE EVENTUALLY.
BZZZZZZZZZ
AHHHH!
I WAS IN THE HOSPITAL FOR THREE WEEKS!
GET OUTSIDE AND FINISH YOUR WORK, NOW!

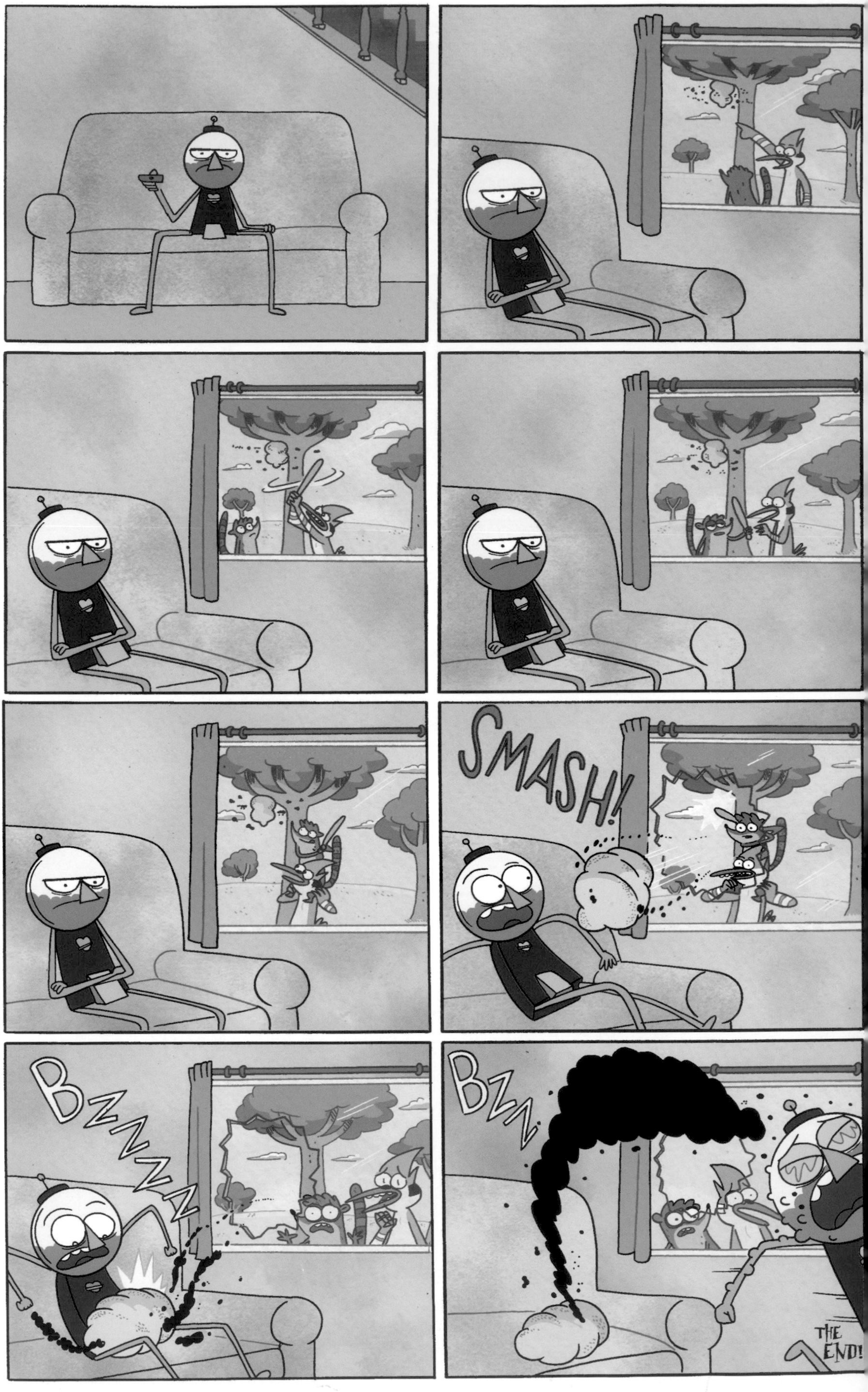
SMASH!
BZZZZZ
BZZ
THE END!

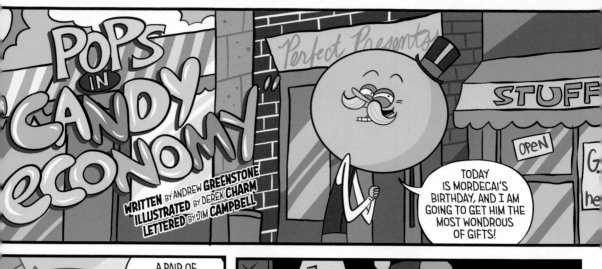

"POPS IN CANDY ECONOMY"
WRITTEN BY ANDREW GREENSTONE
ILLUSTRATED BY DEREK CHARM
LETTERED BY JIM CAMPBELL
Perfect Presents
STUFF
OPEN
TODAY IS MORDECAI'S BIRTHDAY, AND I AM GOING TO GET HIM THE MOST WONDROUS OF GIFTS!
A PAIR OF ROLLING LOAFERS! WHAT A PERFECT PRESENT!
BOX THESE BEAUTIES UP WITH A BOW, MY GOOD MAN!
THAT'LL BE TWENNY BUX.
ALL SALES FINAL
YES, YES, SURELY! DO YOU HAVE CHANGE FOR A PEPPERMINT SWIRL?
POP
POP
WHAT IS THIS, SOME KINDA JOKE?! LOOK, BUDDY, I'M TRYIN' TA RUN A BUSINESS HERE, I AIN'T GOT TIME FER WISE GUYS!
COME BACK WHEN YA GOT SOME **REAL MONEY!**
I SAY!

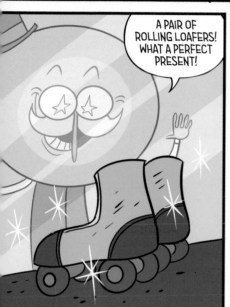

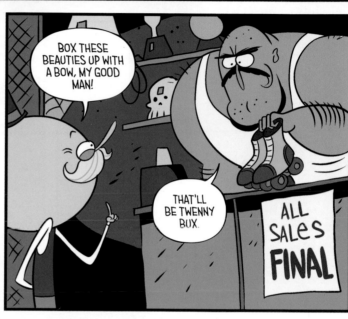

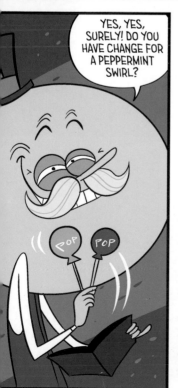

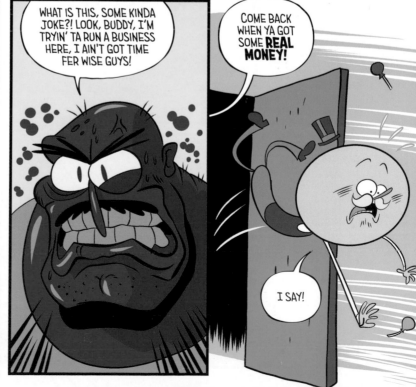

BAD SHOW! I DON'T KNOW HOW THAT PROPRIETOR HOPES TO STAY IN BUSINESS TREATING HIS CUSTOMERS SO SHABBILY.

WELL, I MUSTN'T GIVE UP! THERE'S A PERFECT GIFT FOR MORDECAI OUT THERE, AND IT'S UP TO ME TO FIND IT!

I'M SORRY, OLD CHAP, BUT I AM AFRAID THAT YOU MUST LEAVE THIS HABERDASHERY POSTHASTE!

PHONOGRAPHS, EUPHONIUMS, AND UNITARDS

GET OUTTA HERE, YOU NUT!

...YOU GOTTA BE KIDDING ME.

BAND

WHY WON'T THESE SHOPKEEPS ACCEPT MY TENDER FOR THEIR WARES? MORDECAI'S BIRTHDAY PARTY IS FAST APPROACHING AND I'M AFRAID I'M LEFT BUT ONE RECOURSE.

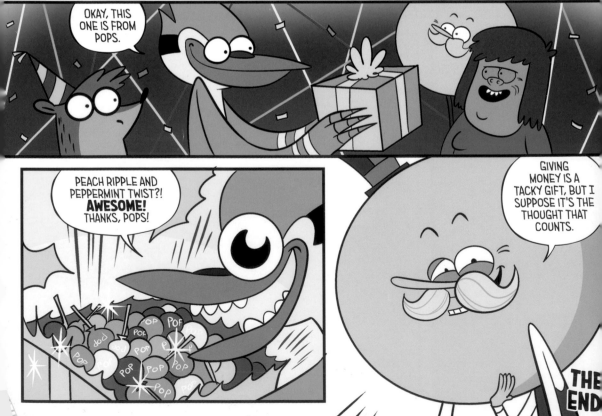

OKAY, THIS ONE IS FROM POPS.

PEACH RIPPLE AND PEPPERMINT TWIST?! **AWESOME!** THANKS, POPS!

GIVING MONEY IS A TACKY GIFT, BUT I SUPPOSE IT'S THE THOUGHT THAT COUNTS.

THE END

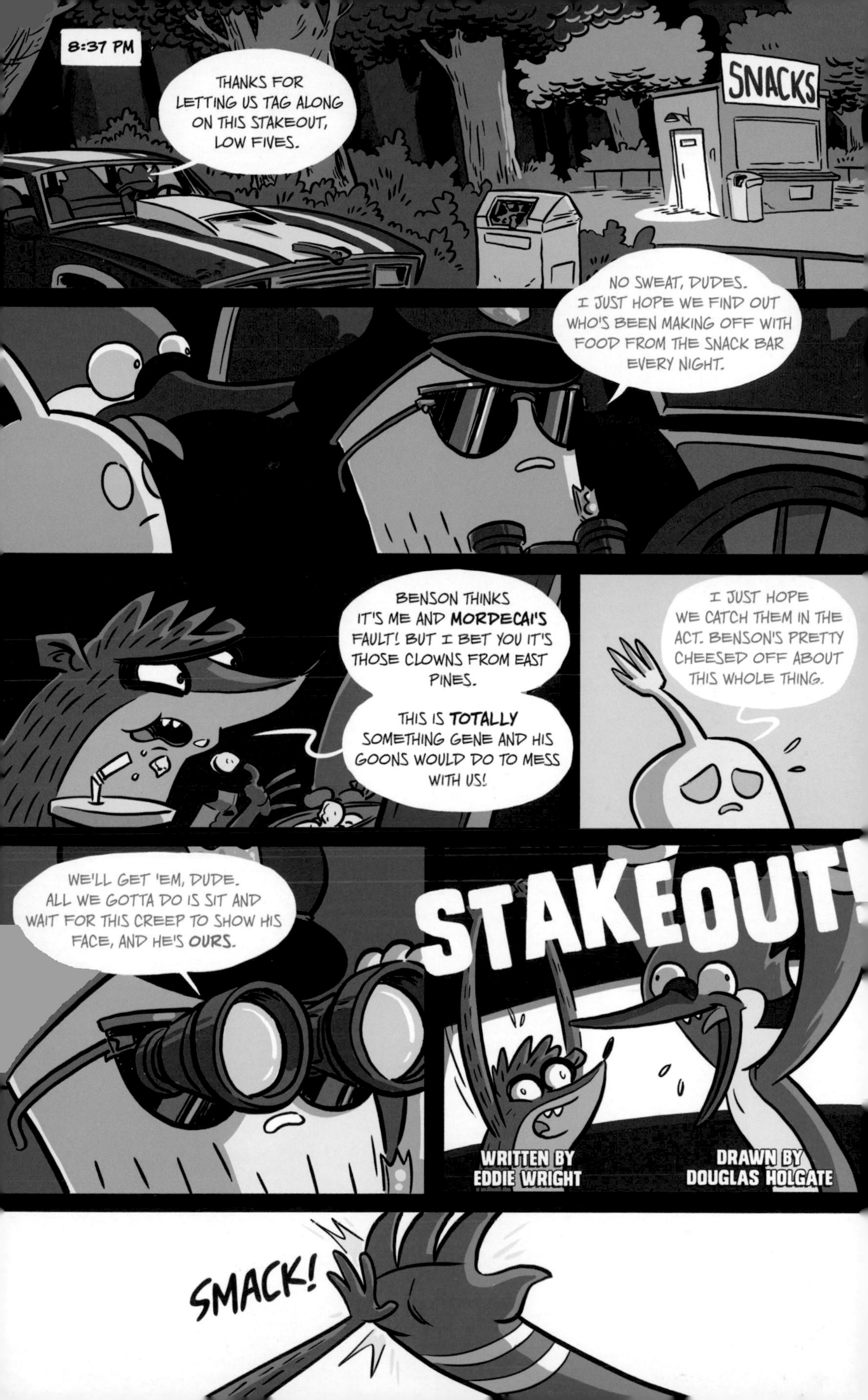
8:37 PM
THANKS FOR LETTING US TAG ALONG ON THIS STAKEOUT, LOW FIVES.
NO SWEAT, DUDES. I JUST HOPE WE FIND OUT WHO'S BEEN MAKING OFF WITH FOOD FROM THE SNACK BAR EVERY NIGHT.
SNACKS
BENSON THINKS IT'S ME AND MORDECAI'S FAULT! BUT I BET YOU IT'S THOSE CLOWNS FROM EAST PINES.
THIS IS TOTALLY SOMETHING GENE AND HIS GOONS WOULD DO TO MESS WITH US!
I JUST HOPE WE CATCH THEM IN THE ACT. BENSON'S PRETTY CHEESED OFF ABOUT THIS WHOLE THING.
WE'LL GET 'EM, DUDE. ALL WE GOTTA DO IS SIT AND WAIT FOR THIS CREEP TO SHOW HIS FACE, AND HE'S OURS.
STAKEOUT!
WRITTEN BY EDDIE WRIGHT
DRAWN BY DOUGLAS HOLGATE
SMACK!

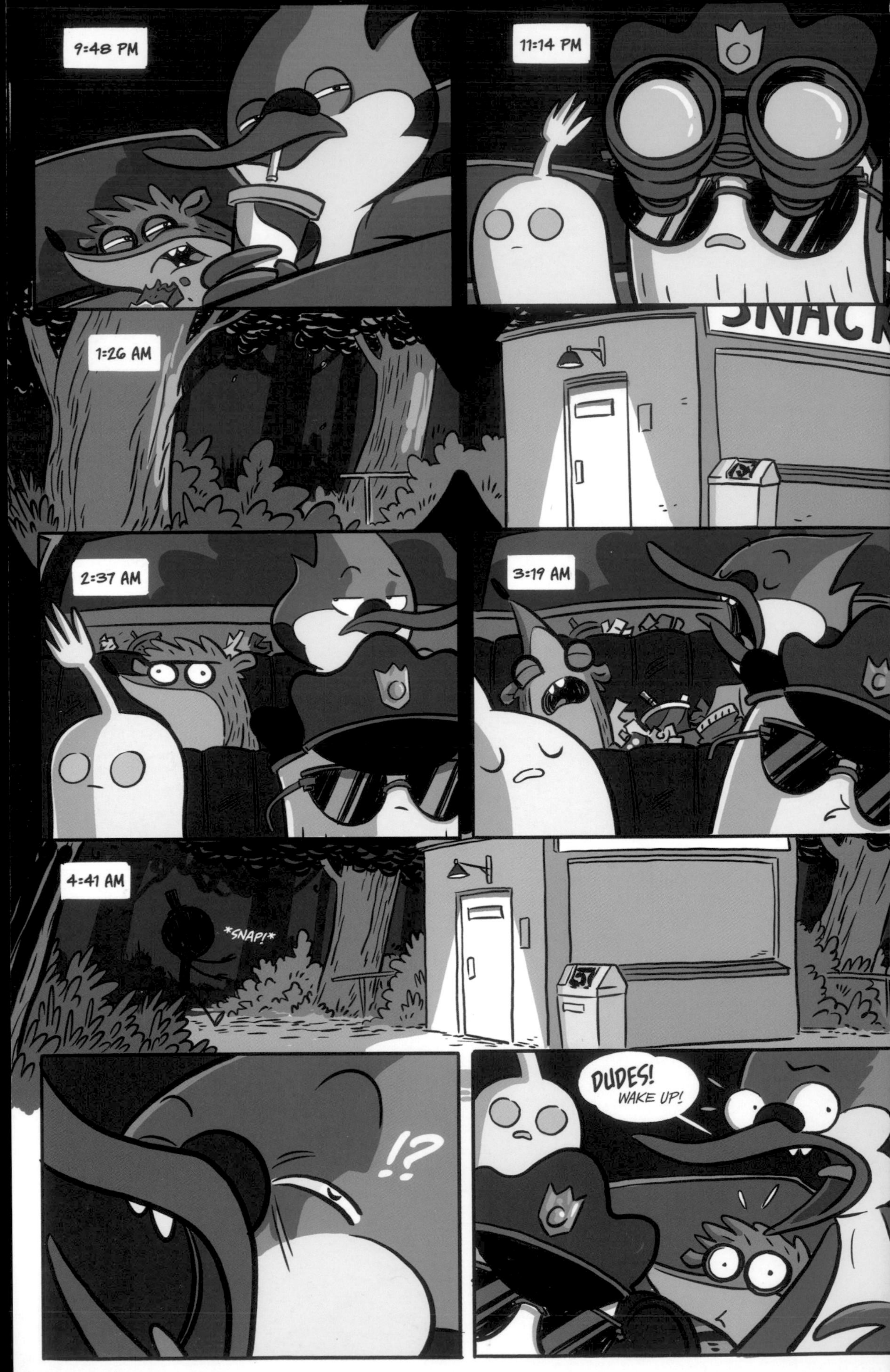
9:48 PM
11:14 PM
SNACK
1:26 AM
2:37 AM
3:19 AM
4:41 AM
SNAP!
!?
DUDES! WAKE UP!

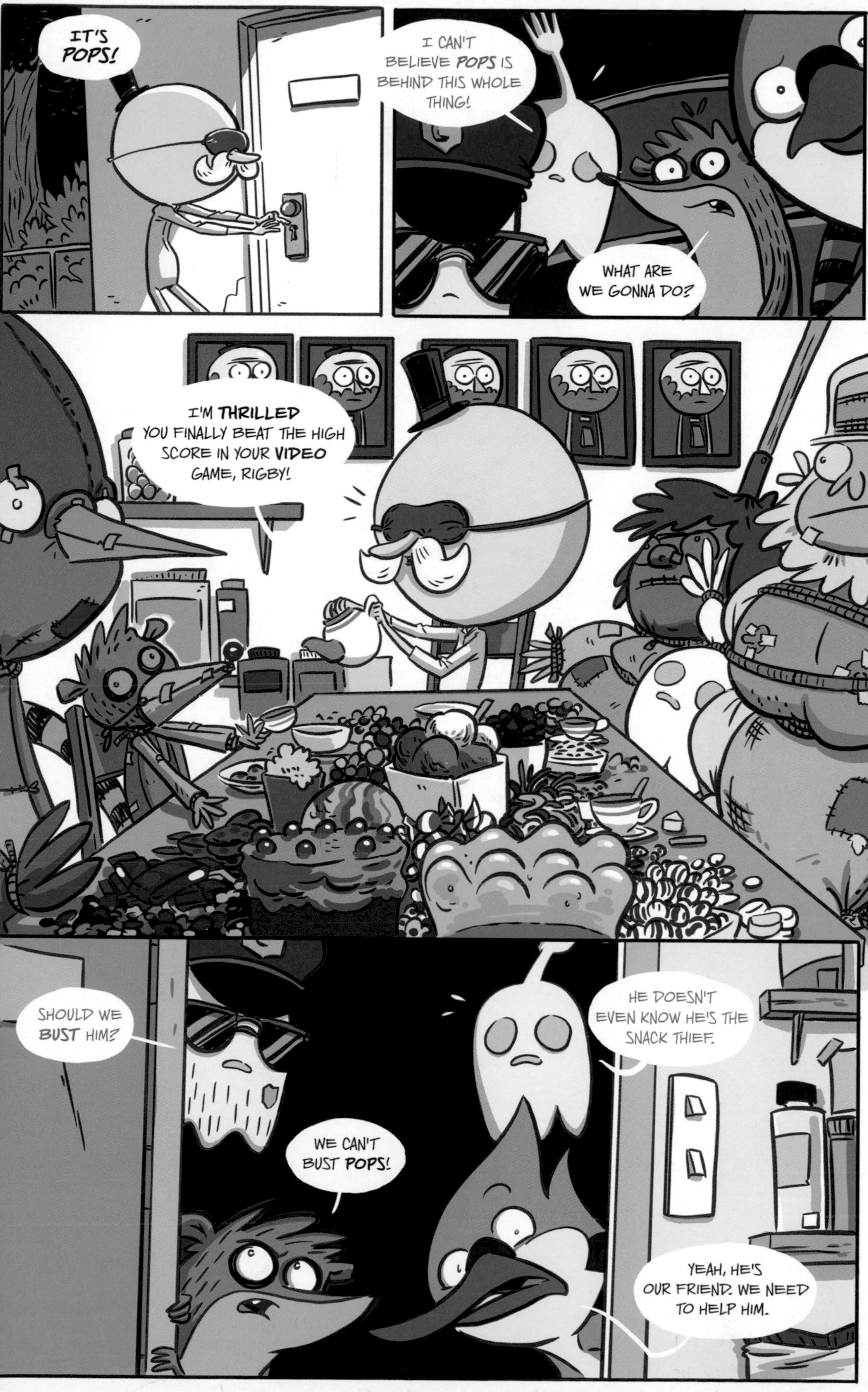
IT'S POPS!
I CAN'T BELIEVE POPS IS BEHIND THIS WHOLE THING!
WHAT ARE WE GONNA DO?
I'M THRILLED YOU FINALLY BEAT THE HIGH SCORE IN YOUR VIDEO GAME, RIGBY!
SHOULD WE BUST HIM?
HE DOESN'T EVEN KNOW HE'S THE SNACK THIEF.
WE CAN'T BUST POPS!
YEAH, HE'S OUR FRIEND. WE NEED TO HELP HIM.

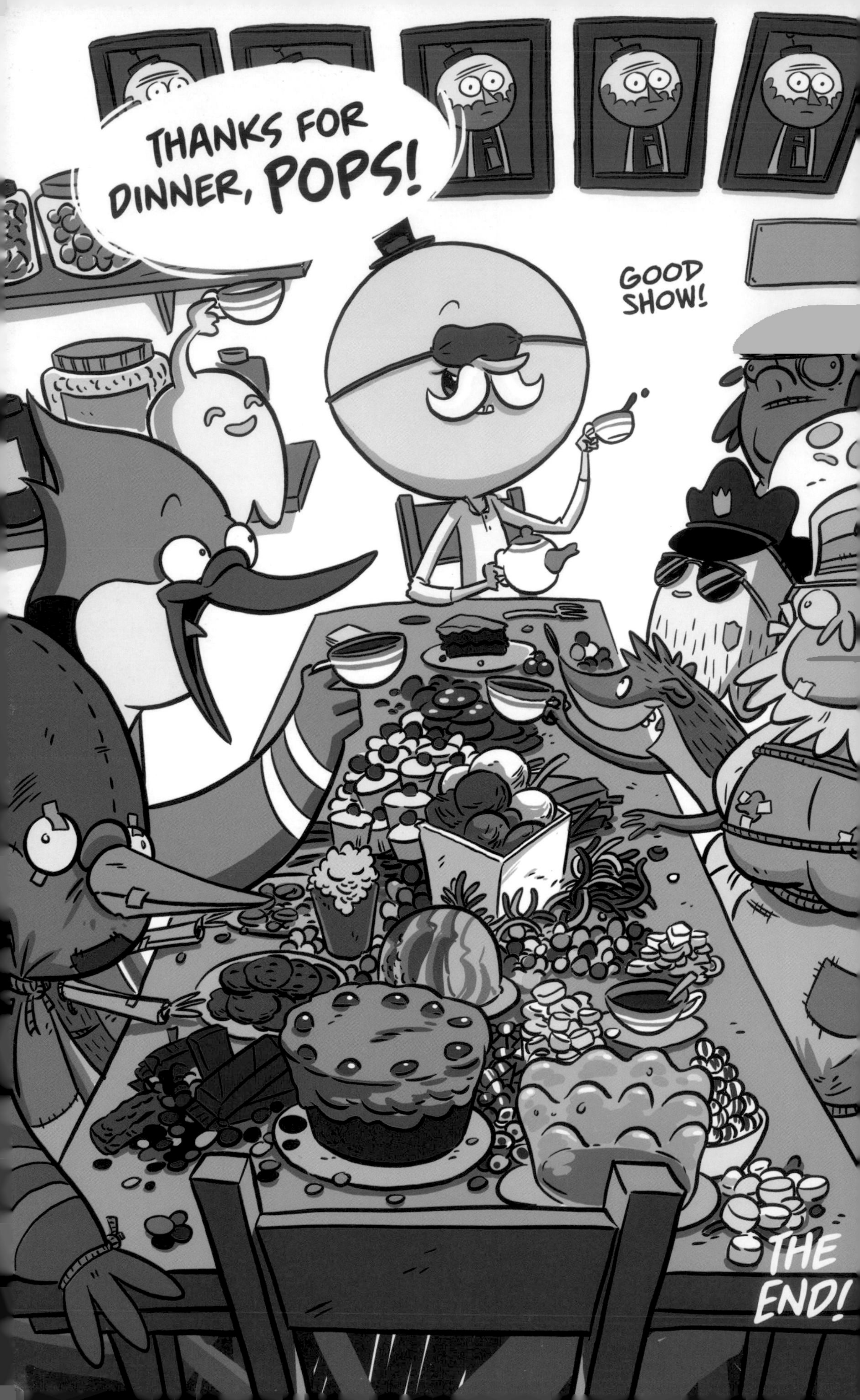
THANKS FOR DINNER, POPS!
GOOD SHOW!
THE END!

COVER GALLERY

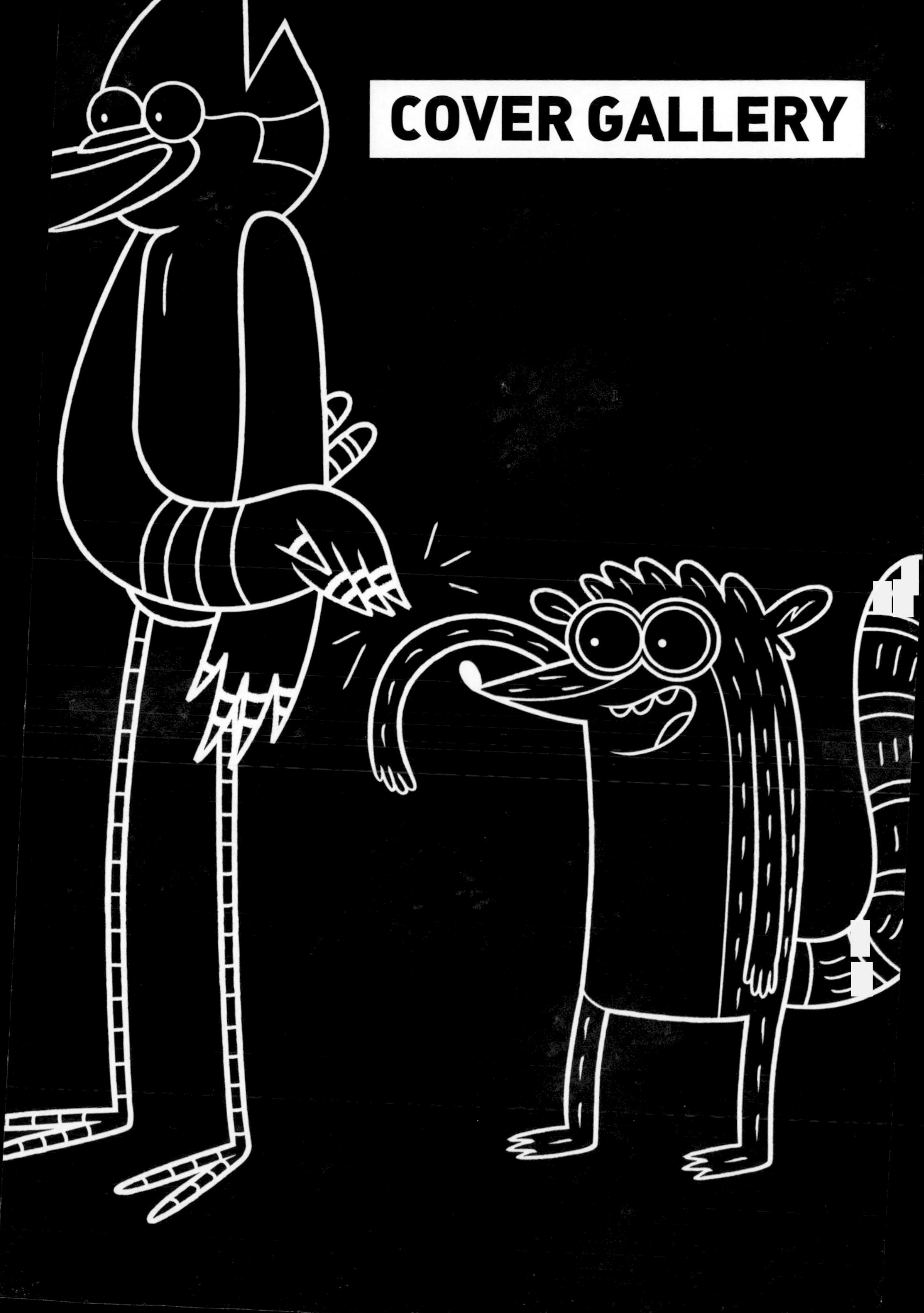

ISSUE TWENTY FIVE Main Cover
PAMELA LOVAS

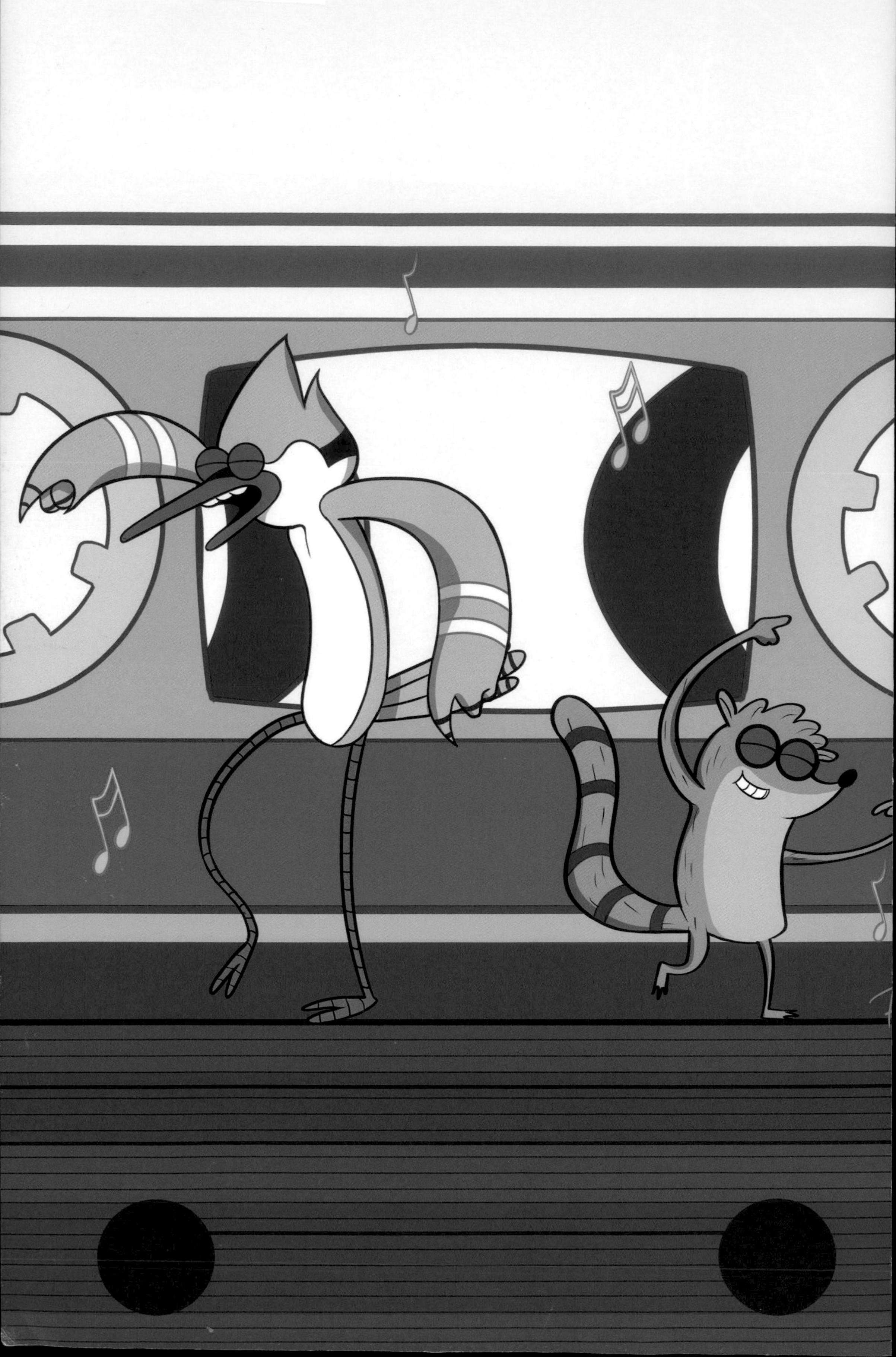

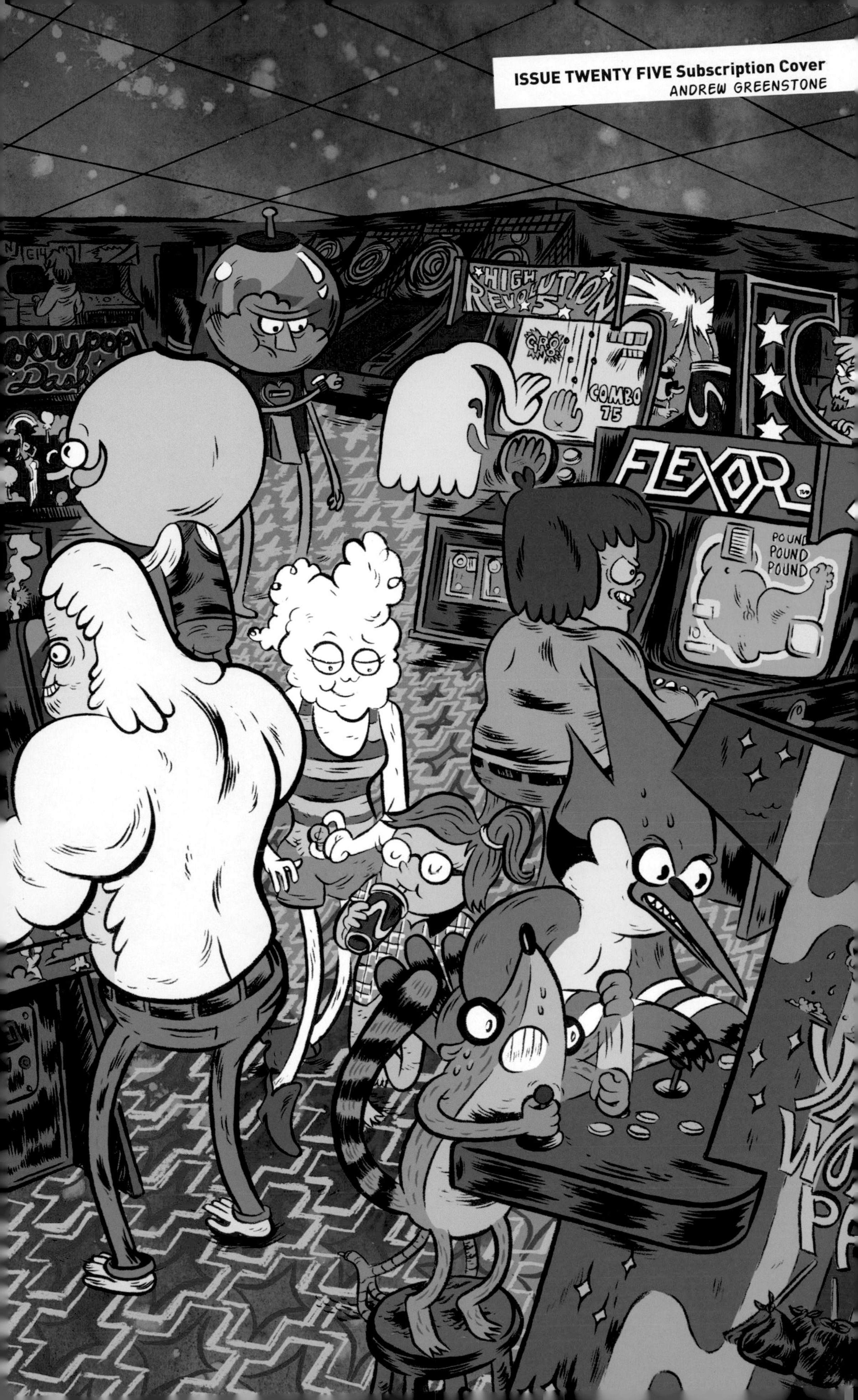
HIGH REVOLUTION 5
COMBO 75
FLEXOR
POUND
POUND
POUND

ISSUE TWENTY FIVE Subscription Cover
ANDREW GREENSTONE

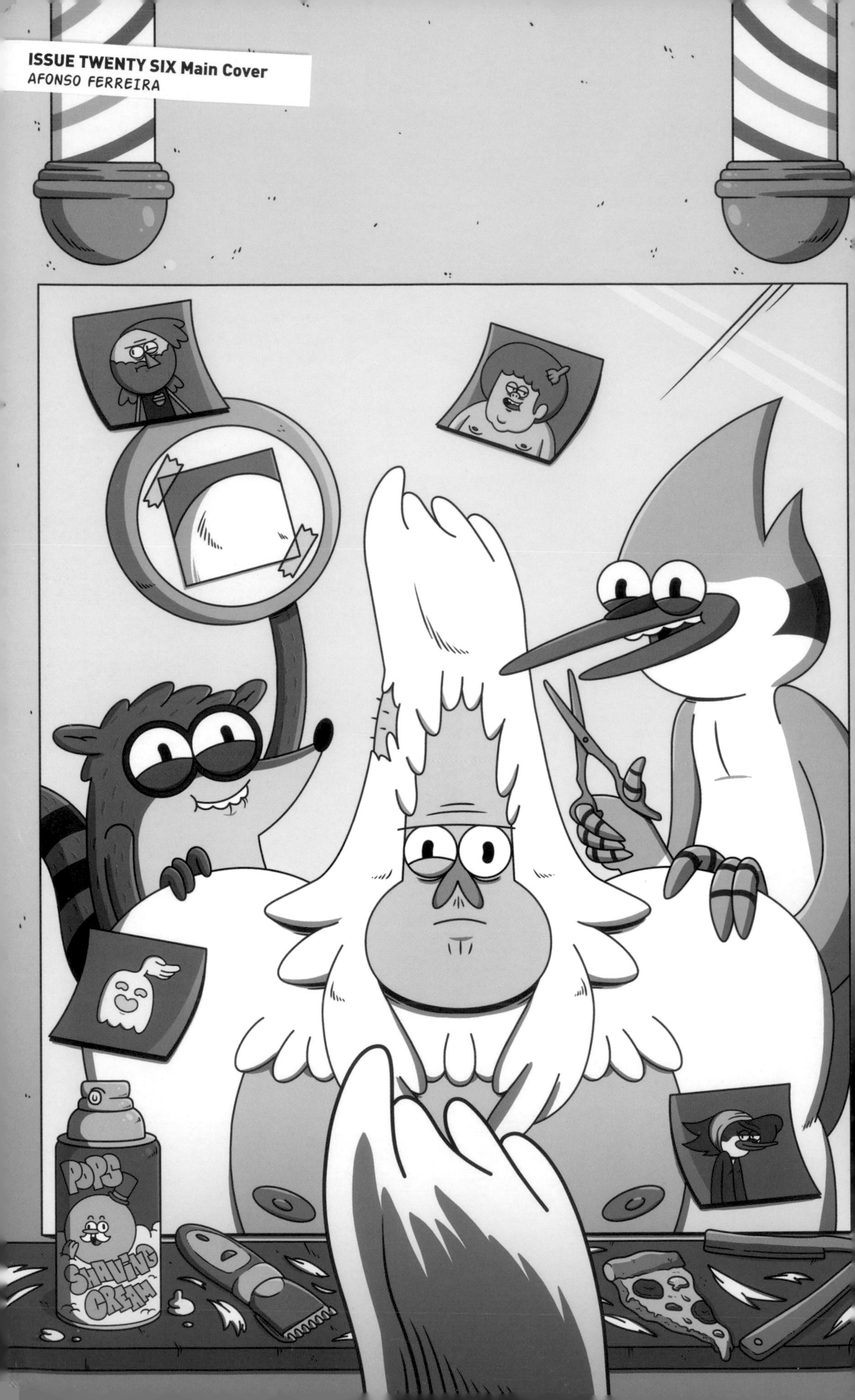

ISSUE TWENTY SIX Main Cover
AFONSO FERREIRA

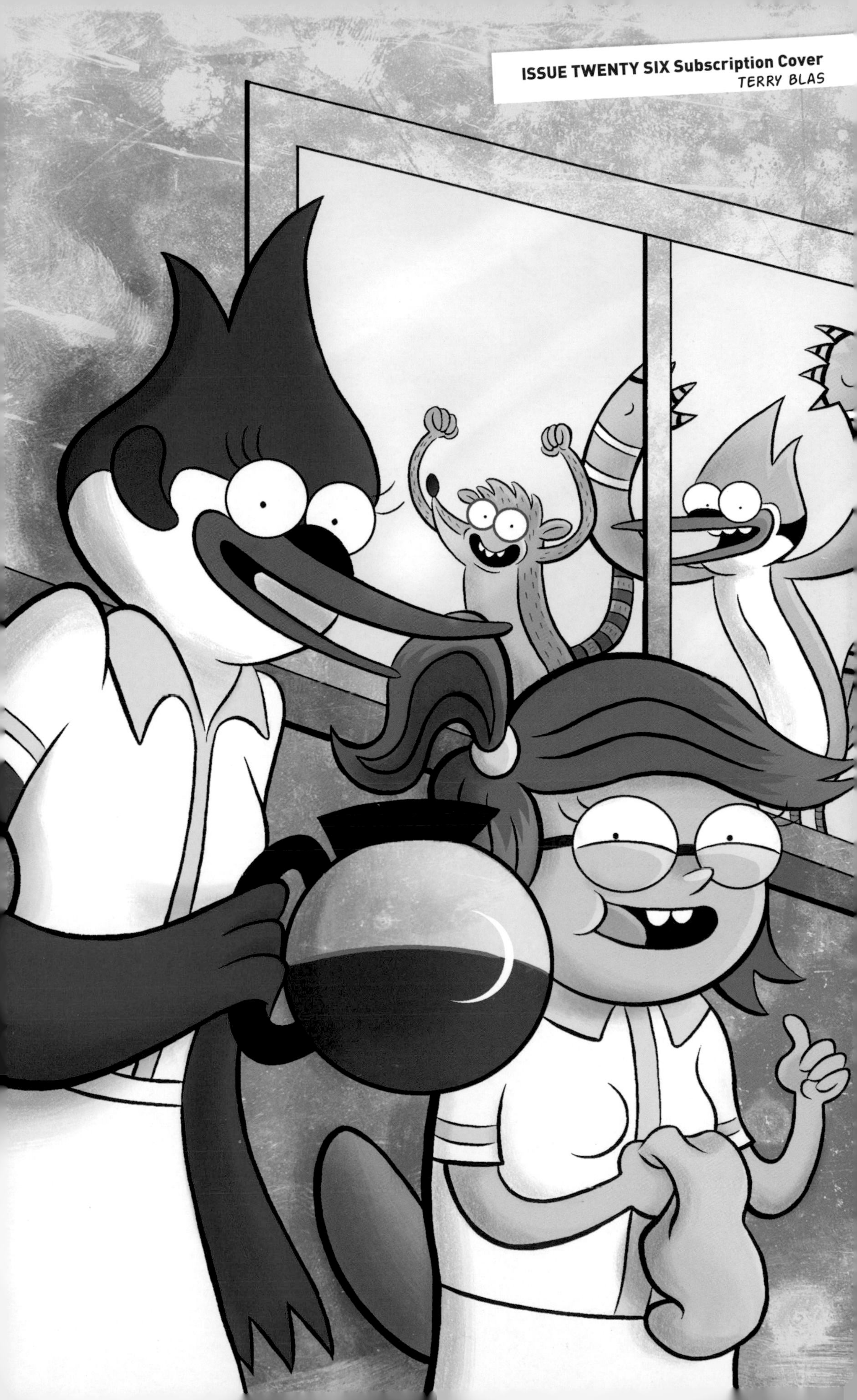

ISSUE TWENTY SIX Subscription Cover
TERRY BLAS

ISSUE TWENTY SEVEN Main Cover
JULIAN ROBINSON & DAN CIURCZAK

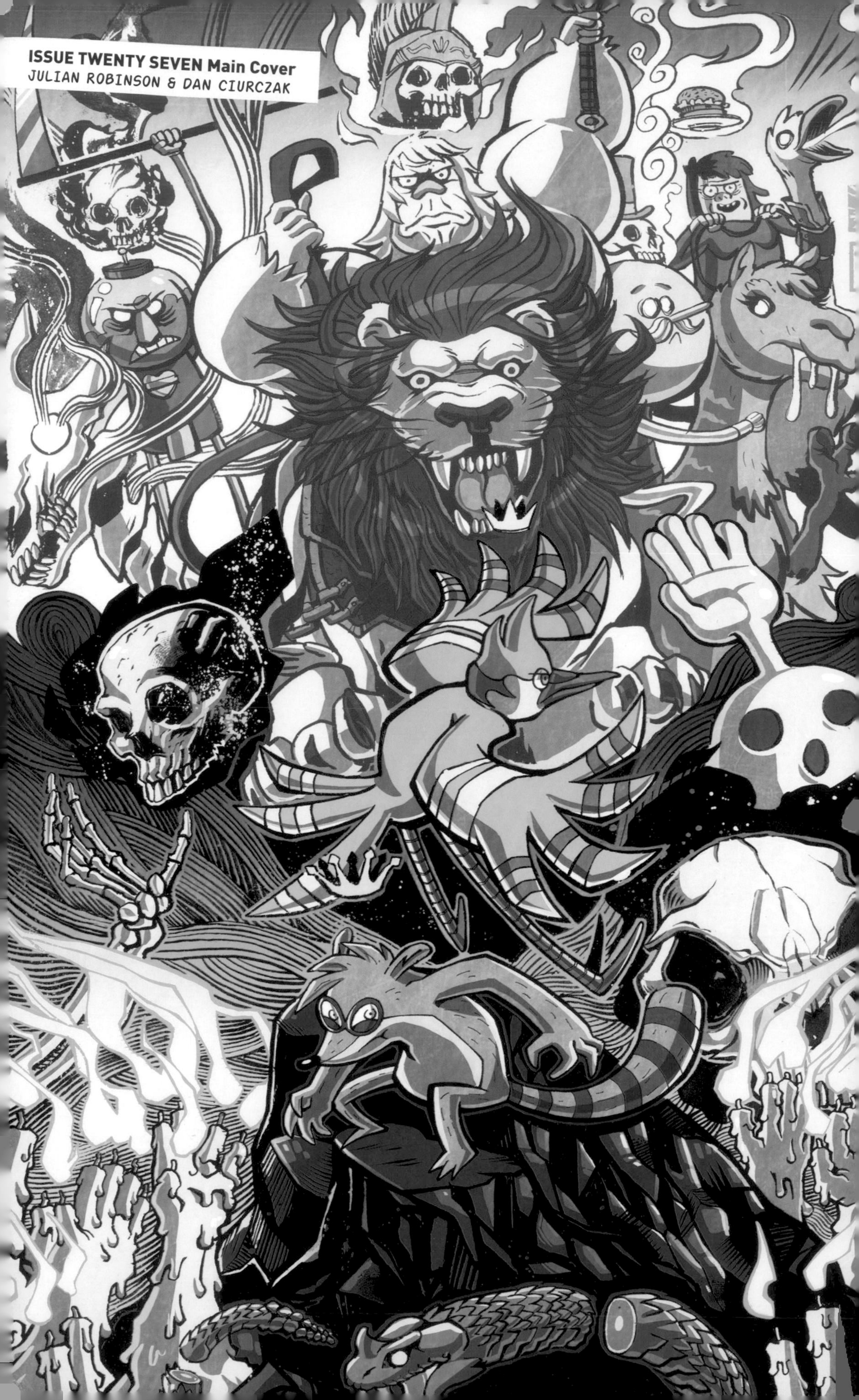

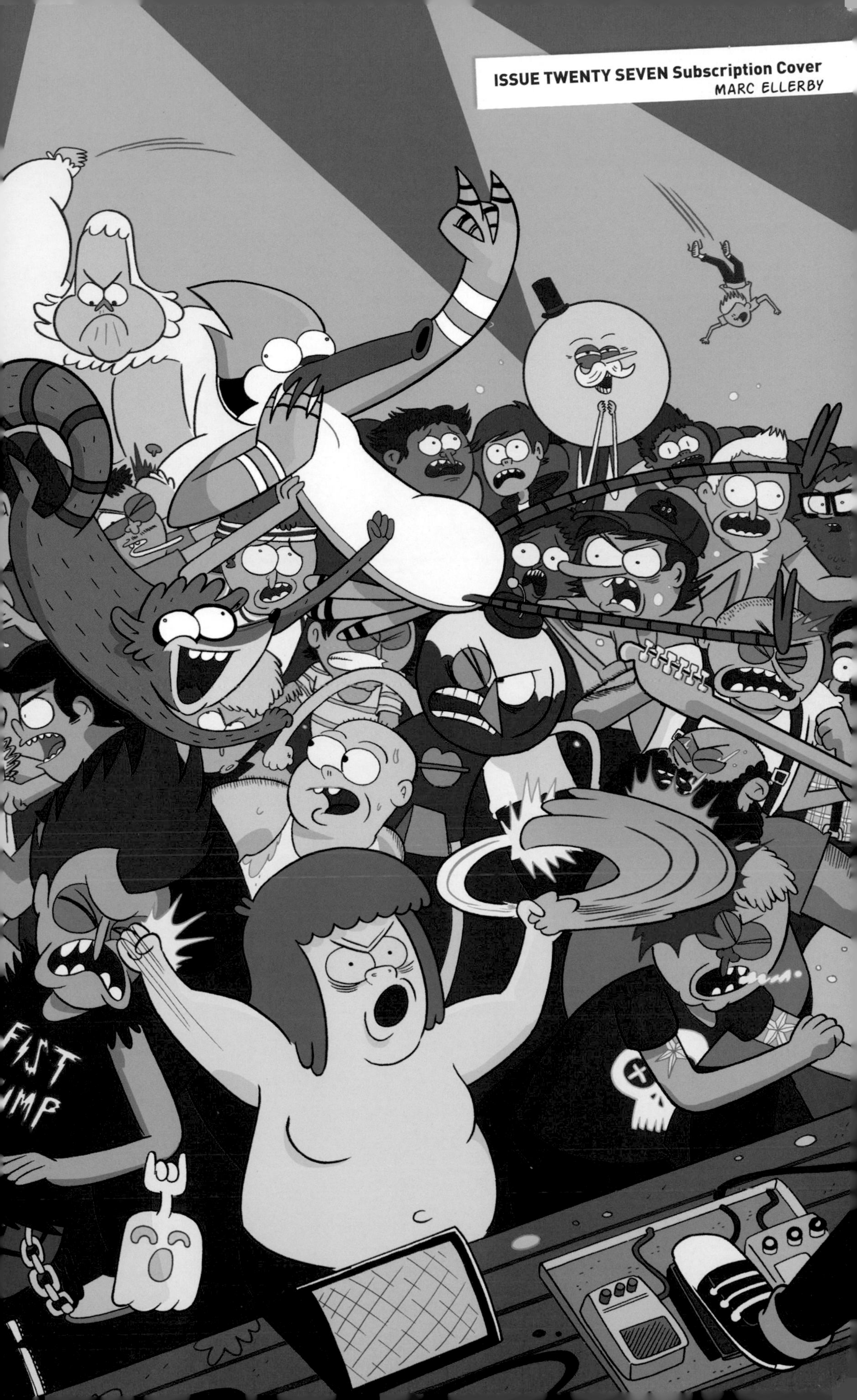

ISSUE TWENTY SEVEN Subscription Cover
MARC ELLERBY

ISSUE TWENTY EIGHT Main Cover
DOUGLAS HOLGATE

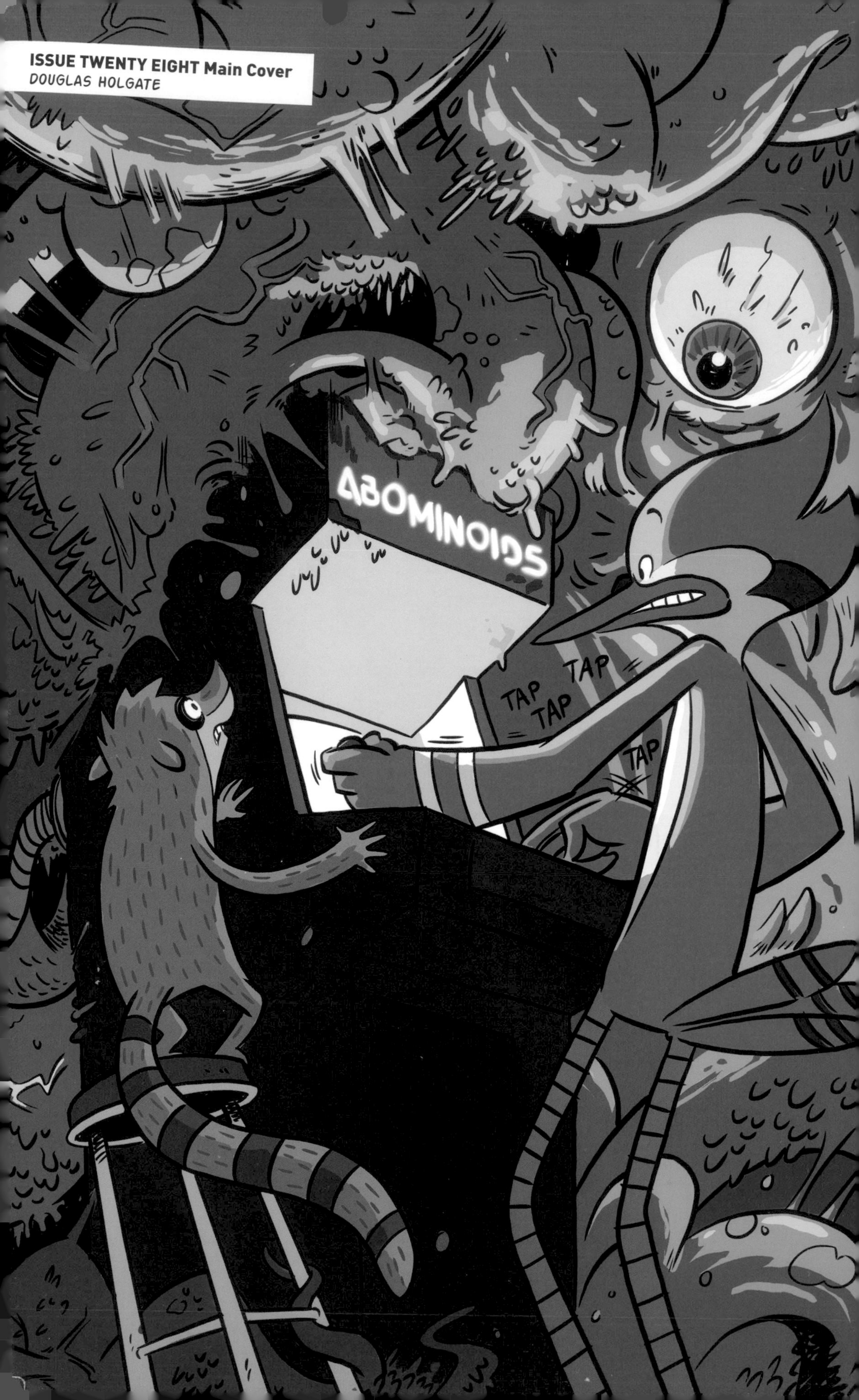
ABOMINOIDS
TAP TAP TAP TAP
TAP

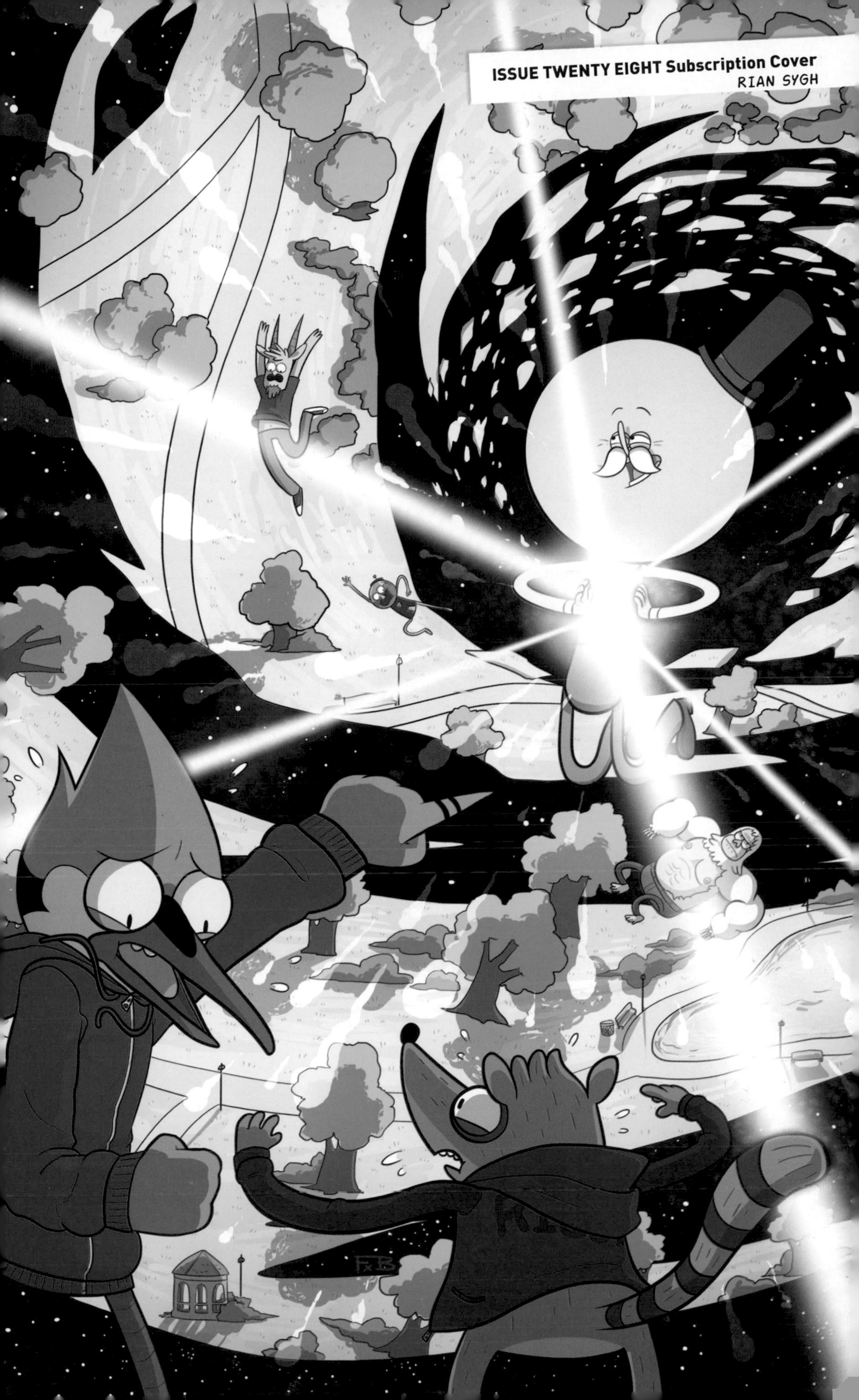

ISSUE TWENTY EIGHT Subscription Cover
RIAN SYGH

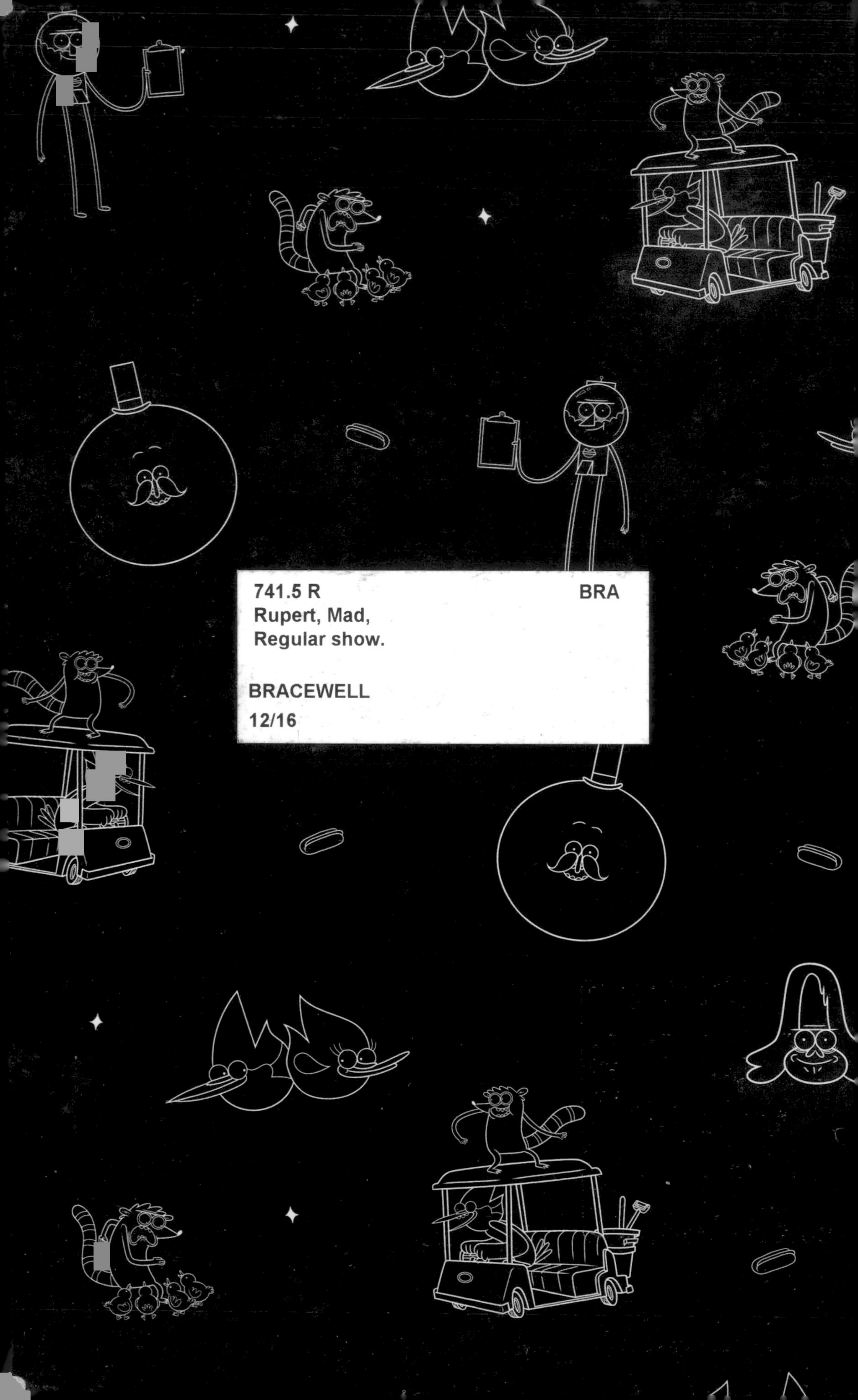